This huge MEGA Bundle of Ga
packed with explicit adult conte
provocative, explicit, or intense
discretion.

CW01547027

BUT If Forbidden is the way
and start reading!

Enjoy this MEGA Collection filled with sinfully delicious erotic short stories in this Hot MEGA Bundle!

Ever dreamed of giving in to your wildest desires, feeling the rush of forbidden pleasure, and diving into your deepest, hottest fantasies?

This book is your ticket to that thrill!

This steamy gay erotica collection packs more than 10 brand-new stories that'll get your heart racing. Each one's loaded with intense, explicit stories, featuring confident alpha guys who take charge and passionate men craving that explosive release.

From steamy seduction to raw desire, these stories will set your kindle on fire.

to raw desire, these stories will leave you breathless and begging for more.

This MEGA COLLECTION includes:

COCKY BASTARD

CAPITOL'S WHORE

PUNISHED BF69

BOUND TO THE BASEMENT

STEAM AND SURRENDER

CURIOUS SOCCER BROS

OFFICE SECRET

BACKSTAGE WRECK220

LEATHER LUST

UNDERWEAR MISMATCH

CHOKEHOLD

Warning: These erotic stories are full of hot sex scenes and are intended for adult readers only.

CONTENTS

COCKY BASTARD

I'm twenty-eight, lean, with a runner's build—long legs, tight abs, and a cock that's gotten me more than a few appreciative looks. My hair's dark, always a little messy, falling into my eyes when I'm too lazy to trim it. I keep my face clean-shaven, mostly because I like the way it shows off my sharp jawline, the kind that makes guys do a double-take. My skin's tanned from weekends at the beach, and I've got a couple of tattoos—a snake curling around my bicep and a dagger on my thigh—that add a bit of edge. I'm not a gym rat, but I'm fit enough to hold my own, and I know how to use what I've got. My eyes, a deep brown, have a glint that says I'm trouble, and I lean into it. Confidence is my currency, and tonight, I'm spending it all on Grindr, scrolling for someone who can handle me.

It's late, the kind of Friday night where the city hums with restless energy, and I'm sprawled on my couch, shirt off, sweatpants low, my phone glowing in the dim light of my apartment. The AC's broken, so the air's thick, my skin already slick with a sheen of sweat. Grindr's open, and I'm thumbing through profiles, half-bored, half-horny, looking for something to spark. Most of the guys are the usual—gym bros with mirror selfies, twinks with filtered faces, or blank profiles with no game. I'm picky, not because I'm vain, but because I know what I want: someone who can take a pounding, someone who'll match my fire without flinching.

Then I see him. His profile pic's just a torso, but fuck, what a torso—broad, thick, with a hint of gray hair dusting his chest. His bio's short: "50, versatile, thick in all the right places. You host." No face, but there's a second pic, a mirror shot from behind, and my cock twitches at the sight. His ass is massive, round, and firm, the kind you want to grab with both hands and bury yourself in. It's not just big—it's sculpted, like he's spent years squatting heavy or maybe just born lucky. My mouth goes dry, and I'm already imagining how it'd feel to spread those cheeks, to see them bounce under my hips.

I tap to message, my fingers quick, my pulse faster. "That ass is fucking unreal. You take it as good as you show it?"

He's online, and the reply comes fast. "Bet I can handle more than you can give, kid. You got the goods to back up that talk?"

I grin, leaning back, my free hand adjusting the growing bulge in my sweats. He's got balls, throwing it back like that. I like it. "Hung and ready to wreck. Send me something to prove you're worth my time."

A minute passes, then my phone pings. It's a private pic, and I open it, my breath catching. He's bent over, one hand pulling a cheek aside, showing off a tight, pink hole that's practically begging for it. His thighs are thick, dusted with more of that gray hair, and I can see the curve of his balls, heavy and low. My cock's fully hard now, straining against my sweats, and I'm already picturing how he'd look spread out on my bed, that ass up, taking every inch I've got.

"Fuck," I type, one-handed, my other hand palming myself. "That's a hole I need to ruin. You want this cock?" I snap a quick pic—my sweats pulled down just enough to show my dick, thick and veiny, the head already slick with precum. I hit send, my heart pounding, knowing I'm playing with fire.

His response is a voice note, and I fumble to plug in my earbuds, not wanting my neighbors to hear. His voice is deep, gravelly, with a hint of a drawl that makes my balls tighten. "Kid, that's a fucking monster. You sure you know how to use it? 'Cause I don't let just anyone near this ass."

I laugh, low and rough, and send another pic, this one from a better angle, my hand wrapped around my shaft, stroking slow to show off the length. "Trust me, I know exactly what to do with it. You host, or you coming to me? I want that ass in my hands tonight."

He types back, “You’re cocky. I like that. My place, one hour. Bring that dick and prove you’re not all talk.” He drops a pin, an address across town, not too far. My pulse spikes, adrenaline mixing with lust. I’m already standing, grabbing a quick shower to rinse off the sweat, my cock half-hard the whole time, imagining that thick ass under my hands, imagining how tight he’ll be when I slide in.

In the shower, the hot water does nothing to calm me down. I’m wired, my mind racing with images—his hole clenching around me, his moans filling the room, the way his ass will jiggle when I slam into him. I dry off, throw on a tight black tee and jeans that hug my thighs, my cock still heavy in my briefs. I check myself in the mirror, running a hand through my damp hair, knowing I look good—hungry, ready to dominate.

The drive to his place is a blur, the city lights streaking past as I weave through traffic, my phone buzzing with another message.

It's him again, another pic—this time a close-up of his ass, one finger teasing his rim, slick with lube. "Getting ready for you," the caption reads, and I have to adjust myself, my jeans too tight now, my cock aching. "Fuck, you're killing me," I type back, my fingers shaky. "Keep that hole ready. I'm close."

His building's a nondescript brick walk-up, the kind that blends into every other in this part of town. I park, take a deep breath, and head up, my heart hammering. The hallway's dim, smelling faintly of weed and old carpet, but I don't care. I find his door, knock twice, and it swings open almost immediately.

He's standing there, and fuck, he's even better than the pics. Taller than me, maybe six-two, with a broad frame that fills the doorway. His hair's short, silver at the temples, and his face is rugged—strong jaw, a few lines that say he's lived hard and liked it. He's in a loose tank and shorts that do nothing to hide that ass, thick and round, stretching the fabric. His eyes, a sharp gray, rake over me, lingering on my crotch, and his lips curve into a smirk that's equal parts challenge and invitation.

"You're the cocky kid from Grindr," he says, his voice that same gravelly drawl from the voice note, sending a shiver down my spine. He steps aside, letting me in, and I can feel his gaze on my back as I walk past, the air between us already crackling.

"Guilty," I say, turning to face him, my own smirk matching his. His apartment's small but clean, a couch, a coffee table, and a door that probably leads to the bedroom. The air's warm, a fan humming in the corner, and I can smell him—musk, soap, and something spicy that makes my mouth water. "You gonna show me that ass in person, or am I working off memory?"

He laughs, a low, dirty sound, and steps closer, close enough that I can feel the heat off his body. "You're bold," he says, his eyes flicking down to my lips, then lower. "But I don't give it up easy. You gotta earn this." He turns, just enough to give me a view of that ass, the shorts riding up to show the curve where thigh meets cheek, and my cock throbs, straining against my jeans.

I step closer, crowding him, not touching yet but letting him feel my presence. "Earn it? Baby, I'm gonna wreck that hole so good you'll be begging for round two." My voice is low, rough with want, and I see the way his shoulders tense, the way his breath hitches. He's not backing down, though—his eyes meet mine, challenging, like he's daring me to make good on my promise.

"Big talk," he says, stepping back until he's against the couch, his hands braced on the armrest. "Show me what you've got, kid.

Strip. Let's see if that cock's as good in person as it looked on my phone."

I don't hesitate. I pull my shirt over my head, tossing it aside, letting him see the lean muscle, the ink on my arm, the way my abs flex as I move. His eyes darken, and I undo my jeans, shoving them down with my briefs, kicking them off. My cock springs free, hard and heavy, the head glistening, and I stroke it once, slow, watching his reaction. His lips part, just a fraction, and I see his shorts tent, his own dick clearly interested.

"Fuck," he mutters, his voice thicker now, and he steps closer, his hand hovering like he wants to touch but isn't sure yet. "That's... a lot to work with."

I grin, closing the distance, my hand brushing his hip, feeling the heat through his shorts. “You’ll take it all,” I say, my fingers slipping under the waistband, tugging just enough to tease. “But first, let’s see that ass. Turn around.”

He hesitates, just for a second, then turns, bending slightly over the couch, giving me a view that makes my cock twitch. Those shorts are obscene, clinging to every curve, and I can’t resist—I hook my fingers in the waistband and pull them down, slow, revealing that perfect, thick ass inch by inch. It’s even better than the pics, round and firm, the skin smooth but dusted with that gray hair, and I can see his hole, tight and pink, just begging for my tongue, my fingers, my cock.

“Fucking hell,” I breathe, my hands on his cheeks, spreading them gently, testing the give. He’s warm, the muscle yielding under my grip, and I can feel him tense, then relax, like he’s already anticipating what's coming. "This ass is gonna be the death of me."

He looks back over his shoulder, that smirk still there but softer, laced with want. "You gonna stand there drooling, or you gonna do something about it?"

I laugh, low and rough, and lean in, my lips brushing the back of his neck, not kissing, just teasing with my breath. "Oh, I'm gonna do plenty," I murmur, my hands kneading his ass, thumbs brushing closer to his hole, feeling it twitch under the pressure. "But I'm taking my time. Gonna make you beg for this cock before I wreck you."

He shudders, pushing back into my hands, and I know I've got him—hooked, ready, and already starting to unravel.

His ass is a fucking masterpiece, thick and round under my hands, the skin hot and slightly slick from the humid air of his apartment. My thumbs graze closer to his hole, circling the tight rim without dipping in, and he lets out a low, frustrated groan, pushing back like he's daring me to go further. The fan in the corner hums uselessly, barely stirring the heavy air, and every breath feels like it's laced with his scent—musky, warm, with a hint of the lube I saw in his Grindr pic. My cock's throbbing, pressed against my thigh, but I'm not rushing this. I want him squirming, needy, before I give him what he's clearly craving.

"Fuck, you're a tease," he growls, his voice thick with that gravelly drawl, head turning just enough for me to catch the glint in his gray eyes. There's a challenge there, but his body's betraying him—his hips shift, chasing my touch, his shorts bunched around his thighs like a surrender. "You gonna keep playing games, or you got the balls to back up that big dick energy?"

I chuckle, low and dirty, my lips brushing the shell of his ear as I lean over him, my chest grazing his back. “Oh, I’ve got the balls,” I murmur, letting my breath fan across his neck, watching goosebumps rise despite the heat. My hands squeeze his cheeks, hard enough to make him hiss, and I spread them wider, exposing that tight, pink hole to the air. “But I’m not fucking you yet. Gonna make you feel every inch of this want first, till you’re begging for my cock to split you open.”

He shudders, a full-body tremor that makes his ass jiggle under my grip, and I can’t resist—I slap one cheek, not hard, just enough to sting, the sound sharp in the quiet room. He gasps, his head dropping forward, hands gripping the couch arm tighter. “Fuck you,” he mutters, but there’s no venom, just a ragged edge of need. “You’re enjoying this too much.”

"Damn right I am," I say, my voice rough as I knead the spot I slapped, soothing the faint red mark. My fingers drift closer to his hole again, one thumb brushing over it, feather-light, feeling it twitch under the touch. He's sensitive, responsive, and it's driving me wild, the way his body's screaming for more even as he tries to play tough. I lean down, my lips grazing the small of his back, tasting the salt of his sweat, and he arches, a soft moan slipping out.

"Don't act like you're not loving it," I say, my hand sliding up his spine, fingers splaying across the broad plane of his back, feeling the muscle shift under my palm. "Your ass is practically begging for me, pushing back like it's got a mind of its own." I press my thumb harder against his rim, not entering, just applying pressure, and he groans, his hips rocking back involuntarily.

“Cocky bastard,” he breathes, but his voice cracks, and I can hear the strain, the way he’s fighting to keep control. He straightens slightly, turning his head to look at me, and fuck, his face is a sight—flushed, lips parted, eyes dark with lust but still sharp, like he’s not ready to give in completely. “You think you’ve got me figured out? I’m not that easy.”

I grin, stepping closer, my cock brushing against the back of his thigh, not deliberate but enough to make him tense, his breath hitching. “Easy? Nah, you’re a challenge. That’s why I’m here.” My hand slides down, cupping his ass again, my other hand trailing to his hip, tugging him back so he’s pressed against me, my dick nestled against the crease of his thigh. The contact’s electric, my precum smearing against his skin, and I can feel his heat, the way his body’s trembling just under the surface.

He twists, half-turning to face me, and grabs my wrist, his grip firm but not pushing me away. "You talk a big game," he says, his voice low, almost a growl, his eyes flicking down to my cock, then back up to mine. "But I'm not some twink you can just bend over and own. You want this ass, you work for it."

The defiance in his tone makes my cock twitch, and I lean in, my lips hovering over his, close enough to feel his breath but not kissing yet. "Oh, I'm gonna work for it," I say, my voice a low rumble. "Gonna make you melt before I even fuck you. You'll be dripping, begging for it, and I'll still take my time." I let my free hand slide to his chest, thumbing his nipple through the tank, feeling it harden under my touch. He gasps, his grip on my wrist tightening, but he doesn't pull away, just stares at me, eyes blazing.

I tug his tank up, exposing his chest—broad, dusted with that gray hair, a little softer than mine but still solid. My fingers trace the line of his pecs, down to his stomach, feeling the slight give, the warmth of his skin. He's watching me, his breath coming faster, and I can see his cock straining against his shorts, a dark spot where he's leaking. "Look at you," I murmur, my hand dipping lower, brushing the waistband but not going further. "Hard as fuck, leaking like a faucet, and I haven't even touched your dick yet."

"Fuck off," he says, but it's half-laughed, his head tipping back as my fingers graze his nipple again, pinching lightly. He's sensitive there, his whole body jerking, and I file that away for later. I step closer, my thigh pressing between his, forcing his legs apart, and he lets me, his shorts slipping lower, barely clinging to his hips now.

"You say that, but your body's telling a different story," I say, my hand sliding to his lower back, pulling him against me so our cocks brush through the fabric of his shorts. The friction's maddening, my dick throbbing, but I keep it slow, deliberate, letting the tension build. "Feel that? My cock's ready to wreck you, but I'm gonna make you ache for it first."

He groans, his hands finding my shoulders, fingers digging in as he rocks against me, subtle but desperate. "You're all talk," he mutters, but his hips betray him, grinding against my thigh, seeking more. I slide my hand down, cupping his ass again, my fingers dipping into the crease, brushing his hole with more purpose now, pressing just enough to make him gasp. His head falls forward, forehead against my shoulder, and I can feel his breath, hot and uneven, against my chest.

“Talk? Nah, this is foreplay,” I say, my lips brushing his ear, my tongue flicking out to trace the lobe. He shivers, his hands sliding down my arms, exploring the muscle, the ink, like he’s mapping me out. “I’m gonna touch every inch of you, make you so fucking needy you’ll be begging for my cock to fill that perfect ass.”

I spin him around again, pressing him against the couch, his chest flat against the armrest, ass out. My hands are on him immediately, kneading those thick cheeks, spreading them to see that hole again, glistening now, ready. I drop to my knees, my face level with his ass, and he tenses, knowing what’s coming. “Relax,” I murmur, my breath hot against his skin, and I lean in, kissing the curve of his cheek, my lips grazing closer to his hole but not touching yet. He moans, low and desperate, his hands gripping the couch like it’s the only thing keeping him grounded.

"You're killing me," he says, his voice muffled against the couch, but there's a laugh in it, a shaky, turned-on edge that makes my cock leak. "Just—fuck, do something."

I smirk, my hands spreading him wider, thumbs brushing his rim, feeling it clench. "Oh, I'm doing plenty," I say, my voice low, rough with want. I kiss closer, my lips grazing the sensitive skin just beside his hole, and he pushes back, needy, his shorts finally falling to his ankles. I tug them off, leaving him bare, and fuck, the sight of him—bent over, ass up, hole twitching—is enough to make me dizzy.

I lean in, my tongue flicking out, just a tease, brushing the edge of his rim. He groans, loud and broken, his hips jerking back, and I hold him still, my hands firm on his thighs. "So fucking sensitive," I murmur, my lips brushing his skin as I speak. "Bet I could make you come just from my tongue in your ass, no cock needed."

“Try it,” he challenges, his voice hoarse, head turning to glance back at me, eyes dark and daring. “See if you can back up that mouth of yours.”

I laugh, the sound vibrating against his skin, and give him what he wants—just a slow, deliberate lick, flat of my tongue dragging over his hole, tasting the clean musk of him. He shudders, a string of curses spilling out, and I do it again, slower, letting him feel every inch of my tongue, teasing without penetrating. His thighs tremble, and I can see his cock, hard and leaking, dangling between his legs, begging for attention.

I pull back, standing, and turn him to face me, my hands on his hips, pulling him close. Our cocks brush again, and I groan, the friction almost too much. “You’re a fucking tease yourself,” I say, my lips hovering over his, my hand sliding to his cock for the first time, stroking slow, feeling the weight of him, the slickness of his precum. “Look at this—hard as steel, dripping for me. You want my mouth on it, don’t you?”

He nods, biting his lip, his hands gripping my arms, nails digging in. “Yeah,” he admits, his voice low, almost a whisper. “Want your mouth, your hands, your—fuck, everything.”

I kiss him then, hard and deep, my tongue fucking his mouth as my hand strokes him faster, my other hand sliding back to his ass, fingers teasing his hole again. He moans into the kiss, his body arching, caught between my hands, my mouth, the tension so thick it’s suffocating.

His moan vibrates against my lips, a desperate edge to it that makes my cock throb harder, pressed against his hip as our mouths clash. The kiss is messy, all tongue and teeth, his taste a mix of salt and heat that’s got me dizzy. My hand’s still wrapped around his dick, stroking slow but firm, feeling the thick weight of him, the way his precum slicks my palm. His ass clenches under my other hand, my fingers teasing his hole, circling the tight rim without pushing in, keeping him on edge. The air's thick, the fan doing fuck-all to cool us down, and every inch of his skin is slick with sweat, making every touch slide like silk.

I pull back from the kiss, my lips grazing his jaw, feeling the faint stubble there, and he tilts his head, giving me access to his throat. "You're fucking killing me," he rasps, his voice rough, laced with that drawl that hits me right in the balls. His hands grip my biceps, nails biting into the ink on my arm, and he's rocking into my hand, chasing the friction. "Gonna make me beg for real, aren't you?"

I smirk, nipping the pulse point under his jaw, feeling it jump against my lips. "Already begging, aren't you?" I murmur, my thumb swiping over the head of his cock, spreading the slickness, making him shudder. “But I’m not done playing. Gonna make you so desperate you’ll be choking on my cock just to get some relief.” My fingers press harder against his hole, just enough to stretch the rim, and he gasps, his hips jerking back, trying to force me inside.

“Fuck you,” he says, but it’s half-laughed, his eyes dark and glassy, locked on mine with a mix of defiance and raw want. “You’re all talk, kid. Show me something real.” His hand slides down my chest, fingers tracing the lines of my abs, then lower, brushing the base of my cock. The touch is light, teasing, but it’s enough to make me groan, my dick twitching against his palm.

I grab his wrist, pinning it to the couch arm, leaning in so our faces are inches apart. “You want real?” I growl, my voice low, vibrating with lust. “Get on your knees. Let’s see how much you love cock.” I release him, stepping back just enough to give him room, my cock jutting out, thick and heavy, the head glistening with precum in the dim light. His eyes drop to it, and fuck, the way he licks his lips—slow, deliberate, like he's already tasting me—makes my balls tighten.

He doesn't hesitate, sliding off the couch and onto his knees, the hardwood creaking under his weight. His hands find my thighs, fingers digging into the muscle, and he looks up at me, that smirk still there but softer, hungrier. "Big fucking cock," he mutters, his voice reverent, like he's admiring a work of art. "Bet it tastes as good as it looks." He leans in, his breath hot against my shaft, and my hand finds his hair, gripping the silver-streaked strands, not guiding yet, just holding.

"Find out," I say, my voice rough, my hips twitching forward just enough to brush his lips. He doesn't need more invitation. His tongue flicks out, lapping at the head, tasting the precum beaded there, and I groan, the wet heat of his mouth sending sparks up my spine. He's slow at first, deliberate, his tongue swirling around the tip, exploring every ridge, every vein, like he's savoring it. "Fuck, that's good," I mutter, my fingers tightening in his hair, urging him closer.

He hums, the vibration shooting through my cock, and takes me deeper, lips stretching around my girth, his tongue flat against the underside. He's good—fucking good—his mouth hot and tight, sucking with just the right pressure, his head bobbing slow but steady. His hands slide up my thighs, one cupping my balls, rolling them gently, the other gripping my hip, fingers digging in like he's anchoring himself. I can see the bulge in his throat as he takes me deeper, his eyes watering but never breaking contact with mine, that spark of challenge still there.

“Goddamn, you love this, don’t you?” I growl, my hips rocking slightly, feeding him more. “Sucking cock like you were born for it, taking it deep like a fucking pro.” He moans around me, the sound muffled but filthy, and it’s all I can do not to thrust hard, to fuck his throat raw. Instead, I let him set the pace, watching his lips slide along my shaft, slick with spit, his cheeks hollowing with every suck.

He pulls off with a wet pop, his lips red and swollen, a string of spit connecting his mouth to my cock. “Fuck, you’re thick,” he says, his voice hoarse, but there’s a grin there, like he’s loving every second. He licks a slow stripe up the underside, from base to tip, his tongue flicking over the slit, and I hiss, my hand tightening in his hair. “Tastes better than I thought,” he adds, his eyes flicking up, teasing, before he dives back in, taking me deeper, his throat constricting around me as he swallows.

I groan, loud and rough, my head tipping back for a second before I force myself to look down, to watch him work. His ass is still bare, those thick cheeks jiggling slightly as he shifts on his knees, and I can't resist—I reach down, grabbing one cheek, squeezing hard, my fingers brushing his hole again. He moans around my cock, the vibration making my toes curl, and I tease his rim, circling slow, feeling it clench under my touch. "You're so fucking needy," I say, my voice thick. "Sucking my cock like it's your last meal, ass begging for my fingers."

He pulls off again, gasping, his hand wrapping around my shaft, stroking slow but firm as he catches his breath. "You're one to talk," he shoots back, his voice wrecked but sharp. "Look at you, leaking like a faucet, groaning like you're already close." His thumb swipes over my head, spreading the precum, and he leans in, licking it off, slow and deliberate, his eyes never leaving mine.

I laugh, the sound rough, and tug his hair, pulling his head back just enough to make him gasp. "Keep talking shit, and I'll fuck that mouth till you can't breathe," I say, but there's no real threat in it—just heat, the kind that's got us both on edge. I push him back down, guiding my cock to his lips, and he opens eagerly, taking me deep, his tongue working overtime, swirling and sucking like he's trying to prove a point.

His hands are everywhere now—one stroking the base of my cock where his mouth can't reach, the other sliding up my thigh, fingers brushing my balls, teasing the sensitive skin behind them. He's relentless, his mouth a fucking furnace, and I can feel the tension coiling low in my gut, the urge to thrust harder, to lose myself in that wet heat. But I hold back, savoring the slow burn, the way his eyes water as he takes me to the hilt, his throat fluttering around me.

I pull him off, my cock slick and throbbing, and haul him to his feet, kissing him hard, tasting myself on his tongue. The kiss is sloppy, desperate, all teeth and spit, and I spin him around, bending him over the couch again, his ass up, hole glistening from my earlier teasing. I drop to my knees, my hands spreading his cheeks, and dive in, my tongue licking a slow, deliberate path over his rim. He cries out, his hips jerking, and I hold him still, my fingers digging into his thighs as I eat him out, my tongue fucking into him, deep and relentless.

"Fuck, fuck, fuck," he chants, his voice breaking, his hands gripping the couch so hard the fabric creaks. His hole clenches around my tongue, hot and tight, and I can taste the lube he used earlier, mixed with his clean musk, driving me wild. I pull back, just enough to speak, my lips brushing his skin. "You taste so fucking good," I growl, my tongue flicking out again, teasing the rim. "Gonna make this ass mine, but not yet. Gonna keep you begging first."

He groans, pushing back against my face, desperate for more. "You're such a prick," he mutters, but it's half-moan, his body betraying him, his cock leaking onto the couch below. "Just—fuck, do something, anything."

I stand, pressing my cock against his ass, not entering, just sliding between his cheeks, the slick friction making us both groan. My hands grip his hips, pulling him back, letting him feel the weight of me, the promise of what's coming. "Oh, I'm doing plenty," I say, my voice low, my lips against his ear. "Gonna make you ache for this cock, make you scream for it before I wreck that perfect fucking ass."

He shudders, his head dropping, breath coming in ragged pants, and I can feel the tension between us, thick and electric, the air heavy with want. We're not done—not even close—and I'm gonna make him feel every second of this heat before I give him what we both need.

His ass is pressed against my cock, the slick slide of my shaft between his thick cheeks driving me to the edge of control. The air's heavy, thick with the scent of sweat and lube, the fan's useless hum doing nothing to cut the heat. His moans are low, desperate, vibrating through the room as he grinds back, his hole twitching against the underside of my dick, begging for more. My hands grip his hips, fingers digging into the meat of him, and I can feel the tremor in his thighs, the way his body's surrendering even as he tries to keep that defiant edge. I'm not fucking him yet—not until he's a mess, until he's moaning like a whore for it.

"Fuck, you're relentless," he pants, his voice rough, that gravelly drawl cracking under the strain. His head's tilted back, resting against my shoulder, and I can see the flush creeping down his neck, his skin glistening in the dim light. "Gonna keep teasing, or you finally gonna give me that cock?" There's a challenge in his tone, but it's shaky, laced with need, and his hips roll back, pressing harder against me, like he's trying to force me inside.

I growl, low and dirty, my lips brushing the nape of his neck, tasting the salt of his sweat. "You want it bad, don't you?" I murmur, my hands spreading his cheeks wider, exposing that tight, pink hole to the air. It's glistening, slick from my tongue and the lube he prepped with, and fuck, it's begging to be wrecked. "But I'm not done with you yet. Gonna devour this ass first, make you scream before I even slide in."

He shudders, a full-body quake that makes his ass jiggle against my cock, and I can't resist anymore. I drop to my knees again, my hands gripping his thighs, pulling them apart to open him up. His hole's right there, perfect and needy, and I lean in, my teeth grazing the curve of one cheek, biting just hard enough to make him gasp. The sound's raw, almost pained, and I soothe it with my tongue, licking a slow path across the mark, feeling his skin prickle under my mouth. "Fuck, this ass," I mutter, my voice muffled against him. "Could eat it for days."

"Do it," he challenges, his voice hoarse, hands braced on the couch arm, knuckles white. "Fucking devour me, kid. Show me you're not all talk." His hips push back, offering himself up, and I don't need more invitation. I bite again, harder this time, sinking my teeth into the meat of his other cheek, and he moans, loud and filthy, his whole body jerking. I lick the sting away, my tongue dragging closer to his hole, circling the rim before diving in, fucking him with slow, deep strokes.

His moans turn into whimpers, high and desperate, and I can feel his thighs trembling under my hands. "Fuck, fuck, you're—shit," he stammers, his voice breaking as I tongue his hole, relentless, tasting the musky heat of him. I pull back just enough to graze my teeth over his rim, not biting but teasing, and he pushes back, needy, his cock leaking onto the couch below. I slide lower, my lips brushing his balls, heavy and tight, and I suck one into my mouth, rolling it gently with my tongue, feeling it pulse against me.

"Goddamn," he groans, his head dropping forward, his body arching like he's offering everything to me. "You're gonna kill me with that mouth." His voice is wrecked, and I can hear the edge of surrender in it, the way he's starting to unravel under my touch. I suck harder, my teeth grazing just enough to make him hiss, then release, licking a slow stripe up to his hole again, keeping him on edge.

I stand, my hands spreading his cheeks wide, thumbs pressing against his rim, stretching it just enough to make him gasp. My cock's throbbing, heavy and slick with precum, and I line it up, the head brushing his hole, not entering yet, just teasing, letting him feel the size of me. "You ready for this?" I growl, my voice low, my lips against his ear. "Gonna spread you open, make you take every fucking inch."

He moans, a whoreish sound that goes straight to my balls, and pushes back, trying to force me inside. "Do it," he says, his voice ragged, almost pleading. "Fuck, stop teasing and give it to me." His hands grip the couch tighter, his ass clenching around nothing, and I can see the desperation in the way his body moves, the way his cock twitches, leaking steadily now.

I spit into my hand, slicking my cock, the wet sound obscene in the quiet room, and press the head against his hole again, slow and deliberate. He's tight, so fucking tight, and I can feel the resistance as I push, just the tip breaching him, stretching his rim. He gasps, a sharp, pained sound that melts into a moan as I hold there, letting him adjust to the size. "Fuck, you're huge," he breathes, his voice trembling, but there's hunger in it, like he's loving the burn.

"Damn right I am," I say, my hands gripping his hips, holding him steady as I push in a little more, slow, inch by inch, watching his hole stretch around me, pink and taut. His moans are louder now, shameless, filling the room, and I lean over, my chest pressed against his back, my lips grazing his shoulder. "Taking it like a fucking whore, aren't you? Moaning for my cock already."

He laughs, a shaky, breathless sound, and turns his head just enough to meet my eyes, his gaze dark and wild. "You love hearing it," he says, his voice rough but teasing. "Bet you're hard as fuck knowing you're wrecking me." His hips rock back, taking me deeper, and I groan, the tight heat of him gripping me like a vice.

I pull back slightly, then push in again, slow, letting him feel every inch, every vein, as I sink deeper. His moans turn into whimpers, high and needy, and I can feel his body opening up, yielding to me. "That's it," I murmur, my hands sliding to his cheeks, spreading them wider to watch my cock disappear inside him. "Fucking perfect, taking me so good. Gonna make you scream before I'm done."

I keep the pace slow, torturous, each thrust deliberate, stretching him, filling him, and his moans are a symphony, raw and unfiltered, like he's lost all control. I lean down, biting his shoulder, not hard but enough to make him gasp, and lick the mark, tasting the salt of his skin. My hands roam, one sliding to his cock, stroking in time with my thrusts, the other gripping his balls, rolling them gently, feeling them tighten under my touch.

“Fuck, you’re—too much,” he gasps, his voice breaking, but he’s pushing back, meeting every thrust, his ass clenching around me, hot and tight. “Keep going, don’t fucking stop.” His words are slurred with pleasure, his body trembling, and I can feel the tension building, the way he’s teetering on the edge of losing it completely.

I pull out, ignoring his whine of protest, and flip him onto his back on the couch, his legs spread wide, his cock hard and leaking against his stomach. His hole’s slick, slightly gaped from my cock, and I line up again, pushing in slow, watching his face contort with pleasure, his eyes rolling back. “Look at you,” I growl, my hands pinning his thighs to the couch, spreading him open. “Moaning like a fucking slut, taking my cock like you were made for it.”

He groans, his hands grabbing my arms, nails digging in as I thrust deeper, slow but relentless, filling him completely. “Fuck, yes,” he moans, his voice high and desperate, his hips arching to meet me. “Harder, give it to me harder.” His cock bounces with every thrust, precum pooling on his abs, and I lean down, licking a stripe across his stomach, tasting the salt and bitterness of him.

I mount him fully now, my body pressed against his, my cock buried deep, and set a rhythm, slow but powerful, each thrust making him moan louder, more shamelessly. His legs wrap around my waist, pulling me closer, and I can feel his hole clenching, his body begging for more. “You’re mine,” I murmur, my lips against his ear, my hand stroking his cock faster now, keeping him on edge. “Gonna fuck you till you’re screaming, till you can’t think of anything but my cock in your ass.”

He's trembling, his moans turning into cries, his body pliant under me, and the tension's electric, the air thick with heat and want. I'm not done—not even close—and I'm gonna keep pushing him, keep making him moan like a whore until he's completely undone.

His cries are obscene now, high and broken, a far cry from that deep, manly drawl he threw at me over Grindr, and fuck, it's driving me wild. Every thrust I give him—slow, deep, deliberate—strips away another layer of that tough-guy bravado, turning him into a moaning, writhing mess beneath me. His legs are splayed wide, hooked around my waist, pulling me deeper as I pound into his ass, my cock buried to the hilt, stretching his tight hole with every inch. The couch creaks under us, the air thick with the scent of sweat, lube, and raw lust, his body slick and trembling under my hands. His cock's leaking a steady stream of precum across his abs, and his moans—God, those moans—are pure whore, desperate and shameless, filling the room like a fucking symphony.

“Listen to you,” I growl, my lips brushing his ear, my voice low and rough as I thrust harder, feeling his hole clench around me, hot and greedy. “That big, tough voice of yours—gone. Now you’re moaning like a slut, begging for my cock to wreck you.” I slam in deep, my balls slapping against his ass, and he cries out, his head tipping back, exposing the pale column of his throat, already marked with a red bite from earlier. I lean down, sinking my teeth into the other side, not hard enough to break skin but enough to make him gasp, his body arching under me like he’s offering himself up.

“Fuck, you’re—shit,” he stammers, his voice high and wrecked, barely coherent as I grind into him, my cock hitting that spot inside that makes his eyes roll back. His hands claw at my shoulders, nails leaving red trails across my ink, and I love it—the sting, the way he’s marking me back, even if it’s just scratches. “You’re too fucking much,” he manages, but it’s half-moan, his hips rocking up to meet my thrusts, his ass taking me like it was made for this.

I grip his hips, my fingers digging in hard enough to bruise, marking him as mine. “Too much? Nah, you’re loving every second,” I say, my voice thick with lust. I pull out slow, letting him feel the drag of my cock, then slam back in, deep and relentless, watching his face contort with pleasure-pain. “Look at you, taking it like a fucking champ, moaning like you’re getting paid for it.” His hole’s so tight, so hot, gripping me like a vice, and I can feel every pulse, every shudder, as I fuck him deeper, claiming every inch of him.

I lean back, pulling his legs higher, draping them over my shoulders to open him up even more. The new angle lets me go deeper, and he screams—a raw, whoreish sound that makes my cock throb harder. “That’s it,” I growl, my hands spreading his cheeks wide, watching my dick disappear into his stretched, pink hole. "Scream for me, baby. Let the whole fucking building know how much you love this cock." I thrust harder, the wet slap of skin on skin echoing, his ass jiggling with every impact, and his moans turn into a string of curses, each one more desperate than the last.

I pull out abruptly, ignoring his whimper of protest, and grab his hair, yanking him up to his knees on the floor. His eyes are glassy, lips swollen from our earlier kisses, and I slap his cheek—not hard, just enough to make his head snap to the side, a sharp sting that makes his cock twitch against his thigh. "Suck it," I order, my voice a low snarl, my hand guiding his face to my cock, slick with lube and his ass. "Taste yourself on me, you filthy fuck."

He doesn't hesitate, his mouth opening wide, taking me in with a hunger that makes my balls tighten. His lips stretch around my girth, his tongue swirling over the head, licking off the mix of lube and his own musk like it's fucking candy. "Fuck, yeah," I groan, my hand tightening in his hair, holding him in place as I thrust shallowly, letting him feel the weight of me. "Suck it like the whore you are, moaning for my cock even now." His eyes flick up, watering but defiant, and he sucks harder, his cheeks hollowing, spit dripping down his chin as he takes me deep, gagging but not stopping.

I lock my thighs around his head, trapping him there, my muscles flexing as I hold him in place, his nose pressed against my pubes, my cock buried in his throat. He moans, the vibration sending sparks up my spine, and I can feel his hands gripping my thighs, not pushing away but pulling closer, like he's loving the way I'm dominating him. "That's right," I say, my voice rough, my hips rocking slightly, fucking his mouth slow and deep. "You're mine now, aren't you? Choking on my dick, loving every second of it."

He hums, a muffled, desperate sound, and I pull back just enough to let him breathe, his lips red and slick, a string of spit connecting his mouth to my cock. "Fuck, you're good at this," he gasps, his voice hoarse, that manly drawl completely gone, replaced by a needy, slutty edge that makes my blood pound. "Making me—fuck, I can't even think straight." His hand wraps around my shaft, stroking as he licks the head, slow and deliberate, his eyes locked on mine, daring me to push him further.

I grin, yanking him back to his feet and spinning him around, bending him over the couch again. His ass is red from my bites, slick and open, and I spread his cheeks wide, my cock brushing his hole, not entering yet, just teasing, letting him feel the size of me again. "You're not thinking straight because you're mine," I growl, my lips against his ear, my hand sliding to his cock, stroking fast, making him moan louder, more desperate. "Gonna fuck you till you're screaming, till you're nothing but a moaning, dripping mess for me."

I push in slow, just the head, stretching his rim again, and he cries out, his voice high and broken, like the whore I'm turning him into. "Fuck, yes," he moans, pushing back, trying to take more, but I hold him still, my hands on his hips, controlling the pace. "Give it to me, please, just—fuck me." His words are slurred, his body trembling, and I can feel the tension between us, electric and suffocating, the air thick with heat and want.

I thrust deeper, slow but relentless, letting him feel every inch, every vein, as I fill him completely. His moans are nonstop now, a filthy litany of need, and I lean over, biting his shoulder again, marking him as mine. My hand strokes his cock in time with my thrusts, keeping him on edge, and I can feel him clenching around me, his hole so tight it's almost too much. "You're fucking perfect," I murmur, my voice rough, my lips brushing his neck. "Taking me like you were born for it, moaning like a slut in heat."

He's shaking, his body pliant under me, his moans turning into screams as I pick up the pace, fucking him deep, my balls slapping against his ass. I slap his cheek again, lighter this time, just enough to make him gasp, and he turns his head, his eyes meeting mine, wild and desperate. "You love this, don't you?" I say, my hand wrapping around his throat, not squeezing, just holding, feeling his pulse race under my fingers. "Love me making you submit, turning you into my little whore."

"Yes," he moans, his voice breaking, his hips rocking back to meet my thrusts, his cock leaking in my hand. "Fuck, yes, I love it." His admission is raw, unfiltered, and it sends a surge of power through me, knowing I've got him completely, body and mind. The tension's unbearable now, the heat of his ass, the sound of his moans, the way he's giving himself over to me—it's all pushing me to the edge, but I'm not done yet. I want him broken, begging, completely mine before this night is over.

His screams echo in the small apartment, a raw, slutty edge to them that makes my cock throb harder, buried deep in his tight ass. The way he's gone from that deep, gravelly voice to these high, desperate moans—fuck, it's like I've cracked him open, turned this rugged, manly guy into a whimpering whore for me. My hand's still on his throat, feeling his pulse race, my other stroking his leaking cock in time with my thrusts, each one slamming him into the couch, his body shaking under the force. The air's thick with the scent of sweat, lube, and raw need, the heat making every touch slick, every sound sharper. I'm not done with him—not even close. I want him completely broken, lost in me, before I let this end.

I pull out, sudden and sharp, ignoring his choked whine, and flip him onto his back, his legs falling open like an invitation. His chest heaves, sweat glistening on his broad pecs, that silver-dusted hair catching the dim light. His cock's hard, red, and dripping, slapping against his abs with every ragged breath. But it's his hole that draws my eyes—pink, slick, slightly gaped from my cock, twitching like it's begging for me to come back. "Fuck, look at that," I growl, my voice rough with lust, my hands grabbing his thighs, spreading them wider. "Your hole's fucking starving for me, isn't it? Practically winking, begging for my dick."

He groans, his head tipping back, hands gripping the couch cushions. "You're such a prick," he rasps, but his voice is wrecked, high and needy, that manly drawl long gone. "Just—fuck, do something, don't just stare." His hips shift, lifting slightly, offering himself up, and the sight of him—so big, so rugged, but so fucking submissive—makes my blood pound.

I don’t make him wait. I dive in, my face buried between his thighs, my tongue licking a slow, deliberate stripe over his hole. It’s hot, musky, slick with lube and my spit from earlier, and I groan against him, the taste driving me wild. I eat him out like I’m starving, my tongue fucking into him, deep and relentless, feeling his rim clench and flutter. His moans are louder now, shameless, a whoreish wail that fills the room. “Fuck, yes,” he cries, his hands flying to my hair, tugging hard, his hips grinding against my face. “Eat me, fuck, don’t stop.”

I don’t. I suck at his rim, my teeth grazing just enough to make him jerk, then plunge my tongue deeper, curling it inside him, tasting every bit of his heat. His thighs tremble around my head, his balls brushing my nose, and I grab them, rolling them gently, feeling them tighten under my touch. “So fucking perfect,” I murmur, my lips brushing his hole as I speak, my breath hot against his skin. “This ass, this hole—made for me to ruin.”

He’s panting, his moans turning into desperate sobs, and I can feel him unraveling, his body pliant, his pride shattered. I pull back, my lips slick, and grab his ankles, lifting his legs high, spreading him wide. His feet are in my face now, strong and masculine, the soles rough but clean, and I can’t resist—I lick one, slow and deliberate, tasting the faint salt of his skin, then suck his big toe into my mouth, my tongue swirling around it. He gasps, a shocked, filthy sound, his cock twitching hard against his stomach. “Fuck, you’re—shit, that’s insane,” he moans, his voice breaking, his eyes wide but dark with lust.

“Love these,” I growl, biting lightly at the arch of his foot, feeling him shudder. “So fucking manly, just like you—except now you’re my whore, aren’t you?” I suck his toe again, hard, then move to the other foot, licking the sole, savoring the way he squirms, his moans getting louder, more desperate. His cock's leaking a steady stream now, pooling on his abs, and I can see his hole clenching, begging for me to fill it again.

I drop his legs, lining up my cock, the head brushing his slick rim. "You ready for this?" I ask, my voice low, my hands spreading his cheeks wide, watching his hole stretch as I push in, slow but relentless. He's so fucking tight, even after all this, and I groan, feeling his heat wrap around me, every inch a struggle and a victory. "Fuck, you're still so tight," I say, my voice rough, my hips rocking forward, sinking deeper. "Taking my cock like a good little slut."

He screams, a raw, whoreish sound that makes my balls tighten, his head thrashing against the couch. "Yes, fuck, give it to me," he moans, his voice high and broken, his hands clawing at my arms, nails digging in. I thrust harder, deeper, my cock buried to the hilt, my balls slapping against his ass with every slam. The couch creaks, threatening to give way, and I lean over, my chest pressed against his, my lips finding his in a desperate, hungry kiss.

Our mouths crash together, tongues tangling, teeth clashing, the kiss sloppy and wild, all spit and need. His moans vibrate against my lips, and I swallow them, fucking him harder, my cock pounding into him, hitting that spot that makes his eyes roll back. "You're mine," I growl into his mouth, my hand sliding to his cock, stroking fast, feeling it pulse in my grip. "Moaning like a fucking whore, taking every inch, loving it."

"Fuck, yes," he gasps, his voice barely recognizable, his lips swollen against mine. "I'm—shit, I'm yours, just don't stop." His hands grab my face, pulling me deeper into the kiss, his tongue fucking my mouth as I pound his ass, the rhythm brutal, relentless. His hole clenches around me, hot and tight, and I can feel him trembling, his body on the edge, his cock throbbing in my hand.

I pull back from the kiss, my lips grazing his jaw, his throat, biting hard enough to leave another mark. “Look at you,” I say, my voice thick with lust, my thrusts slowing just enough to make him whine, desperate for more. “So fucking manly, but now you’re my slut, screaming for my cock, begging for it.” I slam in hard, making him cry out, his legs tightening around my waist, pulling me deeper.

I can feel the tension building, the heat coiling low in my gut, my cock throbbing inside him, so close to the edge. His moans are nonstop, a filthy litany of need, and I know he’s close too, his cock leaking in my hand, his hole clenching with every thrust. “You’re gonna come for me, aren’t you?” I growl, my lips against his ear, my hand stroking him faster, matching the brutal pace of my hips. “Gonna spill all over yourself while I fuck you senseless.”

“Yes, fuck, I’m—shit,” he moans, his voice breaking, his body shaking under me. His hands grab my shoulders, nails digging in, and I can feel him teetering, his hole gripping me like a vice, his cock pulsing in my hand. I’m right there with him, the pressure building, my balls tight, ready to explode, but I hold back, wanting to push him further, to make him scream louder, to own him completely before we both lose it.

The tension’s unbearable, the air thick with heat and want, our bodies slick with sweat, locked together in this desperate, filthy dance. I’m not done—not yet—and I’m gonna keep fucking him, keep making him moan like the whore he’s become, until he’s nothing but mine.

His moans are a fucking drug, high and broken, spilling out of him like he's lost all control, his body shaking beneath me as I pound into his tight ass. The couch groans under the force of my thrusts, his legs clamped around my waist, pulling me deeper, his hole gripping my cock like it's trying to milk me dry. The air's thick, heavy with the scent of sweat, lube, and raw, animalistic need, the heat making every slide of skin slick and electric. His face is a mess—flushed red, lips swollen, eyes glassy but still burning with that spark of defiance that's got me so fucking hard. I'm owning him, turning this rugged, manly guy into my personal whore, and the power of it, the way he's unraveling, is pushing me to the edge.

I lean down, crashing my lips into his, kissing him hard, my tongue fucking his mouth with the same brutal rhythm as my cock in his ass. The kiss is desperate, all teeth and spit, his moans muffled against my lips as I devour him, tasting the salt of his sweat, the faint bitterness of his precum from earlier. His hands grab my face, fingers digging into my jaw, pulling me closer like he's starving for it, and I growl into his mouth, my hips slamming faster, deeper, each thrust making his body jolt, his cock bouncing against his abs, leaking a steady stream.

"Fucking take it," I snarl, breaking the kiss just enough to speak, my lips brushing his, my voice cocky as hell. "You're my slut now, aren't you? Moaning like a whore, taking every goddamn inch like you were born for my cock." I slam in hard, hitting that spot inside him that makes him scream, a raw, filthy sound that echoes in the room. His hole clenches around me, hot and tight, and I can feel every pulse, every shudder, as I fuck him senseless, my balls slapping against his ass with every thrust.

"Fuck, yes," he moans, his voice high and wrecked, barely recognizable from that deep drawl he had on Grindr. "I'm—shit, I'm yours, just don't stop." His words are slurred, desperate, his hands sliding to my shoulders, nails raking across my skin, leaving red trails that sting and make my cock throb harder. He's completely gone, his pride shattered, and the sight of him—so big, so masculine, but moaning like a slut in heat—has me grinning, my ego swelling as much as my dick.

"You love this, don't you?" I growl, my hand wrapping around his cock, stroking fast, matching the relentless pace of my hips. "Love me wrecking your ass, making you scream like a cheap whore." I thrust harder, faster, my cock stretching his hole, filling him completely, and he's crying out now, his moans turning into sobs, his body trembling under me. I lean in again, kissing him fiercely, my tongue plunging deep, swallowing his cries as I pound him, the couch creaking like it's about to break.

His lips are frantic against mine, his tongue sloppy, desperate, and I can feel him teetering, his cock pulsing in my hand, his hole clenching tighter with every thrust. “Gonna come for me?” I murmur, my lips brushing his ear, my voice thick with lust. “Gonna spill all over yourself while I fuck you raw, fill you up with my cum?” I slam in deep, grinding against that spot, and he screams, his head thrashing, his hands clawing at my back like he’s trying to hold on to something, anything.

“Yes, fuck, please,” he moans, his voice breaking, his eyes rolling back as his body arches, his cock jerking in my hand. “I’m—shit, I’m so close.” His words are a plea, a surrender, and I love it, the way I’ve turned him into this writhing, needy mess, his manly facade shattered, replaced by pure, slutty desperation.

I pick up the pace, my hips snapping forward, fucking him so hard the couch slides an inch across the floor. My hand strokes his cock faster, rough and relentless, and I can feel my own release building, the heat coiling low in my gut, my balls tightening.

"You're mine," I growl, my lips against his throat, biting hard enough to leave another mark, claiming him. "Gonna cum inside you, mark you from the inside out, make sure you feel me for days."

He moans, a long, whoreish wail, and I feel his cock pulse, his body tensing as he comes, hot spurts shooting across his abs, his chest, some hitting my hand as I stroke him through it. His hole clenches around me, tight and rhythmic, and it's too much—my cock throbs, and I slam in one last time, burying myself deep as I cum, hard and hot, filling his ass with pulse after pulse. The feeling's electric, my vision blurring for a second as I empty inside him, my groans mixing with his moans, our bodies locked together in the haze of heat and lust.

I collapse against him, our chests heaving, slick with sweat and his cum, my cock still buried in his ass, softening but not pulling out yet. His legs are still wrapped around me, trembling, and I kiss him again, slower this time, but no less hungry, tasting the aftermath on his lips. “Fucking perfect,” I murmur, my voice rough, my hand sliding to his face, thumb brushing his swollen lips. “Took my cock like a champ, moaning like my personal slut.”

He laughs, a shaky, breathless sound, his eyes half-lidded but still sharp, that spark of defiance flickering back. “Cocky bastard,” he mutters, but there’s no heat in it, just a sated, almost fond edge. His hand rests on my chest, fingers tracing the ink there, and I can feel the warmth of him, the way his body’s still shuddering with aftershocks.

I pull out slowly, watching him wince, a trickle of my cum leaking from his stretched hole, and fuck, it’s a sight—his ass red from my bites, slick and used, marked by me in every way. I lean down, kissing his thigh, then his hip, tasting the salt of his skin, and he shudders, his hand tangling in my hair. "You're gonna kill me," he says, his voice hoarse but soft, a smile tugging at his lips.

I grin, standing, pulling him up with me. His legs are shaky, but he steadies himself against the couch, his eyes meeting mine, still dark with want. "Not done with you yet," I say, my voice low, cocky as ever. "Gonna clean you up, then we'll see how much more you can take." His eyes widen, a mix of exhaustion and anticipation, and I know this night's far from over—the tension's still there, simmering, ready to ignite again.

CAPITOL'S WHORE

I'm Luca, 24, slim but toned, with a body carved from years of running and yoga to keep the stress of D.C. at bay. My ass is tight, round, the kind that turns heads in my fitted khakis, and my chest is lean, defined, my abs a subtle ripple under my crisp button-downs. My dark hair's cropped short, framing sharp blue eyes that catch the light, and my smooth jaw gives me a boyish charm that I know disarms people. A single silver stud in my left ear is my only rebellion against the polished look this job demands. I'm a junior aide for a trio of powerful senators, running their errands, scheduling their lives, and keeping their secrets—secrets I know are dirty, whispered in coded glances and locked-door meetings, but I've never been let in on the details.

The Capitol's a pressure cooker, all marble halls and hushed deals, the air thick with ambition, cologne, and the faint tang of whiskey from late-night briefings. Today's a long one—budget talks dragging into the evening, the Senate chamber buzzing with tension, and I'm in Senator Caldwell's office, dropping off a stack of briefing notes. Caldwell's 50, silver-haired, with a jaw like granite and a voice that commands rooms. His suits are tailored to perfection, hugging his broad shoulders, and his dark eyes always seem to linger on me a beat too long, a smirk playing at his lips that makes my stomach flip, my cock twitch despite myself.

"Luca, good work today," he says, leaning back in his leather chair, his tie loosened, a glass of bourbon in his hand. His office smells of polished wood, leather, and his cologne—something sharp, expensive, masculine. "You're always so... thorough." His voice is low, deliberate, his eyes raking over me, lingering on my khakis, the way they cling to my ass, my thighs. My cock stirs, a faint heat building, and I shift, trying to hide it, my face flushing.

"Just doing my job, Senator," I say, my voice steady but my pulse racing, my hands fidgeting with the edge of his desk. I'm straight—or at least I've always thought so—but there's something about his power, the way he owns every room, that gets under my skin, makes my cock harden in my briefs, the fabric suddenly too tight.

He stands, slow, his 6'2" frame towering over me, and steps closer, his bourbon glass clinking on the desk. "You're more than just the job, kid," he says, his voice smooth, dangerous, his hand brushing my shoulder, fingers lingering, the touch sending a jolt straight to my cock. "You ever think about what else you could do for us?" His smirk widens, his eyes dark, and I swallow hard, my throat dry, my cock throbbing now, pressing against my khakis.

Before I can answer, the door opens, and Senator Hayes walks in, 45, leaner than Caldwell but just as commanding, his blond hair streaked with gray, his blue eyes sharp, predatory. His suit's navy, tailored to his slim frame, and his tie's undone, giving him a reckless edge. "Caldwell, you starting without me?" he says, his voice teasing, but his eyes lock on me, raking over my body, lingering on my ass, making my face burn hotter. "Luca, you're looking… tense. Long day?"

"Yeah, long day," I say, my voice catching, my hands gripping the desk to steady myself. Hayes steps closer, his cologne—woodsy, with a hint of citrus—mixing with Caldwell's, the air heavy, electric. My cock's fully hard now, a visible bulge in my khakis, and I know they see it, their smirks telling me they're enjoying this, enjoying me.

"Kid's always working too hard," Caldwell says, his hand still on my shoulder, squeezing now, his thumb brushing the nape of my neck, making me shiver. "Maybe we should help him relax, Hayes. What do you think?" His voice is low, suggestive, and Hayes laughs, a deep, rumbling sound that makes my balls ache, my cock twitching harder.

"Relax, huh?" Hayes says, stepping behind me, his hand grazing my lower back, fingers brushing the waistband of my khakis, the touch light but deliberate. "Bet you've got some tension we could work out, Luca. You ever let loose, or you always this buttoned-up?" His breath's hot against my ear, his hand sliding lower, brushing the curve of my ass, making me gasp, my cock leaking into my briefs.

"I… I'm good," I stammer, my voice shaky, my body betraying me, my hips shifting, pressing back against his hand without meaning to. I'm straight, I tell myself, but their power, their confidence, the way they're circling me like wolves, has my cock throbbing, my head spinning. "Just… doing my job," I say, but it's weak, and they know it, their laughs low, predatory.

"Job's more than fetching coffee," Hayes says, his hand squeezing my ass now, firm, possessive, his fingers digging in through the khakis, making me moan softly, my face burning. "You know what goes on around here, don't you? The late nights, the locked doors. Ever wonder what we're doing?" His voice is smooth, taunting, his hand sliding up, under my shirt, fingers brushing my bare skin, hot and rough, making my breath hitch.

Caldwell steps in front of me, his hand sliding to my chest, palm flat against my pec, thumb brushing my nipple through my shirt, making it harden, sending a jolt to my cock. "You're curious, aren't you, Luca?" he says, his voice low, his eyes locked on mine, dark and commanding. "Bet you've heard the rumors—senators and their... extracurriculars. Want to know what we're really into?" His thumb circles my nipple, slow, teasing, and I'm trembling, my cock so hard it's painful, my briefs damp with precum.

Before I can answer, the door opens again, and Senator Vaughn walks in, 48, stocky but powerful, his dark hair slicked back, his brown eyes sharp, his suit charcoal and crisp despite the late hour. His presence is heavy, commanding, and his smirk is instant, his eyes flicking over me, Caldwell, and Hayes, taking in the scene. “Well, fuck me, what’s this?” he says, his voice rough, amused, his eyes lingering on my bulge, my flushed face. “Luca, you caught in the middle of something?”

“Caught’s one way to put it,” Hayes says, his hand still on my ass, squeezing, his fingers brushing the seam of my khakis, teasing the crack. “Kid’s been working hard. Thought we’d… reward him.” His voice drips with suggestion, his fingers pressing harder, making me moan again, my cock twitching, my head spinning with the weight of their eyes, their hands, their power.

Vaughn steps closer, his cologne—spicy, heavy—mixing with the others, the air thick, suffocating. “Reward, huh?” he says, his hand brushing my jaw, fingers rough, calloused, tilting my chin up to meet his eyes. “You’re a good boy, Luca, but good boys get curious. You wondering what we do behind those locked doors? What gets us off?” His thumb brushes my lips, parting them slightly, and my breath catches, my cock throbbing, my body trembling under their touches.

“I… I don’t know,” I say, my voice hoarse, my hands gripping the desk, my knuckles white. I’m straight, I keep telling myself, but their power, their confidence, the way they’re touching me, owning me, has my cock leaking, my balls aching. “Just… trying to do my job,” I say, but it’s weak, and they laugh, low and knowing, their hands never stopping, Caldwell’s thumb on my nipple, Hayes’ fingers on my ass, Vaughn’s thumb brushing my lips.

"Job's about loyalty," Caldwell says, his voice low, his hand sliding down my chest, fingers brushing the waistband of my khakis, making me gasp. "And you're loyal, aren't you, Luca? Bet you'd do anything we ask." His fingers dip lower, brushing the outline of my cock, hard and straining, and I moan, my hips bucking, my face burning with shame and want.

"Anything," Hayes murmurs, his lips brushing my ear, his hand sliding under my shirt, fingers splaying across my abs, feeling the muscle tense. "Bet you'd look so good on your knees for us, Luca. Ever think about that? Serving your senators?" His hand squeezes my ass harder, his fingers brushing my hole through the khakis, making me shudder, my cock leaking more, soaking my briefs.

Vaughn's thumb presses into my mouth, just enough to make me taste the salt of his skin, and I'm trembling, my body caught between them, their hands, their eyes, their power. "You're shaking, kid," he says, his voice rough, his eyes dark, hungry. "Bet you're hard as fuck right now, aren't you? Straight boy, but you're loving this, loving us." His thumb slides deeper, brushing my tongue, and I moan, my lips closing around it, sucking instinctively, my cock throbbing harder.

"Fuck, look at him," Caldwell says, his voice thick, his hand cupping my bulge now, squeezing, making me groan, my hips bucking into his touch. "Kid's practically begging for it. Bet he's never had it like this, never knew he wanted it." His fingers stroke my cock through my khakis, slow, teasing, and I'm panting, my body trembling, my head spinning with their words, their touches, the way they're unraveling me.

"Never thought you'd be this easy," Hayes says, his voice low, his fingers sliding under my khakis, brushing the edge of my briefs, teasing my hole through the fabric, making me moan louder, my cock leaking, my balls aching. "Straight boy, my ass. You're our little slut now, aren't you, Luca?" His fingers press harder, circling my hole, the pressure intense, and I'm trembling, my body theirs, my cock throbbing with every touch.

I'm caught, surrounded, their hands on me, their power overwhelming, and I'm straight, I swear I am, but their confidence, their control, has me so fucking hard I can't think, can't breathe. The office smells of their colognes, their whiskey, the musky edge of my own arousal, and I know they're not done, know they're going to push me further, and I'm not sure I can stop it—or if I even want to.

Caldwell's hand is on my cock, stroking slow through my khakis, the fabric tight, damp with precum, his fingers tracing the outline, squeezing just enough to make me gasp, my hips bucking into his touch. Hayes' fingers are teasing my hole through my briefs, circling, pressing, the pressure sending sparks up my spine, my ass clenching instinctively. Vaughn's thumb is in my mouth, rough and salty, my lips closing around it, sucking, tasting the faint musk of his skin as his brown eyes burn into mine, dark and commanding. The Senate office is a haze of heat, the air thick with their colognes—spicy, woodsy, sharp—and the musky edge of my own arousal, my cock throbbing so hard it's painful, my balls aching, my body trembling under their touches. Their power, their confidence, has me unraveling, my straight-boy resolve crumbling with every brush of their hands, every filthy word dripping from their lips.

"Fuck, look at this cock," Caldwell murmurs, his voice low, smooth as bourbon, his fingers tightening, stroking harder, making my breath hitch, my cock leaking more, soaking my briefs. His silver hair catches the dim light, his chiseled jaw set, his dark eyes glinting with something predatory, hotter than sin. "Hard as a fucking rock, kid. Bet you've never been this turned on, have you?" His thumb brushes the head of my cock through the fabric, circling the tip, and I moan, my hips jerking, the sensation sharp, electric, my skin burning under his gaze.

Hayes laughs, low and dirty, his blond hair streaked with gray, his lean frame pressed against my back, his fingers still teasing my hole, slipping under my briefs now, brushing bare skin, making me shudder. "He's practically begging for it," he says, his voice a velvet growl, his lips brushing my ear, hot and wet, his stubble scraping my neck. "This tight little cunt's twitching for us, isn't it? Straight boy, my ass." His finger presses harder, not entering but circling, the pressure intense, making my ass clench, my cock throb, my knees weak. His blue eyes are sharp, his smirk wicked, his body radiating a lean, coiled power that's got me dizzy with want.

Vaughn pulls his thumb from my mouth, leaving my lips slick, and grabs my chin, tilting my head up, his stocky frame looming, his charcoal suit hugging his thick shoulders, his brown eyes dark, hungry, like he's ready to devour me. "You're a fucking tease, aren't you?" he says, his voice rough, gravelly, his fingers tightening, his thumb brushing my lower lip, smearing my spit. "Sucking my thumb like it's a cock. Bet you'd look so good with the real thing in your mouth." His other hand slides to my chest, fingers pinching my nipple through my shirt, twisting just enough to make me gasp, my cock jumping in Caldwell's hand, my body trembling under their combined assault.

"Fuck," I groan, my voice hoarse, my hands gripping the desk, my knuckles white, my body caught in their web, their touches overwhelming. I'm straight, I keep telling myself, but their power, their filthy words, the way they're owning me, has my cock leaking, my ass clenching, my skin burning with every touch. "You guys... you're fucking killing me," I say, my voice shaky, my hips bucking into Caldwell's hand, my ass pressing back against Hayes' fingers, my lips tingling from Vaughn's thumb.

"Killing you?" Caldwell says, his smirk widening, his hand sliding under my shirt, fingers splaying across my abs, feeling the muscle tense, his touch hot, possessive. "Nah, kid, we're just warming you up. Bet this tight body's never felt like this—hot, desperate, ready to break." His fingers trail lower, brushing the waistband of my briefs, slipping inside, grazing the base of my cock, skin on skin now, making me moan, my head tipping back, my breath ragged. His silver hair, his chiseled features, his commanding presence are hotter than fuck, and I'm lost in it, my cock throbbing under his touch, my body begging for more.

Hayes' fingers slide deeper under my briefs, brushing my hole, teasing the rim, the sensation sharp, overwhelming, making my ass clench, my cock leak more. "Look at this," he murmurs, his voice thick, his lips brushing my neck, his stubble scraping, sending shivers down my spine. "Your cunt's so fucking eager, twitching like it wants to be filled. Bet you've never even thought about this, have you? Getting worked over by three senators." His finger presses harder, circling, the pressure building, my ass trembling, my cock throbbing in Caldwell's hand, my body caught between them, their heat, their power.

Vaughn's hand slides from my chin to my neck, fingers wrapping lightly, not choking but holding, his thumb brushing the pulse point, feeling it race. "You're shaking, kid," he says, his voice low, rough, his eyes dark, his stocky frame radiating raw, masculine power that's got my cock leaking, my balls aching. "Bet you're thinking about it now, though. Us, taking you apart, making you our little slut." His other hand slides under my shirt, fingers pinching my other nipple, twisting, making me moan louder, my hips bucking, my cock throbbing under Caldwell's strokes, Hayes' fingers teasing my hole.

"Fuck, please," I groan, my voice breaking, my body trembling, my cock so hard it's painful, my ass clenching, begging for more. I'm straight, I swear, but their touches, their words, the way they're circling me, owning me, has me unraveling, my body theirs, my mind spinning. "You're... you're driving me crazy," I say, my voice hoarse, my hands gripping the desk, my knuckles white, my hips bucking into Caldwell's hand, my ass pressing back against Hayes' fingers, Vaughn's grip on my neck tightening just enough to make my head spin.

"Crazy's the point," Caldwell says, his voice smooth, commanding, his fingers stroking my cock faster, skin hot against mine, his thumb circling the head, smearing precum, making me gasp. "You're our boy now, Luca. Loyal, eager, hard as fuck. Bet you'd do anything we say, wouldn't you?" His hand slides lower, cupping my balls, squeezing gently, the sensation sharp, making my cock throb, my breath hitch. His silver hair, his granite jaw, his dark eyes are a fucking vision, and I'm lost in him, in the power he wields, the way he's unraveling me.

Hayes' fingers press harder, one slipping just inside my hole, not deep but enough to make me moan, my ass clenching, my cock leaking more. "Fuck, this cunt's tight," he murmurs, his voice thick, his lips brushing my ear, his breath hot, his stubble scraping my neck. "Bet it'd feel so good wrapped around us, squeezing like it's begging. You want that, don't you? To be our little fucktoy." His finger moves slow, teasing, the sensation intense, my ass trembling, my cock throbbing in Caldwell's hand, my body caught in their grip, their power overwhelming.

Vaughn leans in, his lips brushing my jaw, his stubble rough, his breath hot, his hand sliding from my neck to my chest, fingers splaying across my pecs, pinching both nipples now, twisting, making me cry out, my cock jumping, my body shaking. "You're ours, kid," he says, his voice rough, his eyes dark, his stocky frame pressing closer, his cologne spicy, heavy, mixing with the musk of my arousal. "Bet you're imagining it—us fucking you, filling you up, making you scream. Straight boy, my ass." His fingers twist harder, the pain sharp, blending with pleasure, my cock leaking, my body trembling under their combined assault.

“Fuck, I… I don’t know,” I groan, my voice wrecked, my hips bucking into Caldwell’s hand, my ass pressing back against Hayes’ finger, Vaughn’s hands on my nipples driving me wild. My cock’s throbbing, my balls aching, my body theirs, my mind spinning with their words, their touches, their power. I’m straight, I keep telling myself, but it’s a lie, crumbling under their hands, their filthy promises, the way they’re making me feel—hot, desperate, ready to break.

“Know what I think?” Caldwell says, his voice low, his hand stroking my cock faster, his fingers tight, his thumb brushing the head, making me moan, my hips jerking. “I think you’re dying for it. Dying to be our little slut, to let us take you apart.” His eyes lock on mine, dark, commanding, his silver hair gleaming, his jaw set, hotter than fuck, and I’m lost in him, in the way he’s owning me, his hand relentless, my cock leaking, my body trembling.

Hayes' finger slides deeper, just enough to stretch, the sensation intense, making my ass clench, my cock throb, my breath ragged. "Fuck, you're so ready," he murmurs, his voice thick, his lips brushing my neck, his stubble scraping, his lean frame pressed against me, his power undeniable. "This cunt's begging for us, Luca. Bet you'd scream so pretty for your senators." His finger moves slow, teasing, the pressure building, my ass trembling, my cock leaking more, my body caught in their web, their touches overwhelming.

Vaughn's hands slide lower, fingers brushing the waistband of my khakis, tugging them down slightly, exposing the damp fabric of my briefs, my cock straining, leaking, the air cool against my skin. "Look at this," he says, his voice rough, his eyes dark, his stocky frame looming, his power raw, intoxicating. "Hard and leaking for us. Bet you'd look so good spread out, taking us one by one." His fingers brush my cock, light, teasing, making me moan, my body trembling, my head spinning with their words, their touches, the tension so thick I can't breathe.

Caldwell's hand is relentless, stroking my cock through my soaked briefs, his fingers hot and commanding, while Hayes' finger teases my hole, circling, pressing just inside, the sensation making my ass clench, my breath hitch. Vaughn's hands are on my chest, pinching my nipples, twisting, the sharp pain blending with pleasure, my cock throbbing, leaking, my body trembling under their combined assault. The Senate office smells of their colognes—spicy, woodsy, sharp—and my own musk, the air thick with heat, the tension so intense I'm dizzy, my straight-boy resolve shattering with every touch, every filthy word. Their rugged faces—silver-haired Caldwell with his granite jaw, blond-streaked Hayes with his predatory smirk, stocky Vaughn with his dark, hungry eyes—are hotter than sin, their power overwhelming, my cock aching, my balls tight.

"Time to see what you're hiding under that suit," Caldwell murmurs, his voice smooth, dangerous, his hands moving to my tie, yanking it loose with a swift tug, the silk hissing against my shirt. His stubble scrapes my neck as he leans in, his lips brushing my pulse, the rough hair sending shivers down my spine, my cock jumping in his hand. "Bet you're fucking perfect, kid," he says, his fingers unbuttoning my shirt, slow, deliberate, exposing my chest, my abs, the lean muscle glistening with sweat.

"Fuck, no," I groan, my voice shaky, my hands gripping the desk, trying to resist, but my body betrays me, arching into his touch, my cock throbbing, leaking more. "I'm... I'm straight," I say, but it's weak, and they laugh, low and knowing, their hands never stopping. Hayes' finger slides deeper, stretching my hole, making me moan, my ass clenching, the sensation intense, filthy, making my head spin.

"Straight, huh?" Hayes says, his voice a velvet growl, his lean frame pressed against my back, his stubble scraping my shoulder as he kisses the skin, rough and hot. "This cunt says otherwise, twitching like it's begging." His free hand tugs at my khakis, pulling them down, the fabric pooling around my ankles, leaving me in my briefs, damp and clinging to my cock, the outline obscene. His finger moves slow, teasing my hole, the pressure building, my ass trembling, my cock leaking, my body caught in their grip.

Vaughn's hands slide to my shirt, yanking it off my shoulders, the buttons popping, the fabric hitting the floor. "Look at this body," he says, his voice rough, his brown eyes dark, his stocky frame looming as he leans in, his stubble grazing my chest, making me gasp, my nipples hardening. "Fucking perfect, kid. Bet you taste as good as you look." His tongue flicks out, licking my nipple, the rough hair of his beard scraping my skin, sending jolts to my cock, my moans louder, my resistance crumbling.

"Please," I groan, my voice wrecked, my hands gripping the desk, my body trembling as they strip me bare. Caldwell's hands move to my briefs, tugging them down, my cock springing free, thick and veined, leaking precum in thick beads. The air's cool against my skin, but their hands, their mouths, are hot, overwhelming, their rugged faces—stubble, hard jaws, hungry eyes—driving me wild. "I shouldn't," I say, but it's a lie, my cock throbbing, my ass clenching, my body begging for more.

“Shouldn’t, but you want it,” Caldwell says, his voice low, his silver hair gleaming as he drops to his knees, his stubble scraping my thigh as he leans in, his tongue licking a stripe up my cock, slow, deliberate, tasting the precum. The rough hair of his beard brushes my shaft, the sensation sharp, electric, making me moan, my hips bucking. “Fuck, you taste good,” he murmurs, his lips wrapping around the head, sucking slow, his tongue swirling, the stubble scraping my sensitive skin, driving me crazy.

Hayes pulls his finger out, making me gasp, and drops behind me, his hands spreading my ass, his stubble grazing my cheeks as he leans in, his tongue flicking my hole, hot and wet, the rough hair scraping my skin, sending shivers up my spine. “This cunt’s so fucking tight,” he says, his voice thick, his tongue licking deeper, circling the rim, teasing, the sensation intense, filthy, making my cock throb in Caldwell’s mouth, my moans loud, desperate. His beard scratches my ass, the contrast of rough hair and wet tongue overwhelming, my body trembling, my resistance gone.

Vaughn's lips move to my neck, his stubble scraping my pulse, his tongue licking slow, tasting the sweat, the salt, his hands roaming my chest, pinching my nipples, twisting, making me cry out. "You're ours now," he says, his voice rough, his stocky frame pressing closer, his cologne spicy, heavy, mixing with the musk of my arousal. His beard brushes my skin, rough and hot, as he licks down to my pit, sniffing deep, the musky scent making him groan, his tongue lapping at the hair, tasting the sweat, the raw edge of me. "Fuck, you smell like a man," he says, his voice thick, his stubble scraping my pit, sending jolts to my cock, my body shaking.

"Fuck, stop," I groan, but it's weak, my hips bucking into Caldwell's mouth, my ass pressing back against Hayes' tongue, Vaughn's lips on my pit driving me wild. Their rugged faces, their stubble, their power—it's too much, too good, my cock throbbing, my balls aching, my body theirs. "I'm straight," I say, but it's a whisper, a lie, my moans loud, my body trembling, loving the rough scrape of their beards, the heat of their mouths, the way they're unraveling me.

"Straight boys don't moan like this," Hayes says, his voice muffled against my ass, his tongue probing deeper, licking, sucking, his stubble scraping my cheeks, the sensation intense, making my ass clench, my cock leak more. "This cunt's begging for us, Luca. Bet it'd feel so good wrapped around our cocks." His hands spread my cheeks wider, his tongue pushing inside, the rough hair of his beard scratching my sensitive skin, driving me crazy, my moans louder, my body trembling under his assault.

Caldwell pulls off my cock, his lips slick, his stubble glistening with my precum, and moves to my balls, sucking one into his mouth, his tongue swirling, the rough hair of his beard scraping the sensitive skin, making me gasp, my hips bucking. "Fucking perfect," he murmurs, his voice smooth, his tongue licking up my shaft, tasting every inch, his stubble brushing my cock, the contrast of rough and wet driving me wild. His silver hair, his granite jaw, his commanding presence are hotter than fuck, and I'm lost in him, my cock throbbing, my body begging for more.

Vaughn's lips move to my feet, yanking off my dress shoes, my socks, his hands rough, calloused, gripping my ankles. "Look at these," he says, his voice rough, his eyes dark, his tongue licking the arch of my foot, the rough hair of his beard scraping the sensitive skin, sending jolts to my cock, my moans loud, desperate. The musky scent of my feet, sweaty from a long day, makes him groan, his tongue lapping at my toes, sucking, the sensation intense, filthy, his stubble scratching, driving me crazy. "You taste like a fucking dream," he says, his voice thick, his beard brushing my foot, his hands squeezing my ankles, holding me in place.

Hayes' tongue keeps working my hole, licking deep, the rough stubble scraping my ass, the sensation overwhelming, my cock throbbing in Caldwell's mouth, my body trembling under Vaughn's lips. "Fuck, you guys," I groan, my voice wrecked, my hands gripping the desk, my knuckles white, my body caught in their web, their mouths, their beards. "It's too much," I say, but my hips buck, my ass presses back, my cock leaks, my body loving every second, the rough scrape of their stubble, the heat of their tongues, the power in their touches.

“Too much?” Caldwell says, pulling off my cock, his lips slick, his stubble glistening, his hand stroking me slow, keeping me on edge. “You’re loving it, kid. Moaning like a slut, cock leaking like a faucet.” His tongue licks up my shaft again, slow, deliberate, his stubble scraping, making me moan, my hips bucking. His silver hair, his dark eyes, his commanding presence are driving me wild, my cock throbbing, my balls aching, my body theirs.

Hayes’ tongue probes deeper, his stubble scraping my ass, his hands spreading my cheeks, his lips sucking the rim, the sensation intense, filthy, making my cock leak more, my moans louder. “This cunt’s so fucking ready,” he murmurs, his voice thick, his beard scratching, his tongue licking, teasing, driving me crazy. “Bet you’d scream for us, Luca. Straight boy, my ass.” His finger slides in again, slow, stretching, the pressure building, my ass clenching, my cock throbbing, my body trembling under their assault.

Vaughn’s lips move back to my neck, his stubble scraping my pulse, his tongue licking, tasting the sweat, his hands roaming my chest, pinching my nipples, twisting, making me cry out, my cock jumping in Caldwell's hand, my ass clenching around Hayes' finger. "You're ours," he says, his voice rough, his stocky frame pressing closer, his cologne heavy, mixing with the musk of my arousal. His beard brushes my skin, rough and hot, as he licks my pit again, sniffing deep, groaning, the sensation overwhelming, my body shaking, my cock leaking, my straight-boy resolve gone, lost in their touches, their power, the filthy heat of it all.

Caldwell's lips are on my cock, his stubble scraping the shaft, his tongue swirling around the head, tasting my precum, the rough hair driving me wild, while Hayes' tongue probes my hole, his beard scratching my ass, the wet heat making my body tremble. Vaughn's mouth is on my pit, licking, sniffing, his stubble grazing the sensitive skin, his hands pinching my nipples, twisting, sending jolts to my cock, my moans loud, desperate. The Senate office is a haze of heat, their colognes—spicy, woodsy, sharp—mixing with the musky tang of my sweat, my precum, the air thick with tension, their rugged faces—silver-haired Caldwell, blond-streaked Hayes, stocky Vaughn—hotter than sin, their power overwhelming, my body theirs.

Caldwell pulls off my cock, his lips slick, his stubble glistening with my precum, and stands, his dark eyes burning, his silver hair catching the light. "Time to show us what that mouth can do," he says, his voice smooth, commanding, his hands unbuckling his belt, the metal clinking, his tailored trousers dropping to reveal a thick, veined cock, hard and leaking, the head flushed, glistening. He grabs my hair, yanking my head forward, his cock brushing my lips, the musky scent hitting me hard—sweat, cologne, raw masculinity. "Suck it, kid," he growls, his voice low, his cock slapping my cheek, the wet smack loud, making my face burn, my cock throb, my body weak under his power.

"Fuck, no," I groan, my voice shaky, my hands gripping the desk, my body trembling, but my lips part, my tongue flicking out, tasting the precum on his cock, salty and bitter, the sensation overwhelming. I'm straight, I tell myself, but his power, his rugged jaw, the stubble scraping my cheek as he slaps me again with his cock, has me helpless, my cock leaking, my balls aching. "I... I can't," I say, but it's weak, and he laughs, low and knowing, his hand tightening in my hair, guiding his cock to my lips, pushing the head past, stretching my mouth.

“Suck it like you mean it,” he says, his voice rough, his hips bucking slightly, his cock sliding deeper, filling my mouth, the taste intense, musky, the precum coating my tongue. His stubble grazes my chin as he thrusts, slow, deliberate, the rough hair scraping my skin, making me moan around his cock, my body trembling, overloaded with the heat, the weight, the power of him. I’m sucking now, my lips tight, my tongue swirling, tasting every inch, his groans loud, his hand guiding me, making me take more.

Hayes pulls back from my ass, his tongue leaving my hole slick, tingling, and stands, his lean frame towering, his blond hair streaked with gray, his blue eyes sharp, predatory. His trousers hit the floor, his cock springing free, longer than Caldwell’s, not as thick but veined, leaking, the head flushed. “My turn,” he says, his voice a velvet growl, his hand grabbing my jaw, turning my head, his cock slapping my other cheek, the wet sound sharp, making my face burn hotter, my cock throb harder. “Open up, slut,” he says, his stubble scraping my jaw as he leans in, his cock brushing my lips, the musky scent stronger, mixed with his woodsy cologne.

I moan, my lips parting, my tongue flicking out, tasting his precum, sharper, more bitter than Caldwell's, the sensation dizzying. "No, please," I say, my voice muffled, but my mouth opens wider, his cock sliding in, stretching my lips, filling my mouth, the taste overwhelming, my head spinning. I'm sucking now, my tongue working the underside, feeling the vein pulse, his groans low, his hand in my hair, pulling me down, making me gag, my eyes watering, my cock leaking, my body weak, helpless under their power.

Vaughn steps up, his stocky frame looming, his charcoal suit open, his cock thick, shorter but massive, the head dark, leaking, the musky scent hitting me like a punch—sweat, spice, raw man. "You're taking us all, kid," he says, his voice rough, his brown eyes dark, hungry, his hand grabbing my chin, his cock slapping my face, the wet smack loud, making my cheeks burn, my cock throb, my body trembling. "Suck this cock, show us what a good boy you are." His stubble scrapes my cheek as he leans in, his cock pushing past my lips, filling my mouth, the taste intense, musky, his precum thick, coating my tongue.

I'm overwhelmed, cock after cock, their sizes different—Caldwell's thick, Hayes' long, Vaughn's massive—each one stretching my mouth, the precum mixing, salty, bitter, musky, my head spinning, my body weak, helpless. I'm sucking Vaughn now, my lips tight, my tongue swirling, his groans loud, his hand in my hair, guiding me, his stubble scraping my chin, the rough hair driving me wild. "Fuck, you're good," he growls, his hips bucking, his cock hitting the back of my throat, making me gag, my eyes watering, my cock leaking onto the floor.

Hayes steps behind me, his hands on my ass, spreading my cheeks, his stubble grazing my skin, the rough hair sending shivers up my spine. "This cunt's so fucking ready," he murmurs, his voice thick, his tongue flicking my hole again, teasing, licking, the sensation intense, making my cock throb, my moans muffled around Vaughn's cock. His finger slides in, slow, stretching, the pressure building, my ass clenching, my body trembling, overloaded with their cocks, their mouths, their power.

I pull off Vaughn's cock, gasping, my lips slick, my voice hoarse. "Fuck, stop," I say, my voice breaking, my hands gripping the desk, my body trembling, but my cock's leaking, my ass clenching, my body begging for more despite my words. "I'm… I'm straight," I say, but it's a lie, weak and crumbling, my head spinning, my body theirs. Caldwell laughs, his hand grabbing my hair, pulling my head back, his cock slapping my face again, the wet sound sharp, making me moan, my cock throbbing.

"Straight boys don't suck cock like this," he says, his voice smooth, his silver hair gleaming, his dark eyes burning. His cock pushes back into my mouth, filling it, the taste musky, his stubble scraping my chin, the sensation overwhelming. I'm sucking again, my tongue swirling, tasting his precum, my body weak, my moans muffled, my cock leaking, my balls aching.

Hayes' finger pulls out, and I feel his cock now, the head brushing my hole, hot and slick, teasing, not entering yet, the pressure intense, making my ass clench, my body tremble. “No, stop,” I groan, pulling off Caldwell’s cock, my voice wrecked, my hands gripping the desk, my body shaking. “I can’t… not that,” I say, but my cock’s throbbing, my ass twitching, my body betraying me, wanting it despite my words.

Vaughn grabs my face, his lips crashing into mine, his kiss devouring, his tongue pushing deep, tasting my mouth, my precum, his stubble scraping my lips, my jaw, the rough hair driving me wild. His kiss is rough, hungry, shutting me up, his hands holding my face, his cock brushing my thigh, hot and heavy. “You want it,” he growls against my lips, his voice rough, his brown eyes dark, his stocky frame pressing closer, his power overwhelming. “You’re our slut now, kid. Take it.”

Hayes pushes in, slow, the head of his cock stretching my hole, the pressure intense, burning, making me gasp into Vaughn’s kiss, my body trembling, my cock leaking, my balls aching. “Fuck,” I groan, my voice muffled, Vaughn’s tongue still in my mouth, his stubble scraping, his kiss relentless. Hayes’ cock slides deeper, inch by inch, filling me, the stretch overwhelming, his stubble grazing my ass as he leans in, his breath hot, his groans low, his cock long, hitting deep, making my body shake, my moans loud, desperate.

“Take it, slut,” Hayes says, his voice thick, his hips bucking, his cock sliding deeper, the sensation intense, filthy, my ass clenching, my cock throbbing in Caldwell’s hand, Vaughn’s lips devouring me. I’m overloaded, their cocks, their stubble, their power surrounding me, my body weak, helpless, trembling under their assault, the tension so thick I can’t breathe, my straight-boy resolve gone, lost in the heat, the musk, the raw power of them taking me apart.

Hayes’ cock is deep in my ass, long and relentless, stretching me, the burn blending with pleasure as he thrusts slow, deliberate, his stubble scraping my cheeks, his hands gripping my hips, bruising the skin. Vaughn’s lips devour mine, his tongue plunging deep, tasting my moans, his coarse beard rubbing my jaw raw, while Caldwell’s thick cock fills my mouth, his precum bitter and slick, coating my tongue as I suck, my lips stretched tight, his silver stubble grazing my chin. The Senate office is a furnace, the air thick with their spicy colognes, my sweat, and the musky tang of precum, the desk creaking under my grip, my cock hard as fuck, leaking a steady stream of precum onto the floor, my balls aching, my body trembling under their rugged, powerful assault. I'm straight, or was, but their dominance, their filthy control, has me loving every second, my moans muffled, my ass clenching, my cock throbbing with every thrust, every suck.

"Fuck, this cunt's tight," Hayes growls, his voice a low rumble, his lean frame pressed against my back, his blond hair falling into his sharp blue eyes as he thrusts deeper, his cock hitting that spot that makes my vision blur, my moans louder, vibrating around Caldwell's shaft. His fingers dig into my hips, pulling me back, making me take every inch, the stretch intense, my ass gripping him like a vice. "You're our little slut now, aren't you? Taking my cock like you were born for it."

I pull off Caldwell's cock, gasping, my lips slick, my voice hoarse. "Fuck, it's too much," I say, but my hips buck back, chasing Hayes' cock, my own cock leaking, dripping onto the carpet, my body screaming for more. Vaughn's kiss breaks, his brown eyes dark, his stocky frame looming as he grabs my hair, yanking my head toward his massive cock, thicker than the others, the head dark and leaking, the musky scent hitting me like a drug—sweat, spice, raw man.

"Suck it, boy," Vaughn says, his voice rough, his beard scraping my cheek as he slaps his cock against my lips, the wet smack loud, making my face burn, my cock throb harder. "Show us how much you love being our fucktoy." I moan, my lips parting, his cock pushing in, stretching my mouth, the taste overwhelming—musky, heavy with precum, thicker than Caldwell's, filling me completely. I suck, my tongue swirling, tasting him, my eyes watering, my body trembling, overloaded with their cocks, their power.

Caldwell steps back, stroking his cock, his silver hair gleaming, his dark eyes burning as he watches me suck Vaughn, Hayes fucking my ass slow, deep. "Look at you, taking it from both ends," he says, his voice smooth, commanding, his hand reaching down to pinch my nipple, twisting hard, making me moan around Vaughn's cock, my cock jumping, leaking more. "Never thought you'd be this easy, kid. Our perfect little slut, hard as fuck for us."

Hayes pulls out, his cock slick, glistening, and I whimper at the emptiness, my ass clenching, begging. "Don't whine," he says, his voice thick, his hand slapping my ass, the crack sharp, the sting making my cock leak, my body shake. "Vaughn's turn. Let's see how you handle that thick cock." Vaughn pulls out of my mouth, his cock wet with my spit, and moves behind me, his hands spreading my cheeks, his beard grazing my skin as he leans in, his tongue flicking my hole, teasing, the rough hair sending shivers up my spine.

"Fuck, please," I groan, my voice wrecked, my hands gripping the desk, my cock throbbing, leaking, my body trembling under their control. Vaughn's cock brushes my hole, massive, hot, the head pressing, stretching, the pressure intense, making me gasp, my ass clenching. "Too big," I say, my voice shaky, but my hips push back, my cock leaking, my body wanting it despite my words.

“Take it,” Vaughn growls, his voice rough, his hands gripping my hips, his cock pushing in, slow, stretching me wider than Hayes, the burn sharp, blending with pleasure as he fills me, inch by inch. His beard scrapes my ass, his breath hot, his groans low as he thrusts, deep, relentless, making me cry out, my cock throbbing, leaking onto the floor. “This cunt’s perfect,” he says, his voice thick, his hips snapping, his cock hitting deep, making my vision blur, my moans loud, desperate.

Caldwell grabs my hair, pulling my head up, his cock slapping my face, the wet sound sharp, making my cheeks burn, my cock throb. “Back to work, slut,” he says, his voice smooth, his silver stubble glistening as he pushes his cock into my mouth, filling it, the taste musky, his precum coating my tongue. I suck, my lips tight, my tongue swirling, his groans loud, his hand guiding me, making me take more, my eyes watering, my body trembling, overloaded with Vaughn’s cock in my ass, Caldwell’s in my mouth, Hayes stroking his nearby, watching, his blue eyes sharp, predatory.

“You love this, don’t you?” Hayes says, his voice a velvet growl, his lean frame stepping closer, his hand stroking my back, fingers trailing down my spine, making me shiver. “Straight boy, my ass. You’re leaking like a faucet, taking cock like a pro.” His hand slides to my cock, stroking slow, his fingers slick with my precum, the sensation intense, making me moan around Caldwell’s cock, my ass clenching around Vaughn’s, my body shaking, loving every second, the tension so thick I can’t breathe.

Vaughn’s thrusts speed up, his cock slamming into me, the stretch overwhelming, his beard scraping my ass as he leans in, his breath hot, his groans raw. “Fuck, I’m close,” he says, his voice rough, his hands bruising my hips, his cock hitting that spot, making my cock throb, my precum pooling on the floor. I moan, my body trembling, my mind spinning, caught in their power, their cocks, their rugged faces—stubble, hard jaws, hungry eyes—driving me wild.

“Fuck, no,” I gasp, pulling off Caldwell’s cock, my voice hoarse, my lips slick, as Vaughn’s thrusts grow erratic, his cock pulsing inside me. “Don’t—” But it’s too late, his groan loud, his hips slamming forward, his cock buried deep as he cums, hot and thick, filling my ass, the sensation shocking, overwhelming, my cock throbbing, leaking, my body trembling, my mind reeling. “What the fuck,” I groan, my voice wrecked, my ass clenching around him, the warmth spreading, filthy, intense, making my cock leak more, my balls aching.

Vaughn pulls out, his cock slick, glistening, and Hayes takes his place, his long cock pushing in, the stretch easier now, slick with Vaughn’s cum, making me moan, my body shaking. “Shut up and take it,” Hayes says, his voice thick, his hand slapping my ass, the sting sharp, making my cock jump. Caldwell grabs my hair, pushing his cock back into my mouth, thrusting deep, his stubble scraping my chin, his precum bitter, coating my tongue.

“Suck it good,” Caldwell growls, his voice smooth, his hips bucking, his cock hitting the back of my throat, making me gag, my eyes watering, my cock throbbing, leaking, loving the overload, the power, the filth. Hayes fucks me harder, his cock long, hitting deep, the wet sound of his thrusts obscene, mixing with Vaughn's cum, my ass clenching, my moans muffled around Caldwell's cock.

Hayes' hand strokes my cock, fast, rough, his fingers slick, the sensation intense, making me moan louder, my body trembling, my balls tight. "Gonna make you feel it," he says, his voice a growl, his thrusts brutal, his cock hitting that spot, driving me crazy. Caldwell's cock pulses in my mouth, his groans loud, his hand tightening in my hair, and I know he's close, his precum thick, coating my tongue.

"Fuck, take it," Caldwell says, his voice breaking, his hips bucking, his cock pulsing as he cums, hot and thick, flooding my mouth, the taste bitter, musky, overwhelming. I swallow, choking, my lips slick, my eyes watering, my cock throbbing, leaking, my body shaking as Hayes fucks me harder, his cock relentless, his hand stroking me, keeping me on edge.

Hayes pulls out, his cock slick, and moves in front of me, stroking fast, his blue eyes burning, his blond hair falling into his face. "Open up," he says, his voice thick, and I do, my lips parted, my tongue out, as he cums, thick ropes splattering across my chest, hot and sticky, dripping down my abs, my cock throbbing, leaking, my body trembling under their assault. "Fucking perfect," he murmurs, his hand smearing his cum across my chest, his stubble grazing my shoulder as he leans in, his breath hot.

I'm a mess, my ass dripping with Vaughn's cum, my mouth thick with Caldwell's, my chest slick with Hayes', my cock hard as fuck, leaking, my body trembling, weak, helpless. I'm their slut, used and owned, my straight-boy resolve gone, shattered by their power, their cocks, their rugged faces. The office is quiet now, just our panting, the air heavy with cum, sweat, and cologne, their eyes on me, dark, satisfied, but the tension lingers, their hands still on me, promising more, and I know I'm theirs, completely, utterly fucked.

PUNISHED BF

I'm Jace, 28, lean but ripped, my body carved from years of hitting the gym and fucking my way through life's stresses. My chest is broad, dusted with dark hair, my abs tight, leading to a V that points straight to my thick cock, always ready to go. My arms are corded with muscle, inked with a tribal sleeve on one side, a skull on the other, and my dark brown hair's cropped short, framing hazel eyes that burn with intensity. My jaw's sharp, stubbled, giving me a rugged edge, and my ass, firm and round, fills out my jeans just right. I'm the kind of guy who takes charge, always have, especially with my twink boyfriend, Leo, who's been pushing my buttons lately, testing my patience with his bratty antics.

The apartment's dim, the late-night city lights filtering through the blinds, casting stripes across the hardwood floor. The air's thick with the scent of my cologne—cedar, musk—and the faint tang of whiskey from the glass on the coffee table. Leo's sprawled on the couch, his slim frame barely filling out his tight black tank and ripped skinny jeans, his blond hair messy, falling into his blue eyes that sparkle with defiance. He's 22, all lithe muscle and smooth skin, his ass a perfect bubble that begs to be grabbed, his lips full, always smirking like he knows he's got me wrapped around his finger. Tonight, though, he's gone too far—flirting with some guy at the club, grinding on him right in front of me, daring me to react.

"You think that was cute?" I say, my voice low, a growl that makes his smirk falter, his eyes flicking up to meet mine, a mix of nerves and excitement. I'm standing over him, my black tee clinging to my chest, my jeans low, the bulge of my cock already half-hard, straining against the denim. "Fucking with me like that, Leo?

Dancing with that prick, letting him put his hands on you?" I step closer, my boots heavy on the floor, my hands flexing, itching to grab him, to show him who he belongs to.

He leans back, his tank riding up, exposing a sliver of his smooth abs, his nipples hard through the thin fabric. "What's the big deal, Jace?" he says, his voice teasing, but there's a tremor in it, his eyes darting to my bulge, then back to my face. "Just having fun. You're always so... serious." He bites his lip, that fucking lip that drives me crazy, and shifts, his ass pressing into the couch, his jeans so tight I can see the outline of his cock, small but hard, twitching under my gaze.

"Fun?" I say, my voice dropping, rough, my hand grabbing his chin, tilting his face up, my thumb brushing his lip, rough, calloused, making him gasp. "You think it's fun to make me watch some asshole grind on my boy?" My other hand slides to his throat, not squeezing, just holding, feeling his pulse race, my cock throbbing harder, pressing against my jeans. His eyes widen, but he doesn't pull away, his breath hitching, his cock twitching in his jeans, betraying how much he's loving this.

"I didn't mean—" he starts, but I cut him off, my thumb pressing into his lip, parting them, his breath hot against my skin. "Don't fucking lie," I say, my voice sharp, my hazel eyes burning into his, my hand tightening on his throat, just enough to make him squirm. "You wanted this, Leo. Wanted to push me, see how far you can go. Well, you're gonna find out." My cock's fully hard now, a thick bulge in my jeans, and I know he sees it, his eyes flicking down, his tongue darting out to lick his lips.

He shifts, his ass grinding into the couch, his hands gripping the cushions, his voice shaky but defiant. "What're you gonna do, huh?" he says, his blue eyes sparkling, challenging, his smirk back, but it's nervous, his cock straining against his jeans. "You're always so sweet, Jace. All kisses and cuddles. You gonna spank me or something?" He laughs, but it's breathy, his body leaning into my touch, his nipples hard, poking through his tank, his ass begging to be grabbed.

I lean in, my lips brushing his ear, my stubble scraping his smooth skin, my breath hot, making him shiver. "Spank you?" I say, my voice low, dangerous, my hand sliding from his throat to his chest, pinching his nipple through the tank, twisting hard, making him gasp, his back arching. "Oh, baby, I'm gonna do so much more than that. You've been a brat, and I'm done being gentle." My other hand grabs his thigh, squeezing the lean muscle, my fingers digging in, making him moan, his cock twitching, a damp spot forming on his jeans.

“Fuck, Jace,” he says, his voice breaking, his hands reaching for me, but I grab his wrists, pinning them above his head, my body pressing him into the couch, my cock grinding against his thigh, the denim rough, the friction making me groan. His eyes are wide, his lips parted, his breath ragged, his cock leaking, the scent of his arousal—clean, boyish, with a hint of his citrus body wash—mixing with mine, making the air heavy, electric.

“You think you can play me?” I say, my voice rough, my lips brushing his, not kissing, just teasing, my stubble scraping his lips, making him whimper. “Flirt with some random fuck, make me watch? You’re mine, Leo, and I’m gonna remind you who you belong to.” My hand slides under his tank, fingers splaying across his smooth abs, feeling them tense, his skin hot, slick with sweat. My cock’s throbbing, leaking precum into my boxers, but I’m holding back, wanting to drag this out, make him beg, make him pay.

He squirms, his ass grinding against the couch, his cock straining, his voice shaky but still defiant. “You’re jealous,” he says, his smirk trembling, his blue eyes locked on mine, daring me. “I was just dancing, Jace. Didn’t mean anything. You gonna punish me for that?” His tongue darts out, licking his lips, and I can’t help it—I lean in, biting his lower lip, hard enough to make him gasp, his cock twitching, his body arching into mine.

“Jealous?” I growl, my hand sliding to his ass, squeezing through his jeans, feeling the firm muscle, the perfect curve that drives me fucking crazy. “I don’t get jealous, baby. I get even.” I slap his ass, not hard, but sharp, the sound cracking through the room, making him moan, his eyes fluttering, his cock leaking more, the damp spot growing. “You’re gonna learn what happens when you fuck with me.” My voice is low, my stubble scraping his neck as I kiss the skin, tasting the salt, the citrus, my tongue flicking out, making him shiver.

“Fuck, okay,” he says, his voice breathy, his hands pulling against my grip, but I hold him tight, my body pinning him, my cock grinding harder against his thigh, the friction intense, my balls aching. “I’m sorry, Jace. Didn’t mean to piss you off.” His voice is softer now, less defiant, but his eyes still sparkle, his cock still hard, his ass pressing back into my hand, begging for more despite his words.

“Sorry’s not enough,” I say, my voice rough, my hand sliding under his jeans, fingers brushing the waistband of his briefs, feeling the heat, the smooth skin. “You’re gonna earn it, Leo. Gonna show me you’re mine.” I yank his tank up, pulling it over his head, exposing his smooth chest, his pink nipples hard, his abs glistening with sweat. My lips brush his collarbone, my stubble scraping, my tongue licking, tasting him, his moans louder, his body trembling under me.

"Jace, please," he says, his voice breaking, his hips bucking, his cock straining against his jeans, the damp spot obscene, his blue eyes wide, pleading but still defiant. "I'm yours, okay? Always yours." His hands pull against my grip, his body arching, his ass grinding into my hand, his cock leaking, his scent filling the air, driving me wild.

I let go of his wrists, my hands moving to his jeans, unbuttoning them, yanking them down, his briefs tight, clinging to his small, hard cock, the fabric soaked with precum. "Look at you," I say, my voice thick, my hand cupping his cock, squeezing through the briefs, making him moan, his hips bucking. "Hard as fuck, leaking for me. You love this, don't you? Love pushing me till I snap." My thumb brushes the head of his cock, smearing the precum, the fabric slick, his moans loud, desperate.

"Fuck, yes," he admits, his voice wrecked, his hands grabbing my shoulders, fingers digging into my muscle, his eyes locked on mine, blue and burning. "I love it, Jace. Love you like this, all pissed and rough." His confession hits me like a punch, my cock throbbing, leaking, my hands trembling as I pull his briefs down, his cock springing free, small but hard, leaking, the head flushed, glistening.

I grab his thighs, spreading them, my lips brushing his inner thigh, my stubble scraping his smooth skin, making him shiver, his cock twitching. "You're gonna pay for that," I say, my voice low, my tongue licking a stripe up his thigh, tasting the sweat, the citrus, my hands squeezing his ass, spreading his cheeks, exposing his tight, pink hole. "Gonna fuck you so hard you won't forget who owns this cunt." My breath's hot against his skin, my stubble grazing his balls, making him moan, his cock leaking, dripping onto his abs.

"Jace, fuck," he groans, his voice breaking, his hands gripping my hair, pulling, his hips bucking, his cock begging for attention. "Do it, please. I'm sorry, just... do it." His voice is desperate, his body trembling, his ass clenching under my hands, his scent overwhelming, driving me crazy. The apartment's quiet, just our heavy breathing, the city lights flickering, the tension so thick I can barely think, my cock throbbing, my balls aching, ready to take him apart, to punish him, to make him mine.

Leo's sprawled beneath me, his slim frame trembling, his smooth chest heaving, pink nipples hard, his small cock leaking precum onto his abs, glistening in the dim city light filtering through the blinds. My hands grip his thighs, spreading them wide, my stubble scraping the soft skin of his inner thigh, the rough hair sending shivers through him, his moans soft but desperate. His tight, pink hole is exposed, twitching under my gaze, and my cock throbs in my jeans, leaking, my balls aching, but I'm holding back, dragging this out, making him squirm for pushing me too far. The apartment smells of my cedar musk, his citrus body wash, and the sharp tang of our arousal, the air thick, electric, the tension coiling tighter with every touch, every filthy word.

"You think you can just bat those eyes and get away with it?" I growl, my voice low, rough, my lips brushing his thigh, my tongue flicking out, tasting the sweat, the faint salt of his skin. My hands slide to his ass, squeezing the firm, round cheeks, my fingers digging in, making him gasp, his cock twitching, a bead of precum dripping down his shaft. "Flirting with that fucker, grinding on him like you're not mine." My stubble grazes his balls, the sensitive skin tightening, his moan louder, his hands gripping the couch cushions, knuckles white.

“Jace, I didn’t mean—” he starts, his voice breathy, trembling, but I cut him off, my hand slapping his thigh, not hard but sharp, the sound cracking through the room, his skin pinkening under my palm. “Don’t fucking lie,” I say, my voice thick, my hazel eyes burning into his blue ones, wide and pleading but still sparking with defiance. My fingers trail up his thigh, brushing the base of his cock, light, teasing, making him buck, his moan desperate, his cock leaking more, the damp spot on the couch growing.

“I’m sorry,” he says, his voice breaking, his hips lifting, chasing my touch, his ass clenching under my hands. “I just... wanted to see you like this, all pissed and hot.” His confession makes my cock throb harder, my jeans tight, my balls aching, but I keep my control, my hand sliding to his hip, pinning him down, my thumb brushing the sharp bone, feeling him tremble.

"Hot, huh?" I say, my voice a low rumble, my lips brushing his navel, my stubble scraping his smooth abs, making him shiver, his cock twitching against my chest as I lean over him. "You like me pissed, Leo? Like pushing me till I snap?" My hand slides up his side, fingers tracing the lean muscle, finding his nipple, pinching hard, twisting, making him cry out, his back arching, his cock leaking, dripping onto his skin. His blue eyes flutter, his lips parted, his breath ragged, and I can see he's loving it, loving the edge, the danger.

"Fuck, yes," he admits, his voice shaky, his hands reaching for me, but I grab his wrists again, pinning them above his head with one hand, my body pressing him into the couch, my cock grinding against his thigh through my jeans, the friction intense, making me groan low in my throat. "I love it, Jace. Love you like this, all rough and mean." His voice is desperate, his cock twitching, his ass pressing into my other hand, begging for more.

"Mean's just the start," I say, my voice rough, my lips brushing his ear, my stubble scraping his cheek, the rough hair making him whimper, his body trembling under me. My free hand slides down his chest, fingers splaying across his abs, feeling them tense, his skin hot, slick with sweat. "You're gonna beg before I'm done, baby. Gonna make you wish you never looked at that guy." My fingers brush his cock, light, teasing, not stroking, just grazing the head, smearing the precum, making him moan, his hips bucking, his cock throbbing under my touch.

"Jace, please," he groans, his voice wrecked, his wrists pulling against my grip, his body arching, his ass grinding into my hand, his cock leaking, dripping onto his abs. "Touch me, fuck, just... do something." His blue eyes are wild, his blond hair messy, sticking to his forehead, his smooth skin glistening, and he's so fucking pretty, so desperate, it's driving me crazy, my cock throbbing, my balls aching, but I'm not giving in yet, not letting him off easy.

I release his wrists, my hands moving to his shoulders, squeezing the lean muscle, my thumbs brushing his collarbone, feeling the delicate bone under his smooth skin. "You don't get to call the shots," I say, my voice low, my lips brushing his neck, my tongue licking a stripe up to his jaw, tasting the salt, the citrus, his stubble barely there, soft compared to my rough scruff. My hands slide down his arms, gripping his biceps, small but toned, my fingers digging in, making him gasp, his cock twitching against my thigh as I press closer, my jeans rough against his bare skin.

"Fuck, you're killing me," he says, his voice breathy, his hands grabbing my tee, pulling, his fingers brushing my chest, feeling the hair, the muscle. "I'm yours, Jace, okay? Just... touch me, please." His voice is pleading, but there's still that spark, that bratty edge that makes my cock throb, my hands itch to punish him, to make him mine in every way.

I pull back, my hands grabbing his thighs, spreading them wider, my fingers digging into the soft flesh, my stubble grazing his inner thigh as I lean in, my breath hot against his balls, making them tighten, his cock twitching, leaking more. “You want my hands?” I say, my voice thick, my fingers trailing up his thigh, brushing the base of his cock, teasing, not touching where he wants. “Earn it, Leo. Tell me how fucking sorry you are.” My tongue flicks out, licking the crease of his thigh, tasting the sweat, the musk, his moan loud, his hips bucking, his cock begging for attention.

“I’m so fucking sorry,” he says, his voice breaking, his hands gripping my hair, pulling, his body trembling. “I shouldn’t have danced with him, shouldn’t have pushed you. I’m yours, Jace, all yours.” His confession hits me hard, my cock leaking, my balls aching, but I keep teasing, my lips brushing his balls, my stubble scraping the sensitive skin, making him whimper, his cock dripping, the precum pooling on his abs.

"Good boy," I say, my voice low, my hand sliding to his ass, squeezing the firm cheek, my fingers brushing his hole, tight and pink, twitching under my touch. "But you're not off the hook." My thumb circles his hole, not entering, just teasing, the pressure making him moan, his cock twitching, his body shaking. My other hand slides up his chest, pinching his nipple again, twisting, making him cry out, his back arching, his cock leaking more, the scent of his arousal thick, driving me wild.

"Fuck, Jace, please," he groans, his voice desperate, his hips bucking, his ass pressing into my hand, his cock throbbing, leaking, his blue eyes wide, pleading. "I need you, need your hands, your mouth, fuck, anything." His hands grab my shoulders, fingers digging into my muscle, his body trembling, his smooth skin glistening, and he's so fucking desperate, so mine, it's making my cock throb, my balls ache, my control fraying.

I lean in, my lips brushing his ear, my stubble scraping his cheek, my breath hot, making him shiver. "You need me?" I say, my voice rough, my hand sliding to his cock, finally wrapping around it, stroking slow, his small shaft hot, slick with precum, pulsing in my hand. "You're gonna get me, baby, but it's gonna be my way." My thumb brushes the head, smearing the precum, making him moan, his hips bucking, his cock throbbing, his ass clenching under my other hand, my fingers still teasing his hole.

"Jace, fuck," he says, his voice wrecked, his hands pulling at my tee, trying to get it off, his fingers brushing my chest, feeling the hair, the muscle. I let him, yanking my tee over my head, exposing my broad chest, my abs, the dark hair trailing down to my jeans, my cock straining, leaking, the bulge obscene. His eyes widen, his tongue darting out, licking his lips, his cock twitching in my hand, his moans louder, his body trembling under my touch.

I grab his jaw, tilting his face up, my lips brushing his, not kissing, just teasing, my stubble scraping his lips, making him whimper. “You’re mine,” I say, my voice low, my hand stroking his cock faster, my fingers pressing harder against his hole, teasing, not entering, the tension building, his moans desperate, his body shaking. “And you’re gonna feel it, Leo. Every fucking inch of what you’ve earned.” My hand slides to his neck, squeezing lightly, feeling his pulse race, my cock throbbing, my balls aching, the air thick with our heat, our want, the punishment just beginning.

Leo’s trembling beneath me, his slim frame pinned to the couch, his smooth skin glistening with sweat, his small cock throbbing in my hand, leaking precum that drips onto his abs, pooling in the ridges. My fingers tease his tight hole, circling, pressing, the pressure making him moan, his blue eyes wide, pleading, but still sparking with that bratty defiance that's got my cock hard as fuck, straining against my jeans, leaking into my boxers. My stubble scrapes his jaw as I lean in, my breath hot against his ear, my hand stroking his cock slow, deliberate, keeping him on edge, his moans desperate, his body arching, begging for more. The apartment's a haze of cedar musk, his citrus scent, and the raw tang of our arousal, the city lights casting shadows across his flushed skin, the tension so thick it's suffocating.

"You ready to pay, baby?" I growl, my voice low, rough, my lips brushing his neck, my tongue flicking out, tasting the salt, the faint citrus, his pulse racing under my mouth. My hand leaves his cock, sliding to his thighs, spreading them wider, my fingers digging into the soft flesh, bruising, making him gasp, his cock twitching, leaking more. "You fucked up, Leo, and now you're gonna take it—hard." My other hand grabs his hair, yanking his head back, exposing his throat, my stubble scraping as I bite the skin, hard enough to leave a mark, his moan loud, raw, his body trembling.

“Jace, fuck, please,” he groans, his voice wrecked, his hands gripping my shoulders, fingers digging into my muscle, his cock leaking, dripping onto the couch. “I’m sorry, okay? Just... do it, I’m yours.” His voice is desperate, his blue eyes burning, but there’s still that edge, that spark that says he’s loving this, loving pushing me to the edge, and it’s driving me fucking crazy, my cock throbbing, my balls aching.

I stand, yanking my jeans down, my cock springing free, thick and veined, the head flushed, leaking precum, the musky scent hitting the air. His eyes widen, his tongue darting out, licking his lips, his cock twitching at the sight. “On your knees,” I say, my voice rough, commanding, grabbing his hair, pulling him off the couch, his slim body pliant, his knees hitting the hardwood floor. “You’re gonna suck this cock, Leo, and you're gonna do it right." I slap his cheek with my cock, the wet smack loud, making his face flush, his moan soft, his cock leaking more, dripping onto the floor.

"Fuck, Jace," he says, his voice shaky, his hands grabbing my thighs, feeling the muscle, his fingers trembling. "I... I'll do it, okay?" His lips part, his tongue flicking out, brushing the head of my cock, tasting the precum, salty and bitter, making him moan, his eyes fluttering. I grab his hair tighter, pushing my cock past his lips, filling his mouth, the heat and wet tightness making me groan, my hips bucking slightly, my cock hitting the back of his throat.

"Suck it, slut," I growl, my voice thick, my hand guiding his head, making him take more, his lips stretching, his tongue swirling, tasting me, his moans muffled, vibrating around my cock. His smooth face, his soft lips, contrast with my rough stubble, my hard grip, and it's fucking perfect, his blue eyes watering, his cock throbbing, leaking, his body trembling as he sucks, eager but overwhelmed. "You love this, don't you? Sucking my cock after fucking with me." I thrust deeper, making him gag, his eyes tearing up, but he doesn't stop, his tongue working, his lips tight, his moans desperate.

I pull out, my cock slick with his spit, and slap his face again, the wet sound sharp, making him gasp, his cheeks red, his cock leaking more. "Get up," I say, my voice rough, yanking him to his feet, his slim body trembling, his cock hard, dripping. I push him back onto the couch, face down, his ass up, perfect and round, his hole tight, pink, twitching under my gaze. "You're gonna take this cock, Leo, and you're gonna feel every fucking inch." I grab a bottle of lube from the side table, slicking my fingers, my cock, the scent sharp, mixing with our musk.

"Jace, wait," he says, his voice shaky, his hands gripping the cushions, his ass clenching, but his cock's leaking, his body begging despite his words. "Be... be gentle, okay?" His voice is soft, pleading, but his eyes, glancing back at me, are wild, wanting, and I know he's lying, know he wants it rough, wants the punishment he earned.

"Gentle's not what you get tonight," I say, my voice low, my fingers sliding to his hole, circling, pressing, the lube slick, making him moan, his ass twitching. "You wanted to play, baby, so now you play my way." I push a finger in, slow, stretching him, the tightness gripping me, his moan loud, his body trembling, his cock leaking onto the couch. My other hand slaps his ass, hard, the crack echoing, his cheek jiggling, red from the sting, his moan sharper, his cock twitching.

"Fuck, Jace," he groans, his voice breaking, his hips pushing back, taking my finger deeper, his ass clenching, his cock throbbing. "It's… it's too much," he says, but his body says different, his moans desperate, his ass grinding, his cock leaking, dripping, his smooth skin glistening with sweat. I add another finger, stretching him wider, the lube slick, the sensation intense, making him cry out, his back arching, his hands clawing the cushions.

"Too much?" I say, my voice thick, my lips brushing his ear, my stubble scraping his neck, making him shiver. "You're taking it like a fucking champ, Leo. This tight cunt's begging for my cock." I thrust my fingers deeper, curling, hitting that spot, making him moan louder, his cock leaking, his body shaking. My other hand grabs his hair, yanking his head back, my lips brushing his jaw, my tongue licking the sweat, the citrus, his moans raw, desperate.

“Jace, please,” he groans, his voice wrecked, his ass clenching around my fingers, his cock throbbing, leaking, his body trembling under my grip. “I’m sorry, okay? Just... fuck me, please.” His voice is desperate, his blue eyes glancing back, wild, pleading, his smooth skin flushed, his blond hair messy, sticking to his forehead, and he’s so fucking pretty, so mine, it’s driving me wild, my cock throbbing, leaking, my balls aching.

I pull my fingers out, his hole twitching, slick with lube, and line my cock up, the head brushing his hole, teasing, not entering yet, the pressure making him moan, his hips pushing back, begging. “You want this cock?” I say, my voice rough, my hand slapping his ass again, the sting sharp, his cheek red, his moan loud, his cock leaking more. “Beg for it, Leo. Tell me how bad you need it.” My other hand grabs his hip, holding him still, my cock teasing his hole, the heat, the tightness driving me crazy, my precum mixing with the lube.

"Fuck, I need it," he says, his voice breaking, his hands gripping the couch, his ass pushing back, his cock throbbing, leaking. "Jace, please, fuck me, I'm yours, I need your cock, please." His voice is raw, desperate, his body trembling, his smooth skin glistening, his blue eyes burning with want, and it's too much, his submission, his need, pushing me to the edge, my cock throbbing, my balls aching, the tension unbearable.

I push in, slow, the head of my cock stretching his hole, the tightness gripping me, making me groan, my hips bucking slightly, his moan loud, raw, his body trembling. "Fuck, you're tight," I growl, my voice thick, my hands gripping his hips, bruising, my cock sliding deeper, inch by inch, the lube slick, the heat overwhelming. His ass clenches, his moans desperate, his cock leaking, dripping onto the couch, his body shaking under me.

"Jace, fuck," he groans, his voice wrecked, his hips pushing back, taking more, his ass gripping my cock, the sensation intense, making my head spin. "It's so big, fuck, it hurts," he says, but his cock's throbbing, leaking, his moans begging for more, his body surrendering, loving it. I thrust deeper, my cock filling him, my hips snapping, the wet sound of skin on skin filling the room, his moans loud, raw, his body trembling.

I grab his hair, pulling him up, his back against my chest, my cock still buried in his ass, thrusting slow, deep, making him cry out, his cock leaking, his abs slick with precum. "Open your mouth," I say, my voice rough, my hand sliding to his jaw, turning his head, my cock brushing his lips, slick with lube, precum, his eyes watering, his moans muffled as I push in, filling his mouth, his tongue swirling, tasting me, his ass clenching around my cock.

“Suck it, slut,” I growl, my voice thick, thrusting into his mouth, slow, deliberate, his lips stretching, his tongue working, his moans vibrating around my cock. My other hand strokes his cock, fast, rough, his small shaft pulsing, leaking, his moans louder, his body trembling, caught between my cock in his ass and his mouth, the tension overwhelming, the apartment filled with the sounds of our heat, our need, the punishment far from over.

Leo’s ass grips my cock, tight and hot, clenching with every brutal thrust, his slim body trembling beneath me, his back pressed against my chest, his smooth skin slick with sweat. My thick cock fills his mouth, stretching his lips, his tongue swirling, tasting the precum and lube, his moans muffled, vibrating against my shaft, sending jolts to my balls, already aching, heavy with need. His small cock throbs in my hand, leaking precum that drips onto his abs, pooling in the ridges, his hips bucking, chasing my strokes. The apartment’s a furnace, the air thick with cedar musk, his citrus scent, and the raw, filthy tang of our arousal, the city lights casting jagged shadows across his flushed skin, his blond hair matted to his forehead, his blue eyes watering, wild with desperation and defiance. The tension’s unbearable, my cock throbbing, my balls tight, but I’m dragging this out, making him feel every second of his punishment for pushing me too far.

“Fuck, you’re taking it like a slut,” I growl, my voice rough, my hips snapping, my cock slamming deep into his ass, the wet slap of skin on skin echoing, his moans sharp, raw, his hole clenching tighter, driving me wild. I pull out of his mouth, my cock slick with his spit, glistening, and slap his cheek with it, the wet smack loud, making his face flush deeper, his eyes fluttering, his small cock twitching in my hand. “You love this, don’t you? Getting fucked raw, owned by my cock.” My hand strokes his shaft faster, my thumb smearing the precum over the head, making him cry out, his body shaking, his ass grinding back, begging for more.

“Jace, fuck, please,” he groans, his voice wrecked, hoarse from moaning, his hands clawing at my arms, fingers digging into the muscle, leaving red marks on my inked skin. “It’s too much, you’re too big,” he says, but his hips buck, his ass clenching, his cock leaking, dripping, his body betraying his words, loving the brutal stretch, the rough edge of my punishment. His smooth chest heaves, his pink nipples hard, his abs slick with precum, and he’s so fucking pretty, so desperate, it’s pushing me to the edge, my cock throbbing, my balls aching.

“Too much?” I say, my voice thick, my lips brushing his ear, my stubble scraping his jaw, the rough hair making him shiver, his moans louder. “You earned this, Leo, flirting with that prick, making me watch.” My hand tightens on his cock, stroking hard, fast, the slick sound obscene, matching the brutal rhythm of my thrusts, my cock hitting that spot deep inside him, making him cry out, his body trembling, his hole gripping me like a vice. “You’re mine, baby, and you’re gonna feel it till you can’t fucking walk.” I bite his neck, hard, my teeth sinking in, tasting the salt, the citrus, his moan sharp, his cock twitching in my hand.

“Fuck, Jace, I’m yours,” he gasps, his voice breaking, his hands grabbing my hair, pulling, his body arching, his ass pushing back, taking my cock deeper, the stretch intense, filthy. “I’m sorry, okay? Just… don’t stop, please.” His blue eyes glance back, wild, pleading, but still sparking with that bratty edge that drives me fucking crazy, my cock throbbing, my balls aching, my control fraying with every clench of his tight cunt.

I flip him onto his back, his legs spreading wide, his hole slick with lube, twitching, begging for my cock. I grab his thighs, pushing them up, his knees near his chest, his ass open, vulnerable, his small cock hard, leaking, dripping onto his abs. “Look at this cunt,” I growl, my voice thick, my cock brushing his hole, teasing, not entering yet, the pressure making him moan, his hips bucking, his cock throbbing in my hand. "So fucking tight, begging for me to wreck it." I slap his ass, hard, the crack sharp, his cheek jiggling, red from the sting, his moan loud, desperate, his cock leaking more, dripping onto his smooth skin.

"Jace, please, fuck me," he groans, his voice raw, his hands gripping the couch, knuckles white, his body trembling, his blue eyes burning with need. "I need it, need your cock, please." His voice is desperate, his smooth chest heaving, his nipples hard, his abs slick, and he's so fucking gorgeous, so mine, it's driving me wild, my cock throbbing, my balls aching, ready to give him what he's begging for.

I push in, slow at first, the head of my cock stretching his hole, the tightness gripping me, making me groan, my hips bucking, his moan loud, raw, his body shaking. "Take it, slut," I growl, my voice thick, my cock sliding deeper, filling him, the lube slick, the heat overwhelming, his ass clenching, his cock throbbing in my hand. I thrust hard, brutal, my hips snapping, my cock slamming into him, hitting that spot, making him cry out, his moans sharp, desperate, his body trembling under me.

“Fuck, yes,” he groans, his voice wrecked, his hips bucking, meeting my thrusts, his ass gripping my cock, the sensation intense, filthy, driving me crazy. “Harder, Jace, fuck me harder,” he says, his voice breaking, his hands clawing at my back, nails scraping, leaving trails of heat, his cock leaking, dripping, his abs slick with precum. I stroke his cock faster, my hand rough, my thumb pressing into the head, making him moan louder, his body shaking, his hole clenching tighter, pushing me closer to the edge.

“You’re gonna cum for me,” I say, my voice rough, my thrusts brutal, my cock slamming deep, the wet sound of skin on skin filling the room, his moans loud, raw, his body trembling. “Gonna cum with my cock in your tight cunt, show me you're mine." My hand strokes his cock in time with my thrusts, fast, relentless, his small shaft pulsing, leaking, his moans desperate, his blue eyes fluttering, his body arching, his ass clenching, driving me wild.

"Jace, fuck, I'm close," he groans, his voice breaking, his hands gripping my shoulders, fingers digging in, his body trembling, his cock throbbing in my hand, leaking, dripping, his abs slick, glistening. "Don't stop, please, make me cum," he says, his voice raw, his hips bucking, his ass clenching, his moans loud, desperate, his body surrendering, loving every brutal thrust, every rough stroke.

I thrust harder, my cock slamming into him, hitting that spot, my hand stroking his cock, fast, rough, the slick sound obscene, his moans louder, his body shaking. "Cum for me, Leo," I growl, my voice thick, my stubble scraping his neck as I lean in, biting the skin, tasting the sweat, the citrus, his moan sharp, his cock pulsing, his body trembling. His ass clenches tight, his cock throbs, and he cums, hard, thick ropes of cum shooting across his abs, splattering his chest, his moans loud, raw, his body shaking, his hole gripping my cock, pushing me closer to the edge.

"Fuck, yes," I groan, my voice rough, my thrusts brutal, my cock slamming deep, his ass clenching, milking me, the sensation intense, filthy, driving me wild. His cum glistens on his smooth skin, his chest heaving, his blue eyes wild, locked on mine, and it's too much, his submission, his tight cunt, his desperate moans. I thrust harder, my balls tight, my cock throbbing, and I cum, hard, hot and thick, filling his ass, the warmth spreading, my groans loud, raw, my hips bucking, milking every drop, his ass clenching, taking it all.

“Jace, fuck,” he groans, his voice wrecked, his body trembling, his cock still twitching, leaking, his abs slick with his cum, his hole dripping with mine. I collapse over him, my chest heaving, my cock still buried in his ass, the heat overwhelming, our sweat mixing, the air thick with cedar, citrus, and the musky tang of cum. His hands slide to my back, fingers tracing the muscle, his breath ragged, his blue eyes soft now, no defiance, just surrender, his body pliant, mine.

“You’re mine,” I say, my voice low, my lips brushing his, my stubble scraping his lips, making him shiver. “No more fucking games, Leo. You pull that shit again, and I’ll fuck you till you can’t move.” My hand slides to his cock, soft now, slick with cum, stroking gently, making him moan, his body trembling, sensitive, spent.

“I’m yours,” he murmurs, his voice soft, his hands pulling me closer, his lips brushing mine, his breath hot, his body warm against me. “No one else, Jace. Just you.” His confession hits me hard, the tension easing, the apartment quiet now, just our breathing, the city lights flickering, the heat of our bodies lingering, the punishment complete, his submission absolute, our bond sealed in the filthy, brutal heat of it all.

BOUND TO THE BASEMENT

I’m not the kind of guy who blends into the background. At twenty-six, I’ve got a lean, wiry build from years of climbing—muscles taut, not bulky, with a smattering of dark hair across my chest that trails down to a treasure line I keep trimmed just so. My jaw’s sharp, framed by a scruffy beard I’ve let grow out, and my hazel eyes have a glint that says I’m trouble before I even open my mouth. My hair's a mess of black curls, always a little too long, falling into my face when I'm up to no good—which is often. I've got a smirk that's gotten me into more beds than I can count, and a cocky streak that makes me think I can handle anything. Tonight, I'm dressed to kill: tight black jeans that hug my ass, a fitted leather harness that shows off my pecs, and boots that thud with purpose when I walk. I know I look good. I always do.

The club's called Iron Veil, a seedy spot tucked in the industrial district where the air smells like rust and regret. It's not my usual haunt—too hardcore for the casual hookups I'm used to—but I'd heard whispers about the basement. A dungeon, they called it, where the real players go to break limits and chase highs that make your pulse race. I'm not here for the drinks or the dance floor upstairs. I'm here for the rush, the kind that comes from pushing boundaries I've only ever teased at. I'm a sub, sure, but I'm not some whimpering pet. I like to play hard, talk back, make the dom work for it. Tonight, I'm feeling reckless, and I want to see how far I can go.

The bouncer at the main door barely glances at my fake ID—some half-assed thing I'd thrown together with a buddy's printer. He's more interested in the line of wannabe kinksters behind me, all leather and latex, trying too hard to look like they belong. I slip past, heart thumping, and head straight for the unmarked door at the back of the club. It's tucked behind a curtain, barely noticeable unless you know what you're looking for. The rumors said you need a special invite to get into the basement, but I'm not big on rules. Never have been.

The door's heavy, metal, cold under my fingers as I push it open. A narrow staircase spirals down into darkness, the air growing thicker with every step. It smells like sweat, leather, and something sharper—maybe fear, maybe anticipation. My boots echo on the concrete steps, and I can feel my cock twitching already, just from the vibe. I'm not supposed to be here, and that makes it so much fucking hotter.

At the bottom, there's another door, this one guarded by a guy who looks like he could bench press me without breaking a sweat. He's all muscle, shaved head, and a scowl that says he's not impressed by my pretty face. "Invite," he grunts, holding out a meaty hand.

I flash my best grin, the one that usually gets me out of trouble. "Must've slipped my mind," I say, leaning in just enough to let my harness creak, drawing his eye. "But I'm good for it, yeah? Promise I'll behave."

His eyes narrow, but I can tell he's sizing me up, not just for trouble but for something else. I'm used to that look—guys wondering how I'd look on my knees. "No invite, no entry," he says, but there's a flicker of something in his voice. He's not as stone-cold as he wants to be.

"C'mon, man," I purr, stepping closer, letting my fingers brush the edge of his vest. "I'm just here to play. You gonna make me beg already?"

He snorts, but I see the crack in his armor. "You're trouble," he mutters, then jerks his head toward the door. "One chance. Fuck up, and you're out on your ass."

I wink at him, already buzzing with the win. "You got it, big guy." The door swings open, and I step into the basement, my pulse hammering like a drum.

The dungeon's everything I'd imagined and more. Dim red lights cast shadows across a maze of equipment—racks, crosses, benches, all gleaming steel and worn leather. The air's heavy with the scent of wax and musk, and the low hum of moans and murmurs fills the space. There's a crowd, but it's not packed—just a handful of players, all serious, no posers. I spot a woman in a latex catsuit wielding a flogger, her sub trembling under her strikes. A guy in a corner's got another man cuffed to a wall, whispering something that makes the bound guy's head tip back in surrender. It's raw, electric, and I'm already half-hard just taking it in.

I weave through the room, keeping my head high, my smirk in place. I'm not here to gawk—I'm here to play. My eyes land on a steel rack in the far corner, all sharp angles and cold metal, ropes dangling from its frame like an invitation. It's empty, waiting, and I feel a pull in my gut. That's where I want to be. Bound, tested, pushed to the edge.

Then I see him. He's standing near the rack, arms crossed, watching the room like he owns it. He's older than me, maybe mid-thirties, with a build that says he works out but doesn't live at the gym. His chest is broad, covered in a tight black shirt that clings to every line of muscle, and his leather pants sit low on his hips, showing off a V that makes my mouth water. His face is all hard angles—strong jaw, sharp cheekbones, and eyes so dark they seem to swallow the light. There's a paddle tucked into his belt, its handle worn from use, and a coil of rope slung over his shoulder. He's a dom, no question, and the kind who doesn't fuck around.

Our eyes meet, and I feel a jolt, like he's already got me pinned. I don't look away, though—I never do. Instead, I saunter over, letting my hips roll just enough to catch his attention. "Nice setup," I say, nodding at the rack, my voice low and teasing. "You gonna put it to use, or is it just for show?"

His lips twitch, but it's not a smile. It's something darker, like he's already imagining what he'd do to shut me up. "You got a mouth on you," he says, his voice deep, rough, like gravel. "You always this bold, or is it just for me?"

I grin, stepping closer, close enough to smell the leather and sweat on him. "Only when I see something I want," I shoot back, letting my eyes drag down his body, slow and deliberate. "And I'm thinking you might be it."

He doesn't flinch, doesn't blush—just studies me like I'm a puzzle he's about to take apart. "You don't belong here," he says, not a question. "No invite, no collar. You're sneaking in where you shouldn't be."

I shrug, unbothered. "Maybe I like the risk. Maybe I'm just looking for someone who can handle me."

His eyes darken, and I know I've got him. He steps forward, closing the distance, and I have to tilt my head back to meet his gaze. He's taller than me, broader, and the way he looms makes my cock throb in my jeans. "You think you can handle me?" he asks, his voice low, dangerous. "Because I don't play gentle, kid."

"Kid?" I laugh, sharp and cocky. "I'm not your kid. And I don't want gentle. I want you to try and break me."

That does it. I see the spark in his eyes, the challenge accepted. He grabs my wrist, not hard enough to hurt but firm enough to make my breath catch. "You're gonna regret that mouth," he says, but there's a hunger in his tone that says he's looking forward to it. "Safe word?"

"Red," I say, quick and sure. I've done this enough to know the rules, even if I like bending them.

He nods, once, then pulls me toward the rack. My heart's pounding now, my skin tingling with anticipation. The crowd fades into the background as he positions me in front of the steel frame, its cold surface glinting under the red lights. “Strip,” he orders, stepping back to watch.

I raise an eyebrow, playing it cool even as my pulse races. “Right here? In front of everyone?”

His jaw tightens, and I know I’ve pushed a button. “You wanted to play, sub,” he says, his voice like a whip. “So play. Strip. Now.”

I hold his gaze, letting the moment stretch, then slowly peel off my harness, letting it drop to the floor with a soft thud. My jeans are next, the zipper loud in the quiet corner as I slide them down, kicking them off along with my boots. I’m left in nothing but black briefs, my cock already straining against the fabric. I don’t cover myself—fuck that. I stand tall, letting him see every inch of me, daring him to make the next move.

He doesn't rush. He circles me, slow, predatory, his eyes raking over my body like he's memorizing every line. "Not bad," he says, almost to himself, then grabs the rope from his shoulder. "Hands behind your back."

I obey, but not without a smirk. "Yes, sir," I say, dripping with sarcasm, just to see how he'll react.

He doesn't take the bait, but I catch the flicker of amusement in his eyes. He's good at this, controlled, not letting me get under his skin. Yet. The rope's rough against my wrists as he binds them, his fingers quick and sure, pulling the knots tight but not cruel. I test them, tugging slightly, and feel the bite of the hemp against my skin. It's secure. No getting out unless he lets me.

He moves to my front, grabbing another length of rope, and starts looping it around my chest, weaving it into a harness that frames my pecs and digs into my shoulders. Every tug of the rope sends a shiver through me, the pressure grounding but teasing, making me hyper-aware of every inch of my body. He's close now, his breath hot against my neck as he works, and I can smell the faint spice of his cologne mixed with leather. My cock's fully hard now, tenting my briefs, and I know he sees it. He doesn't comment, just keeps tying, his hands brushing my skin just enough to drive me fucking crazy.

"On the rack," he says, stepping back. His voice is calm, but there's an edge to it, like he's holding himself back. I step up to the steel frame, the cold metal chilling my bare feet. He guides me into position, spreading my legs to hook my ankles to the rack's base with more rope. My arms are pulled up and back, secured to the top bar, leaving me stretched, exposed, every muscle taut. I'm vulnerable, but I'm not scared. I'm fucking alive, every nerve singing with the thrill of it.

He picks up the paddle, testing its weight in his hand, and my mouth goes dry. It's not some flimsy toy—this thing's solid, leather-wrapped, made to sting. He steps closer, close enough that I can feel the heat of his body, and leans in, his lips brushing my ear. "You wanted to play hard," he murmurs, his voice low and rough. "Let's see how much you can take."

My breath hitches, and I grin, even as my heart pounds. "Bring it on," I say, my voice steady despite the fire in my veins. I'm ready for this—ready for him to push me, to test me, to see how far I can go before I break.

The paddle hovers in his hand, its leather surface catching the dim red glow like a promise of pain. My skin prickles, not from the chill of the steel rack but from the way his eyes pin me, dark and unyielding, stripping me bare without touching me. The ropes bite into my wrists and chest, a constant reminder of my surrender, but I'm still smirking, still daring him to make me flinch. He hasn't earned that yet.

"You're too fucking smug," he says, his voice a low growl that vibrates through the humid air. He steps closer, the paddle tapping lightly against his thigh, a rhythmic threat. "Think you're untouchable, don't you?"

I tilt my head, letting my curls fall into my eyes, and flash him a grin that's all teeth. "Untouchable? Nah. Just waiting for you to prove you're worth my attention."

His jaw tightens, a muscle ticking under the stubble, and I know I've hit a nerve. Good. I want him rattled, want him to feel the same heat coiling in my gut. He doesn't respond right away, just circles me again, slower this time, his boots scuffing the concrete floor. The dungeon's sounds—moans, the sharp crack of a whip, the low hum of murmured commands—fade into a dull roar as my world narrows to him. To the way his fingers flex around the paddle's handle, to the faint sheen of sweat on his collarbone where his shirt gapes open.

He stops behind me, close enough that I can feel the warmth radiating off him, but not close enough to touch. It's maddening. "You talk like you're in charge," he says, his breath grazing the back of my neck, sending a shiver down my spine that I can't hide. "But you're not. Not here. Not with me."

I twist my head, just enough to catch his eye over my shoulder. “Then why’re you still talking?” I taunt, my voice rougher than I mean it to be. “Thought you were gonna make me regret my mouth.”

He chuckles, a dark, velvet sound that makes my cock throb against the tight fabric of my briefs. “Oh, I will,” he says, and then his hand is on me—not the paddle, not yet, but his fingers, calloused and warm, gripping the back of my neck. It’s not gentle, but it’s not cruel either—just firm enough to make me feel the weight of his control. My breath catches, and I hate how obvious it is, how my body betrays me before I can play it cool.

“Already squirming?” he murmurs, his thumb pressing into the base of my skull, sending a jolt of heat straight to my groin. “And I haven’t even started.”

I grit my teeth, refusing to give him the satisfaction of a response, but my body's not as stubborn. My hips shift, involuntary, straining against the ropes that hold my ankles to the rack. He notices—of course he does—and his hand slides down, fingers trailing along my spine, slow and deliberate, like he's mapping every vertebra. Each touch is a spark, igniting nerves I didn't know could feel this alive. My skin's too tight, too hot, and I'm fighting the urge to arch into his hand, to chase the contact.

"Sensitive," he says, almost to himself, as his fingers dip lower, skimming the waistband of my briefs. He doesn't go further, just lets his touch linger there, teasing the edge of what I want. What I need. "Bet you're loud when you're pushed."

"Bet you're all talk," I shoot back, my voice rough with want, but I keep the edge sharp, defiant. "You gonna tease me all night, or you got something real to show me?"

He steps around to face me, and fuck, he's close now, close enough that I can see the flecks of amber in his dark eyes, the faint scar cutting through his left eyebrow. The paddle's still in his hand, but he sets it down on a nearby table with a deliberate slowness that makes my stomach twist. He's toying with me, drawing it out, and it's working. My pulse is a drumbeat in my ears, my cock aching against the fabric trapping it.

"Real?" he repeats, his voice low, dangerous, like a blade sliding against silk. He reaches out, and this time his hand finds my chest, fingers splaying over the ropes that crisscross my pecs. His touch is firm, possessive, his thumb brushing over my nipple, and I can't stop the sharp inhale that escapes me. "This real enough for you?"

I swallow hard, trying to keep my smirk in place, but it's faltering. His thumb circles, slow and relentless, and the sensation's like a live wire, shooting straight through me. "Getting there," I manage, but my voice is shakier than I'd like, and he knows it.

He leans in, his lips brushing my ear again, and I can feel the heat of his breath, the scratch of his stubble against my jaw. "You're gonna learn to watch that mouth," he whispers, and then his hand slides lower, fingers grazing the taut skin of my abdomen, stopping just above the bulge in my briefs. My hips jerk forward, instinctive, desperate for more, but the ropes hold me fast, keeping me exactly where he wants me.

"Fuck," I mutter, half a curse, half a plea, and he laughs again, that low, dark sound that makes me want to both punch him and beg him to keep going.

"Already cursing?" he says, stepping back just enough to look me over, his eyes lingering on the obvious strain in my briefs. "You're not as tough as you think, are you?"

I glare at him "'Tough enough to handle you," I say, but the words come out breathless, and I know I'm losing ground. He's unraveling me, piece by piece, and I'm letting him.

He picks up the paddle again, and my heart stutters. He doesn't swing it, though—just runs the flat of it along my thigh, the leather cool and smooth against my overheated skin. The anticipation's worse than the strike would be, and he knows it. He's playing with my head as much as my body, keeping me on edge, making me wait. "You want this?" he asks, tapping the paddle lightly against my inner thigh, close enough to my cock that I tense, every muscle coiling tight.

"What I want," I say, forcing my voice to stay steady, "is for you to stop fucking around and do something."

His eyes flash, and for a second, I think I've pushed too far. But then he grins, sharp and predatory, and steps closer, the paddle still in one hand while the other grabs my chin, forcing me to meet his gaze. His grip's rough, fingers digging into my jaw, but it's the kind of rough that makes my blood sing. "Careful what you wish for," he says, his voice a low rumble that I feel in my bones. "You're not ready for everything I've got."

I try to pull my chin free, but his grip tightens, and I'm caught, pinned by his hand and his eyes and the fucking ropes that keep me spread out for him. "Try me," I say, and it's half a challenge, half a surrender, because I'm starting to realize I might've bitten off more than I can chew. And I'm loving every second of it.

He lets go of my chin, but only to trail his hand down my throat, fingers curling lightly around it, not squeezing, just resting there, a reminder of his control. My pulse hammers against his palm, and I know he feels it, knows he's got me right where he wants me. His other hand brings the paddle up, dragging it across my chest, the leather catching on the ropes, tugging them just enough to make me gasp. The sensation's sharp, electric, and I'm starting to lose track of where teasing ends and torment begins.

"You're shaking," he says, and there's a mocking edge to his voice that makes me want to prove him wrong, but I can't. My body's betraying me, trembling under his touch, under the weight of his gaze. He leans in again, his lips so close to mine I can almost taste them, but he doesn't kiss me. Instead, he drags the paddle down my side, slow and deliberate, letting it graze the sensitive skin over my ribs, my hip, until it's resting just above my cock, the pressure maddeningly light.

"Fuck, just—do it," I say, my voice cracking, and I hate how desperate I sound, but I can't help it. He's got me wound so tight I'm ready to snap, and he hasn't even hit me yet.

"Do what?" he asks, and the bastard's smirking now, enjoying this way too much. He slides the paddle lower, just brushing the bulge in my briefs, and my hips buck, the ropes digging into my ankles as I strain against them. "This?" he asks, pressing the paddle harder, just enough to make me groan, low and raw, before he pulls it away.

"You're a fucking tease," I pant, my chest heaving, sweat beading on my forehead. My cock's throbbing, trapped, and every nerve in my body's screaming for more—more touch, more pain, more him.

"And you're a brat who needs to learn patience," he says, but there's a heat in his voice now, a crack in his control that tells me I'm getting to him too. He steps back, giving me a moment to catch my breath, but it's not a reprieve—it's a pause, a chance for him to decide what comes next. He sets the paddle down again, picking up a coil of rope instead, and my stomach flips. More restraints? Fuck, I'm already trussed up like a prize, but the thought of him binding me tighter, making me even more helpless, sends a fresh wave of heat through me.

He moves behind me again, and I feel the rope slide across my lower back, cool and rough, as he starts weaving it around my thighs. His fingers brush my skin with every loop, every knot, and it's deliberate—he's making sure I feel every touch, every tug. The rope pulls tight, forcing my legs to spread wider, and I bite my lip to stifle a moan. The vulnerability's intoxicating, like I'm handing over pieces of myself with every knot he ties.

"You're quiet now," he says, his voice close, too close, his breath hot against my shoulder. "Where's that smart mouth gone?"

I force a laugh, but it's shaky, strained. "Waiting for you to give me something worth talking about," I say, but the words lack their earlier bite. He's winning, and we both know it.

He finishes the knots, stepping back to admire his work, and I can feel his eyes on me, burning into my skin. I'm stretched out, bound, every muscle taut and trembling, and I've never felt more exposed—or more alive. He moves to my side, his hand grazing my hip, fingers dipping just under the waistband of my briefs, not pulling them down, just teasing, always fucking teasing. "You're gonna beg before I'm done with you," he says, and it's not a threat—it's a promise.

I meet his eyes, my chest tight with anticipation, and manage a grin. "Gonna take more than that to make me beg," I say, but my voice is hoarse, and I'm not sure I believe it anymore.

His fingers linger at the waistband of my briefs, a maddening pressure that's gone as quick as it came, leaving me straining against the ropes, my skin buzzing like a live wire. The dungeon's heat clings to me, sweat slicking my chest where the ropes dig in, and his eyes—those fucking eyes—rake over me like I'm a canvas he's about to paint with pain and pleasure. He steps closer, his presence a wall of heat and leather, and I can smell the sharp tang of his sweat, the faint musk of arousal that mirrors my own. My cock's so hard it's painful, trapped in the tight fabric, and every shift of my hips makes the ropes bite deeper, grounding me even as they drive me wild.

"You're still talking tough," he says, his voice a low rasp that curls around my spine, "but your body's telling a different story." His hand grazes my thigh, not the paddle, not the rope, just the rough pads of his fingers, tracing the edge of the knots he's tied. It's deliberate, each touch calculated to make me squirm, and fuck, it's working. My breath hitches, and I bite the inside of my cheek to keep from moaning, but he sees it. He always sees it.

"Got nothing to say?" he taunts, his lips curling into a smirk that's equal parts cruel and enticing. He leans in, his face so close I can feel the heat of his breath against my jaw, and for a second, I think he's gonna kiss me, claim that last bit of control. But he doesn't. Instead, his hand slides up my chest, fingers catching on the ropes, tugging just enough to make my nipples harden under the pressure. "Thought you were gonna make me work for it."

I force a grin, though it's shaky, my voice rough with need. "You're the one stalling, big guy. Scared you can't keep up?"

His eyes flash, dark and dangerous, and I know I've poked the bear. Good. I want him unhinged, want him to match the fire burning through me. He steps back, grabbing the paddle again, and my heart stutters, anticipation coiling tight in my gut. But instead of swinging it, he drags the leather edge along my inner thigh, slow and teasing, stopping just short of my cock. The cool surface against my overheated skin is torture, and my hips jerk forward, chasing the contact, only to be stopped by the ropes.

"Fuck," I hiss, the word slipping out before I can stop it, and his smirk widens, triumphant.

"Language," he chides, but there's a hunger in his voice now, a crack in his control that makes my pulse race. He sets the paddle down, and before I can brace myself, his hands are on me, one gripping my hip, the other sliding up to my throat again, fingers curling just tight enough to make my breath catch. "You're gonna learn to wait," he says, his thumb pressing against my pulse point, feeling the frantic beat. "Gonna learn to take what I give you."

I swallow hard, my throat working under his hand, and manage a defiant, "Then give me something worth taking."

He laughs, low and rough, and then his mouth is on me—not my lips, but my neck, teeth grazing the sensitive skin just below my ear. It's not a kiss; it's a claim, sharp and possessive, and I can't stop the moan that rips out of me, low and desperate. His tongue flicks out, tasting the salt of my sweat, and my head tips back, ropes creaking as I strain against them. My cock throbs, leaking now, the wet spot on my briefs obvious, and he hasn't even touched me there yet.

"Fuck, you're responsive," he murmurs against my skin, his voice vibrating through me, and then his teeth sink in, not hard enough to break skin but enough to make me gasp, my body arching into him. His hand on my hip slides lower, fingers dipping just under the waistband again, teasing the coarse hair there, and I'm shaking now, every nerve screaming for more. "Look at you," he says, pulling back to meet my eyes, his own dark with want. "All that bravado, and you're already falling apart."

"Not falling apart," I pant, but it's a lie, and we both know it. My chest heaves, the ropes digging into my pecs, and I'm hyper-aware of every point of contact—his hand on my throat, his fingers teasing my waistband, the faint burn of the bite mark on my neck. I'm drowning in sensation, and he's barely started.

He steps back, and I nearly whine at the loss of his touch, but then he's kneeling, right in front of me, his face level with my crotch. My breath stops, my entire body tensing as he looks up at me, that smirk still in place. "You want my mouth?" he asks, his voice like gravel, and his fingers hook into the waistband of my briefs, pulling them down just enough to free my cock. It springs out, hard and leaking, the tip glistening in the dim light, and I can't help the groan that escapes me.

"Fuck, yes," I say, my voice raw, but he doesn't move, just lets his breath ghost over my cock, warm and teasing, close enough to drive me insane but not enough to give me what I want. My hips strain forward, but the ropes hold me fast, and I'm helpless, completely at his mercy.

“Beg for it,” he says, his eyes locked on mine, and there’s no mistaking the command in his voice. It’s not a suggestion—it’s a demand, and my pride wars with the need coiling tight in my gut.

“Fuck you,” I say, but it’s weak, more a reflex than a real defiance, and he knows it. His hand slides up my thigh, fingers brushing the sensitive skin just below my balls, and I shudder, a low moan spilling out before I can stop it.

“That’s not begging,” he says, and then his tongue flicks out, just a quick swipe across the tip of my cock, and it’s like lightning, sharp and electric, making my whole body jerk. “Try again.”

I grit my teeth, my pride screaming at me to hold out, but my body’s betraying me, trembling under his touch. “Please,” I mutter, the word tasting like surrender, but it's not enough for him.

"Louder," he says, and his hand wraps around my cock, not stroking, just holding, his grip firm and warm, and I'm losing it, my head spinning with need.

"Please," I say again, louder this time, my voice cracking, and he rewards me with another slow lick, his tongue flat and deliberate, dragging from base to tip. I moan, loud and unashamed, my hips bucking against the ropes as he works me, his mouth hot and wet, teasing but not enough, never enough.

"Good boy," he murmurs, and the praise hits me like a drug, making my cock twitch in his hand. He pulls back, standing, and I'm left panting, my body screaming for more. But he's not done—

he grabs a small bottle from the table, lube, I realize, and my heart skips. He slicks his fingers, his movements slow and deliberate, and I know what's coming, know it's gonna push me to the edge.

"Relax," he says, his voice softer now, but still commanding, as he moves behind me. His hand slides down my back, over the ropes, until his fingers find my ass, circling my hole with a slick, teasing pressure. I tense, instinctive, but his other hand grips my hip, steadying me. "Breathe," he says, and I do, forcing air into my lungs as his finger presses in, slow and relentless, stretching me open.

"Fuck," I gasp, the intrusion sharp but so fucking good, my body clenching around him as he works his finger deeper, curling it just right to hit that spot that makes my vision blur. My cock leaks onto the floor, untouched, and I'm moaning now, shameless, every thrust of his finger pulling sounds from me I didn't know I could make.

"You like that," he says, not a question, and his voice is thick with arousal, his control fraying at the edges. He adds another finger, the stretch burning, and I'm panting, my head falling back against the rack as he fucks me with his hand, slow and deep, each movement precise, calculated to drive me wild.

"Yes," I choke out, my voice wrecked, and I'm beyond caring about pride now, beyond anything but the need for more. His fingers twist, scissoring, opening me up, and I'm trembling, my thighs shaking against the ropes, my cock throbbing with every thrust.

He leans in, his lips brushing my ear again, his breath hot and ragged. "You're so fucking tight," he murmurs, and there's a hunger in his voice that matches mine, a need that says he's as caught up in this as I am. "Gonna make you feel every inch of this."

I moan, loud and desperate, as he adds a third finger, the stretch almost too much, but it's perfect, the burn blending with pleasure until I can't tell them apart. My body's his now, every nerve singing under his touch, and I'm begging without words, my hips rocking back as much as the ropes allow, chasing the sensation.

"Not yet," he says, pulling his fingers out, and I whine, actual fucking whine, at the loss. He steps around to face me, his eyes dark and wild, his shirt clinging to his chest with sweat. He's hard, I can see it, the bulge in his leather pants obvious, and it makes my mouth water, makes me want to drop to my knees if I weren't tied up.

"You're not done," he says, grabbing my chin again, forcing me to meet his gaze. "Not even close." His thumb brushes my lips, and I open my mouth, sucking it in, tasting salt and lube, and his eyes darken, his breath hitching. "Fuck, you're trouble," he mutters, and then he's kissing me, finally, his mouth hard and demanding, teeth clashing as he claims me, and I'm lost, drowning in the taste of him, the heat, the need.

He pulls back, both of us panting, and grabs the paddle again, his eyes promising more, promising everything. "Ready for the real fun?" he asks, and I nod, too far gone to speak, ready for whatever he's got, ready to break under him and love every fucking second of it.

His kiss leaves me reeling, lips bruised and tingling, the taste of him—sweat and heat and something darker—lingering on my tongue. My cock's throbbing, dripping onto the concrete floor, and the ropes bite into my skin, a constant reminder of how fucking helpless I am. He's got me pinned, body and mind, and the way his eyes burn into mine says he's done teasing. He steps back, his chest heaving, sweat gleaming on his collarbone where his shirt's unbuttoned just enough to make my mouth water. The bulge in his leather pants is obscene, straining against the zipper, and I can't look away, my hole clenching at the thought of what's coming.

"You want it bad, don't you?" he growls, his voice rough, frayed at the edges like he's barely holding it together. He grabs the lube again, slicking his fingers with a slow, deliberate motion that makes my stomach twist. "Gonna fuck you till you can't think straight."

“Promises, promises,” I rasp, but my voice is wrecked, all bravado gone, and he knows it. My thighs tremble against the ropes, my body screaming for him to follow through. He smirks, dark and filthy, and steps behind me, his hand finding my ass again, fingers circling my hole, still slick from before. I’m open, ready, but the anticipation’s killing me, every nerve on edge as he teases, just brushing the sensitive rim.

“Fuck, just do it,” I groan, my head falling back, ropes creaking as I strain against them. My cock’s so hard it hurts, leaking steadily now, and I’m past caring how desperate I sound.

He doesn’t answer, just presses a finger in, quick and deep, curling it against that spot that makes my vision blur. I moan, loud and shameless, my hips rocking back as much as the ropes allow. He adds another finger, stretching me wider, the burn sharp and perfect, and I'm panting, sweat dripping down my chest, pooling where the ropes dig into my pecs. "So fucking tight," he mutters, his voice thick with lust, and I can hear the strain in it, the way he's fighting to keep control.

"More," I demand, my voice raw, and he laughs, a low, dirty sound that makes my cock twitch. He pulls his fingers out, and I whine at the loss, but then I hear the clink of his belt, the slow drag of his zipper, and my heart slams against my ribs. He's freeing himself, and fuck, I wish I could see it, but the ropes keep me facing forward, stretched out and exposed. I feel the heat of him behind me, the brush of his leather pants against my thighs as he steps closer, and then his cock—hard, thick, slick with lube—presses against my hole.

"Ready?" he asks, but it's not a question, not really. His hand grips my hip, fingers digging in hard enough to bruise, and I nod, breathless, my body screaming for it. He doesn't ease in—he thrusts, hard and deep, filling me in one brutal stroke, and I cry out, the stretch overwhelming, pain and pleasure crashing together until I can't tell them apart.

"Fuck!" I gasp, my body clenching around him, trying to adjust to the size of him, the way he's splitting me open. He's big, bigger than I expected, and the burn's intense, but it's so fucking good, every nerve lighting up as he holds still, letting me feel every inch.

"Take it," he growls, his hand sliding up to my throat, fingers curling around it, not squeezing, just claiming. He pulls back, slow and deliberate, then slams in again, and I moan, loud and broken, my cock bouncing untouched, dripping onto the floor. The ropes hold me tight, keeping me in place as he sets a punishing rhythm, each thrust deep and relentless, hitting that spot that makes my knees buckle.

“Goddamn, you’re tight,” he mutters, his voice rough, almost feral, and I can feel him losing it, his control slipping with every thrust. His hand on my hip slides around, fingers wrapping around my cock, stroking in time with his thrusts, and I’m gone, lost in the sensation, my body shaking as he fucks me raw. The dungeon’s sounds—moans, whips, the hum of lust—fade into nothing, my world narrowing to the feel of his cock in my ass, his hand on my dick, the ropes cutting into my skin.

“Harder,” I pant, because I’m a greedy bastard, and I want more, want him to break me. He groans, low and guttural, and obliges, his thrusts turning brutal, each one driving the air from my lungs. His hand tightens on my cock, stroking faster, rougher, and I’m moaning nonstop now, sounds I didn’t know I could make, raw and desperate. My balls draw up, tight and aching, and I’m close, so fucking close, but he slows down, teasing, dragging it out.

"Not yet," he says, his voice a command, and I whine, actually fucking whine, my body trembling with need. He pulls out, and I curse, my hole clenching around nothing, aching for him to fill me again. But then he's kneeling behind me, hands spreading my cheeks, and his tongue—fuck, his tongue—licks a hot, wet stripe across my hole, and I cry out, the sensation so intense it's almost too much.

"Jesus fuck," I gasp, my head falling forward, ropes creaking as I strain against them. His tongue works me open, licking and probing, teasing the sensitive rim before pushing inside, and I'm shaking, my cock leaking steadily, the pleasure so sharp it's almost painful. He's relentless, eating me out like he's starving, his hands gripping my thighs, keeping me spread for him. The sounds he's making—wet, filthy, hungry—drive me wild, and I'm begging now, words spilling out without thought.

“Please, fuck, please, don’t stop,” I moan, and he hums against me, the vibration sending a jolt through my body. He pulls back, just enough to bite the curve of my ass, hard enough to make me yelp, and then he’s standing again, slicking his cock with more lube before pressing it against my hole.

“You beg so pretty,” he says, his voice thick with arousal, and then he’s pushing in, slower this time, letting me feel every inch, every vein, as he fills me up. I moan, long and low, my body yielding to him, the stretch easier now but no less intense. He starts moving, deep and steady, each thrust hitting that spot that makes my vision blur, and his hand finds my cock again, stroking in time with his hips.

“Fuck, you feel good,” he growls, his breath hot against my neck, and I can feel him losing it, his thrusts getting sloppier, more desperate. My body's on fire, every nerve screaming, and I'm so close, teetering on the edge, but he keeps me there, his hand slowing on my cock, keeping me from tipping over.

"Please," I beg, my voice wrecked, and he laughs, dark and filthy, his teeth grazing my shoulder. "Please what?" he asks, thrusting harder, deeper, and I cry out, my body clenching around him.

"Let me come," I gasp, and he groans, his hand tightening on my cock, stroking faster now, rough and relentless. "Fuck, please, I need it."

"That's it," he says, his voice raw, and he's pounding into me now, each thrust shaking the rack, the ropes biting into my skin as I take everything he gives me. My balls tighten, the pressure building, and then I'm coming, hard and sudden, cum shooting across the floor as I cry out, my body shaking, clenching around his cock. He groans, low and guttural, and thrusts through my orgasm, dragging it out until I'm trembling, oversensitive, every touch like a spark.

He's not done, though. He pulls out, and I'm panting, my body limp against the ropes, but he's not finished with me. He slicks his cock again, pressing it against my hole, and I moan, still sensitive but wanting more, always more. "You're gonna take it again," he says, and then he's pushing in, slower this time, letting me feel the stretch, the way he fills me completely.

"Fuck, yes," I groan, my head falling back as he starts moving, deep and deliberate, each thrust drawing a moan from me. His hand slides up my chest, pinching my nipple hard, and I gasp, the pain blending with pleasure, pushing me higher. He's relentless, fucking me with a single-minded focus, his breath ragged, his groans mixing with mine.

“You’re mine,” he growls, his hand gripping my throat again, and I nod, too far gone to argue, my body his to use, to break. He thrusts harder, faster, and I can feel him getting close, his cock throbbing inside me, his grip tightening. “Gonna fill you up,” he says, and the words push me over the edge again, a second orgasm ripping through me, weaker but no less intense, my cum spilling onto the floor as I cry out.

He groans, loud and raw, and then he’s coming, his cock pulsing inside me, filling me with heat as he thrusts through it, his body shaking against mine. We’re both panting, sweat-soaked, the air thick with the scent of sex and leather. He stays inside me for a moment, catching his breath, his hand still on my throat, grounding me as I come down from the high.

Finally, he pulls out, slow and careful, and I whimper at the loss, my body aching, spent. He steps around to face me, his eyes softer now but still burning, and he cups my jaw, thumb brushing my lips. "You took that like a fucking champ," he says, and there's a hint of pride in his voice that makes my chest tighten.

I grin, weak but cocky, because I'm still me, even after all that. "Told you I could handle you," I say, my voice hoarse, and he laughs, shaking his head.

"We're not done yet," he says, and my heart skips, because fuck, I know he means it, and I'm already craving more.

STEAM AND SURRENDER

I'm not the kind of guy who blends into the background. At forty-two, I've carved out a presence that demands attention—six-foot-three, broad shoulders, a chest that's still thick with muscle from years of lifting heavy and living hard. My hair's gone salt-and-pepper, cropped close to my scalp, and my jaw's lined with a coarse stubble that scratches when I run my hand over it, which I do often, like a reflex. My eyes, a sharp hazel, catch everything—every glance, every flinch, every bead of sweat. My body's a roadmap of ink and scars, each one a story of fights, fucks, or both. I'm not pretty, not by a long shot, but there's a rawness to me, a kind of unpolished power that makes guys look twice, whether they want to or not. In the dim light of this seedy bathhouse, my skin gleams under the sheen of sweat, and I know I'm a fucking force.

The sauna's a haze of heat and shadow, tucked in the back of this rundown joint on the edge of town. The air's thick, heavy with steam and the musky scent of men—sweat, skin, and something primal that hangs like a promise. The walls are slick with condensation, the wooden benches worn smooth by years of bodies sliding across them. It's not my first time here. This place, with its flickering neon sign out front and its labyrinth of dark hallways, is a playground for guys like me—hunters who know what they want and take it without asking. Tonight, I'm on the prowl, my towel slung low around my hips, barely clinging to the V of my pelvis, the coarse hair there peeking out like a tease.

I push through the heavy glass door into the sauna, and the heat hits me like a fist, wrapping around my chest, sinking into my bones. The room's small, maybe ten by ten, with tiered benches climbing up to a shadowed corner where the steam's thickest. A single bulb flickers overhead, casting jagged light across the bodies sprawled out—some lounging, some waiting, all of them sizing each other up like wolves. I scan the room, my eyes cutting through the haze. There's a couple of older guys, soft-bellied and uninterested, and a wiry dude with a nervous tic, his eyes darting away when I meet them. Not my type. I want someone who'll feel the weight of me, someone who'll squirm under my grip but won't back down too easy.

Then I see him. He's tucked against the far wall, half-hidden in the steam, his back pressed to the slick tiles like he's trying to disappear. Young—mid-twenties, maybe—lean but not scrawny, with a runner's build that says he's quick but not strong enough to outmuscle me. His hair's dark, wet with sweat, clinging to his forehead in messy strands. His skin's pale, almost glowing in the dim light, and his chest rises and falls too fast, like he's already on edge. He's got a towel wrapped tight around his waist, but it's slipping, showing the sharp cut of his hipbones, the faint trail of hair leading down to a bulge that's impossible to miss. His eyes, wide and blue, flicker toward me, then away, but not before I catch the spark of curiosity, the hint of want. He's perfect.

I don't rush. I never do. I let the heat do its work, let it soften him up, make his skin flush and his breaths shallow. I take a step closer, my bare feet silent on the wet floor, and settle onto the bench across from him, spreading my legs wide so the towel rides up, exposing the thick muscle of my thighs. I lean back, arms stretched along the back of the bench, my chest flexing just enough to draw his gaze. He's trying not to look, but he can't help it. His eyes keep slipping, darting to my pecs, my abs, the bulge under my towel that's growing harder the longer I stare at him. I let him feel it, the weight of my attention, like a hand pressing down on his chest.

"You new here?" My voice is low, rough, cutting through the hiss of the steam. He flinches, just a little, and his fingers tighten on the edge of his towel. He's nervous, but not scared. Good.

"Yeah," he says, his voice softer than I expected, with a slight tremble that makes my cock twitch. "First time."

I nod, slow, like I'm considering something, but really I'm just letting him stew. "Hot as fuck in here, isn't it?" I say, leaning forward, elbows on my knees, my eyes locked on his. He shifts, his thighs pressing together like he's trying to hide what's going on under that towel. Too late, kid. I already saw the way it tented when I spoke.

"Yeah," he mumbles, glancing at the door like he's thinking about bolting. But he doesn't move. He stays put, pinned by the heat and something else—something that's got his pulse hammering in his throat. I can see it, the quick flutter under his skin, and it makes me want to press my thumb there, feel it jump under my touch.

I stand, slow and deliberate, letting the towel slip just enough to show the base of my cock, thick and heavy against my thigh. His eyes widen, and he swallows hard, his Adam's apple bobbing. I take a step toward him, then another, closing the distance until I'm standing over him, my shadow falling across his lap. He's trapped now, the corner of the sauna boxing him in, the bench behind his knees, my body blocking the only way out. The air between us is electric, thick with heat and the sharp scent of his sweat, his arousal.

"Relax," I say, my voice a low growl, and I lean in, one hand bracing against the wall above his head. My other hand hovers near his shoulder, not touching, not yet, but close enough that he can feel the heat of my palm. “You’re gonna like this.”

His breath hitches, and his eyes flick up to mine, wide and searching, like he’s trying to figure out if he’s in over his head. He is, but that’s what makes this fun. I can see the fight in him, the way his jaw tightens, the way his hands clench into fists on his thighs. He’s not sure if he wants to push me away or pull me closer, and that indecision is fucking delicious.

I lean closer, my lips brushing just past his ear, close enough that he can feel my breath on his skin. “You feel that?” I murmur, letting my voice drop to a rumble. “The way the heat’s got you all soft and open? Makes it hard to think, doesn’t it?” I shift my weight, letting my thigh brush against his knee, just a graze, but enough to make him jump. His towel’s slipping now, barely holding on, and I can see the outline of his cock, hard and straining against the fabric.

He doesn't answer, but his chest is heaving, his skin flushed red from the heat and something else. I straighten up, just enough to look down at him, to let him feel the full weight of my size, my presence. I'm not touching him, not yet, but I don't need to. The air's doing it for me, wrapping around him, pressing him down, making him feel small. My hand moves to my towel, adjusting it just enough to let him see more, to let him know exactly what he's dealing with. His eyes drop to my crotch, and his lips part, just a fraction, but it's enough to tell me he's hooked.

"You're not going anywhere," I say, and it's not a question. It's a fact. The corner's tight, the steam's thick, and I'm a fucking wall between him and the door. His eyes dart to it again, but there's no conviction there, no real intent to run. He's caught, and he knows it. His cock's betraying him, twitching under that flimsy towel, and I can practically taste the want rolling off him.

I lower myself onto the bench beside him, close enough that our thighs touch, my skin hot and slick against his. He tenses, but he doesn't pull away. Good boy. I lean in again, my voice a low, dirty whisper. "You ever been pinned like this before? Trapped with nowhere to go, just you and a man who knows exactly what you need?" My hand moves to his thigh, not grabbing, just resting there, heavy and unyielding. His muscle jumps under my palm, and I can feel the heat of him, the way his body's screaming for more even if his mouth won't say it.

He's trembling now, just a little, but it's enough to make my blood pound. I want to rip that towel off, want to see his cock spring free, want to feel it pulse in my hand. But not yet. The buildup's too good, the way his eyes keep flicking to mine, the way his breath catches every time I move. I'm in control here, and he's learning that fast. The sauna's working its magic, softening him up, making his skin slick and his resolve weak. I can wait. I've got all night to break him down, to make him beg for it

. I let my fingers dig in just a fraction, testing the give of his quad muscle, feeling the tremor that runs through him like a current. He's got that lean, taut build—wiry from whatever cardio bullshit keeps him slim, but there's no real bulk to push back against me. My palm's rough, callused from years of gripping barbells and steering wheels, and I know he feels every ridge as I slide it higher, inch by inch, stopping just shy of where his towel bunches up. The steam curls around us, making everything slick, amplifying the heat until it's like we're breathing fire. His skin's fever-hot under my touch, and I can smell him now—clean sweat mixed with that faint, boyish musk that's got my pulse thudding low in my gut.

"Why so tense?" I murmur, my mouth close enough to his ear that my lips nearly brush the lobe. I don't whisper; I let my voice rumble, deep and gravelly, like it's coming from somewhere inside his chest. "You act like you've never had a man's hand on you before. Or maybe you have, and that's why you're shaking—like you know what's coming but can't decide if you crave it or fear it."

He lets out a shaky breath, his eyes half-lidded now, staring straight ahead at the opposite wall where the wood's warped from endless moisture. "I... I don't know you," he says, but it's not a protest. It's weak, threaded with something hungry, like he's fishing for reassurance or maybe just stalling. His voice cracks a little on the last word, and fuck, that does it for me—the vulnerability wrapped in defiance.

I chuckle, low and dark, letting my thumb trace a slow circle on his inner thigh, feeling the fine hairs there stand up. "You don't need to know me, kid. Not my name, not my story. All you need to know is how this feels." I press harder, my fingers splaying out, claiming more territory, and he shifts involuntarily, his knee knocking against mine. The contact sends a jolt through me, but I keep it reined in, savoring the slow burn. My other arm's still braced on the wall above him, caging him in, my bicep flexing just enough to remind him of the strength coiled there. He's got nowhere to go, the corner pressing into his back, the bench creaking under our combined weight.

His hand twitches on his lap, like he's debating whether to shove me off or grab hold, but it stays put, knuckles whitening. "This place... it's intense," he mutters, glancing sideways at me, those blue eyes flickering with a mix of challenge and surrender. "People just... do this? Corner someone and—"

"And what?" I cut him off, my hand sliding up another inch, fingertips brushing the hem of his towel. The fabric's damp, clinging to him, and I can feel the heat radiating from underneath, the subtle throb that tells me he's as hard as I am. I don't go further, not yet; instead, I let my nails graze lightly, a tease that makes his breath hitch audibly. "Take what they want? Yeah, they do. And you walked in here knowing that, didn't you? Eyes wide open, towel barely on, looking like fresh meat in a den of wolves."

He swallows, his throat working, and I watch the bead of sweat trace down from his temple, over his jaw, pooling in the hollow of his collarbone. God, I want to lick it off, taste the salt of him, but restraint's my weapon right now. "Maybe I didn't think it'd be like this," he admits, his voice gaining a edge, like he's trying to reclaim some ground. "You just... assume I want it? That I'm okay with you touching me like—"

"Like I own you?" I finish for him, my grip tightening on his thigh, pulling his leg a fraction closer to mine. Our skins stick together in the humidity, a wet slide that's almost obscene. I lean in, my nose brushing his hairline, inhaling the shampoo scent clinging to him—something citrusy, clean, contrasting the filthy air around us. "Your body's saying yes louder than your mouth's saying no. Look at you—chest heaving, cock twitching under that towel like it's begging for attention. You could've yelled, pushed me away, bolted for the door. But here you are, letting my hand creep higher, wondering how far I'll go."

He turns his head just enough that our faces are inches apart, his breath mingling with mine in the steamy haze. There's fire in his eyes now, a spark of resistance that makes this all the sweeter. "You're cocky as hell," he says, but there's a breathy quality to it, like the words are costing him. His hand finally moves, not to stop me, but to rest on the bench beside him, fingers curling into the wood as if anchoring himself.

I grin, feeling the stubble on my chin scrape against his cheek as I pull back slightly. "Cocky? Nah, just observant." My free hand comes down now, slow and deliberate, tracing the line of his shoulder, down his arm, feeling the goosebumps rise despite the sweltering heat. His bicep's firm, but it yields under my squeeze, and I linger there, kneading like I'm appraising him. "See this? Your skin's telling tales. Every little shiver, every catch in your breath—it's all screaming for more. But I'm not rushing. We've got time for you to admit it."

The sauna door creaks open somewhere behind us, letting in a burst of cooler air that swirls the steam, but it slams shut quick, voices murmuring low before fading. We're not alone, but in this corner, it feels like we are—the shadows and fog creating a bubble where rules don't apply. He glances toward the sound, his body tensing again, but my hand on his thigh anchors him, a firm reminder. "What if someone sees?" he whispers, but it's not fear; it's thrill, edged with that same hunger.

"Let 'em watch," I growl, my fingers dipping under the towel's edge now, just the tips, brushing the soft skin where thigh meets groin. He gasps, a sharp intake that echoes in the quiet, and his hips shift forward involuntarily, chasing the touch. Fuck, that's beautiful—the way he fights it but can't help responding. My other hand moves to his chest, palm flat over his pec, feeling the rapid thud of his heart. His nipple's hard under my thumb, and I circle it lazily, watching his eyes flutter. "Imagine their eyes on you, seeing how you arch into my hand, how your cock leaks just from this. Turns you on, doesn't it? Being on display, but only for me to touch."

He bites his lip, stifling a sound that's half-moan, half-denial, his head tipping back against the wall with a thud. "You're twisting everything," he manages, but his voice is ragged now, breath coming in pants. His hand lifts, hesitating, then lands on my forearm—not pushing, just holding, fingers digging in like he's caught between stopping me and urging me on. The contact's electric, his touch tentative but warm, and it sends a surge straight to my groin.

"Twisting? Or just pointing out the obvious?" I press my thumb harder against his nipple, pinching lightly, and he jerks, a low whimper escaping. I release, then soothe with a flat palm, sliding down to his abs, tracing the faint ridges there, slick with sweat. My thigh presses against his, forcing his legs apart a bit more, and I feel the brush of his towel against my own, the heat building to unbearable. "Feel that? How your body's opening up, relaxing into it even as your mind spins. You're dripping, aren't you? I can smell it—that sharp, needy scent cutting through the steam."

He shakes his head, but it's feeble, his eyes locked on mine now, pupils blown wide. "Stop talking like that," he says, but there's no conviction, just a plea laced with want. His fingers tighten on my arm, sliding up to my bicep, exploring the muscle there with a curiosity that betrays him. "It's... too much. The heat, you—everything's blurring."

"Good," I reply, my voice dropping to a husky murmur as I lean in again, my lips ghosting over his neck without touching, just breathing hot against his pulse point. It jumps under the assault, and I let my hand on his thigh venture higher, fingers curling around the inner seam, inches from his balls. The towel's tented obscenely now, a dark spot blooming where he's leaking, and I hover there, letting him feel the promise. "Let it blur. Let go of that tight-ass control. I'm not gonna fuck you yet—not until you're grinding against me, whispering how bad you need it. But I'll touch you everywhere else, make you ache for it."

His free hand comes up, cupping the back of my neck suddenly, pulling me closer—not for a kiss, but like he needs the anchor. His fingers tangle in the short hair there, tugging lightly, and fuck, that pulls a growl from me. "You're an asshole," he breathes, but his hips roll just a fraction, seeking friction, and his eyes are dark with lust. "Pushing all these buttons, making me—"

"Making you what?" I challenge, my hand slipping fully under the towel now, palm pressing flat against his lower belly, fingers splayed wide, feeling the coarse hair and the base of his cock throb against my wrist. I don't stroke, don't grab—just hold, letting the pressure build, the tease of what's so close. His abs contract under my touch, and he arches, a soft curse slipping out. The steam thickens as someone pours water on the rocks, hissing loud, enveloping us further, making every sensation sharper.

"Making me want to hate you," he confesses, his voice breaking on a laugh that's more gasp, his nails scraping my scalp. "But I can't. Not when it feels like this—like you're unraveling me thread by thread."

I press down harder on his belly, feeling his cock jump against my arm, and slide my other hand up his side, thumbing the dip of his ribs, then back to his chest, rolling his nipple between fingers. He's panting openly now, body slick and pliant, leaning into every touch like he's starving. "That's the point, kid. Unravel you slow, watch you come apart. Tell me—how's that cock feeling? Heavy? Aching? Bet it's dripping down your balls, making a mess."

He groans, low and tortured, his head falling forward onto my shoulder, breath hot against my skin. "Yes," he admits, the word muffled, his hand sliding down my back, gripping my towel like he's holding on for life. "Fuck, yes. But you're killing me—touch it, please, just—"

"Not yet," I say firmly, pulling my hand back just enough to make him whine, then replacing it higher, fingers brushing the underside of his shaft through the towel's fold. The indirect contact makes him buck, and I hold him down with my weight, thigh pinning his. Tension coils between us, thick as the air, every denied touch ratcheting it higher. "Beg a little more. Show me how bad you need my grip around that pretty cock of yours."

He lifts his head, eyes meeting mine, fierce and desperate. "You're enjoying this too much," he accuses, but his hips grind subtly, seeking more, his fingers digging into my back hard enough to leave marks.

"Damn right I am," I retort, my mouth curving into a smirk as I let my fingers dance lighter, teasing the length without mercy, feeling him pulse and strain. The sauna's a pressure cooker now, our breaths syncing in ragged harmony, the world narrowing to this corner, this game of push and pull. He's mine to toy with, and I'm just getting started.

His whine's still ringing in my ears, a desperate edge to it that makes my cock throb against the damp towel. I can feel the heat of him, the way his body's practically vibrating under my hands, caught between defiance and surrender. My fingers linger just shy of wrapping around his shaft, teasing through the towel's thin barrier, feeling the pulse of him, hot and insistent. The sauna's a furnace now, steam curling thick, making every breath heavy, every touch slick and amplified. His nails dig harder into my back, leaving half-moon marks I'll feel later, and his hips jerk again, chasing my hand like he's starving for it.

"You're cruel," he gasps, his voice raw, eyes blazing with a mix of accusation and need. His head's still tilted against my shoulder, lips so close to my neck I can feel their heat, the faint brush of his breath making my skin prickle. "Teasing like that—fuck, just do something."

I chuckle, the sound low and filthy, and slide my hand fully under the towel now, letting my knuckles graze the length of his cock, slow and deliberate. It's thick, harder than I expected, slick with precum that smears against my skin. I don't grip him yet, just let the contact linger, a promise of what's coming. "Cruel? Kid, I'm just warming you up. You think this is torture? Wait till I've got you bent over, begging for my cock in your ass."

His breath catches, a sharp hitch that turns into a moan as I finally curl my fingers around him, loose but firm, giving one slow stroke from base to tip. His cock pulses in my hand, leaking more, and I swipe my thumb over the head, spreading the slickness, feeling him shudder. "Fuck," he whispers, his lips brushing my collarbone, not quite a kiss but close enough to make my blood surge. His hand slides up my neck, fingers tangling in my hair again, tugging hard like he's trying to ground himself.

I tilt his chin up with my free hand, forcing his eyes to meet mine. They're glassy, pupils blown, but there's still that spark of defiance, like he's daring me to push harder. I lean in, my lips hovering over his, not touching, just breathing the same air, letting the tension coil tighter. "You taste that?" I murmur, my voice a low growl. "The way the air's thick with want? Your cock's telling me everything your mouth won't." I stroke him again, tighter this time, and his hips buck, a soft curse spilling from him.

He surges forward suddenly, closing the gap, his lips crashing into mine. It's not gentle—teeth clash, his tongue hot and desperate, tasting of salt and need. I kiss him back, hard, my hand tightening on his cock as I angle his head with my other, deepening the kiss until it's all tongue and heat and the faint scrape of his stubble against mine. He moans into my mouth, the sound vibrating through me, and I swallow it, my tongue fucking his mouth like a preview of what's to come.

I pull back just enough to see his face—flushed, lips swollen, eyes half-shut but locked on mine. "You kiss like you're starving," I say, my thumb brushing his lower lip, still wet from my mouth. "Bet you suck cock like that too, don't you? Hungry, sloppy, taking it deep."

His eyes widen, but he doesn't deny it. Instead, he licks his lips, a slow, deliberate move that makes my cock ache. "Maybe you'll find out," he shoots back, his voice steadier now, laced with a challenge that makes me grin. He's finding his footing, pushing back just enough to keep this interesting.

I don't answer with words. Instead, I tug his towel free, letting it fall to the bench, exposing him completely. His cock juts up, thick and flushed, the head glistening in the dim light. I don't give him time to think—my hand wraps around him again, stroking slow but firm, while my other hand slides down his back, fingers dipping into the crease of his ass. He tenses, but doesn't pull away, his breath hitching as my fingertip brushes his hole, not pushing in, just circling, teasing the sensitive skin.

"Fuck, you're tight here," I growl, my lips brushing his ear. "Bet it's gonna feel like heaven when I'm buried inside you." I press just a little harder, feeling the muscle clench under my touch, and he arches, his cock jerking in my hand. His hands grip my shoulders now, nails biting in, and he's panting, his body caught in a feedback loop of pleasure and anticipation.

I shift, pulling him off the bench and onto my lap, his thighs straddling mine. The movement's quick, almost rough, and he gasps as our cocks brush through the thin layer of my towel. I yank it off, letting it drop, and now it's just skin on skin, his cock sliding against mine, hot and slick with sweat and precum. The sauna's heat makes everything feel molten, like we're melting into each other. I grip his hips, guiding him to grind against me, slow and deliberate, watching his face contort with pleasure.

"Feel that?" I say, my voice thick with lust. "Two hard cocks, sliding together, leaking all over each other. You're making a fucking mess, kid." I pull him closer, one hand sliding up his spine, the other cupping his ass, squeezing hard enough to leave marks. He moans, loud this time, and I feel the vibration against my chest as he buries his face in my neck, lips grazing my skin.

"God, you're—fuck," he stammers, his hips moving faster now, chasing the friction. His mouth finds my jaw, kissing sloppily, teeth nipping as he works his way down to my throat. I tilt my head back, giving him access, and he takes it, sucking hard enough to leave a bruise. The sting sends a jolt straight to my cock, and I growl, my fingers digging into his ass, spreading him open.

"Get down there," I order, pushing him off my lap and onto his knees between my thighs. The bench creaks as he settles, his hands gripping my knees for balance. His eyes are on my cock now, thick and heavy, the head slick with precum. He hesitates, just for a second, and I grab his hair, not pulling, just holding, guiding his face closer. "Show me how hungry you are. Suck it like you mean it."

He doesn't need more encouragement. His lips part, and he takes me in, slow at first, his tongue swirling around the head, tasting me. The wet heat of his mouth is fucking electric, and I groan, my hand tightening in his hair. He's good—better than good—his tongue working the underside, lips stretching around my girth as he takes me deeper. He gags a little, but doesn't stop, his hands braced on my thighs as he bobs, sloppy and eager, spit dripping down his chin.

"Fuck, that's it," I rasp, my hips twitching up, feeding him more. "Take it all, kid. Let me feel that throat." He moans around me, the vibration sending sparks up my spine, and I guide his head, setting a rhythm that's just shy of too much. His eyes flick up, meeting mine, and there's something raw there—submission, but with that same spark of defiance, like he's proving he can handle me.

I pull him off with a wet pop, his lips red and swollen, and haul him back up, kissing him hard, tasting myself on his tongue. The kiss is messy, all teeth and spit, and I flip us so he's back against the wall, my body pinning him. I slide down, kissing a trail down his chest, nipping at his nipples until he's squirming, then lower, my tongue tracing the line of his abs. When I reach his cock, I don't tease—I take him in, sucking hard, my hands spreading his thighs wide. He cries out, hips bucking, and I pin him down, my fingers digging into his hips as I work him, tongue flicking over the slit, tasting his precum.

"Fuck, please," he gasps, his hands in my hair, pulling hard. "Don't stop—God, your mouth—"

I pull off, grinning up at him, my lips slick. "Not stopping, kid. Just getting you ready." I spin him around, pressing his chest to the wall, his ass out. The steam makes his skin glisten, and I spread his cheeks, my tongue finding his hole, licking slow and deep. He moans, loud and broken, his legs trembling as I work him open, my hands gripping his thighs to keep him steady. The taste of him—musky, clean, desperate—drives me wild, and I eat him out like I'm starving, my tongue fucking into him until he's shaking, babbling curses.

I stand, pressing my cock against his ass, not entering, just sliding between his cheeks, slick with spit and sweat. "You want this?" I growl, my lips against his ear, one hand wrapping around his cock, stroking in time with my grinding. "Want me to fuck you right here, make you scream in this fucking sauna?"

"Yes," he moans, pushing back against me, his voice wrecked. "Fuck, yes, please—"

I spin him again, lifting him onto the bench, his legs over my shoulders. I slide my cock against his, grinding hard, our precum mixing as I kiss him, swallowing his moans. Then I shift, lining up, my tip pressing against his hole, not entering yet, just teasing, letting the pressure build. "Not yet," I murmur, my hand stroking him faster, keeping him on edge. "Gonna make you come apart first, then I'll fuck you senseless."

He's trembling, his body open and pliant, every touch pushing him closer to breaking. The sauna's a haze of heat and want, and we're lost in it, bodies slick, tension electric.

His legs tremble over my shoulders, his body pinned against the slick sauna wall, every inch of him taut with need. My cock presses against his hole, not breaching yet, just grinding, the slick head catching on his rim, teasing the tight muscle until he's gasping, his hands clawing at my arms. The steam swirls thick around us, amplifying every sensation—the wet slide of skin, the sharp scent of his arousal, the way his breath hitches in time with my slow, deliberate thrusts against him. My hand's still wrapped around his cock, stroking in rhythm, keeping him teetering on the edge, his precum dripping over my fingers, mixing with the sweat that coats us both.

"Fuck, you're cruel," he pants, his voice raw, eyes locked on mine, wild with desperation. "Just—do it. Stop teasing and fuck me." There's a challenge in his tone, a spark of defiance that makes my blood roar, even as his body yields, hips rolling to meet my pressure.

I smirk, leaning in to bite his lower lip, not gentle, tasting the salt of his sweat. "Begging already? Thought you had more fight in you." My tip presses harder, just enough to stretch him, but I pull back, dragging a frustrated groan from his throat. I slide my hand up his chest, pinching a nipple hard, watching his head tip back, exposing the pale column of his throat. "You'll get my cock when I say, kid. When you're so fucking desperate you're crying for it."

He growls, a low, broken sound, and grabs my face, pulling me into a kiss that's all teeth and hunger, his tongue pushing against mine like he's trying to take back control. I let him have the moment, savoring the way he fights, but I'm the one in charge here. I break the kiss, gripping his jaw, holding his gaze. "You want it bad, don't you? Want me to split you open, pound you till you can't walk straight."

"Yes," he hisses, his nails digging into my shoulders, leaving red crescents. "Fuck, yes, I want it. Stop fucking around and give it to me." His hips buck, trying to force me inside, and the raw need in his voice sends a jolt straight to my cock.

I don't make him wait any longer. I spit into my hand, slicking myself up, the wet sound obscene in the humid air, and line up, pushing in slow but relentless. His hole's tight, clenching around my head as I breach him, and he gasps, a sharp, pained sound that melts into a moan as I sink deeper. "Fuck, you're tight," I growl, my hands gripping his hips, holding him steady as I bottom out, my balls pressed against his ass. He's trembling, his breath coming in ragged pants, and I can feel every shudder of his body, every pulse of his muscles around me.

“Move,” he demands, but it’s half-plea, his legs tightening around my shoulders, pulling me closer. His cock’s leaking steadily now, smearing against his stomach, and I reach down, stroking him in time with my first thrust, slow but deep, making him feel every inch.

I set a brutal pace, pulling out almost all the way before slamming back in, the wet slap of skin echoing in the sauna. His moans are loud, unrestrained, bouncing off the slick walls, and I don’t care who hears. “That’s it,” I grunt, my voice rough with effort. “Take it like you were made for it. Fucking perfect, gripping my cock like a vice.” Each thrust drives him up the wall, his shoulders scraping the tiles, his hands scrabbling for purchase on my arms.

I shift, pulling his legs down and flipping him onto his stomach over the bench, his ass up, face pressed into the wood. The new angle lets me go deeper, and I don't hold back, pounding into him with a rhythm that's all dominance, my hands spreading his cheeks to watch my cock disappear inside him. "Look at that," I murmur, my voice thick with lust. "Your hole's swallowing me, begging for more. You love this, don't you? Being fucked raw in a filthy sauna."

"Fuck, yes," he moans, his voice muffled against the bench, his hips pushing back to meet my thrusts. His fingers grip the edge, knuckles white, and I can see the sweat dripping down his spine, pooling in the dip of his lower back. I lean over, licking a stripe up his spine, tasting the salt, and bite the nape of his neck, hard enough to make him cry out.

I pull out, ignoring his whimper of protest, and haul him up, turning him to face me. “Ride me,” I order, sitting on the bench and pulling him onto my lap. He straddles me, his thighs trembling as he lowers himself, guiding my cock back inside with a shaky hand. The slide is smooth, slick with spit and sweat, and he groans, head falling back as he takes me deep. I grip his hips, guiding him, but let him set the pace, watching his face twist with pleasure as he grinds down, his cock bouncing against my stomach.

“Fuck, you’re deep,” he gasps, his hands on my shoulders, nails biting in as he rides me, slow at first, then faster, chasing the friction. His ass clenches around me, hot and tight, and I can feel my own release building, the heat coiling low in my gut. I grab his cock, stroking rough and fast, matching his rhythm. “You gonna come for me?” I growl, my lips against his ear. “Gonna spill all over my hand while I fuck you senseless?”

He nods, frantic, his movements erratic now, hips slamming down as he chases it. I thrust up to meet him, hard and relentless, and he cries out, his body tensing as he comes, hot spurts coating my hand, his stomach, dripping onto my thighs. The sight of him unraveling, the way his hole pulses around me, pushes me over the edge. I grip his hips, slamming him down one last time, and come hard, pumping deep inside him, filling him with heat. He moans, low and broken, collapsing against my chest, his breath hot against my neck.

We stay like that for a moment, panting, slick with sweat and cum, the sauna's heat wrapping around us like a second skin. His body's limp, pliant, and I run a hand down his back, feeling the aftershocks ripple through him. "Good boy," I murmur, my voice softer now, but still edged with that possessive growl. He shudders at the words, his lips brushing my collarbone in a ghost of a kiss.

I ease him off me, careful, watching the way he winces as my cock slips free, a trickle of cum leaking down his thigh. He's a mess—hair plastered to his forehead, skin flushed, lips swollen—and it's fucking beautiful. I pull him close, kissing him slow, deep, tasting the salt of his sweat, the faint bitterness of his cum on his lips from where I'd smeared it earlier. "You took that like a champ," I say, my thumb brushing his jaw. "Bet you're already thinking about next time."

He laughs, a shaky, breathless sound, his eyes half-lidded but sharp with that same spark of defiance. "You're so fucking full of yourself," he mutters, but there's no heat in it, just a sated kind of amusement. His hand rests on my chest, fingers tracing the ink there, and I can feel the tension still simmering, not gone, just banked for now.

I stand, pulling him up with me, and grab our towels, tossing his over his shoulder. The sauna door creaks open again, a burst of cooler air cutting through the haze, but I don't care who's watching. I lean in, my lips brushing his ear one last time. "Don't go far, kid.

CURIOUS SOCCER BROS

I'm twenty-two, lean and wiry from years of tearing up the soccer field, my legs ropy with muscle, my abs tight from endless sprints. My skin's tanned from hours under the sun, a light sheen of sweat always clinging to me after practice, making my dark hair stick to my forehead in messy strands. I keep it short, practical, but it's always a little wild, like I just rolled out of bed—or off the field. My jaw's sharp, dusted with stubble I'm too lazy to shave, and my green eyes have a glint that says I'm always up to no good. I'm not the biggest guy—five-foot-ten, maybe 160 pounds—but I'm quick, agile, and I've got a cock that's gotten me more than a few appreciative glances in the showers. Confidence is my game, and I play it well, especially in the locker room, where the air's thick with testosterone and the kind of energy that makes you do stupid shit.

Practice was brutal today, the kind of grueling session that leaves your legs burning and your blood pumping. The sun was relentless, beating down on the field, and now, in the locker room, the air's heavy with steam and the sharp tang of sweat. It's just past dusk, the fluorescent lights buzzing overhead, casting harsh shadows across the tiled walls and benches. The team's mostly cleared out, leaving just me and him, the last stragglers peeling off sweaty kits and tossing them into lockers. He's across the room, stripping down, and I can't help but watch, my eyes drawn to him like a magnet.

He's my age, maybe a year younger, with a body built for speed—lean like me, but broader in the shoulders, his chest defined from all those headers he's so damn good at. His hair's blond, damp with sweat, clinging to his scalp in a way that makes you want to run your fingers through it. His skin's pale, flushed pink from exertion, and his blue eyes catch the light when he glances my way, a smirk playing on his lips like he knows I'm looking. He's got that cocky vibe, the kind that says he's used to getting what he wants, and fuck, it's hot.

I'm down to my jock, the straps digging into my hips, my cock half-hard already just from the adrenaline and the sight of him tugging off his shorts. He's in his briefs, tight black ones that hug his ass and show off the bulge of his dick, thick and obvious even through the fabric. I lean against my locker, towel slung over my shoulder, and catch his eye, grinning. "Fucking hell, man, you look like you ran a marathon out there," I say, my voice light but laced with a tease. "Sweating like a pig, and still strutting like you own the place."

He laughs, a sharp, easy sound, and tosses his shin guards into his bag. "Says the guy who missed that shot in the last drill," he fires back, stepping closer, his briefs riding low, showing the cut of his hipbones. "Bet you're too wiped to even get it up right now." His eyes flick down, lingering on my jock, and there's a glint there—playful, but with an edge that makes my pulse kick up.

I step closer, closing the gap between us, the locker room suddenly feeling smaller, the air thicker. "Wanna bet?" I say, my grin widening, my hand adjusting my jock just enough to make the bulge more obvious. "I'm packing more than you, and I'm not even trying." It's a joke, but it's not—there's a challenge in it, the kind of dumb, horny shit guys say when the testosterone's still pumping and the room's too quiet.

He raises an eyebrow, his smirk growing, and steps right up to me, close enough that I can smell the sweat on him, sharp and clean, mixed with the faint cedar of his body wash. "Bullshit," he says, his voice dropping lower, teasing but with a heat that wasn't there before. "You think you're bigger? Prove it, hotshot." He hooks a thumb in the waistband of his briefs, tugging them down just an inch, showing the dark blond hair at the base of his dick, and my mouth goes dry.

I laugh, but it's rough, my cock twitching in my jock. "Alright, fucker, you're on," I say, and before I can overthink it, I shove my jock down, letting it fall to my ankles. My cock springs free, half-hard and heavy, the head already slick with a bead of precum. I stroke it once, casual, like it's no big deal, but my eyes are locked on his, daring him to match me.

His eyes widen, just for a second, before that smirk comes back, cockier than ever. "Not bad," he says, his voice low, almost a growl. He shoves his briefs down, kicking them aside, and fuck, his cock's a sight—thick, veiny, maybe a touch shorter than mine but fatter, the head flushed red and glistening. He gives it a slow stroke, mirroring me, and the air between us crackles, the locker room's fluorescent hum fading into nothing. "Still think you're winning?" he asks, stepping closer, his cock bobbing with the movement, inches from mine.

I grin, my heart pounding, the heat pooling low in my gut. "Fuck yeah, I'm winning," I say, but my voice is rougher now, the teasing edge giving way to something hungrier. I step closer, our cocks almost touching, the space between us electric. "But let's see who's got more game." I reach out, bold as fuck, and wrap my hand around his dick, giving it a slow, firm stroke. His breath hitches, his eyes darkening, but he doesn't pull away—instead, he leans into it, his hips shifting forward.

"Fuck, you don't mess around," he mutters, his voice thick, that cocky smirk faltering as I stroke him again, my thumb swiping over the head, spreading his precum. His cock's hot, pulsing in my hand, and I can feel my own dick throbbing, fully hard now, brushing against my thigh. "Thought you were just joking," he adds, but his hand's on my cock now, mirroring my move, his grip tight and sure, stroking slow but deliberate.

"Joking's over," I say, my voice low, my eyes locked on his. His hand feels fucking good, rough from years of gripping a ball, and every stroke sends a jolt through me, making my balls tighten. The locker room's quiet except for our breathing, heavy and uneven, the steam from the showers curling around us like a haze. “You’re hard as fuck for me, aren’t you?” I tease, my hand speeding up, feeling his cock twitch in my grip. “Bet you’ve been thinking about this all practice, watching me run.”

He laughs, but it’s shaky, his hand matching my pace, stroking me faster, his thumb circling my head, slick with precum. “You’re one to talk,” he shoots back, his voice rough, his eyes flicking down to my cock, then back up. “Leaking like a fucking faucet, acting all cocky while your dick’s begging for it.” He steps closer, our cocks brushing now, the contact sending a spark up my spine, and I groan, low and rough, my hand tightening on him.

“Fuck you,” I say, but there’s no heat in it—just lust, raw and unfiltered. I lean in, my lips hovering over his, not kissing yet, just breathing the same air, the tension so thick it’s suffocating. His hand’s relentless, stroking me with a rhythm that’s got me on edge, and I can feel his cock pulsing in my grip, his precum slicking my fingers. “You want more, don’t you?” I murmur, my voice a low growl, my lips brushing his jaw, feeling the stubble there. “Want me to make you feel it, right here in the fucking locker room.”

He groans, his head tipping back, giving me access to his throat, and I nip at it, not hard, just enough to make him gasp. “You’re such a prick,” he says, but his voice is wrecked, his hips rocking into my hand, chasing the friction. “But yeah, fuck, I want it.” His hand slows, teasing now, his thumb pressing against my slit, making me hiss. “What’s it gonna be, hotshot? You gonna keep talking, or you gonna do something?”

I grin, my heart pounding, the heat between us unbearable. I push him back against the lockers, the metal clanging under his weight, and drop to my knees, my hand still on his cock, stroking slow. His dick's right in my face, thick and red, the head glistening, and I can smell him—sweat, musk, and that faint cedar from his body wash. "Gonna do plenty," I say, my voice rough, my eyes flicking up to his. "Gonna make you beg for it, then we'll see who's really winning."

He's breathing hard, his hands braced against the lockers, his cock twitching in my hand as I lean in, my lips brushing the head, not sucking yet, just teasing with my breath.

His cock twitches in my hand, slick with precum, the head brushing my lips as I kneel before him, the locker room's steamy air wrapping around us like a fever. His chest heaves, those broad shoulders pressed back against the cold metal of the lockers, his blue eyes dark with a mix of shock and hunger. The fluorescent buzz overhead is drowned out by our ragged breathing, the heat of our bodies cutting through the lingering scent of sweat and grass from practice. My own dick's rock-hard, straining against the air, pulsing with every beat of my heart as his hand still lingers on it, his grip loose now but still there, teasing, like he's testing how far this game can go. We're both straight, got girlfriends waiting at home, but right now, in this hazy, testosterone-soaked moment, none of that matters. It's just us, the tension, and the forbidden thrill of crossing a line we've never touched before.

"Fuck, man, you're really doing this," he says, his voice low, rough, with a nervous edge that makes my cock throb harder. His hand tightens on my dick for a second, a reflexive squeeze, and I groan, the sound low and raw, my lips still hovering over his cock, close enough to feel the heat radiating off it. "What about—shit, you know, your girl?" There's a flicker of guilt in his tone, but it's drowned out by the way his hips shift, pushing his cock closer to my mouth, like his body's making decisions his brain hasn't caught up to.

I smirk, my breath hot against his tip, making him shudder. "What about yours?" I shoot back, my hand stroking him slow, deliberate, feeling the thick vein pulse under my fingers. "You're the one leaking all over my hand, acting like you don't want this." I give his cock a gentle tug, my thumb circling the head, spreading his precum, and he gasps, his head thudding back against the locker with a dull clang. "Don't play innocent now. You started this, sizing me up like it's a fucking contest."

He laughs, a shaky, breathless sound, his hand sliding to my shoulder, fingers digging in like he's trying to ground himself. "Started it? You're the one who whipped it out first, hotshot," he says, his voice teasing but thick with want, his eyes flicking down to my cock, then back to my face. "Fuck, this is crazy. We're not—shit, we're not supposed to be doing this." But his hand's back on my dick, stroking slow, his fingers exploring the length like he's curious, like he's never touched another guy before and can't stop himself now.

I lean in closer, my lips brushing the head of his cock, not sucking yet, just teasing with the lightest graze, tasting the salt of his precum. He moans, a low, desperate sound that sends a jolt straight to my balls, and I pull back, grinning up at him. “Not supposed to, but you’re fucking loving it,” I say, my voice rough, my hand speeding up on his cock, making his hips buck. “Look at you, hard as fuck, moaning like you’re dying for it. Bet your girl doesn’t make you squirm like this.”

He groans, his hand sliding to my hair, tugging lightly, not pushing me away but not guiding me closer either—just holding, like he’s caught between want and restraint. “Fuck you, man,” he mutters, but there’s no bite in it, just a shaky laugh, his eyes half-lidded, dark with lust. “You’re so fucking cocky. Bet you’re thinking about your girl right now, too, trying to pretend this ain’t turning you on." His thumb brushes my slit, slow and deliberate, and I hiss, my hips jerking into his hand, my cock leaking more.

I stand, pulling him with me, our bodies close, cocks brushing against each other, the contact sending a spark through me that makes my breath catch. "Oh, it's turning me on," I admit, my voice low, my lips inches from his, the air between us electric. "But not because of her. It's you, all fucking flushed and needy, acting like you don't want my hands all over you." I grab his ass, firm and round from years on the field, and squeeze, pulling him closer so our cocks grind together, slick with precum, the friction fucking maddening.

He gasps, his hands grabbing my biceps, nails digging in as he rocks against me, subtle but desperate. "Fuck, you're—shit, you're making this hard," he says, his voice cracking, a mix of nerves and hunger. "We're straight, man, we shouldn't—fuck, why's this feel so good?" His cock slides against mine, hot and heavy, and I can feel the tension in him, the way he's fighting it but losing, his body betraying every word.

I laugh, rough and low, my hands roaming his back, fingers tracing the dip of his spine, feeling the sweat there, the heat of his skin. "Feels good 'cause it's fucking hot," I say, my lips brushing his jaw, not kissing, just teasing, feeling the stubble scrape against me. "You, me, all this pent-up shit from practice—it's like we're wired for it. Bet you've been checking me out in the showers, wondering what it'd be like." My hand slides to his chest, thumbing his nipple, hard and sensitive, and he moans, his head tipping back, giving me access to his throat.

"Fuck off," he says, but it's weak, his voice trembling as my thumb circles his nipple, making him arch into my touch. "You're the one always strutting around, showing off that dick like it's a fucking trophy." His hand's back on my cock, stroking faster now, his fingers tight, exploring every inch like he's memorizing it. "Bet you've been thinking about this, too, jerking off to the idea of us messing around."

I grin, my hand sliding to his ass again, kneading the muscle, my fingers brushing the crease, teasing closer to his hole but not touching yet. "Maybe I have," I say, my voice a low growl, my lips grazing his ear, making him shiver. "Maybe I've been watching you bend over to tie your cleats, imagining what that ass looks like bare, wondering how you'd moan with my hands on you." I squeeze his ass harder, pulling him against me, our cocks grinding together, the slick friction making us both groan.

He's panting now, his hands roaming my chest, fingers tracing the lines of my abs, hesitant but curious, like he's never touched a guy like this but can't stop himself. "This is fucked up," he mutters, but his hips rock forward, chasing the contact, his cock leaking against mine. “My girl’d kill me if she knew—fuck, why can’t I stop?” His voice is shaky, but his hands are bold, one sliding to my hip, the other stroking my cock again, slow and teasing, like he’s testing how far he can push this.

I grab his wrist, pinning it to the locker behind him, leaning in so our faces are inches apart, our breaths mingling. “Stop? You don’t wanna stop,” I say, my voice rough, my free hand sliding to his cock, stroking slow, feeling it pulse in my grip. “You’re hard as fuck, leaking all over me, acting like you don’t want my mouth on you next.” I lean closer, my lips brushing his, not kissing yet, just hovering, letting the tension build. His eyes flutter, his breath hitching, and I can feel his resolve crumbling, his body screaming for more.

"Fuck, you're a bastard," he says, but it's half-laughed, his voice thick with want, his free hand grabbing my ass, mirroring me, his fingers digging in like he's claiming me back. "You're gonna ruin me, aren't you? Make me do shit I've never even thought about." His cock twitches in my hand, and I stroke faster, my thumb swiping over the head, making him moan, a low, desperate sound that goes straight to my balls.

"Ruin you? Nah, I'm just waking you up," I say, my lips brushing his jaw again, my teeth grazing the stubble, making him shudder. "Bet you've been curious, wondering what it's like to get this close, to feel another guy's cock against yours." I grind against him, our dicks sliding together, slick and hot, and he groans, his head thudding back against the locker. My hand slides to his balls, rolling them gently, feeling them tighten under my touch, and he's trembling now, his moans louder, more desperate.

"You're so fucking full of yourself," he says, but his voice is wrecked, his hand stroking my cock faster, matching my pace, like he's trying to keep up, to prove he's not just along for the ride. "Bet you're thinking about sucking me off, too, aren't you? Can't stop staring at my dick." His eyes flick down, catching the way I'm looking at his cock, thick and red, leaking steadily now, and he smirks, a shaky, cocky grin that makes my pulse race.

I laugh, low and dirty, and push him harder against the lockers, my body pinning his, our cocks trapped between us, grinding slow and deliberate. "Oh, I'm thinking about it," I admit, my voice a growl, my hand sliding to his hip, fingers digging in. "Thinking about how you'd taste, how you'd moan with my mouth on you, begging for more like a needy little fuck." I lean in, my lips brushing his ear, my breath hot against his skin. “But first, I’m gonna make you squirm, make you admit you want this as bad as I do.”

He groans, his hand tightening on my cock, his other sliding to my chest, pushing back just enough to meet my eyes. “You’re fucking insane,” he says, but his voice is trembling, his body arching into mine, his cock leaking against my stomach. “We’ve got girls, man, we’re not—fuck, why’s this so hot?” His words are a mix of guilt and hunger, but his hands don’t stop, his fingers exploring, teasing, like he’s as curious as I am, as caught up in this forbidden heat.

The tension’s unbearable, the locker room a haze of steam and want, our bodies pressed together, slick with sweat, cocks grinding, hands roaming. We’re both straight, both got lives outside this room, but right now, it’s just us, the thrill of touching what we shouldn't, the tease of what's coming next, and I'm gonna keep pushing him, keep playing this game, until we're both too far gone to care.

His body's pressed against mine, the metal lockers cold against his back, our cocks grinding together, slick with precum and sweat, the air thick with the musky scent of our arousal. His blond hair's damp, sticking to his forehead, and his blue eyes are dark, pupils blown, flickering with a mix of nerves and raw hunger. My hand's on his cock, stroking slow, feeling the thick pulse of him, while his fingers dig into my hips, pulling me closer, like he's torn between pushing me away and begging for more. We're both straight, got girlfriends waiting for us, but in this steamy, testosterone-charged locker room, that feels like a distant memory. The tension's electric, our breaths ragged, the fluorescent buzz drowned out by the sound of our panting, the wet slide of skin on skin.

“Fuck, man, you’re driving me insane,” he mutters, his voice rough, a shaky edge to it that makes my cock throb harder. His hand’s still on my dick, stroking with a hesitant curiosity that’s got me on edge, his fingers exploring every inch like he’s never touched another guy before. “We shouldn’t—shit, this is so fucked up.” But his hips rock forward, grinding his cock against my hand, betraying every word, and I can see the guilt warring with the lust in his eyes.

I grin, my lips brushing his jaw, feeling the stubble scrape against me, my voice low and teasing. “Fucked up? Maybe. But you’re hard as hell, leaking all over me, acting like you don’t want my mouth on you.” I pull back just enough to meet his eyes, my hand slowing on his cock, teasing the head with my thumb, spreading his precum. He groans, his head thudding back against the locker, his hands gripping my shoulders, nails biting into my skin. “Bet you’ve been wondering what it’d feel like, haven’t you? My lips around your dick, sucking you dry.”

He laughs, a nervous, breathless sound, but his hips buck into my hand, chasing the friction. "You're so fucking cocky," he says, his voice trembling, but there's a smirk tugging at his lips, that cocky vibe he's got on the field still flickering through. "Bet you're dying to taste me, too, talking all that shit." His hand speeds up on my cock, his grip tightening, and I hiss, the pleasure shooting through me, making my balls tighten.

"Fuck yeah, I am," I admit, my voice a low growl, and I don't give him a chance to respond. I drop to my knees, the tiled floor cool against my skin, and grab the waistband of his briefs, yanking them down just enough to free his cock. It springs out, thick and heavy, wider than I expected, the head flushed red and glistening with precum. It's fucking massive, thicker than mine, veiny and pulsing, and my mouth waters at the sight. "Goddamn," I mutter, my hands on his thighs, feeling the muscle tense under my fingers. “This is a fucking monster.”

He groans, his hands flying to the locker behind him for support, his cock twitching as my breath hits it. “Fuck, man, you don’t have to—” he starts, but his words cut off with a sharp gasp as I lean in, my tongue flicking out to taste the bead of precum at his slit. It’s salty, sharp, and fuck, I love it, the taste hitting me like a drug. I swirl my tongue around the head, slow and deliberate, savoring every inch, feeling the ridges, the veins, the way it pulses against my lips.

“Shit, shit, shit,” he chants, his voice high and desperate, his hips jerking forward involuntarily. I grab his hips, holding him steady, and take him deeper, my lips stretching around his girth, my tongue flat against the underside, licking every inch as I slide down. He’s so fucking thick, filling my mouth, the weight of him heavy on my tongue, and I moan, the vibration making him shudder. "Fuck, you're—God, that's good," he groans, his hands tangling in my hair, tugging lightly, not guiding but just holding, like he's afraid to let go.

I pull back, just enough to look up at him, my lips slick, his cock glistening with my spit. "Taste so fucking good," I say, my voice rough, my hand wrapping around the base of his dick, stroking where my mouth can't reach. "Bet you've never had it this good, have you? Not with your girl, not with anyone." I dive back in, sucking hard, my tongue swirling around the head, then taking him deep, feeling him hit the back of my throat. He's wider than I thought, stretching my jaw, but I love it—the challenge, the way he's unraveling under me.

He's moaning now, loud and shameless, his hands tightening in my hair, his hips starting to move, thrusting shallowly into my mouth. “Fuck, you’re—shit, you’re too good at this,” he gasps, his voice wrecked, his eyes half-lidded but locked on mine, watching me take him. I can feel him losing it, the way his thighs tremble, the way his cock pulses, leaking more precum onto my tongue. I suck harder, my lips tight, my tongue working overtime, licking every inch, savoring the taste, the heat, the way he’s filling my mouth.

I pull off with a wet pop, my hand stroking him fast, keeping him on edge. “Look at you,” I say, my voice low, cocky as hell. “Moaning like a fucking slut, thrusting into my mouth like you can’t get enough.” I lean in, licking a slow stripe up the underside, from base to tip, feeling him shudder, his hands gripping my hair tighter. “Bet you’re thinking about how much you want this, even with your girl waiting at home.”

“Fuck you,” he mutters, but it’s weak, his voice trembling, his hips rocking forward, chasing my mouth. “You’re loving this too, you prick. Bet you’re hard as fuck, sucking me off like you were born for it.” His hand slides to my shoulder, then lower, brushing my cock, and I groan, the contact sending a jolt through me, my dick throbbing against his fingers.

I grin, my lips brushing his cock as I speak. “Damn right I’m hard,” I say, my hand speeding up on his dick, my other sliding to his balls, rolling them gently, feeling them tighten. “Hard from watching you fall apart, from tasting this fucking cock.” I take him back in, deeper this time, my throat relaxing as I swallow around him, feeling him hit the back, gagging slightly but not stopping. His moans turn into cries, high and desperate, and I can feel him thrusting harder, his hips moving on instinct, fucking my mouth like he’s lost all control.

I let him, my hands gripping his thighs, letting him set the pace, his cock sliding in and out, slick with spit and precum. The taste is overwhelming—salty, musky, perfect—and I'm drunk on it, my own cock leaking onto the floor, my hips rocking unconsciously, chasing the pleasure. He's pounding my mouth now, not rough but relentless, his moans a mix of curses and gasps, his hands pulling my hair, guiding me deeper. "Fuck, fuck, you're—shit, I can't—" he stammers, his voice breaking, his body trembling as I suck him harder, my tongue swirling, my lips tight.

I pull off again, just to tease, my hand stroking fast, keeping him on edge. "You're fucking gone, aren't you?" I say, my voice rough, my eyes locked on his, watching his face contort with pleasure. "Thrusting into my mouth like a needy fuck, loving every second." I lean in, licking his slit, slow and deliberate, tasting the fresh bead of precum, and he cries out, his hips bucking, his hands clawing at my shoulders.

“Goddamn, you’re—fuck, you’re killing me,” he groans, his voice high and wrecked, his cock twitching in my hand. “Don’t stop, please, just—fuck.” His words are a plea, and I love it, the way he’s begging, the way his straight-guy bravado has crumbled into this desperate, horny mess. His hand’s back on my cock, stroking fast, matching my pace, and I groan, the pleasure spiking, my balls tightening.

I take him back in, sucking hard, my tongue working every inch, my throat relaxing to take him deeper. He’s thrusting harder now, fucking my mouth with abandon, his moans loud and shameless, filling the locker room. The tension’s unbearable, the heat between us suffocating, our bodies slick with sweat, cocks pulsing, hands roaming. We’re both straight, both got lives outside this room, but right now, it’s just us, lost in this forbidden, filthy pleasure, and I'm gonna keep driving him crazy, keep pushing him, until we're both too far gone to stop.

His cock fills my mouth, thick and heavy, the salty tang of his precum coating my tongue as I suck him hard, my lips stretching around his girth. His moans are loud, desperate, echoing off the locker room tiles, his hips thrusting shallowly, fucking my mouth like he's lost all control. The air's thick with steam and sweat, the musky scent of him—grass, salt, and that sharp, manly cedar from his body wash—driving me wild. My own cock's throbbing, leaking onto the floor, my hand stroking it in time with his thrusts, the pleasure spiking through me. We're both straight, both got girlfriends, but right now, in this haze of post-practice heat, that feels like a distant fucking dream. His blond hair's damp, sticking to his forehead, his blue eyes dark with lust, and I'm drunk on the sight of him unraveling, his straight-guy cool shattered into needy moans.

I pull off with a wet pop, my lips slick, his cock glistening with my spit, and look up at him, grinning, my voice rough. “Fuck, you taste good,” I say, my hand still wrapped around his base, stroking slow, keeping him on edge. “Moaning like you’re dying for it, thrusting into my mouth like you can’t get enough.” His chest heaves, his hands still tangled in my hair, tugging lightly, and I can see the mix of shock and hunger in his eyes, like he’s still processing how we got here.

He laughs, a shaky, breathless sound, his hands tightening in my hair, pulling me back toward his cock. “Fuck you, man,” he says, his voice hoarse but playful, that cocky smirk flickering back. “You’re loving this too, sucking me off like you’ve been waiting for it all fucking practice.” His hips shift, his cock brushing my lips again, and I can feel the heat of him, the way he’s trembling, caught between nerves and want. “Your turn,” he says, his voice dropping lower, a teasing edge to it that makes my pulse race. "Fair's fair, right? Get that mouth on me, let's see how you handle it."

I raise an eyebrow, my grin widening, but I don't argue. Instead, I stand, grabbing his shoulders and spinning him around, pushing him back against the lockers with a dull clang. His eyes widen, but he doesn't resist, his cock still hard, bobbing between us, slick from my mouth. "You want my mouth again?" I say, my voice low, teasing, my hand sliding to his hip, fingers digging into the muscle. "Nah, you're gonna suck me now. Let's see if you can keep up." I step back, my cock jutting out, thick and veiny, the head glistening with precum, and I stroke it once, slow, watching his reaction.

His eyes flick down, lingering on my dick, and I see his throat bob, a mix of nerves and curiosity flashing across his face. "Fuck, you're serious," he mutters, but there's a spark in his eyes, that same competitive edge we have on the field, like he's not backing down from a challenge. He drops to his knees, the tiles creaking under him, and grabs my thighs, his hands rough from years of soccer, fingers digging in like he's anchoring himself. "Alright, hotshot," he says, his voice shaky but bold, his lips inches from my cock. "Let's see if you taste as good as you talk."

He leans in, his breath hot against my tip, and I groan, my hand finding his blond hair, tangling in the damp strands. His lips brush my cock, tentative at first, just a graze, and the contact sends a jolt through me, my balls tightening. "Fuck, don't tease," I growl, my voice rough, my fingers tightening in his hair, urging him closer. He laughs, a low, nervous sound, but then his tongue flicks out, licking the head, tasting the precum beaded there, and I hiss, the pleasure sharp and immediate.

"Goddamn," he mutters, his voice muffled against my cock, and then he takes me in, his lips wrapping around the head, sucking lightly, his tongue swirling like he's testing the waters. The heat of his mouth is fucking electric, wet and tight, and I groan, my hips rocking forward instinctively, wanting more. His hands grip my thighs harder, steadying himself, and he takes me deeper, his lips stretching around my girth, his tongue flat against the underside, licking every inch.

"Fuck, yeah," I say, my voice thick, my hand guiding his head, not pushing but encouraging, feeling him bob on my cock. "Suck it like you mean it, man. Show me you can handle it." He moans, the vibration shooting through me, and I can feel him getting into it, his mouth working harder, sucking with more confidence, his tongue exploring the veins, the ridges, like he's savoring it. The scent of him hits me harder now—sweat, musk, that raw, manly smell that's all him, mixed with the faint cedar lingering on his skin, and it's driving me fucking crazy.

He pulls back, just enough to catch his breath, his lips red and slick, a string of spit connecting his mouth to my cock. "Fuck, you're thick," he says, his voice hoarse, his eyes flicking up to mine, wide but hungry. "Tastes—shit, tastes better than I thought." He dives back in, taking me deeper, his throat relaxing as he swallows around me, gagging slightly but not stopping, his hands sliding to my balls, rolling them gently, feeling them tighten under his touch.

I groan, loud and rough, my head tipping back for a second before I force myself to look down, to watch him work. His blond hair's a mess in my hand, damp strands slipping through my fingers as I guide him, his lips stretched wide, his cheeks hollowing with every suck. "Goddamn, you're good at this," I say, my voice rough, my hips starting to move, thrusting shallowly into his mouth. "Sucking my cock like you've been dreaming about it, like you're fucking starving." He moans again, the sound muffled, and I can feel him getting lost in it, his tongue working overtime, licking every inch, savoring the taste.

I'm pounding his mouth now, not hard but relentless, my cock sliding in and out, slick with his spit, his throat fluttering around me. The pleasure's insane, my balls tight, my cock throbbing, and I fucking love it—the way he's taking me, the way he's moaning around my dick, his hands gripping my thighs like he's holding on for dear life. "Fuck, you love this, don't you?" I growl, my hand tightening in his hair, pulling just enough to make him gasp around me. "Straight guy my ass—sucking me like you were born for it, moaning like a fucking slut."

He pulls off, gasping, his lips swollen, his hand wrapping around my cock, stroking fast to keep me on edge. "Fuck you," he says, but it's half-laughed, his voice wrecked, his eyes dark with lust.

“You’re loving it just as much, leaking all over my tongue, thrusting like you can’t control yourself.” He leans in, licking a slow stripe up the underside, from base to tip, his tongue flicking over the slit, and I groan, my hips bucking, chasing his mouth.

“Damn right I’m loving it,” I say, my voice rough, my hand guiding his head back to my cock. “Love watching you choke on my dick, love that fucking smell of you driving me crazy.” I push him down, his lips wrapping around me again, and he sucks hard, his tongue swirling, his throat relaxing to take me deeper. The scent of him—sweaty, masculine, raw—fills my senses, mixing with the steam, the heat, and I’m lost in it, my hips thrusting faster, fucking his mouth with abandon.

He’s moaning nonstop now, the vibrations sending sparks up my spine, his hands roaming my thighs, my balls, like he can’t get enough. I can feel him getting off on it, his cock hard and leaking against his thigh, and I know he's as gone as I am, both of us caught in this forbidden, filthy heat. The tension's unbearable, the locker room a haze of steam and want, our bodies slick with sweat, cocks pulsing, mouths working. We're straight, got lives outside this room, but right now, it's just us, lost in this crazy pleasure, and I'm gonna keep pushing him, keep driving him wild, until we're both too far gone to care.

His mouth is a furnace around my cock, hot and wet, his lips stretched wide as he sucks me with a hunger that's got my head spinning. His blond hair's a mess in my hand, damp strands slipping through my fingers as I guide him, my hips thrusting shallowly, fucking his throat with a rhythm that's got me teetering on the edge. The locker room's a haze of steam and sweat, the air thick with his scent—raw, masculine, a mix of grass, cedar, and pure, unfiltered arousal that's driving me fucking wild. His moans vibrate around my dick, low and desperate, sending sparks up my spine, and I can feel him losing it, his hands gripping my thighs, nails digging in as he takes me deeper, gagging but not stopping.

We're both straight, got girlfriends waiting at home, but right now, in this sweaty, testosterone-soaked moment, that's the last thing on my mind. It's just him, me, and this insane, forbidden heat.

"Fuck, you're so good at this," I groan, my voice rough, my hand tightening in his hair, pulling just enough to make him moan louder, the sound muffled around my cock. His tongue swirls over the head, licking every inch, savoring the precum leaking from my slit, and I can feel my balls tightening, the pressure building low in my gut. "Sucking me like you've been dreaming about it, like you're fucking starving for my cock." His eyes flick up, watery but dark with lust, and there's a spark there—part defiance, part surrender—that makes my dick throb harder.

He pulls back slightly, his lips slick with spit, his hand wrapping around my base, stroking fast to keep me on edge. "Goddamn, you're leaking so much," he mutters, his voice hoarse, that cocky smirk flickering but shaky, like he's as caught up in this as I am. "Bet you're close, aren't you? Can't handle my mouth, huh?" His tongue darts out, licking the head again, slow and deliberate, and I hiss, my hips bucking, chasing the wet heat of his lips.

"Fuck you," I growl, but it's half-laughed, my hand guiding him back to my cock, urging him to take me deeper. "You're the one moaning like a slut, sucking me like you can't get enough." He dives back in, his mouth tight and relentless, his tongue working overtime, and I'm thrusting harder now, fucking his mouth with abandon, the pleasure so intense it's almost painful. His hands slide to my balls, rolling them gently, feeling them tighten, and I can feel the edge creeping closer, my cock pulsing, ready to explode.

But then he stiffens, his moans turning into a choked, desperate sound, and I feel it before I see it—his body shakes, his hips jerking, and suddenly he's cumming, hard and fast, his cock untouched but spilling thick ropes across the floor, some hitting his thighs, his briefs still bunched around his knees. "Fuck, fuck, fuck," he gasps, pulling off my cock with a wet pop, his lips red and swollen, his eyes wide with shock as his orgasm rips through him. His cum keeps coming, more than I expected, thick and white, splattering the tiles, his uniform shorts, even catching the edge of his shin guards still tangled at his ankles.

I'm frozen for a second, my cock throbbing in the air, slick with his spit, as I watch him unravel. "What the fuck," I mutter, my voice rough, but I'm so fucking horny it hurts, my dick twitching at the sight of him—his face flushed, his chest heaving, cum dripping down his thighs, staining the black fabric of his briefs. His eyes meet mine, wide and dazed, a mix of embarrassment and raw need, and it's the hottest fucking thing I've ever seen, this straight guy losing it like this, cumming just from sucking my cock.

"Shit, I—" he starts, his voice shaky, his hand reaching for his cock, still hard despite the mess, like he's not done yet. "I didn't mean to—fuck, that was intense." He's panting, his blond hair plastered to his forehead, and I can see the guilt flickering in his eyes, the thought of his girlfriend probably creeping in, but his hand's already moving, stroking himself, slick with his own cum.

I grin, my cock aching, and step closer, my hand wrapping around my dick, stroking slow, keeping myself on edge. "Look at you, making a fucking mess," I say, my voice low, teasing, but there's a heat in it, a hunger that matches his. "Cumming like that, just from my cock in your mouth? You're hornier than I thought." I reach out, grabbing his wrist, stopping his hand, and smear some of his cum across my fingers, using it as lube to stroke my own cock. The slickness, the warmth of it, makes me groan, the pleasure spiking, and I can see his eyes widen, his lips parting as he watches me.

"Fuck, that's—" he starts, but his voice cracks, his hand twitching like he wants to touch me again. "You're using my cum, you fucking perv," he says, but there's a laugh in it, shaky and turned-on, his eyes locked on my hand, watching me stroke myself with his release. His cock's still hard, leaking more, and I can tell he's caught in the same haze I am, guilt and want warring in his head but his body screaming for more.

I step closer, my cock brushing his thigh, the contact sending a jolt through me. "Perv? Says the guy who just came buckets from sucking dick," I shoot back, my voice rough, my hand speeding up, the slick sound of his cum on my cock filling the room. "Bet you're still thinking about it, wanting more, aren't you?" I grab his hand, guiding it to my cock, letting him feel the mix of his cum and my precum, and he groans, his fingers wrapping around me, stroking slow but firm, like he can't help himself.

"Fuck, man, this is so messed up," he mutters, but his hand doesn't stop, his eyes dark with lust, his cock twitching against his thigh. "My girl's gonna—shit, I don't even know." His voice is trembling, but his fingers are bold, stroking me faster, his thumb circling my head, making me moan, low and rough. The scent of him—sweat, cum, that raw, manly musk—fills my senses, driving me closer to the edge, and I can see he's right there with me, his hand moving on instinct, like he's as lost in this as I am.

I grab his shoulders, pushing him back against the lockers, my cock still in his hand, and lean in, my lips hovering over his, not kissing but close enough to feel his breath, hot and uneven. "Messed up? Maybe," I say, my voice a low growl, my hips rocking into his hand, chasing the pleasure. "But you're loving it, stroking me with your cum, acting like you don't want to taste me again." My hand slides to his cock, stroking him back, using his cum as lube, and he moans, his head tipping back, his body arching into my touch.

"Fuck, you're—God, you're gonna make me cum again," he groans, his voice high and desperate, his hand speeding up on my cock, matching my pace. I can feel the pressure building, my balls tight, my cock pulsing in his grip, and I'm right there, the pleasure so intense it's almost blinding. I stroke him faster, my hand slick with his cum, and he's trembling, his moans turning into cries, his cock leaking more, ready to explode again.

I can't hold back anymore. The sight of him—his cum-soaked uniform, his flushed face, his blond hair a mess—pushes me over the edge. I groan, loud and rough, my cock pulsing as I cum, hard and fast, thick ropes shooting across his chest, splattering his abs, his briefs, mixing with his own mess. He gasps, his eyes wide, his hand still stroking me through it, milking every drop, and then he's cumming again, his cock jerking in my hand, spilling more onto his thighs, the floor, a fucking mess of heat and need.

We're both panting, frozen for a moment, our hands still on each other, cum dripping everywhere—his uniform, my thighs, the tiles. The air's heavy, the scent of cum and sweat overwhelming, and then the reality hits like a cold shower. His eyes meet mine, wide and stunned, the lust fading into something else—guilt, maybe, or just plain awkwardness. "Fuck," he mutters, pulling his hand back, wiping it on his shorts, his face flushed red. "What the fuck did we just do?"

I laugh, shaky, stepping back, my cock softening, the mess on my thighs cooling fast. "Got carried away," I say, trying to keep it light, but my voice is rough, the weight of it sinking in. "Guess we're not telling the girls about this one." I grab my jock from the floor, pulling it on, the fabric sticking to my skin, and he does the same, tugging his briefs up, the cum stains glaring under the fluorescent lights.

"Yeah, no shit," he says, his voice low, avoiding my eyes as he grabs his towel, wiping at the mess on his chest, his shorts. The locker room's quiet now, the steam settling, the buzz of the lights louder than ever. He looks at me, just for a second, and there's a flicker of something—maybe want, maybe regret—before he turns away, grabbing his bag. "This... stays here, right?"

I nod, my throat tight, the high of the moment crashing hard. "Yeah, stays here," I say, pulling on my shorts, the awkwardness thick between us. We don't say anything else, just pack up in silence, the weight of what we did hanging heavy, our straight lives waiting outside the locker room door.

OFFICE SECRET

I'm thirty-two, lean but toned, with a swimmer's build—long limbs, defined abs, and a chest that fills out my tailored suits just right. My dark brown hair's neatly styled, swept back with a touch of gel, though a few strands always fall loose by the end of the day, giving me a slightly roguish edge. My hazel eyes are sharp, catching every detail, and my clean-shaven face shows off a jawline that's gotten me more than a few lingering glances. I'm openly gay, always have been, and I carry it with a confidence that's as much a part of me as the bespoke navy suit I'm wearing today, the silk tie knotted tight, the polished oxfords gleaming under the office lights. My name's Julian, and I'm the senior marketing lead, which means I spend my days charming clients and my nights charming whoever catches my eye at the bar. Right now, though, it's not a client or a bar hookup I'm focused on—it's Marcus, the straight-laced finance guy across the office, who's got my cock twitching every time he walks by.

The office is quiet tonight, the hum of computers and the faint buzz of fluorescent lights the only sounds in the open-plan space. It's late, well past eight, and most of the team's gone home, leaving just me and Marcus burning the midnight oil on a deadline. The floor-to-ceiling windows show the city skyline, all twinkling lights and dark glass, but my eyes are on him, sitting at his desk, his broad shoulders straining the seams of his charcoal suit jacket. Marcus is a few years older, maybe thirty-five, bulkier than me, with a linebacker's build—wide chest, thick arms, and a waist that's still trim despite the muscle. His black hair's cropped short, flecked with early gray at the temples, and his strong jaw is shadowed with just enough stubble to make you want to run your fingers over it. His dark brown eyes are intense, always focused, but there's a warmth there when he lets his guard down, which isn't often. He's married, got a wife and a kid, the picture of straight suburban life, but there's something in the way he looks at me sometimes—quick, guarded glances—that says he's not as straight as he thinks.

He's loosening his tie now, the burgundy silk sliding through his fingers, and I can't help but watch, my pulse kicking up as he undoes the top button of his crisp white shirt, revealing a sliver of tanned skin. I'm at my desk, pretending to review a campaign brief, but my eyes keep drifting to him, to the way his suit hugs his thighs, the way his polished black dress shoes catch the light. My own suit feels tighter than usual, my cock half-hard just from the sight of him, and I shift in my chair, trying to focus on the screen in front of me.

"Still here, Julian?" he calls out, his voice deep, with a hint of a smile, breaking the silence. He leans back in his chair, stretching, and the movement pulls his jacket open, showing the way his shirt clings to his pecs, the faint outline of his nipples through the fabric. "Thought you'd be out charming some guy at a club by now."

I grin, leaning back in my own chair, my tie still knotted but loosened, my suit jacket draped over the back. "And miss the chance to keep you company?" I say, my voice light but laced with a tease, my eyes locking on his. "Nah, I'm good right here, watching you wrestle with those spreadsheets in that sexy suit." It's bold, flirty, the kind of line I toss out to test the waters, and I see his eyes widen just a fraction, a flush creeping up his neck.

He laughs, a low, nervous sound, and adjusts his tie, his fingers lingering on the silk like he's buying time. "Sexy suit, huh? Didn't know you were into corporate chic," he says, his tone playful but guarded, his eyes flicking to mine, then away, like he's not sure how to handle the compliment. He stands, shrugging off his jacket, and hangs it on the back of his chair, the movement making his shirt pull tight across his chest, showing off the bulk of his muscles. My mouth goes dry, my cock twitching harder, and I stand too, moving toward the coffee machine near his desk, just to get closer.

"Corporate chic's my thing when it looks like that," I say, leaning against the counter, my eyes raking over him, taking in the way his trousers hug his thick thighs, the bulge at his crotch that's impossible to ignore. "That suit's doing you favors, Marcus. Bet your wife loves peeling it off you." I'm pushing it, I know, but there's a thrill in it, in seeing how far I can go before he shuts me down—or doesn't.

He freezes for a second, his hand pausing on the stack of papers on his desk, and I catch the way his throat bobs, the way his eyes flick to my lips, then back to his screen. "You're trouble, you know that?" he says, his voice lower now, rougher, and he adjusts his cufflinks, the silver glinting under the lights. "My wife's got no complaints, but I'm not sure she'd appreciate you talking like that." There's a warning in his tone, but it's weak, and the way he's looking at me—quick, heated glances—says he's not as offended as he's pretending to be.

I step closer, close enough that I can smell his cologne, spicy and warm, mixed with the clean sweat of a long day. "Trouble's my middle name," I say, my voice a low drawl, my fingers brushing the edge of his desk, inches from his hand. "But come on, Marcus, you're telling me you've never wondered? Never thought about what it'd be like to let loose, just a little, with someone who knows how to have fun?" I lean in, my tie dangling, the silk brushing his arm, and I see his fingers twitch, like he's fighting the urge to touch it.

He laughs again, but it's strained, his eyes darting to my tie, then to my chest, where my shirt's unbuttoned just enough to show a hint of skin. "You're relentless," he says, standing now, towering over me with that bulky frame, his dress socks sliding silently on the carpet. "I'm straight, Julian. Got a wife, a kid, the whole deal. You know that." But his voice wavers, and he's not moving away, his body angled toward me, his hands flexing at his sides like he's not sure what to do with them.

"Straight, sure," I say, my grin widening, my hand reaching out to tug lightly at his tie, the silk smooth under my fingers. "But you're standing here, letting me get this close, not exactly running for the door." I pull the tie gently, just enough to make him step closer, and he does, his polished shoes brushing mine, the air between us crackling. His eyes are dark, pupils blown, and I can see the conflict there—guilt, curiosity, and a whole lot of want he's trying to bury.

"Fuck, you're bold," he mutters, his voice rough, his hands hovering like he wants to push me away but can't quite bring himself to do it. "What are you trying to do, get me fired? Or just fuck with my head?" He's trying to keep it light, but his breath's uneven, his chest rising faster, and I can see the bulge in his trousers growing, straining against the tailored fabric.

I let go of his tie, letting it fall back against his chest, but I don't step back, keeping the space between us tight. "Not fucking with your head," I say, my voice low, my eyes locked on his. "Just seeing how far you'll let this go. You're curious, aren't you? Wondering what it'd feel like to let go, to let me touch you, right here in this fancy office." My hand brushes his arm, just a graze, feeling the heat of his skin through his shirt, and he flinches but doesn't pull away, his eyes flicking to my hand, then back to my face.

"You're insane," he says, but it's half-laughed, his voice thick with something that's definitely not rejection. He adjusts his tie again, his fingers fumbling, and I catch the way his trousers tent, his cock clearly hard now, pressing against the zipper. "My wife—she'd lose her mind if she knew I was even talking to you like this." But he's leaning in now, just a fraction, his body betraying him, his dress socks sliding closer on the carpet.

I grin, my hand sliding to his wrist, feeling his pulse race under my fingers, my thumb brushing the cuff of his shirt, the silk cufflink cool against my skin. "She doesn't have to know," I murmur, my voice a low growl, my lips inches from his ear. "Just you and me, Marcus, in these suits, in this office. Bet you've never been this hard at work before." I let my hand drift lower, brushing his hip, not touching his cock but close enough to make him gasp, his eyes fluttering shut for a second.

"Fuck, Julian," he breathes, his voice shaky, his hands clenching into fists at his sides. "You're gonna get us both in trouble." But he's not moving, his body angled toward me, his cock straining against his trousers, and I can see the want in his eyes, the way he's fighting it but losing, his straight life crumbling under the weight of this moment.

I step closer, our shoes touching now, my tie brushing his chest, the silk whispering against his shirt. "Trouble's worth it sometimes," I say, my hand sliding to his chest, feeling the hard muscle under the fabric, the faint thump of his heart. "Bet you're thinking about it—my hands on you, peeling off this suit, seeing what's under all that straight-guy armor." My fingers tug at his tie again, loosening it just a bit, and he groans, low and rough, his hands finally moving, grabbing my arms, not pushing me away but holding me there, like he's caught in the same haze I am.

The tension's electric, the office a bubble of heat and want, our suits crisp but starting to rumple, our bodies close, cocks hard, the air heavy with the promise of what's coming. He's straight, got a life I'll never fit into, but right now, it's just us, the thrill of this forbidden game, and I'm gonna keep pushing, keep teasing, until he gives in completely.

Our bodies are close, my tie brushing his chest, the silk whispering against his crisp white shirt as I lean in, my fingers grazing his arm, feeling the heat of his skin through the fabric. His hands grip my biceps, not pushing me away but holding me there, his breath uneven, his eyes dark with a mix of guilt and raw want. The office is a cocoon of tension, the city skyline glittering beyond the windows, the fluorescent lights casting sharp shadows across his broad frame. His charcoal suit hugs his bulky muscles, his burgundy tie loosened just enough to show a sliver of tanned skin at his throat, and his cock is straining against his trousers, a thick bulge that's impossible to ignore. My own suit feels tight, my cock hard and aching, the navy fabric clinging to my thighs as I press closer, the air between us electric with the promise of something neither of us should want.

"Fuck, Julian, you're pushing it," he mutters, his voice low and rough, that deep tone cracking with nerves. His hands flex on my arms, his polished cufflinks glinting as he shifts, like he's fighting the urge to pull me closer or shove me back. "We're at work, man. This is—fuck, this is crazy." But his eyes betray him, flicking to my lips, then down to my tie, lingering on the way my shirt pulls tight across my chest. His face is flushed, a pink creeping up his neck, and I can see the struggle—his straight life, his wife, his kid, all clashing with the heat in his gaze.

I grin, my fingers tugging his tie just a bit more, loosening it further, the silk sliding through my hands like a tease. "Crazy's my specialty," I say, my voice a low drawl, my lips inches from his ear, close enough to feel his shudder. "You're hard as fuck, standing here letting me touch you. Bet you're imagining what happens if I undo this tie, peel off that suit, get my hands on that cock." My hand slides to his chest, feeling the hard muscle under his shirt, the faint thump of his heart racing, and he groans, low and desperate, his hands tightening on my arms.

Before he can respond, the sharp buzz of the intercom cuts through the haze, making us both freeze. "Julian, Marcus, conference room in five," the boss's voice crackles, clipped and no-nonsense. "Emergency meeting with the execs. Don't be late." The line clicks off, and the silence that follows is deafening, our breaths loud in the empty office. His eyes meet mine, wide and startled, the lust still there but now mixed with panic, like he's just remembered where we are.

"Fuck," he breathes, stepping back, his hands dropping from my arms as he adjusts his tie, his fingers fumbling, trying to restore order. His trousers are still tented, his cock not getting the memo, and I can't help but smirk, adjusting my own suit, smoothing the navy fabric over my thighs, my cock still half-hard and obvious if anyone looks too close.

"Saved by the bell," I say, my voice teasing, but I keep my eyes on him, watching the way he tries to pull himself together, his face red, his hands shaking as he grabs his jacket from the chair. "Don't think this is over, though. We're just getting started." I wink, grabbing my own jacket, and head for the conference room, leaving him to follow, knowing he's rattled, knowing I've got him hooked.

The conference room is all sleek glass and polished wood, the long table surrounded by leather chairs, the city lights reflecting off the windows like a backdrop. The execs are already there, murmuring over reports, the boss at the head of the table, his gray suit pristine, his voice droning about quarterly projections. I take a seat across from Marcus, the table wide enough to keep us apart but close enough for me to see every detail—his flushed cheeks, the way his tie's still slightly askew, the nervous way he adjusts his cufflinks. His eyes avoid mine, fixed on the papers in front of him, but I can see the tension in his shoulders, the way his hands grip the table's edge like he's holding on for dear life.

I slip off one polished oxford under the table, the move subtle, my socked foot brushing the carpet as I stretch my leg out, finding his ankle. He stiffens, his eyes flicking up to mine, a quick, panicked glance before he looks away, his face reddening further. I grin, keeping my expression neutral for the execs, my hands folded on the table, but my foot slides higher, tracing the curve of his calf through his dress sock, the wool soft but warm from his skin. “Market trends are shifting,” the boss is saying, flipping through slides, but I’m barely listening, my focus on the way Marcus’s jaw clenches, his fingers tightening on his pen.

“Relax,” I mouth silently, my foot sliding higher, nudging his trouser leg up, exposing the tanned skin of his shin. His eyes dart to mine again, a mix of shock and heat, and I can see him fighting it, trying to stay composed as my toes graze his knee, slow and deliberate, the touch light but electric. His breath hitches, just a fraction, but I catch it, my cock twitching in my trousers at the sight of him unraveling, right here in front of everyone.

“You okay, Marcus?” one of the execs asks, noticing his flush, and he coughs, shifting in his seat, his hands fumbling with his papers.

“Yeah, just—warm in here,” he mutters, his voice strained, and I bite my lip to keep from laughing, my foot sliding higher, brushing the inside of his thigh now, the muscle tense under my touch. The boss drones on, oblivious, and I lean forward slightly, pretending to study the slide deck, while my foot creeps closer to his crotch, the wool of my sock catching on the fabric of his trousers.

“Focus, man,” I whisper, low enough that only he can hear, my foot nudging higher, grazing the bulge in his trousers, and he flinches, his pen clattering to the table. The execs glance over, but he waves it off, his face now a deep red, his eyes locked on his papers like they’re his lifeline. I press harder, my toes massaging his cock through the fabric, feeling the thick, hard shape of him, still rock-hard from our earlier moment. The tension’s unbearable, my own cock aching in my suit, but I keep my face neutral, my foot working slow, deliberate circles, feeling him twitch under the pressure.

"Fuck," he breathes, so quiet it's barely audible, but I catch it, and it's enough to make my pulse race. My foot slides higher, pushing his trouser leg up further, exposing more of his thigh, and I can feel the heat of his skin through my sock, the muscle flexing as he tries to stay still. His hands grip the table, knuckles white, and I can see the sweat beading at his temples, his tie now completely crooked, a stark contrast to his usual polished look.

"You're killing me," he mouths, his eyes meeting mine for a split second, dark and desperate, and I grin, my foot pressing harder, massaging his bulge with more purpose now, feeling it pulse under my toes. The boss is talking about revenue streams, but it's background noise, drowned out by the silent battle across the table—his straight resolve cracking, my gay confidence pushing him to the edge.

I lean back in my chair, my hands still folded, my expression calm, but my foot's relentless, tracing the outline of his cock, feeling it strain against his trousers, the fabric damp with precum. He shifts, trying to adjust himself, but it only presses his bulge harder against my foot, and a low, accidental moan slips from his lips, sharp and needy, cutting through the room. The execs pause, heads turning, and his face goes crimson, his hands fumbling to grab his water glass, knocking it over in his panic.

"Everything alright, Marcus?" the boss asks, frowning, and he nods quickly, his voice tight.

"Yeah, just—uh, bumped my knee," he says, his eyes darting to me, a mix of panic and fury, but the heat's still there, undeniable. I pull my foot back, slipping my shoe back on under the table, my grin hidden behind a sip of coffee, but my cock's throbbing, the thrill of pushing him like that making my blood pound.

The meeting drags on, but the air between us is electric, his eyes avoiding mine but his body still tense, his tie askew, his trousers still tented. The tension's thicker than ever, the office a pressure cooker of want and risk

The meeting drags on, the boss's voice a monotonous drone about profit margins, but all I can focus on is Marcus across the table, his face still flushed, his burgundy tie crooked, his hands gripping his pen like it's the only thing keeping him grounded. My foot's back in my oxford now, but the memory of his cock, hard and pulsing under my sock, lingers, making my own dick throb in my navy suit trousers. His eyes avoid mine, darting to his papers, the window, anywhere but me, but I can see the tension in his broad shoulders, the way his thick thighs shift under the table, like he's still feeling my touch. The air's thick with unspoken want, the office lights harsh against the dark city skyline outside, and I'm itching to pick up where we left off, to push him further, to see how much of his straight-guy armor I can crack.

Finally, the boss wraps up, dismissing us with a curt nod, and the execs shuffle out, their briefcases snapping shut, voices fading down the hall. Marcus lingers, pretending to organize his papers, but I know he's stalling, waiting for me to make a move. I stand, smoothing my suit jacket, my silk tie catching the light as I saunter toward the door, throwing him a glance over my shoulder. "You coming, or you planning to sleep here?" I say, my voice low, teasing, and his eyes snap to mine, dark and conflicted, before he grabs his jacket and follows.

We're barely out of the conference room when he grabs my arm, his grip firm, and yanks me into a small office down the hall, the door clicking shut behind us. The room's dim, lit only by a desk lamp and the glow of the city through the blinds, the air heavy with the scent of his cologne—spicy, warm, mixed with the clean sweat of a long day. He pins me against the wall, his bulk looming over me, his charcoal suit jacket open, his shirt clinging to his pecs. "What the fuck were you doing in there, Julian?" he hisses, his voice low but sharp, his face inches from mine, his breath hot. "Rubbing my dick under the table? You trying to get us fired?"

I grin, unfazed, my hands resting lightly on his hips, feeling the heat of him through his trousers. "What we both want," I say, my voice a low drawl, my eyes locked on his, watching the way his pupils dilate, the way his flush deepens. "Don't act like you didn't love it, Marcus. You were hard as fuck, moaning like you couldn't help it." I lean in, my lips brushing his, not quite a kiss, just a tease, and he tenses, his hands still pinning my shoulders, but he doesn't pull away.

"Fuck you," he growls, but it's shaky, his voice cracking with a mix of anger and need. He pushes me back, hard enough to make my back hit the wall, but there's no real force in it, just a desperate attempt to regain control. "I'm straight, Julian. I've got a wife, a kid. This isn't me." His eyes are wild, his tie loose, the top button of his shirt undone, showing a glimpse of tanned skin dusted with dark hair, and his cock's still tenting his trousers, betraying every word.

I step forward, closing the gap again, my grin wicked, my hand sliding to his chest, feeling the hard muscle under his shirt, the rapid thud of his heart. "Not you? Bullshit," I say, my voice low, my fingers tugging at his tie, pulling it free with a slow, deliberate slide of silk. "You're standing here, hard as a rock, letting me get this close. You want this, Marcus, even if you're too scared to admit it." I lean in, kissing him hard, my lips crashing into his, my tongue pushing past his hesitation, tasting the faint mint of his breath, the heat of his mouth.

He groans, a low, desperate sound, and for a second, he kisses me back, his lips moving against mine, rough and hungry, his hands tightening on my shoulders. But then he pushes me again, breaking the kiss, his chest heaving, his face redder than ever. "Fuck, stop," he says, his voice hoarse, but his hands don't let go, still gripping my arms, like he's torn between shoving me away and pulling me closer. "This is—fuck, this is wrong."

I laugh, soft and dirty, stepping right back into his space, my hand bold, sliding down to grab his bulge, feeling the thick, hard shape of his cock through his trousers. "Wrong? Feels pretty fucking right to me," I murmur, my fingers squeezing lightly, stroking through the fabric, and he gasps, his hips jerking into my hand, his eyes fluttering shut. “Look at you, leaking already, ready to burst just from my hand.” I lean in again, kissing him slower this time, my tongue teasing his, my lips soft but insistent, and he moans into my mouth, his resistance crumbling, his body melting against mine.

This time, he doesn’t push back. His hands slide to my waist, hesitant at first, then bolder, gripping the fabric of my suit, pulling me closer as he kisses me back, hard and desperate, his tongue tangling with mine. The kiss is messy, all heat and spit, our teeth clashing as we devour each other, the office a haze of want and risk. My hand’s still on his cock, stroking through his trousers, feeling it pulse, the fabric damp with precum, and his hands roam my chest, tugging at my tie, loosening it with a clumsy pull.

"Goddamn, Julian," he mutters against my lips, his voice wrecked, his hands fumbling with my shirt buttons, popping one open, then another, exposing my chest. His fingers graze my skin, hesitant but curious, tracing the lines of my abs, and I groan, the touch sending a jolt straight to my cock. "This is—fuck, I shouldn't, but you're making it so fucking hard to stop." His eyes meet mine, dark and wild, and I can see the guilt there, the thought of his wife flickering, but it's drowned out by the need, the way his cock twitches in my hand.

I grin, my lips brushing his jaw, feeling the stubble scrape against me as I undo his shirt buttons, one by one, revealing his broad chest, dusted with dark hair, the muscle thick and defined. "Hard's the point," I say, my voice a low growl, my hand sliding inside his shirt, feeling the heat of his skin, the hard ridge of his pecs. "You want this, Marcus. Want me to peel this suit off you, touch every inch, make you feel shit your wife never could." My fingers find his nipple, pinching lightly, and he moans, loud and needy, his hips bucking into my hand.

"Fuck, you're—shit," he gasps, his hands grabbing my jacket, yanking it off my shoulders, letting it fall to the floor. His fingers fumble with my shirt, pulling it open, buttons straining, and I laugh, helping him, shrugging it off so we're both bare-chested, our ties dangling loose, our trousers tented with hard cocks. His hands roam my back, hesitant but growing bolder, feeling the lean muscle, the sweat slicking my skin, and I push him against the desk, the edge biting into his thighs as I kiss him again, deeper, my tongue fucking his mouth, swallowing his moans.

I pull back, just enough to grab his belt, unbuckling it with a sharp tug, the leather sliding through my fingers. "Gonna make you lose it," I murmur, my lips against his ear, my hand sliding inside his trousers, brushing his cock through his briefs, feeling the thick, pulsing heat. "Gonna touch you till you're begging, till you forget everything but me." His belt clatters to the floor, and I undo his trousers, letting them pool at his ankles, his black dress socks and polished shoes stark against the carpet.

He groans, his hands gripping my hips, pulling me closer, his cock straining against his briefs, a wet spot spreading. "You're a fucking menace," he says, but it's half-moaned, his voice trembling, his hands tugging at my belt now, clumsy but determined. "I'm—fuck, I'm not supposed to want this." But he's undoing my trousers, pushing them down, his fingers brushing my cock through my boxer briefs, and I groan, the contact electric, my hips rocking into his hand.

We're kissing again, desperate and sloppy, our hands roaming, tugging at ties, shirts, briefs, the office a mess of discarded suits and rising heat. His cock's free now, thick and veiny, leaking against my thigh, and I grab it, stroking slow, feeling it pulse in my hand. He moans into my mouth, his hands on my ass, squeezing through my briefs, and the tension's unbearable, the air thick with want, our bodies slick with sweat, ready to explode but not there yet, not until I push him further, make him mine in this forbidden, filthy moment.

Our mouths crash together, a frenzy of heat and spit, my tongue plunging deep, tasting the faint mint of his breath as he moans into me, his hands clawing at my hips, pulling me closer. The office is a haze of discarded suits—my navy jacket crumpled on the floor, his charcoal trousers pooled around his polished shoes, his burgundy tie dangling loose against his bare chest. My shirt's half-off, buttons popped, my tie a silky noose around my neck, and his thick fingers are fumbling with my boxer briefs, grazing my cock, sending jolts of pleasure through me. His cock's free, hard and heavy against my thigh, leaking precum that slicks my skin, and I'm stroking him, slow and firm, feeling the pulse of his veins under my fingers. The air's thick with the scent of his cologne—

spicy, warm, mixed with the raw musk of his arousal—and the city lights outside cast shadows across his bulky frame, highlighting every ridge of muscle, every bead of sweat.

I pull back from the kiss, my lips swollen, his eyes dark and wild, his face flushed redder than ever. "Fuck, Marcus, you're losing it," I murmur, my voice a low growl, my hand tightening on his cock, stroking faster, making him groan, his hips bucking into my grip. "All that straight-guy bullshit, and look at you—hard as fuck, moaning like you're mine." I drop to my knees, the carpet rough against my skin, and grab his thighs, pulling him closer, his cock right in my face, thick and veiny, the head flushed red and glistening with precum.

"Julian, shit," he breathes, his voice shaky, his hands hovering like he's not sure whether to push me away or pull me closer. "This is—fuck, we can't—" But his words cut off with a sharp gasp as I lean in, my tongue flicking out to taste the bead of precum at his slit. It's salty, sharp, with a musky edge that's so fucking him—manly, raw, like the scent of his sweat and cologne dialed up to eleven. I groan, the taste hitting me like a drug, and wrap my lips around the head, sucking lightly, feeling the weight of him on my tongue.

"Goddamn," he moans, loud and desperate, his hands flying to my hair, tangling in the dark strands, tugging just enough to make my cock throb in my briefs. His dick's a fucking masterpiece—thick, veiny, so damn masculine, the kind of cock that screams power, and I'm drunk on it, taking him deeper, my lips stretching around his girth. I swirl my tongue over the head, tasting more precum, and it's better than I expected, rich and heady, making my mouth water as I suck harder, my tongue tracing every vein, every ridge, savoring the heat, the pulse.

He's losing it, his moans turning into cries, his hips thrusting shallowly, fucking my mouth like he can't help himself. "Fuck, Julian, you're—shit, you're too good at this," he groans, his voice wrecked, his hands tightening in my hair, guiding me deeper. I take him all the way, my throat relaxing, feeling him hit the back, gagging slightly but not stopping, loving the way he fills my mouth, the way he's unraveling. His cock's so veiny, so thick, it's a challenge, but I'm up for it, sucking with everything I've got, my tongue working overtime, my lips tight and wet.

I pull off with a wet pop, my lips slick with his precum, and stand, grabbing his tie to pull him into a kiss. My mouth's full of his taste, salty and musky, and I shove my tongue into his mouth, letting him taste himself, the kiss sloppy and desperate, all teeth and heat. He moans into it, his hands grabbing my face, kissing me back with a hunger that's got my cock aching, leaking in my briefs. "Fuck, that's me," he mutters against my lips, his voice hoarse, a mix of shock and lust as he tastes his own precum, his tongue tangling with mine, chasing more.

I grin, breaking the kiss, my lips brushing his jaw, feeling the stubble scrape against me. “Yeah, that’s you, Marcus,” I say, my voice low, teasing, my hand stroking his cock again, keeping him on edge. “Taste good, don’t you? Bet you’re loving this, straight guy or not.” I kiss him again, harder, my tongue fucking his mouth, swallowing his moans as his hands roam my chest, tugging at my tie, pulling it free with a silky slide. His shirt’s completely open now, his chest broad and hairy, sweat glistening on his pecs, and I push him back against the desk, the edge biting into his thighs.

His hands slide to my ass, squeezing through my briefs, his fingers bold but hesitant, like he’s still grappling with the fact that he’s touching another guy. “Fuck, you’re—shit, this is insane,” he says, his voice trembling, but his hands don’t stop, kneading my ass, pulling me closer so our cocks grind together, the friction making us both groan. “I shouldn’t be—fuck, why’s this so good?” His eyes are wild, his face flushed, and I can see the guilt flickering, the thought of his wife, his kid, but it’s drowned out by the need, the way his cock pulses against mine.

I laugh, low and dirty, my hand sliding to his ass now, squeezing the firm muscle through his briefs, feeling it clench under my touch. “You like it, don’t you?” I murmur, my lips against his ear, my fingers teasing closer to his crack, not pushing in but brushing the crease. “All that straight bullshit, and you’re moaning for my hands on your ass. Bet you’d love more.” I nip his earlobe, making him shudder, and then I pull back, dropping to my knees again, my hands tugging his briefs down further, exposing his ass, round and muscular, dusted with dark hair.

“Julian, wait—” he starts, his voice panicked, but I don’t listen, my hands spreading his cheeks, revealing his tight, pink hole, glistening slightly from sweat. I lean in, my tongue flicking out, licking a slow stripe over his rim, and he cries out, a raw, desperate sound that echoes in the small office. “Fuck, no, you can’t—” he gasps, but his hips push back, betraying him, chasing my tongue as I lick again, slow and deliberate, tasting the clean musk of him, so fucking masculine it makes my cock throb harder.

“Relax,” I murmur, my lips brushing his hole, my tongue teasing the rim, feeling it clench under my touch. “You’re loving this, Marcus. Moaning like a fucking slut for me.” I dive in, my tongue fucking into him, deep and relentless, and he’s trembling now, his hands gripping the desk, his moans loud and shameless. His hole’s tight, hot, and I’m lost in it, licking and sucking, savoring the way he opens up, the way his body surrenders. His cock’s leaking, dripping onto the carpet, and I reach around, stroking him, my hand slick with his precum, keeping him on edge.

"Goddamn, Julian," he moans, his voice high and wrecked, his hips rocking back against my face, his ass clenching around my tongue. "This is—fuck, I shouldn't, but—shit." His words are slurred, his straight resolve shattered, and I can feel the release in him, the way he's giving in, letting himself go in a way he never has. My own cock's aching, leaking in my briefs, and I'm drunk on the taste of him, the scent of his sweat and cologne, the way he's unraveling under my tongue.

I pull back, standing, my lips slick, and kiss him again, hard and desperate, letting him taste his own ass on my tongue. He groans into the kiss, his hands grabbing my ass again, squeezing hard, like he's claiming me back. The tension's electric, the office a haze of heat and want, our bodies slick with sweat, cocks hard, suits half-off. He's straight, got a life I'm not part of, but right now, he's mine, moaning and groping like he can't get enough, and I'm gonna keep pushing, keep driving him wild, until we're both too far gone to stop.

His hands are still on my ass, fingers digging into the muscle through my briefs, his grip tight but trembling, like he's caught between diving in and pulling back. The office is a pressure cooker, the air thick with the scent of our sweat, his spicy cologne, and the raw musk of arousal that's got my head spinning. His lips are parted, breath ragged, his dark eyes locked on mine, flickering with guilt but burning with want. My hand's still wrapped around his cock, stroking slow, keeping him on the edge, the thick vein pulsing under my fingers, his precum slicking my palm. His briefs are bunched at his thighs, his charcoal trousers a crumpled heap around his polished dress shoes, black dress socks stark against the carpet. My own navy suit's a mess—jacket on the floor, shirt open, tie loose like a silk leash dangling against my chest.

“You’re shaking, Marcus,” I murmur, my voice low, teasing, my lips brushing the stubble on his jaw, feeling it scrape rough against me. “All that big, straight talk, and you’re trembling like a virgin. You want this so bad, don’t you?” My thumb swipes over the head of his cock, smearing precum, and he groans, a deep, guttural sound that hits me right in the gut, making my own dick throb harder in my briefs.

“Fuck you, Julian,” he rasps, but there’s no bite in it, just raw need, his hands sliding up my back, fingers catching on the damp fabric of my open shirt. “You’re—shit, you’re pushing me too far.” His voice cracks, and he leans in, his forehead brushing mine, his breath hot and uneven. His hands roam higher, grazing the nape of my neck, tangling in my hair, tugging just enough to make me hiss. He’s not shoving me away anymore; he’s holding on, like I’m the only thing keeping him upright.

I grin, my lips grazing his ear, nipping the lobe, feeling him shudder. “Too far? Nah, you’re right where you wanna be.” My hand slides lower, cupping his balls through the briefs still clinging to his thighs, feeling their weight, the heat, the way they tighten under my touch. He gasps, his hips jerking forward, his cock grinding against my wrist. “Feel that? You’re so fucking hard, leaking all over me. Bet you’re dying to know what else I can do with these hands.” I squeeze lightly, rolling his balls, and his knees buckle slightly, his hands gripping my shoulders for balance.

“Goddamn it,” he mutters, his voice a low growl, his fingers digging into my skin, leaving marks I’ll feel tomorrow. “You’re—fuck, you’re gonna ruin me.” His eyes meet mine, dark and desperate, the guilt still there but drowning in the heat, the need. His tie’s completely undone now, hanging loose around his neck, the burgundy silk catching the dim light of the desk lamp. I grab it, twisting it around my fist, pulling just enough to make him lean closer, our chests brushing, my bare skin against his, the coarse hair on his pecs tickling my nipples.

"Ruin you?" I chuckle, my voice a low purr, tugging the tie again, making his breath hitch. "I'm just getting you started, big guy." I let go of his cock, my hands sliding to his hips, pushing his briefs down further, letting them drop to his ankles. His cock springs free, thick and heavy, slapping against his thigh, and I step closer, my own bulge pressing against his, the friction through my briefs making me groan. "Fuck, Marcus, look at you. All that muscle, that perfect fucking cock, and you're letting me touch you like this. You're not so straight now, are you?"

He groans, his hands sliding to my waist, fingers hooking into the waistband of my briefs, tugging them down just enough to expose the base of my cock, the dark hair there damp with sweat. "You're such a fucking tease," he says, his voice rough, almost angry, but his hands don't stop, pulling my briefs lower, his fingers grazing the sensitive skin of my shaft. "I shouldn't—fuck, I shouldn't want this, but—" His words cut off as I grab his wrists, pinning them against the desk, leaning in to kiss him again, my tongue plunging deep, swallowing his protests.

The kiss is feral, all teeth and hunger, his stubble burning my lips as I bite his lower lip, tugging it gently. He moans, loud and shameless, his body arching into mine, his cock brushing my thigh, leaving a slick trail of precum. I release his wrists, my hands roaming his chest, thumbs circling his nipples, feeling them harden under my touch. "You're moaning like you're made for this," I murmur against his mouth, my fingers pinching his nipples, making him gasp, his hips bucking. "Bet you've never been this hard for your wife."

“Don’t—fuck, don’t bring her into this,” he snaps, but his voice is weak, his hands grabbing my ass again, squeezing hard, pulling me so our cocks grind together, the friction electric. “You’re—shit, you’re making me crazy.” His fingers dig into my cheeks, spreading them slightly through my briefs, and I groan, the sensation shooting straight to my dick. His touch is clumsy, unsure, but it’s bold, like he’s testing how far he can go, how much he can let himself want.

I pull back, just enough to look at him, his face flushed, eyes wild, his broad chest heaving under the open shirt. “Crazy’s good,” I say, my voice low, my hand sliding to his neck, feeling his pulse race under my thumb. “Crazy’s what makes you grab my ass like that, makes you want to rip these briefs off me.” I lean in, kissing his neck, sucking hard enough to leave a mark, tasting the salt of his sweat, the spice of his cologne. He moans, his head tilting back, giving me more access, his hands sliding up my back, tugging at my shirt, pulling it off completely.

"Fuck, Julian," he breathes, his hands roaming my bare back, fingers tracing the lean muscle, the sweat slicking my skin. "You're—shit, you're too much." His voice is wrecked, his hands trembling as they slide to my chest, thumbs brushing my nipples, sending sparks through me. He's touching me like he's never touched a guy before, hesitant but hungry, his fingers exploring every inch, like he's memorizing me.

I grab his tie again, pulling him closer, my lips brushing his ear. "Too much? You're the one groping me like you can't get enough." My hand slides to his ass, squeezing the firm muscle, my fingers teasing closer to his crack again, brushing the crease through the thin layer of sweat-damp hair. He shudders, his cock twitching against my thigh, and I grin, my other hand stroking his chest, pinching his nipple hard, making him cry out, a sharp, needy sound that echoes in the small office.

“You’re gonna kill me,” he says, his voice high and desperate, his hands fumbling with my briefs, pushing them down further, exposing my cock fully. It springs free, hard and leaking, brushing against his, and we both groan, the contact electric, raw. His fingers wrap around me, hesitant at first, then tighter, stroking slow, feeling the weight, the heat. “Fuck, you’re—shit, you’re big,” he mutters, his voice shaky, his eyes wide as he looks down, watching his own hand on my cock, like he can’t believe he’s doing this.

I laugh, low and dirty, my hand sliding to his cock again, stroking in time with his, our rhythms matching, the air thick with the sound of our breaths, our moans. “Big, huh? You’re not doing so bad yourself,” I say, my thumb swiping over his slit, making him gasp, his hips jerking. “Feel that? You’re leaking like a fucking faucet, Marcus. All for me.” I lean in, kissing him again, my tongue deep, tasting his desperation, his hands stroking me faster, his fingers clumsy but eager, learning fast.

We're grinding together now, cocks brushing, hands roaming, ties dangling like silk lifelines in the chaos. His hands slide to my ass again, squeezing hard, pulling me closer, his fingers teasing my crack now, brushing my hole through the sweat-soaked fabric of my briefs. I moan into his mouth, the sensation intense, my cock throbbing in his hand. "Fuck, yeah, touch me there," I murmur, my lips against his, my hand stroking his cock faster, feeling it pulse, ready to explode but not yet, not until I've got him begging.

He pulls back, his eyes wild, his chest heaving, his tie a crumpled mess around his neck. "This is—fuck, Julian, this is too much," he says, but his hands don't stop, one stroking my cock, the other gripping my ass, his fingers bolder now, pressing against my hole, not pushing in but teasing, testing. "I'm—shit, I'm not supposed to feel like this." His voice is trembling, but his touch is sure, his fingers exploring, learning, driving me wild.

"Feel like what?" I tease, my hand sliding to his neck, pulling his tie tight, making him gasp. "Like you wanna fuck me? Like you wanna lose it right here, in this office, with me?" I kiss his throat, sucking hard, leaving another mark, feeling his pulse race under my lips. His cock twitches in my hand, leaking more, and I stroke faster, my thumb circling the head, making him moan, loud and shameless, his hips rocking into my grip.

"Goddamn, yes," he groans, his voice breaking, his hands grabbing my face, pulling me into another kiss, desperate and sloppy, his tongue fucking my mouth, his stubble burning my lips. "I want—fuck, I want you so bad." His words are a confession, raw and unguarded, and it's like a dam breaking, his straight resolve shattered, his body all mine. His hands slide to my hips, pulling me closer, our cocks grinding together, the friction unbearable, the tension building, ready to snap but holding, just barely.

I pull back, my lips swollen, my breath ragged, and grab his tie again, yanking it hard, making him stumble forward, his chest crashing into mine. “Then show me,” I growl, my hand stroking his cock, keeping him on edge, my other hand sliding to his ass, squeezing hard, fingers teasing his hole again, making him shudder. “Show me how bad you want it, Marcus. Let go. Be mine.” The office is a haze of heat and want, our bodies slick with sweat, suits in ruins, cocks hard, hands groping, and I know I’ve got him, right on the edge, ready to fall.

My own tie's loose, my briefs barely clinging to my hips, my cock hard and aching under his touch, the friction of his calloused fingers driving me wild.

"Fuck, Marcus, you're learning fast," I murmur, my voice thick, my lips brushing his ear, nipping the lobe again, feeling him shiver. "Stroking me like you've done this before. Bet you're imagining fucking me, aren't you?" My hand twists on his cock, a slow, deliberate stroke, my thumb circling the head, smearing precum, and he groans, his hips bucking, his fingers tightening on my shaft.

"Shut up," he rasps, but it's half-moaned, his voice wrecked, his eyes dark and wild, locked on mine. "You're—fuck, you're making it impossible to think." His hand speeds up on my cock, his grip firmer now, less hesitant, like he's chasing the high, the thrill of touching me. His other hand slides deeper, fingers slipping under the waistband of my briefs, brushing the bare skin of my ass, teasing closer to my hole, making my breath hitch.

I grin, grabbing his tie again, pulling it tight, making him gasp as I drag him closer, our lips inches apart. “Don’t need to think,” I say, my voice a low growl, my hand stroking his cock faster, matching his rhythm on mine. “Just feel this. Feel how fucking good it is.” I kiss him hard, my tongue plunging deep, tasting the desperation in his moans, the faint salt of his sweat. His fingers press harder against my hole, not pushing in but circling, teasing, and I moan into his mouth, my cock throbbing in his hand, leaking precum that slicks his fingers.

He pulls back, his chest heaving, his eyes wild with a mix of panic and lust. “Fuck, Julian, I’m—I’m too close,” he says, his voice trembling, his hand slowing on my cock, like he’s trying to hold back. “This is—shit, I can’t stop, but I—” His words cut off as I grab his ass, squeezing hard, my fingers digging into the muscle, pulling him closer so our cocks grind together again, the friction making us both groan.

“Then don’t stop,” I murmur, my lips brushing his jaw, kissing the stubble, feeling it scrape against me. “Let it happen, Marcus. Let me make you feel good.” I slide my hand to his neck, tugging his tie again, using it like a leash to pull him into another kiss, slow and dirty, my tongue teasing his, swallowing his moans. His hands are everywhere—stroking my cock, gripping my ass, fingers teasing my hole, his touch bold but still tinged with that straight-guy hesitation, like he’s amazed he’s doing this.

I push him back against the desk, the edge biting into his thighs, his cock brushing my thigh, leaving a wet trail. “Fuck, you’re so hard for me,” I say, my voice low, my hand stroking his cock again, slow and deliberate, keeping him on edge. “Bet you’ve never been this turned on, have you? Not with her, not with anyone." My other hand slides to his chest, pinching his nipple, rolling it between my fingers, and he cries out, a sharp, needy sound that makes my cock twitch.

"Goddamn it, Julian," he groans, his hands grabbing my hips, pulling me closer, his fingers digging into my skin. "You're—fuck, you're right, okay? I've never—shit, this is insane." His voice is high, desperate, his eyes flickering with guilt but burning with want, his cock pulsing in my hand, ready to explode but holding, just barely. His fingers slide to my ass again, bolder now, slipping under my briefs, brushing my hole directly, the contact making me gasp, my hips rocking back against his hand.

"Yeah, that's it," I moan, my lips against his neck, sucking hard, leaving another mark, tasting the salt of his skin. "Touch me like that. Show me how bad you want this." I stroke his cock faster, my thumb circling the head, feeling it pulse, and he moans, his fingers pressing harder against my hole, circling, teasing, driving me wild. The tension's unbearable, the office a haze of heat and want, our bodies slick with sweat, ties dangling, briefs barely on, cocks hard and leaking, hands groping, pushing each other closer to the edge.

His fingers are still teasing my hole, circling with a boldness that's got my head spinning, his touch rough but precise, like he's learning me inch by inch. The desk creaks under his weight, his thighs spread, his cock throbbing in my hand, slick with precum that drips onto my wrist. His burgundy tie's a crumpled mess, hanging loose, and his shirt's a lost cause, open and clinging to his sweaty chest, the dark hair matted, his nipples hard from my earlier teasing. My own briefs are barely on, my cock hard and leaking, brushing against his thigh as I lean in, my lips grazing his ear, my breath hot against his skin.

“Fuck, Marcus, you’re driving me crazy,” I murmur, my voice thick, my hand stroking his cock, slow and deliberate, keeping him teetering on the edge. “Those fingers—shit, you’re gonna make me lose it.” I nip his earlobe, feeling him shudder, his fingers pressing harder against my hole, not pushing in but teasing, the pressure sending sparks through me. His other hand’s on my cock, stroking with a rhythm that’s surer now, his grip tight, his thumb swiping over the head, making me groan, my hips bucking into his hand.

“You’re—fuck, you’re the one driving me crazy,” he says, his voice hoarse, cracking with need, his eyes dark and wild, locked on mine. “I’m not—shit, I’m not supposed to want this, but—” His words cut off as I tug his tie, pulling him into another kiss, my tongue plunging deep, tasting the raw heat of him, the faint musk of his arousal. His fingers slide deeper, brushing my hole directly now, the contact electric, making me moan into his mouth, my cock throbbing in his hand.

I pull back, my lips swollen, my breath ragged, and grab his wrists, pinning them to the desk, leaning in so our foreheads touch, our breaths mingling. "You want it," I growl, my voice low, my eyes boring into his. "You're so fucking hard, touching me like this, moaning like you're mine. Say it, Marcus. Say you want me." My hand strokes his cock faster, my thumb circling the head, feeling it pulse, and he groans, his hips bucking, his fingers twitching against the desk.

"Fuck, Julian, I—I want you," he gasps, his voice breaking, his face flushed, his eyes wild with a mix of shame and desire. "I shouldn't, but—goddamn it, I want you so bad." His words are a surrender, raw and desperate, and it’s like a switch flips, his hands breaking free from my grip, grabbing my face, pulling me into a kiss that’s all teeth and hunger, his tongue fucking my mouth, swallowing my moans.

I laugh into the kiss, my hand sliding to his ass, squeezing hard, fingers teasing his crack again, brushing his hole, making him shudder. “That’s it,” I murmur, my lips brushing his, my hand stroking his cock, keeping him on edge. “Let go, Marcus. Let me have you.” I kiss his neck, sucking hard, leaving another mark, feeling his pulse race under my lips, his cock twitching in my hand, leaking more precum, staining the carpet.

His hands slide to my hips, pulling my briefs down completely, letting them fall to my ankles, my cock springing free, brushing his thigh. “Fuck, you’re—shit, you’re perfect,” he mutters, his voice trembling, his hands roaming my ass, squeezing, his fingers teasing my hole again, bolder now, pressing harder. "I can't—fuck, I can't stop touching you." His touch is desperate, hungry, his fingers circling my hole, making me moan, my cock throbbing against his thigh.

"Then don't," I growl, grabbing his tie again, yanking it hard, pulling him closer, our cocks grinding together, the friction making us both groan. "Touch me, Marcus. Feel me. Let's see how much you can take." I kiss him again, deep and sloppy, my tongue teasing his, my hand stroking his cock, keeping him on edge, the tension building, ready to snap but holding, just barely.

His hands are relentless now, one stroking my cock, the other teasing my hole, his fingers circling with a confidence that's got my knees weak. The office is a haze of heat and want, the desk creaking under his weight, his tie a crumpled mess, his shirt open, his chest glistening with sweat. My own tie's loose, my briefs gone, my cock hard and leaking, brushing his thigh as I lean in, kissing his neck, sucking hard, tasting the salt of his skin, the spice of his cologne. His cock's still in my hand, thick and pulsing, leaking so much precum it's slicking my fingers, dripping onto the carpet.

"Fuck, Julian, I need—" he starts, his voice hoarse, breaking, his eyes wild, locked on mine. "I need you to—shit, put it in." His words hit like a shockwave, raw and desperate, his face flushed with a mix of nerves and need. He's trembling, his hands gripping my hips, pulling me closer, his cock grinding against mine, the friction unbearable.

I grin, my lips brushing his ear, my hand stroking his cock, keeping him on edge. “You sure, big guy?” I murmur, my voice low, teasing, my fingers teasing his hole again, brushing the rim, making him shudder. “You want my cock in you? Right here, in this office?” I kiss his jaw, feeling the stubble scrape, my other hand sliding to his chest, pinching his nipple, making him gasp.

“Yes, fuck, yes,” he groans, his voice high and desperate, his hands grabbing my ass, pulling me closer, his fingers digging into my skin. “I’m—shit, I’m nervous, but I want it. I want you.” His eyes meet mine, dark and wild, the guilt still there but drowned out by the need, the want, the raw hunger in his gaze.

I kiss him hard, my tongue plunging deep, swallowing his moans as I push him back against the desk, his thighs spreading, his cock throbbing against my thigh. I pull back, grabbing my cock, stroking it slow, letting him see it, the head flushed and leaking, ready for him. “Relax,” I murmur, my voice low, my hand sliding to his hole, teasing it with my fingers, feeling it clench, hot and tight. “I’m gonna make you feel so fucking good, Marcus.”

I press the head of my cock against his hole, not pushing in yet, just teasing, feeling the heat, the tightness, the way he tenses but doesn’t pull away. “Fuck, you’re tight,” I groan, my hand stroking his cock, keeping him on edge, my other hand gripping his thigh, spreading him wider. He’s trembling, his breath ragged, his hands grabbing the desk, knuckles white, his tie dangling loose, a silk lifeline in the chaos.

“Julian, shit, just—do it,” he gasps, his voice breaking, his eyes wild, locked on mine. “I’m ready, fuck, I want it.” His words are a plea, raw and desperate, and I can feel his need, his surrender, the way his straight resolve has shattered, leaving him open, vulnerable, mine.

I push in, slow and deliberate, the head of my cock breaching his hole, and he cries out, a sharp, needy sound that echoes in the office. “Fuck, fuck,” he moans, his hands grabbing my arms, gripping tight, his body tense but opening for me, taking me inch by inch. It’s tight, hot, so fucking perfect, and I groan, my hips rocking forward, pushing deeper, feeling him clench around me, his heat pulling me in.

“Goddamn, Marcus, you’re taking it so well,” I murmur, my voice thick, my hand stroking his cock, keeping him on edge as I push deeper, slow and steady, letting him adjust. His moans are loud, shameless, his hips rocking back, meeting my thrusts, his body surrendering completely. “Fuck, you feel so good, so tight.”

He groans, his hands sliding to my tie, grabbing it, yanking it hard, pulling me closer, his eyes wild with need. “Harder,” he gasps, his voice wrecked, his body trembling, his cock pulsing in my hand. “Fuck me harder, Julian, please.” His words are a shock, raw and desperate, and I grin, my hips snapping forward, pounding into him, the desk creaking under the force, his moans filling the office, loud and needy.

I lean in, licking his back, tasting the salt of his sweat, the spice of his cologne, my tongue tracing the curve of his spine, feeling the muscle flex under my lips. “Fuck, you’re so hot like this,” I growl, my hips pounding harder, deeper, his hole clenching around me, so tight it’s driving me wild. His hands tug my tie, pulling me closer, his moans high and desperate, his body rocking back, meeting every thrust, taking me deeper, harder.

“Goddamn, Julian, don’t stop,” he moans, his voice slurred, drowned in pleasure, his eyes fluttering shut, his face flushed, his tie a crumpled mess in his fist. “Fuck, it’s so good, you’re so fucking good." His words hit me like a drug, fueling me, and I pound harder, my cock driving into him, the friction electric, the heat overwhelming, my hand stroking his cock in time with my thrusts, keeping him on edge.

I lick his back again, my tongue tracing the sweat-slicked muscle, savoring the taste, the raw masculinity of him, my hips never slowing, pounding relentless, his moans louder, needier, filling the office. "You love this, don't you?" I murmur, my lips against his skin, my hand tugging his tie, pulling it tight, making him gasp. "Love me fucking you, making you mine." I nip his shoulder, feeling him shudder, his hole clenching tighter, his cock pulsing in my hand, ready to explode but holding, just barely.

"Fuck, yes," he cries, his voice high, desperate, his hands gripping my tie, yanking it hard, pulling me closer, his body rocking back, taking every thrust, every inch, his pleasure drowning out everything else. The office is a haze of heat and want, our bodies slick with sweat, ties dangling, cocks throbbing, and I'm lost in him, in the way he's giving in, the way he's mine, right here, right now, in this forbidden, filthy moment.

His moans are a symphony of surrender, raw and jagged, filling the small office as I thrust into him, my cock buried deep, his tight heat gripping me like a vice. The desk groans under our weight, its polished surface slick with sweat, his broad frame rocking back to meet every snap of my hips. His burgundy tie is a twisted knot in his fist, his shirt splayed open, revealing the glistening expanse of his chest, dark hair matted, nipples hard from my earlier teasing. My own tie dangles loose, a navy silk pendulum swinging with each thrust, my briefs long gone, my cock throbbing inside him, the friction electric, unbearable. His dress socks slide on the carpet, his polished shoes scuffed from our frantic movements, and his charcoal trousers are a crumpled heap around his ankles, his briefs tangled with them, exposing his thick thighs, dusted with hair, flexing with every thrust.

"Fuck, Julian, you're—shit, you're wrecking me," he gasps, his voice a low, broken growl, his head thrown back, exposing the taut line of his throat, glistening with sweat. His hands clutch my tie, yanking it hard, pulling me closer, his lips crashing into mine in a kiss that's all teeth and desperation, his tongue plunging deep, tasting of mint and raw need. I groan into his mouth, my hips driving harder, deeper, the slick sound of skin on skin echoing in the room, mixing with the faint buzz of the desk lamp and the distant hum of the city beyond the blinds.

"Wrecking you? You're fucking loving it," I murmur against his lips, my voice thick, my tongue flicking out to trace the stubble along his jaw, tasting the salt of his sweat, the sharp edge of his cologne. My hand strokes his cock, slick with precum, matching the rhythm of my thrusts, feeling it pulse, thick and heavy, ready to burst. "Look at you, taking my cock like you were made for it, moaning like you're mine." I nip his lower lip, sucking it hard, and he moans louder, his hips bucking back, his hole clenching around me, pulling me deeper, making my head spin.

"Goddamn it, don't—fuck, don't stop," he pleads, his voice high and wrecked, his hands sliding to my ass, fingers digging into the muscle, pulling me closer, urging me to go harder. His touch is desperate, no longer hesitant, his straight-guy armor shattered, replaced by a raw, primal need that's got my blood pounding. I lean in, licking a slow stripe up his neck, savoring the salty tang, the heat of his skin, my tongue tracing the pulse hammering under his jaw. He shudders, his cock twitching in my hand, leaking more precum, dripping onto the desk, staining the wood.

"You're so fucking tight," I growl, my hips snapping forward, pounding into him, the desk rattling, papers sliding to the floor in a cascade of forgotten work. My hand twists on his cock, stroking faster, my thumb circling the head, smearing precum, and he cries out, a sharp, needy sound that hits me right in the gut. “Bet you’ve never felt this, huh? Never had anyone fuck you like this, make you lose it like this.” I kiss him again, deep and sloppy, my tongue fucking his mouth, swallowing his moans, his stubble burning my lips as he kisses back, hungry, reckless.

“Fuck, Julian, I—I can’t hold it,” he gasps, his voice breaking, his eyes wild, locked on mine, pupils blown wide with lust. His hands grab my shoulders, nails biting into my skin, leaving marks I’ll feel later, and his hips rock back, meeting every thrust, his hole clenching tighter, driving me closer to the edge. “You’re—shit, you’re too much, I’m gonna—” His words cut off with a moan, loud and shameless, his body trembling, sweat dripping from his brow, catching in the dark hair at his temples.

I grin, my lips brushing his ear, nipping the lobe, feeling him shudder. "Gonna come for me, Marcus? Gonna lose it while I'm fucking you?" I thrust harder, deeper, my cock hitting that spot inside him that makes his moans turn to cries, his body arching, his cock pulsing in my hand. My other hand slides to his chest, pinching his nipple, rolling it between my fingers, and he gasps, his hips bucking wildly, his hole clenching so tight it's almost too much.

"Yes, fuck, yes," he moans, his voice slurred, drowned in pleasure, his hands yanking my tie again, pulling me into another kiss, his lips desperate, his tongue chasing mine. His cock throbs in my hand, the head flushed red, leaking so much it's slicking my fingers, and I stroke faster, matching the relentless rhythm of my thrusts, pushing him closer, closer, until he's teetering on the edge.

"Come on, big guy," I murmur, my voice a low growl, my lips against his neck, sucking hard, leaving another mark. "Let go. Come for me, right here, right now." I pound into him, my cock driving deep, the friction electric, the heat overwhelming, and he cries out, a raw, desperate sound that fills the office, his body convulsing, his hole clenching around me as he comes, hot and thick, spilling over my hand, splattering onto the desk, his cock pulsing with every wave.

"Fuck, Julian!" he gasps, his voice high, broken, his hands gripping my tie, yanking it hard, pulling me closer as he rides out his orgasm, his body shaking, sweat dripping, his chest heaving. The sight of him—broad, muscular, unraveling under me—pushes me over the edge, and I groan, my hips snapping forward, my cock pulsing as I come inside him, filling him with hot, thick spurts, the sensation so intense it whites out my vision for a second.

We're both panting, slick with sweat, our bodies pressed together, my cock still buried in him, his hole twitching around me, milking every last drop. His hands loosen on my tie, sliding to my chest, fingers tracing the lean muscle, the sweat-slicked skin, like he's grounding himself in the aftermath. I lean in, kissing him slow, soft, my tongue teasing his, tasting the lingering mint, the raw musk of our sex. He kisses back, hesitant now, the guilt creeping back into his eyes, but his hands don't let go, still resting on my hips, like he's not ready to break the connection.

"Fuck," he breathes, his voice shaky, his forehead resting against mine, his breath hot and uneven. "That was—shit, that was too much." His eyes flicker, dark and conflicted, the reality of what we've done sinking in, his straight life crashing back like a tidal wave. I pull out slowly, making him wince, a soft groan escaping his lips, and I grin, wiping my hand on his crumpled shirt, the fabric stained with his cum, his sweat.

"Too much? You loved every second," I say, my voice low, teasing, as I step back, grabbing my briefs from the floor, pulling them on, the fabric clinging to my damp skin. He's still leaning against the desk, his trousers and briefs around his ankles, his cock softening, glistening with cum, his tie a crumpled mess. He looks wrecked, vulnerable, and it's fucking beautiful, the way his broad frame trembles, the way his eyes avoid mine, like he's afraid of what he'll see.

"We—fuck, we can't tell anyone," he says, his voice low, urgent, as he pulls up his briefs, his trousers, fumbling with the belt, his hands shaking. "My wife, my kid—Julian, please, you can't say a word." His eyes meet mine, wide and panicked, the lust fading, replaced by raw fear, the weight of his life pressing down on him.

I grin, smoothing my tie, slipping my shirt back on, buttoning it with deliberate slowness. "Your secret's safe with me, Marcus," I say, my voice calm, reassuring, but with a teasing edge that makes his flush deepen. "Relax, big guy. Nobody's gonna know." I step closer, brushing a stray lock of hair from his forehead, my fingers lingering, feeling the heat of his skin. "But you might wanna check your underwear before you head home."

He frowns, confused, glancing down as he adjusts his trousers, tucking in his shirt. "What the—?" He freezes, his hands pausing at his waistband, realizing the briefs he's wearing aren't his—mine, navy and snug, clinging to his thick thighs, a size too small. His eyes snap to mine, wide with panic, and I laugh, low and dirty, pulling my own trousers up, his black briefs hugging my hips, the fabric warm from his body, a secret trophy of this moment.

“Guess we got a little mixed up in the heat,” I say, winking, grabbing my jacket from the floor, slipping it on. “Let’s see if your wife notices you’re wearing my underwear. Might make for an interesting night.” I saunter toward the door, throwing him a final glance, catching the way his face pales, his hands fumbling with his tie, trying to restore order to his disheveled appearance.

“Julian, fuck, you’re not gonna tell, right?” he calls after me, his voice high, desperate, as he follows, his shoes scuffing the carpet, his belt still unbuckled. “Please, man, I’m serious.”

I pause at the door, turning to face him, my grin wicked, my eyes locking on his. “I’m not gonna tell,” I say, my voice low, reassuring, but with a spark of mischief. “But you better hope she doesn’t notice you’re wearing my briefs. Might be hard to explain.” I wink, pushing the door open, stepping into the hall, leaving him standing there, flushed and rattled, his tie askew, his trousers barely holding up.

The office is silent now, the hum of computers gone, the fluorescent lights dimmed, the city skyline glittering beyond the windows. I head for the bathroom, my cock still tingling from the intensity, my body buzzing with the thrill of what we did. His briefs feel strange, tight, a reminder of him, of the way he moaned, the way he came apart under me. I splash water on my face, the cold shocking my skin, and glance in the mirror, my hair mussed, my tie loose, my lips swollen from his kisses. The reflection smirks back at me, satisfied, knowing I've got him hooked, knowing this isn't the last time.

I adjust my jacket, smooth my tie, and step back into the hall, the office empty, the air still heavy with the scent of our sex.

BACKSTAGE WRECK

I'm Zane, 29, lean and ripped from years of hauling gear and living on the road. My body's all sinew and muscle, not bulky but cut, with a tight ass that fills out my black jeans and a chest that strains my worn-out band tees. My dark hair's long, tied back in a messy bun, strands always falling into my hazel eyes, which I've been told have a hungry edge. A few tattoos snake up my arms—skulls, flames, a lyric from a song I'll never admit I regret—and my hands are calloused from years of lugging amps and coiling cables. I'm the head roadie for Black Serpent, the biggest rock band in the country, and I've spent the last five years in the shadow of their frontman, Cole, the kind of guy who makes your cock twitch just by walking into a room.

Tonight's a sold-out show, 20,000 screaming fans packed into the arena, the air vibrating with the thrum of guitars and the roar of the crowd. Backstage is a fucking zoo—techs running around, groupies trying to sneak past security, and the smell of beer, sweat, and cigarette smoke thick in the air. I'm in Cole's dressing room, checking his gear, my hands moving over his custom Les Paul, making sure it's tuned to perfection. The room's a mess—empty whiskey bottles, half-smoked joints, and a leather couch that's seen more action than a porn set. My black tee's clinging to my chest, damp with sweat from hauling equipment all day, and my jeans are low, showing the waistband of my boxers, the outline of my cock already half-hard just from being in his space.

Cole bursts in, the door slamming behind him, his presence like a fucking lightning bolt. He's 35, tall, with a body carved from years of strutting stages—broad shoulders, pecs that pop under his open leather vest, and abs you could grate steel on. His dark blond hair's slicked back, wet with sweat, and his green eyes are sharp, glinting with that rockstar fire that makes fans drop their panties and guys question their sexuality. His tight leather pants hug his thighs, his cock a thick bulge that's impossible to ignore, and his boots clomp heavy on the floor. He smells like whiskey, sweat, and the faint musk of leather, and my cock twitches harder, pressing against my jeans as he tosses his mic on the table and grabs a bottle of Jack.

"Fucking killed it out there," he says, his voice rough, raw from belting lyrics for two hours. He takes a swig, his throat working, a bead of sweat rolling down his neck, catching in the blond hair on his chest. "You good, man? Kept my shit tight, as always?" He's talking to me, but his eyes are roaming, lingering on my arms, my chest, the way my jeans sit low on my hips.

"Always, boss," I say, my voice low, a smirk tugging at my lips as I lean against the table, my hands brushing the guitar strings, making them hum. "Your axe was singing tonight. Crowd was losing their fucking minds." I'm close to him, closer than I need to be, my body angled so he can see the bulge in my jeans, the way my tee clings to my pecs. I've been his roadie since the band blew up, loyal as fuck, always there to fix his gear, his mic, his fucking life, and over the years, the tension's been building, a slow burn that's got my cock hard every time he looks at me like that.

He laughs, a deep, throaty sound, and steps closer, the bottle dangling from his fingers. "You're the only one I trust, you know that?" he says, his eyes locking on mine, green and piercing, like he's seeing right through me. "Five years, and you've never fucked up. That's rare as shit in this game." He's close now, close enough that I can smell the whiskey on his breath, the sweat on his skin, and my cock's throbbing, my balls aching, but I keep it cool, my smirk steady.

“Just doing my job,” I say, but my voice is rough, thick with the heat building between us. I shift, my hip brushing his, and he doesn’t pull away, just takes another swig, his eyes flicking to my crotch, then back to my face. “You need anything else tonight? Mic’s good, guitar’s tight, but I can... handle whatever you want.” I let the words hang, heavy with intent, my eyes on his lips, his jaw, the way his stubble catches the dim light of the dressing room.

He grins, slow and dangerous, setting the bottle down with a clink. “You’re always so fucking ready, aren’t you?” he says, his voice low, a growl that makes my cock jump. He steps closer, his leather vest brushing my arm, his body heat hitting me like a wave. “What’s got you so worked up, huh? The crowd? Or something else?” His eyes drop to my bulge again, lingering, and I know he sees it, knows he’s the reason I’m hard as fuck.

"Maybe it's you," I say, my voice dropping, bold as hell, my hand brushing his arm, feeling the hard muscle under the leather. "You out there, owning that stage, looking like that. Hard not to notice." I'm pushing it, testing him, my heart pounding, my cock straining against my jeans, the air thick with the smell of his sweat, the whiskey, the faint tang of his cologne.

He doesn't back off, just smirks, his eyes darkening, and steps even closer, his thigh brushing mine, his cock a thick outline in his leather pants. "You're a cocky fucker," he says, but there's no heat in it, just amusement, and something else—want, raw and unfiltered. "Five years, and you're still looking at me like that. What's it gonna take, man?" He's teasing, but his voice is rough, his breath hot, and I can feel the tension coiling, ready to snap.

I laugh, low and rough, leaning in, my lips close to his ear, my breath brushing his skin. "Maybe I'm waiting for you to make a move, rockstar," I say, my voice thick, my hand sliding to his waist, resting just above his belt, feeling the heat of him through the leather. "You're the one strutting around like you own the world. Own me too, why don't you?" My cock's throbbing, my balls aching, and I'm so close I can taste his sweat, feel the pulse in his neck.

He groans, a low, guttural sound, and grabs my wrist, not pulling my hand away but holding it there, his grip strong, calloused. "You're playing with fire, man," he says, his voice rough, his eyes locked on mine, green and burning. "You keep talking like that, I might just take you up on it." His thumb brushes my wrist, a small move but enough to make my cock leak, my jeans damp at the tip.

"Fucking do it then," I say, my voice a growl, stepping into his space, my chest brushing his, my hand sliding lower, brushing the edge of his bulge, feeling the heat, the hardness. He doesn't stop me, just breathes harder, his eyes flicking to my lips, his jaw tight. The dressing room's loud with the hum of the crowd outside, the thump of music from the crew tearing down the stage, but in here, it's just us, the air thick with sweat, whiskey, and the musky edge of our arousal.

He leans in, his lips so close I can feel his breath, but he doesn't kiss me, just hovers, teasing, his hand still on my wrist, his cock pressing against my thigh through his leather pants. "You want this bad, don't you?" he says, his voice low, taunting, and I can hear the smirk in it, the rockstar swagger that's got me so fucking hard I can't think straight. "All these years, hauling my shit, staring at my ass. Bet you've been jerking off to me every night."

"Guilty," I say, my voice thick, my hand sliding up his chest, feeling the hard muscle, the sweat-slicked hair under my fingers. "You're a fucking tease out there, Cole. Strutting around, that cock in those pants. You know what you do to me." I'm bold now, my hand cupping his bulge, feeling the weight, the heat, and he groans, his hips bucking slightly, pushing into my hand.

"Fuck, man," he says, his voice rough, his hand grabbing my shoulder, squeezing hard. "You're gonna get us in trouble." But he's not stopping me, not pulling away, and I can feel his cock twitch under my hand, hard as fuck, leaking through the leather. My own cock's screaming, my jeans tight, my balls aching, and I'm so close to ripping his pants off, but I hold back, wanting to drag this out, make him want it as bad as I do.

I step back, just enough to break the contact, and grab a joint from the table, lighting it with a flick of my lighter. The smoke curls up, mixing with the smell of whiskey and sweat, and I take a drag, my eyes on him, watching the way his chest heaves, his cock straining against his pants. "Take a hit," I say, holding it out, my voice low, teasing. "Might loosen you up, rockstar." I'm playing with him, keeping the tension high, my cock throbbing at the thought of what's coming.

He takes the joint, his fingers brushing mine, lingering, and takes a drag, his eyes never leaving mine. He exhales, the smoke curling around his face, and steps closer again, his body heat hitting me like a wave. "You're a fucking menace," he says, but he's grinning, his voice rough, his hand brushing my arm, sliding to my waist, pulling me closer. "What's it gonna take, huh? You want me on my knees for you?"

My cock jumps at the thought, my breath catching, but I keep my smirk, leaning in, my lips brushing his ear. "Maybe I want you bent over that couch, rockstar," I say, my voice a growl, my hand sliding to his ass, squeezing the firm muscle through his leather pants. "Bet that tight cunt of yours would feel so fucking good around my cock." I'm pushing it, hard, and he groans, his hand tightening on my waist, his cock pressing against my thigh, telling me he's just as fucking turned on.

The dressing room's a pressure cooker, the thrum of the crowd outside fading, the world narrowing to just us, our breath, our heat, the smell of smoke and sweat. His hand slides to my chest, pushing me back against the table, his eyes dark, hungry, and I know we're seconds away from crossing the line, from turning this buildup into something raw, filthy.

His body pins me against the table, his leather vest rough against my tee, his cock hard and pressing into my thigh through his pants, the heat of it making my own dick throb painfully in my jeans. The dressing room's dim, the air thick with the hum of the arena outside, fans chanting his name, but in here, it's just the sound of our breathing, heavy and ragged, the faint creak of the table under my weight. His green eyes are locked on mine, dark and intense, his breath hot against my face, whiskey-laced and sharp. His hand's on my chest, fingers splayed, pressing me back, but not hard enough to hurt—just enough to make it clear he's in control, or thinks he is.

"You've been eyeing me like this for years, haven't you?" he says, his voice low, gravelly from the show, a smirk curling his lips as his thumb brushes my nipple through the thin fabric of my tee. It hardens instantly, a jolt shooting straight to my cock, and I suck in a breath, my hands gripping the table's edge, knuckles white. "Always so fucking attentive. Fixing my gear, watching my back. Bet you've imagined this a thousand times."

I grin, but it's strained, my heart pounding, my cock straining against my zipper. "More like a million," I say, my voice rough, thick with want, my eyes flicking to his lips, full and parted, still red from the mic. "You prance around on stage, all sweat and swagger, that cock in those tight pants. How's a guy supposed to ignore that?" My hand moves, slow, deliberate, sliding up his arm, feeling the corded muscle under his vest, the slick sweat on his skin. He doesn't stop me, just watches, his eyes darkening, his breath hitching when my fingers brush the edge of his pec, the coarse hair there rough against my palm.

He laughs, a low, rumbling sound that vibrates through me, his hand sliding lower, fingers tracing the ridges of my abs through my tee, slow and teasing, making my skin tingle. "You're a bold little shit," he says, his voice dropping an octave, his thumb dipping under the hem of my shirt, brushing bare skin, the contact like a spark. "All these groupies throwing themselves at me, and you're the one who's got my attention. What makes you think you can handle me, roadie?" His fingers circle my navel, light, barely there, but it's enough to make my cock leak, a damp spot forming in my boxers.

I lean into his touch, my hips shifting, brushing his thigh, feeling the hard muscle there. "Because I've been handling your shit for five years," I say, my voice low, challenging, my hand sliding to his waist, fingers hooking into his belt loop, tugging him closer. "Your guitars, your mics, your ego. Bet I can handle that cock too." My thumb brushes the edge of his bulge, not grabbing, just teasing, feeling the heat through the leather, the way it twitches under my touch. He groans, soft but deep, his eyes fluttering for a second, his hand pressing harder against my abs, fingers splaying wider, possessive.

"Fuck, you talk a big game," he mutters, his voice rough, his other hand coming up to grip my jaw, tilting my face up, his thumb brushing my lower lip, rough and calloused from playing guitar. "But you're shaking, man. Nervous?" His eyes search mine, green and piercing, a smirk playing on his lips, but there's heat there, real fucking want, and it's making my pulse race, my cock throb harder.

"Not nervous," I say, my voice thick, my tongue darting out to lick his thumb, tasting the salt of his skin, the faint bitterness of stage grime. "Just fucking hard for you." I suck his thumb into my mouth, slow, my tongue swirling around it, my eyes locked on his, watching the way his pupils blow, his breath catching. He groans, his hips bucking slightly, his cock pressing harder against my thigh, the leather warm and tight.

"Jesus," he breathes, his voice cracking, his hand on my abs sliding lower, fingers brushing the waistband of my jeans, dipping just under, teasing the trail of hair leading down. "You're a tease, aren't you? Sucking my thumb like it's my cock." His words are low, dirty, and it's got me moaning around his thumb, my hand squeezing his bulge harder, feeling the thick length of him, the way he pulses under my palm.

I pull off his thumb with a wet pop, my lips slick, my breath ragged. “Bet your cock tastes better,” I say, my voice low, my hand stroking his bulge slow, deliberate, feeling every inch through the leather. “All that sweat from the show, that rockstar musk. I’d suck it so fucking good.” My fingers trace the zipper, not pulling it down, just teasing, and he hisses, his hips pushing into my hand, his fingers dipping lower under my jeans, brushing the base of my cock through my boxers.

“Fuck, you’re killing me,” he says, his voice rough, his hand gripping my jaw tighter, pulling me closer, his lips hovering over mine, so close I can feel his breath. “You want my cock that bad? Years of hauling my gear, and this is what you’ve been after?” His fingers slide lower, cupping my cock through the fabric, squeezing just enough to make me gasp, my hips bucking into his touch, my cock leaking more, the dampness spreading.

“Yeah,” I admit, my voice thick, my hand sliding up his vest, fingers brushing his nipple, pinching lightly, making him groan. “Watching you up there, owning that stage, that body all sweat and power. Makes my cock hard every fucking night.” I lean in, my lips brushing his ear, my breath hot, my hand stroking his bulge faster, feeling him harden even more, the leather stretching tight. “Bet you’re leaking for me right now, rockstar. That thick cock dripping in those pants.”

He curses, low and rough, his hand squeezing my cock harder, his thumb brushing the head through my boxers, making me moan, my body trembling. “You’re a dirty fucker,” he says, but he’s grinning, his eyes dark, his hips grinding into my hand, chasing the friction. “All that time, and you never said shit. What changed?”

His fingers trace the length of my cock, slow, teasing, making my breath hitch, my hips bucking.

“Tonight,” I say, my voice ragged, my hand sliding to his ass, squeezing the firm muscle through the leather, pulling him closer. “You out there, all lit up, that energy. I want it. Want you.” My fingers dig in, feeling the heat, the way he tenses, his cock pressing against mine through our pants, the friction making us both groan. His hand’s still on my cock, stroking slow, his thumb circling the head, smearing the precum through the fabric.

He leans in, his lips brushing mine, not kissing, just hovering, his breath mixing with mine, whiskey and sweat. “You think you can take me?” he says, his voice low, taunting, his hand squeezing my cock, making me gasp. “Big talk for a roadie. Bet you’d beg for it, on your knees, that tight ass in the air.” His words are dirty, rough, and it’s got me moaning, my hand sliding up his back, under his vest, feeling the slick sweat, the hard muscle.

“Fuck yeah,” I say, my voice thick, my lips brushing his, my tongue darting out to lick his lower lip, tasting the salt. “I’d beg. For that cock, that mouth. Whatever you want.” My hand slides to his chest, fingers tweaking his nipple, pinching hard, making him hiss, his hips bucking, his cock grinding against mine. The tension’s unbearable, our bodies pressed together, hands teasing, lips hovering, the air thick with our sweat, our need.

He groans, his hand sliding out of my jeans, gripping my hip, pulling me tighter, his cock hard and hot against mine. “You’re gonna drive me fucking crazy,” he says, his voice rough, his lips brushing mine again, his tongue flicking out, tasting me. “All these years, and now you’re here, touching me like this. What if I told you I’ve noticed? The way you look at me, that hunger in your eyes.”

My heart pounds, my cock throbbing, my hand sliding to his neck, fingers tangling in his sweat-damp hair. “Then fucking do something about it,” I say, my voice a growl, my lips inches from his, my body trembling with the effort not to close the distance, to keep this tension boiling. “You’re the rockstar. Take what you want.” My thumb brushes his lip, parting it, and he sucks in a breath, his eyes fluttering, his hand sliding to my ass, squeezing hard, making me groan.

He laughs, low and rough, his fingers digging into my ass, pulling me against him, our cocks grinding through the fabric, the friction intense, making us both moan. “You’re a tease,” he says, his voice thick, his lips brushing mine, his tongue darting out to lick my lower lip, slow and deliberate. “But I like it. Makes me want to pin you down, make you beg for my cock." His hand slides up my back, under my tee, fingers tracing my spine, making my skin tingle, my cock leak more.

I moan, my hand cupping his face, thumb brushing his stubble, rough and prickly. "Do it then," I say, my voice ragged, my hips grinding against his, feeling the thick length of him, the heat. "Pin me. Make me beg. I want it." My fingers trace his jaw, down his neck, feeling the pulse there, fast and hard, matching mine. The dressing room's spinning, the thrum of the crowd outside a distant hum, our world narrowing to this—our breath, our touch, the unbearable tension coiling tighter.

He grabs my wrist, pinning it to the table, his body pressing me back, his cock hard against mine, his lips so close I can taste his breath. "You're mine tonight," he says, his voice a growl, his free hand sliding to my thigh, squeezing, his fingers brushing the edge of my bulge. "Gonna make you feel every fucking inch." His thumb brushes my cock through my jeans, light, teasing, making me gasp, my body arching into him.

"Fuck, Cole," I moan, my voice breaking, my free hand gripping his vest, pulling him closer, our lips brushing, not kissing, just teasing, the tension so thick it's suffocating. "Touch me. Please." My hips buck, chasing his hand, and he grins, his fingers squeezing my thigh, inching higher, but not quite there, keeping me on the edge, making me ache.

"Not yet," he says, his voice low, taunting, his lips brushing mine again, his tongue flicking out, tasting. "Gonna make you wait, roadie. Make you beg for it." His hand slides up, cupping my ass, squeezing hard, his fingers digging in, making me moan louder, my cock throbbing, my body trembling with need. The buildup's killing me, the touch, the words, the way he's playing me like one of his guitars, and I'm so fucking hard, so desperate, but I love it, love the tension, the way it's coiling, ready to snap.

Cole's fingers wrap around my cock, skin hot and rough, stroking slow, his thumb circling the head, smearing the precum that's leaking like a faucet. His leather pants are open, my hand inside, gripping his thick shaft, feeling it pulse, hot and veined, the head slick under my thumb. The dressing room's air is thick, heavy with our sweat, the whiskey on his breath mixing with the musky tang of our arousal, the faint hum of the crew outside a distant buzz. His green eyes lock on mine, dark and hungry, his lips curled in that rockstar smirk that's got me throbbing harder, my balls aching.

"Fuck, you're leaking for me," he murmurs, his voice low, gravelly, his stroke tightening, making me gasp, my hips bucking into his hand. "All that talk, and look at you—cock so hard it's begging.

You want my mouth on it, don't you? Want me to suck you like one of those groupies out there?"

I groan, my hand stroking his cock faster, feeling it twitch, the leather of his pants rough against my wrist. "Yeah, but I want yours first," I say, my voice rough, thick with need, my thumb pressing into his slit, making him hiss. "Bet that rockstar cock tastes like sweat and sin. Let me get on my knees for you, Cole. Been dreaming about choking on it for years."

He laughs, low and dirty, his hand sliding out of my jeans, fingers glistening with my precum, and he brings them to my lips, pushing them in. I suck, tasting myself, salty and bitter, my tongue swirling around his fingers, his eyes darkening as he watches. "You're a greedy fucker," he says, his voice rough, pulling his fingers out with a pop, his hand grabbing my hair, tugging hard. "But yeah, get on your knees. Show me how bad you want this cock."

I drop, my knees hitting the carpet, the dressing room floor rough under me, my hands on his thighs, feeling the muscle flex through the leather. His cock's right there, thick and heavy, veined, the head flushed and leaking, the musky scent of him hitting me hard—sweat, leather, and that raw, primal edge that's got my mouth watering. I lean in, my tongue flicking the head, tasting his precum, bitter and slick, coating my tongue, and he groans, his hand tightening in my hair, guiding me.

"Fuck, yeah," he says, his voice low, commanding, his hips bucking slightly, pushing the head past my lips. I suck slow, my tongue swirling around the tip, savoring the taste, the heat, my hands sliding up his thighs, squeezing the muscle. He's huge, stretching my lips, and I take him deeper, my throat relaxing, sucking harder, the wet sound of my mouth filling the room. "Goddamn, you're good at this," he groans, his voice rough, his fingers tugging my hair, pulling me down, making me gag a little, but I don’t stop, sucking deeper, my tongue working the underside, feeling the vein pulse.

I pull back, gasping, my lips slick, and lick down his shaft, tasting the sweat, the leather tang from his pants, my hands pushing his thighs apart wider. “You taste so fucking good,” I say, my voice hoarse, my lips brushing his balls, heavy and full, the musky scent stronger here, making my cock throb in my jeans. I suck one into my mouth, my tongue swirling, tasting the salt, the sweat, and he moans, loud, his hips bucking, his hand in my hair pulling me closer.

“Fuck, roadie,” he says, his voice breaking, his thighs trembling under my hands. “You’re gonna make me lose it.” I move lower, my tongue sliding behind his balls, teasing the sensitive skin, the musky scent overwhelming, driving me crazy. I spread his thighs wider, my hands gripping the muscle, and lick lower, my tongue flicking his hole, tasting the sweat, the faint leather tang, and he gasps, his body tensing, his moans louder, more desperate.

“Jesus fuck,” he groans, his voice raw, his hips lifting, pushing against my tongue. I’m eating his ass now, my tongue circling the rim, pressing, the taste intense—musky, salty, with the edge of his sweat—and he’s moaning like a slut, his hands gripping the table behind him, his cock twitching above me, leaking precum onto his abs. I spread his cheeks with my hands, my fingers digging into the firm muscle, and push my tongue deeper, teasing, licking, sucking the rim, feeling him clench, his moans loud and broken.

“You like that, rockstar?” I say, my voice muffled against his ass, my tongue flicking fast, making him shudder. “Bet no groupie’s eaten your ass like this. Tastes so fucking good, all sweaty and hot.” I lick deeper, my tongue probing, the musky scent filling my senses, my cock throbbing so hard I'm dizzy, my jeans damp with precum. He's trembling, his thighs shaking, his moans desperate, his hand reaching down to stroke his cock slow, matching my rhythm.

"Fuck, don't stop," he says, his voice wrecked, his hips grinding against my face, chasing my tongue. "You're a filthy bastard, but goddamn, it's good." I keep going, my tongue working his hole, circling, pressing, the taste overwhelming, the heat of him making my cock leak more. My hands squeeze his ass, spreading him wider, my fingers brushing his hole, teasing, not entering yet, building the tension, making him beg.

I pull back, my lips slick, my breath hot against his skin, and stand, my hands on his thighs, pushing him back onto the couch. "Turn over," I say, my voice rough, commanding, and he does, his body pliant, his ass up, the leather pants bunched around his knees. I drop behind him, my hands spreading his cheeks, and dive in again, my tongue licking his hole, deep and slow, tasting him fully, the musky scent stronger, driving me wild. He's moaning louder, his hand stroking his cock under him, his body shaking, the tension so thick it's suffocating.

"God, you're killing me," he groans, his voice raw, his hips pushing back, fucking himself on my tongue. I lick harder, my tongue pressing inside, the tightness gripping me, the taste intense, salty and hot, my hands squeezing his ass, my fingers digging in. My cock's screaming, leaking, but I'm lost in this, in making him moan, in the way his body's surrendering, the rockstar reduced to whimpers under my tongue.

I slide a finger in, slow, the oil from earlier making it slick, and he gasps, his hole clenching, his moans desperate. "Fuck, yes," he says, his voice breaking, his hips bucking. I finger him slow, my tongue still licking around it, the taste, the heat overwhelming, my free hand stroking his thigh, feeling the muscle tense. “More,” he mutters, his voice thick, and I add another finger, stretching him, my tongue teasing the rim, making him cry out, his body trembling.

“Bet you’ve never been this open,” I say, my voice low, my fingers curling inside him, hitting that spot, making him gasp, his cock leaking onto the couch. “All that stage presence, and here you are, ass up for your roadie. You love it, don’t you? Being my slut.”

“Fuck you,” he says, but it’s breathless, his hips grinding back, taking my fingers deeper, his moans loud, desperate. I pull my fingers out, my tongue replacing them, licking deep, the taste so fucking good I’m addicted, my cock throbbing, my balls aching. He’s shaking, his moans raw, the tension building, the air heavy with our sweat, the musky scent of his ass, his cock.

I stand, my hands on his hips, flipping him onto his back again, his cock hard and leaking, his abs slick with precum. I unbutton my jeans, pulling them down, my cock springing free, thick and veined, leaking at the tip. “You ready for this?” I say, my voice rough, stroking my cock slow, my eyes on his, dark and hungry. “Gonna fuck you, Cole. Make you scream my name.”

He grins, shaky, his hand reaching for my cock, squeezing, making me groan. “Do it,” he says, his voice low, challenging, his legs spreading, his hole slick from my tongue. I line up, the head of my cock brushing his hole, teasing, not entering yet, the tension so thick I can barely breathe. “Fuck me, roadie. Show me what you got.”

I push in, slow, the head stretching him, the heat gripping me tight, and he gasps, his eyes fluttering, his hands gripping my arms, nails digging in. “Fuck,” he groans, his voice raw, his ass clenching around me as I slide deeper, inch by inch, the slickness from my spit and his sweat making it smooth but intense. “You’re so fucking big,” he says, his voice breaking, his hips bucking, taking more, his cock twitching against his abs.

I thrust slow at first, deep, feeling every clench, every pulse, my hands on his thighs, pushing them wider, his hole gripping my cock like a vice. “Take it,” I growl, my voice rough, my hips snapping harder, my cock filling him, making him moan loud, desperate. “You’re so tight, Cole. Like a fucking virgin cunt.” I thrust deeper, my cock hitting that spot, making him cry out, his body shaking, his moans raw and broken.

“Fuck, yes,” he groans, his voice wrecked, his hands sliding to my ass, pulling me deeper, his hips meeting my thrusts. I’m fucking him harder now, my cock slamming into him, the wet sound of skin on skin filling the room, his moans loud, his body trembling. The tension's unbearable, my balls tight, my cock throbbing, but I'm not done, not yet, wanting to make him lose it completely.

My cock's buried deep in Cole's tight ass, the heat and grip of him making my head spin as I thrust hard, my hips slamming against his, the slickness of spit and sweat making every slide filthy, intense. His moans are loud, raw, like a fucking whore, his muscular body trembling beneath me, legs spread wide, his hole clenching around my shaft with every thrust. The dressing room's a haze of whiskey, sweat, and musk, the faint thrum of the crew outside barely audible over his groans, the slap of skin on skin, the wet sound of my cock fucking his tight cunt. His green eyes are half-lidded, burning with lust, his blond hair slick with sweat, sticking to his forehead, his leather vest open, chest heaving, abs glistening with precum from his thick cock bouncing against them.

“Fuck, you’re so deep,” he groans, his voice gravelly, wrecked from screaming lyrics and now from me, his hands gripping my biceps, nails digging into my skin, leaving red marks. “You’re tearing me apart, you bastard.” His hips buck up, meeting my thrusts, his ass squeezing my cock, making me growl, my balls aching, my cock throbbing so hard it’s almost painful.

“Love it, don’t you?” I say, my voice low, rough, my lips brushing his ear, my breath hot against his sweat-slicked skin. “Rockstar cunt taking my cock like it’s made for it.” I thrust harder, deeper, my cock hitting that spot that makes him cry out, his moans sharp, desperate, his body arching under me. I grab his hair, yanking his head back, exposing his throat, and bite the skin, hard enough to make him hiss, his hole tightening around me, driving me fucking crazy.

"Goddamn, you're a filthy fuck," he says, his voice breaking, but he's grinning, his eyes wild, his hips grinding back, chasing my cock. "Knew you'd be like this—talking shit, fucking me raw." His hand slides to my ass, squeezing, pulling me deeper, his fingers digging into the muscle, making me groan. I slap his thigh, the sound sharp, his skin reddening under my palm, and he moans louder, his cock leaking more, smearing across his abs.

"Filthy's my specialty," I growl, my hand sliding to his chest, pinching his nipple, twisting just enough to make him gasp, his ass clenching tighter. "Look at you, Cole, moaning like a slut, that tight cunt begging for more." I thrust faster, my hips snapping, my cock slamming into him, the wet sound of our bodies obscene, filling the room. His moans are loud, raw, his body trembling, his cock bouncing with every thrust, thick and veined, the head flushed, leaking precum in thick beads.

I lean down, my tongue licking a stripe up his neck, tasting the salt, the musk, his stubble scraping my lips. “You taste like fucking trouble,” I say, my voice thick, my teeth grazing his jaw, my thrusts slowing but deeper, making him feel every inch. His hand slides to my neck, pulling me into a kiss, his lips rough, hungry, his tongue pushing into my mouth, tasting of whiskey and sweat, his moans vibrating against me. I kiss him back, hard, my tongue battling his, my cock still fucking him deep, his ass gripping me like he never wants me to stop.

“Fuck, you’re gonna ruin me,” he murmurs against my lips, his voice wrecked, his hand sliding down my back, nails scratching, leaving trails of heat. “Keep going, you prick. Make me feel it.” His hips buck harder, his ass taking my cock deeper, his moans louder, more desperate, like he’s losing control, and it’s driving me fucking insane, my balls tight, my cock throbbing, the tension so thick I can barely breathe.

I pull back, grabbing his legs, pushing them higher, his knees almost to his chest, his hole open, slick, and I thrust harder, my cock slamming into him, making him cry out, his voice raw, broken. “Take it, rockstar,” I growl, my hand slapping his ass, the crack loud, his cheek jiggling, red from the sting. “Scream for me, let the whole fucking crew hear you.” He moans louder, his head tipping back, his hands gripping the couch, knuckles white, his cock leaking so much it’s pooling on his abs, glistening in the dim light.

“Fuck you,” he gasps, but it’s breathless, his eyes burning, his hips bucking, meeting every thrust. “You’re such a cocky bastard... but goddamn, it’s good.” His voice is thick, his words slurring with pleasure, and I grin, my hand sliding to his cock, stroking slow, matching my thrusts, feeling it pulse, hot and heavy in my palm. He groans, his body trembling, his ass clenching, making my cock throb harder, my balls aching, but I'm holding back, wanting to push him further, make him break.

I pull out, my cock slick, glistening, and flip him onto his stomach, his ass up, perfect and muscular, slick with sweat and spit. "Spread for me," I say, my voice rough, my hands on his cheeks, spreading them, his hole tight, pink, glistening. I dive in, my tongue licking slow, tasting the musk, the sweat, the faint tang of my own precum from fucking him. He moans, loud, his hips pushing back, fucking himself on my tongue, his hands gripping the couch, his body shaking.

"Jesus, you're killing me," he groans, his voice raw, his ass clenching around my tongue as I lick deeper, circling the rim, teasing, sucking. The taste is intense, salty and hot, his musk overwhelming, driving me wild. My cock's throbbing, leaking, but I'm focused on him, on making him moan, on the way his body's surrendering. “Fuck, your tongue… you’re too fucking good,” he says, his voice breaking, his hips grinding, his cock trapped against the couch, leaking more.

“Love this tight cunt,” I say, my voice muffled, my tongue probing deeper, my hands squeezing his cheeks, spreading him wide. “Bet you’ve never had it like this, rockstar. All those groupies, and none of them can eat your ass like me.” I lick harder, my tongue pressing inside, feeling him clench, his moans loud, desperate, his body trembling under me. I slide a finger in, slow, slick from my spit, and he gasps, his hole gripping me, his hips bucking.

“Fuck, yes,” he groans, his voice wrecked, his hand reaching back, grabbing my hair, pulling me closer. “Don’t stop, you bastard. Keep going.” I finger him slow, my tongue still licking, teasing the rim, the taste, the heat driving me crazy. My free hand strokes my cock, slow, keeping myself on edge, my balls tight, my cock leaking onto the floor.

I pull back, my lips slick, and climb over him, lining my cock up again, pushing in slow, the head stretching his hole, making him moan, his body arching. “Take it,” I say, my voice rough, my cock sliding deeper, filling him, his ass gripping me tight. I thrust hard, my hips snapping, my cock slamming into him, making him cry out, his moans loud, raw, like he’s lost all control. “You’re my fucking slut now,” I growl, my hand slapping his ass, the sound sharp, his cheek red, jiggling under my palm.

“Goddamn, you’re relentless,” he says, his voice breaking, his hips bucking back, taking my cock deeper, his moans desperate. “Fuck me harder, you prick. Make me feel it.” I do, my thrusts brutal, my cock hitting deep, his ass clenching, his body shaking, his cock leaking onto the couch. The tension’s unbearable, the air thick with our sweat, the musky scent of his ass, his cock, the whiskey on his breath.

I pull out, my cock slick, and grab his hair, pulling him up, his body pliant, his eyes wild. "On your knees," I say, my voice rough, stroking my cock fast, my balls tight, ready to explode. He drops, his lips parted, his tongue out, and I'm stroking harder, the head of my cock brushing his lips, teasing. "Want it in your mouth, rockstar?" I say, my voice thick, my hand in his hair, holding him there.

"Fuck, yes," he groans, his voice raw, his eyes locked on my cock, his lips brushing the head, tasting my precum. "Give it to me, you bastard." I push in, my cock sliding past his lips, hot and wet, his tongue swirling, sucking hard, making me groan, my hips bucking. He's sucking like he's starving, his hands on my thighs, squeezing, his moans vibrating around my cock.

I'm right there, my balls tight, my cock throbbing, and I pull out, stroking fast, my hand a blur. "Open wide," I growl, and he does, his tongue out, his eyes burning, and I cum hard, thick ropes of cum shooting into his mouth, splattering his lips, his tongue, dripping down his chin. "Fuck," I groan, my voice raw, my hips jerking, milking every drop, his tongue licking, swallowing, tasting me, his eyes locked on mine, wild and hungry.

He's panting, his lips slick with my cum, his cock still hard, leaking, and I'm not done, the tension still crackling, the air heavy with what's next. I grab his vest, pulling him up, kissing him hard, tasting my cum on his lips, his tongue, and he groans, his hands gripping my ass, pulling me closer, our cocks brushing, the heat between us far from over.

LEATHER LUST

I'm thirty-six, built like a linebacker who's traded the field for the gym—broad shoulders, thick pecs, and a narrow waist carved from years of heavy lifting and strict discipline. My chestnut hair's cropped close, with a slight wave, a few gray strands creeping in at the sides, giving me a rugged edge. My hazel eyes are sharp, always watching, catching every glint of desire in a crowded room. My jaw's chiseled, dusted with a five o'clock shadow that's more grit than polish, and my lips curve into a smirk that's gotten me into trouble more times than I can count. I'm gay, unapologetic, and I've got a thing for leather—black, sleek, tight, the kind that hugs muscle and smells like sin. Tonight, I'm in my element, clad in a black leather jacket, open to show my bare chest, the sheen of sweat catching the dim light, and leather pants that cling to my thighs, my cock already half-hard, straining against the zipper, no underwear, just the raw feel of leather on skin. My boots, polished to a mirror shine, thud softly on the club floor, and a leather cuff on my wrist completes the look, a signal to those who know.

The club's a dungeon of pulsing bass and flickering neon, the air thick with the scent of sweat, bourbon, and leather, the kind of place where desires are laid bare under strobe lights. It's past midnight, the crowd a mix of hard bodies and hungry eyes, leather vests and chaps mingling with bare skin and chains. I'm leaning against the bar, a whiskey in hand, the glass cold against my palm, when I spot him across the room, moving through the crowd like he owns it. He's younger, maybe thirty, with a body that's all lean muscle, like a panther—sleek, powerful, built for speed. His black hair's slicked back, a few strands falling over his forehead, framing eyes so dark they're almost black, smoldering with a mix of confidence and curiosity. His skin's a warm tan, smooth except for a faint scar on his cheek, giving him a dangerous edge. His lips are full, curled into a half-smile, and he's wearing a leather harness that crisscrosses his bare chest, accentuating his defined pecs, his nipples hard in the cool air. Black leather pants hug his thighs, the bulge obvious, thick and promising, and his boots are scuffed, like he's been in places rougher than this. He's straight, or so he's told the guys at the bar, but the way his eyes keep finding mine, lingering on my bare chest, my leather-clad cock, says he's not so sure tonight.

I take a sip of whiskey, the burn sharp, and let my gaze rake over him, slow and deliberate, catching the way his throat bobs, his fingers flexing around his beer bottle. My cock twitches, pressing harder against the leather, the material creaking as I shift my weight, the friction sending a jolt through me. "You keep staring, man," I call out, my voice low, carrying over the thump of the music, my smirk widening as his eyes snap to mine, a flush creeping up his neck. "Something you like?" I set my glass down, stepping away from the bar, my boots thudding on the floor, closing the distance between us, the crowd parting like they know what's coming.

He laughs, a short, nervous sound, his fingers tightening around the bottle, his eyes flicking to my chest, the leather jacket open, my nipples hard from the cool air and the thrill of his gaze. "Just—fuck, just checking out the scene," he says, his voice deep, with a gravelly edge that hits me right in the gut, making my cock throb, the leather pants tight, almost painful. "You're, uh, hard to miss in that getup." His eyes linger on my pants, the bulge obvious, and I catch the way his own cock stirs, the leather stretching, a faint outline of the head showing through.

"Hard to miss, huh?" I grin, stepping closer, close enough to smell the leather of his harness, the clean sweat of his skin, a hint of sandalwood from whatever cologne he's wearing. "You're not doing so bad yourself, that harness showing off those pecs." I let my fingers brush the strap of his harness, just a graze, feeling the smooth leather, the heat of his skin underneath, and he tenses, his breath hitching, but he doesn't pull away. My cock's fully hard now, straining against the leather, the zipper biting into my skin, and I shift, letting him see the bulge, the way the leather molds to every inch.

He swallows hard, his eyes flicking to my crotch, then back to my face, his flush deepening, his lips parting slightly. "Fuck, man, you don't hold back, do you?" he says, his voice quieter now, a tremor in it, like he's fighting something inside, his straight-guy facade cracking under the weight of my gaze. His hand shifts, brushing his own bulge, adjusting it, and I catch the faint sheen of sweat on his chest, the harness gleaming, his nipples peaking harder, begging to be touched.

“Hold back? Not my style,” I say, my voice a low drawl, my hand lingering on his harness, my thumb brushing the leather, grazing the edge of his pec, feeling the muscle flex under my touch. “Bet you’re wondering what this leather feels like, sliding off, my hands on you instead.” I lean in, my breath hot against his ear, not touching but close enough to make him shiver, his beer bottle trembling in his hand. “Or maybe you’re thinking about my cock, hard as fuck in these pants, just for you.”

“Fuck off,” he mutters, but it’s weak, more reflex than conviction, and his eyes betray him, darting to my bulge again, lingering on the tight leather, the outline of my cock clear, throbbing, leaking precum that’s starting to dampen the inside of my pants. “I’m not—shit, I’m not into that,” he says, but his voice shakes, and he’s not moving away, his body angled toward me, his bulge growing, the leather pants stretching tight, showing every inch of his hard cock.

I chuckle, my hand sliding to his shoulder, feeling the leather harness, the heat of his skin, my fingers tracing the strap, slow and deliberate, making his breath hitch. “Not into it? Bullshit,” I say, my voice low, teasing, my thumb brushing his collarbone, feeling the pulse racing under his skin. “Your cock’s saying something else, man. Bet it’s rock-hard, leaking in those pants, just from me standing here.” I step closer, our boots almost touching, the air between us electric, thick with the scent of leather and sweat, my cock aching, the leather creaking with every move.

“You’re—fuck, you’re trouble,” he says, his voice hoarse, his hand twitching like he wants to touch me but can’t quite cross that line. His eyes flick to my lips, then lower, to the open jacket, my bare chest, the sweat beading on my pecs, and I catch the way his cock twitches, the leather pants straining, a faint wet spot forming where he's leaking. "I've got a girlfriend, you know," he adds, but it's half-hearted, like he's trying to remind himself, his eyes locked on mine, dark and hungry, the guilt fading under the heat.

"Girlfriend, huh?" I grin, my hand sliding to his chest, brushing the harness, my fingers grazing his nipple, hard and sensitive, making him gasp, his hips jerking slightly. "She's not here, is she? Just you and me, in all this leather, with your cock begging for attention." I pinch his nipple through the harness, just enough to make him moan, a low, needy sound that hits me right in the dick, making it throb harder, the leather pants so tight it's almost unbearable.

"Goddamn it," he groans, his hand finally moving, brushing my hip, hesitant, his fingers grazing the leather of my pants, feeling the heat, the hardness underneath. "You're—shit, you're making it hard to think." His touch is clumsy, unsure, but it's there, his fingers lingering, tracing the seam of my pants, brushing the bulge, making my cock twitch, leaking more, the precum soaking the leather inside.

I lean in, my lips inches from his, not kissing but teasing, my breath hot against his mouth, the scent of whiskey and leather mixing with his sandalwood. “Don’t need to think,” I murmur, my voice a low growl, my hand sliding to his neck, feeling the pulse hammering under my fingers, my thumb brushing the stubble along his jaw. “Just feel this. Feel how fucking good it is.” I tug at his harness, pulling him closer, our chests brushing, his bare skin against my open jacket, the leather creaking, his nipple grazing mine, sending a jolt through me.

“Fuck, man,” he breathes, his hand bolder now, sliding to my waist, fingers digging into the leather, pulling me closer, his bulge brushing my thigh, the leather pants slick with sweat, his cock hard, straining, leaking. “This is—fuck, this is crazy.” His eyes meet mine, wild, conflicted, but his hand doesn't stop, sliding lower, brushing the bulge in my pants, feeling the outline of my cock, making me groan, my hips rocking into his touch.

I grin, my hand sliding to his ass, squeezing the firm muscle through the leather, feeling it clench under my touch, the material warm, slick with sweat. "Crazy's what makes your cock so hard, leaking in that leather," I say, my voice low, my fingers teasing the seam of his pants, brushing the crease of his ass, making him shudder. "Bet you're imagining me peeling these off, getting my hands on that dick, making you moan louder than you ever have." I lean in, my lips brushing his ear, nipping the lobe, tasting the sweat, the heat, and he moans, his hand tightening on my bulge, stroking through the leather, clumsy but eager.

"You're—shit, you're gonna get me in trouble," he says, his voice trembling, his hand sliding under my jacket, brushing my bare chest, fingers tracing the lines of my pecs, thumbs grazing my nipples, sending sparks through me. “I’m not—fuck, I’m not supposed to want this.” His eyes flick to my lips, then lower, to the bulge in my pants, the leather stretched tight, the outline of my cock clear, throbbing, leaking more, the precum soaking the inside.

“Then stop me,” I challenge, my voice low, my hand squeezing his ass, pulling him closer, our bulges grinding together, the leather creaking, the friction electric, making us both groan. “Push me away, tell me you don’t want this.” I kiss his neck, sucking lightly, tasting the salt, the sandalwood, my tongue flicking out, feeling his pulse race under my lips. His hand tightens on my bulge, stroking harder, his fingers bold now, tracing the length of my cock through the leather, making my head spin.

He doesn't push me away. Instead, his hand slides to my chest, pinching my nipple, rolling it between his fingers, making me moan, my hips bucking into his touch. "Fuck, I—I want it," he admits, his voice breaking, his eyes wild, locked on mine. "You're—shit, you're making me want it so bad." His words are a surrender, raw and desperate, and it's like a switch flips, his hand sliding to my ass, squeezing the leather, his fingers teasing the seam, brushing my crack, making my cock throb, aching for more.

I laugh, low and dirty, my lips brushing his jaw, kissing the stubble, tasting the sweat. "That's it, big guy," I murmur, my hand sliding inside his harness, brushing his bare chest, pinching his nipple, making him gasp, his hips bucking. "Show me how bad you want it." I tug at his pants, pulling the zipper down just enough to expose the base of his cock, the dark hair damp with sweat, his cock straining, leaking through the leather, and he moans, loud and needy, his hand tightening on my bulge, stroking faster, the club a haze of leather and lust, the tension unbearable, electric, ready to snap but holding, just barely.

His hand is on my bulge, fingers tracing the outline of my cock through the tight leather pants, his touch bold but trembling, like he’s teetering on the edge of surrender. The club pulses around us, the bass thumping through the floor, the air thick with the scent of leather, sweat, and bourbon, the neon lights casting jagged shadows across his tanned skin. His leather harness gleams, crisscrossing his bare chest, his nipples hard, peeking through the straps, his pecs flexing with every ragged breath. My jacket’s open, my bare chest slick with sweat, the leather pants creaking as my cock strains, leaking precum that soaks the inside, the zipper biting into my skin. His pants are unzipped just enough to show the dark hair at the base of his cock, the bulge massive, throbbing, a wet spot spreading where he’s leaking, his boots scuffed, planted firm on the floor, his thighs tense, powerful.

"Fuck, you're—shit, you're making me crazy," he rasps, his voice low, cracking with need, his dark eyes locked on mine, pupils blown wide, flickering with guilt but burning with want. His fingers dig into the leather, stroking my cock through the fabric, slow and deliberate, making my hips buck, my cock throbbing harder, aching for more. "This is—fuck, I shouldn't be doing this." His words are shaky, but his hand doesn't stop, sliding to my hip, fingers brushing the bare skin above my waistband, sending a jolt through me, my breath hitching.

I grin, my hand sliding to his chest, fingers hooking under the harness, tugging it, pulling him closer, our bodies inches apart, the heat radiating off his skin, the leather creaking. "Shouldn't? Your cock's saying something else," I murmur, my voice a low growl, my lips brushing his ear, nipping the lobe, tasting the salt of his sweat, the faint sandalwood of his cologne. "Bet it's leaking like a faucet, begging for my hands." My fingers graze his nipple through the harness, pinching lightly, and he gasps, his hips jerking, his bulge brushing my thigh, the leather slick with sweat, the friction electric.

“Goddamn it,” he groans, his hand sliding to my ass, squeezing the leather, fingers digging into the muscle, pulling me closer, our bulges grinding together, making us both moan, low and needy. “You’re—fuck, you’re too much.” His voice trembles, his fingers bolder now, slipping under the waistband of my pants, brushing the bare skin of my hip, the contact sending sparks through me, my cock throbbing, leaking more, the precum soaking the leather inside. His eyes flick to my lips, then lower, to the open jacket, my bare chest, the sweat beading on my pecs, and I catch the hunger in his gaze, the straight-guy facade cracking.

I laugh, low and dirty, my hand sliding to his neck, feeling the pulse hammering under my fingers, my thumb brushing the stubble along his jaw. “Too much? You’re the one groping my ass like you can't get enough," I say, my voice a low purr, my fingers tugging the harness, pulling him closer, our chests brushing, his bare skin hot against mine, the leather straps rough against my nipples. "Bet you're imagining peeling this leather off me, getting your hands on my cock." I lean in, my lips grazing his throat, kissing the sweat-slicked skin, tasting the salt, the sandalwood, and he moans, his hand tightening on my ass, his fingers teasing the seam, brushing my crack through the leather.

"Fuck, man," he breathes, his voice hoarse, his hand sliding to my chest, fingers brushing my nipple, pinching lightly, making me groan, my hips bucking into his touch. "This is—shit, this is insane." His eyes meet mine, wild, conflicted, but his hand doesn't stop, sliding lower, brushing the bulge in my pants again, stroking the outline of my cock, making my head spin. His cock twitches against my thigh, the leather pants stretched tight, the wet spot growing, his precum soaking through, and I grin, my hand sliding to his ass, squeezing hard, feeling the muscle clench under the leather.

“Insane’s good,” I murmur, my lips brushing his ear, my tongue flicking out, tasting the sweat, the heat, making him shudder. “Insane’s what makes you grab me like this, your cock hard as fuck, leaking in that leather.” My fingers tease the zipper of his pants, pulling it lower, exposing more of his bulge, the black hair at the base of his cock damp with sweat, his cock straining, thick and veiny, begging to be touched. “Bet you’re dying to feel my hands on you, stroking that dick, making you moan louder than you ever have.” I kiss his collarbone, sucking lightly, leaving a faint mark, feeling his pulse race under my lips.

“You’re—fuck, you’re gonna get us caught,” he says, his voice trembling, but his hand slides to my back, fingers digging into the muscle, pulling me closer, our bulges grinding together, the leather creaking, the friction making us both groan. "I've got a girlfriend, man. This is—shit, this is wrong." His words are weak, the guilt about his girlfriend fading under the heat, the want, the way his cock pulses against my thigh, leaking more, the wet spot stark against the leather.

"Wrong?" I chuckle, my hand sliding inside his harness, brushing his bare chest, pinching his nipple, rolling it between my fingers, making him gasp, his hips bucking. "Feels pretty fucking right to me." I lean in, kissing his chest, my tongue flicking over his nipple, sucking hard, tasting the sweat, the musk, and he moans, loud and needy, his hand tightening on my bulge, stroking faster, his fingers bold now, tracing the length of my cock through the leather. "Look at you, leaking already, ready to burst just from my touch," I murmur, my lips against his skin, my hand squeezing his ass, fingers teasing the crease through the leather, making him shudder.

“Goddamn, you’re—shit, you’re relentless,” he groans, his hand sliding under my jacket, brushing my bare abs, fingers tracing the lines of muscle, the sweat slicking my skin. “I’m not—fuck, I’m not supposed to feel like this.” His touch is bolder, his fingers slipping lower, brushing the waistband of my pants, teasing the bare skin above, sending a jolt through me, my cock throbbing, leaking more, the precum soaking the leather inside. His eyes meet mine, dark and wild, the guilt drowning in the lust, the need, the way our bodies are pressed together, leather on leather, cocks hard, hands groping.

I grin, my hand sliding to his face, cupping his jaw, my thumb brushing his lips, feeling the soft, full curve, the faint stubble scraping my skin. “Feel like what? Like you wanna rip this leather off me, get your hands on my cock?” I murmur, my voice low, my lips inches from his, not kissing but teasing, my breath hot against his mouth. "Bet you're imagining it, my hands on your dick, my tongue on your hole, making you scream." I tug at his harness, pulling him closer, our bulges grinding harder, the leather creaking, the friction electric, making us both moan, low and needy.

"Fuck, stop," he says, but it's half-hearted, his voice trembling, his hand sliding to my ass again, squeezing hard, fingers digging into the leather, teasing the seam, brushing my crack, making my cock throb, aching for more. "This is—fuck, this is too much." His eyes flick to my lips, then lower, to the open jacket, my bare chest, the sweat beading on my pecs, and I catch the hunger, the curiosity, the straight-guy resolve crumbling under the weight of this moment.

"Then make me," I challenge, my voice low, my hand sliding to his bulge, cupping it through the leather, feeling the thick, pulsing heat, the fabric slick with precum. "Push me away, tell me you don't want this." I stroke slow, deliberate, my thumb circling the head through the leather, and he gasps, his hips bucking into my hand, his eyes fluttering shut for a second, his breath ragged. I lean in, kissing his neck, sucking hard, leaving a mark, tasting the salt, the sandalwood, feeling his pulse race under my lips.

He doesn't push me away. Instead, his hand slides to my chest, pinching my nipple, rolling it between his fingers, making me groan, my hips bucking into his touch. "Fuck, I—I want it," he admits, his voice breaking, his eyes wild, locked on mine. "You're—shit, you're making me want it so bad." His words are a surrender, raw and desperate, and it's like a dam breaking, his hand sliding to my bulge again, stroking harder, his fingers bold, tracing the length of my cock through the leather, making my head spin.

I laugh, low and dirty, my lips brushing his jaw, kissing the stubble, tasting the sweat. “That’s it, big guy,” I murmur, my hand sliding inside his pants, brushing the base of his cock, the dark hair damp with sweat, his cock straining, leaking more, soaking the leather. “Show me how bad you want it.” I tug at his harness, pulling him closer, our chests pressed together, his bare skin hot against mine, the leather straps rough, his nipple grazing mine, sending sparks through me. His hand tightens on my bulge, stroking faster, his fingers teasing the zipper, brushing the bare skin above, making my cock throb, leaking more, the precum soaking the leather inside.

“Goddamn, you’re—fuck, you’re gonna ruin me,” he groans, his voice hoarse, his hand sliding to my back, fingers digging into the muscle, pulling me closer, our bulges grinding together, the leather creaking, the friction unbearable. “I shouldn’t—shit, I shouldn’t be doing this.” His eyes meet mine, wild, conflicted, but his touch is sure, his fingers slipping under the waistband of my pants, brushing the bare skin of my hip, teasing closer to my cock, making me moan, my hips rocking into his touch.

I grin, my hand sliding to his ass, squeezing hard, fingers teasing the crease through the leather, brushing his crack, making him shudder. "Ruin you? I'm just giving you what you want," I murmur, my lips kissing his chest, my tongue flicking over his nipple, sucking hard, tasting the sweat, the musk, savoring the way his body arches, his cock twitching against my thigh. "Bet you're dying for more, aren't you? My hands on your cock, my tongue on your hole, making you lose it." I kiss his collarbone, sucking lightly, leaving another mark, feeling his pulse race under my lips.

"Fuck, yes," he moans, his voice high, desperate, his hands grabbing my face, pulling me closer, our lips inches apart, not kissing but teasing, his breath hot against my mouth. "You're—

shit, you're making me want it so bad." His words are a confession, raw and filthy, and I grin, my hand stroking his bulge, keeping him on edge, my fingers teasing the base of his cock, feeling it pulse, thick and heavy, the leather slick with precum.

His lips are inches from mine, his breath hot and ragged, the sandalwood scent of his cologne mixing with the raw musk of sweat and leather, driving my cock wild, throbbing against the tight leather pants, precum soaking the inside. The club pulses around us, the bass vibrating through the floor, neon lights casting jagged shadows across his tanned skin, his leather harness gleaming, straps digging into his pecs, nipples hard and begging. My jacket's open, my bare chest slick with sweat, the leather cuff on my wrist creaking as I flex my hand, my cock straining, the zipper biting into my skin. His pants are unzipped, the base of his cock exposed, dark hair damp, his bulge massive, leaking through the leather, a wet spot spreading, his boots scuffed, thighs tense, quivering with need.

“Fuck, you’re—shit, you’re making me lose it,” he groans, his voice hoarse, cracking with desire, his dark eyes wild, locked on mine, pupils blown. His hand’s on my bulge, stroking through the leather, fingers bold but trembling, tracing the thick outline of my cock, making my hips buck, my breath hitching. “This is—fuck, I can’t stop.” His fingers dig into my ass, squeezing the leather, teasing the seam, brushing my crack, sending sparks through me, my cock throbbing harder, aching for more.

I grin, my hand grabbing his harness, yanking him closer, our chests colliding, his bare skin hot against mine, the leather straps rough, scraping my nipples. “Lose it? You’re already fucking gone,” I growl, my lips brushing his jaw, tasting the stubble, the salt of his sweat, my tongue flicking out, licking a slow stripe up his neck. “Your cock’s leaking like a slut, begging for me.” I slap his ass, hard, the sound sharp over the club’s bass, making him gasp, his hips jerking, his bulge grinding against my thigh, the leather slick with precum.

"Goddamn it," he moans, his hand sliding to my chest, fingers pinching my nipple, rolling it, sending a jolt straight to my cock, making me groan, low and needy. "You're—fuck, you're too much." His voice trembles, but his fingers are bold, slipping under my jacket, brushing my abs, tracing the sweat-slicked muscle, his touch hungry, no longer hesitant. I grab his wrist, pinning it above his head against the wall, the power shift making his eyes widen, his breath hitching, his cock twitching against my thigh, leaking more.

"Too much?" I chuckle, my voice a low purr, my free hand sliding to his armpit, fingers brushing the coarse hair, damp with sweat, the musky scent hitting me hard, raw and masculine, making my cock throb. "You're the one grinding on me, your dick hard as fuck in that leather." I lean in, my nose burying in his pit, inhaling deep, the smell intoxicating, sweat and musk and sandalwood, driving me wild. I lick the hair, tasting the salt, the raw heat, and he moans, loud and desperate, his body arching, his pinned wrist flexing against my grip.

"Fuck, man," he gasps, his voice high, wrecked, his free hand grabbing my hair, tugging hard, pulling me closer, his pit pressed against my face. "You're—shit, you're filthy." His words are slurred, drowned in lust, his cock pulsing against my thigh, the leather pants stretched tight, the wet spot growing, his precum soaking through. I pull back, slapping his face lightly, just enough to sting, his eyes flashing with shock and heat, his lips parting, begging for more.

"Filthy? You love it," I growl, my lips crashing into his, the kiss hard and sloppy, all teeth and tongue, tasting the sweat, the musk, swallowing his moans. My hand slides to his bulge, stroking through the leather, feeling the thick, veiny heat, my thumb circling the head, smearing precum, making him cry out into my mouth, his hips bucking. “Bet you’re imagining my mouth on your cock, sucking you dry,” I murmur against his lips, my hand releasing his wrist, sliding to his other pit, fingers digging into the damp hair, inhaling the scent, licking the sweat, savoring the taste, raw and primal.

“Goddamn, yes,” he moans, his voice breaking, his hands grabbing my jacket, yanking it open further, fingers roaming my chest, pinching my nipples, making me groan, my cock throbbing, leaking more, the leather pants soaked inside. “You’re—fuck, you’re driving me insane.” His touch is desperate, his fingers bold, slipping lower, brushing the zipper of my pants, teasing the bare skin above, sending a jolt through me, my hips rocking into his hand.

I pull back, grabbing his harness, spinning him around, pushing him face-first against the wall, his ass out, the leather pants tight, hugging his cheeks, his hole hidden but begging. "You want insane?" I growl, my hand slapping his ass again, harder, the sound echoing, making him moan, his body trembling, his cock twitching against the wall. "I'll give you fucking insane." I lean in, kissing his neck, sucking hard, leaving a mark, my tongue licking the sweat, tasting the sandalwood, my hand sliding to his pit again, inhaling deep, the musky scent driving my cock wild, throbbing against the leather.

"Fuck, do it," he groans, his voice high, desperate, his hands braced against the wall, his ass pushing back, grinding against my bulge, the leather creaking, the friction electric. "I'm—shit, I want it so bad." His words are a surrender, raw and filthy, his body trembling, his pit damp under my fingers, the scent intoxicating, making my head spin. I slap his ass again, the leather stinging my palm, and he cries out, his hips bucking, his cock leaking, soaking the front of his pants.

I drop to my knees, my lips kissing the back of his thigh, tasting the leather, the sweat, my tongue licking a slow stripe up to his ass, nipping the leather, feeling the muscle clench underneath. “Fuck, you smell so good,” I growl, my nose pressing against his ass, inhaling the leather, the musk, the raw heat of him, my cock throbbing, aching to be free. I tug at his pants, pulling them lower, exposing the base of his ass, the dark hair damp, his hole hidden but close, begging for my tongue. I lick the bare skin, tasting the sweat, the musk, and he moans, loud and needy, his hands clawing at the wall, his body trembling.

“Goddamn, you’re—fuck, you’re killing me,” he gasps, his voice wrecked, his ass pushing back, chasing my tongue, his cock twitching, leaking more, dripping onto the floor. I stand, grabbing his harness, yanking him back against me, my bulge grinding against his ass, the leather slick, the friction making us both groan. “Do it, man—fuck, I need it,” he pleads, his voice high, desperate, his body trembling, his pit exposed as he raises his arm, the musky scent hitting me again, driving me wild.

I lean in, burying my face in his pit, inhaling deep, licking the damp hair, tasting the salt, the musk, my tongue relentless, savoring the raw masculinity of him. “You need my cock, don’t you?” I growl, my lips against his skin, my hand sliding to his bulge, stroking hard, feeling it pulse, thick and veiny, the leather soaked with precum. I slap his face again, lightly, the sting making his eyes flash, his lips parting, his moan loud, echoing over the club’s bass. “Say it, big guy. Tell me you want my cock.”

“Fuck, yes,” he moans, his voice breaking, his hands grabbing my jacket, pulling me closer, our lips crashing together, the kiss feral, tongues fucking, tasting sweat, musk, leather. “I want it—shit, I want your cock.” His words are raw, desperate, his body surrendering, his cock pulsing in my hand, leaking more, soaking the leather. I grin, my hand sliding to his ass, squeezing hard, fingers teasing his crack through the leather, brushing his hole, making him shudder, his moans louder, needier.

I push him to his knees, his face level with my bulge, the leather pants stretched tight, my cock throbbing, leaking, the precum soaking the inside. “Suck it,” I growl, my voice low, commanding, my hand grabbing his hair, tugging hard, making him moan, his lips parting, his eyes wild, locked on my bulge. I unzip my pants, my cock springing free, thick and veiny, slick with precum, and he gasps, his breath hot against the head, his tongue flicking out, tasting me, the contact electric, making my hips buck.

“Fuck, you’re—shit, you’re huge,” he groans, his voice trembling, his hands grabbing my thighs, fingers digging into the leather, his tongue licking the head, slow and hesitant, tasting the precum, sharp and musky. I moan, my hand tightening in his hair, guiding him, my cock throbbing, aching for his mouth. He sucks the head, his lips stretching, his tongue swirling, clumsy but eager, and I groan, my hips rocking, fucking his mouth, the wet heat driving me wild.

“Goddamn, that’s it,” I growl, my voice thick, my hand slapping his ass again, the leather stinging, making him moan around my cock, the vibration sending sparks through me. I pull back, my cock slick with his spit, glistening, and push him back against the wall, his ass out, his pants low, his hole exposed, pink and tight, begging for me. “You’re gonna take my cock, aren’t you?” I murmur, my hand stroking my cock, slick with his spit, pressing it against his hole, not pushing in, just teasing, feeling the heat, the tightness.

“Yes, fuck, yes,” he moans, his voice high, desperate, his hands braced against the wall, his ass pushing back, his hole clenching, begging for my cock. I slap his ass again, hard, the sound sharp, making him cry out, his body trembling, his cock leaking, dripping onto the floor. I lean in, kissing his neck, sucking hard, leaving a mark, my tongue licking the sweat, tasting the sandalwood, my cock pressing harder against his hole, breaching it, slow and deliberate, making him gasp, a sharp, needy sound that fills the club.

“Fuck, you’re tight,” I groan, pushing in deeper, inch by inch, feeling his hole clench, hot and slick, pulling me in. He moans, loud and shameless, his hands clawing at the wall, his body trembling, his cock pulsing, leaking more, dripping onto the floor. “Taking my cock so well,” I murmur, my lips kissing his back, licking the sweat, tasting the musk, my hips rocking slow, letting him adjust, savoring the tightness, the heat. I slap his ass again, the leather stinging, and he cries out, his hole clenching tighter, making my cock throb, aching to pound harder.

"Goddamn, fuck me," he pleads, his voice wrecked, his hips bucking back, meeting my thrusts, his hole pulling me deeper, his cock bouncing, leaking onto the floor. I grin, my hand sliding to his pit again, inhaling deep, licking the damp hair, tasting the salt, the musk, my tongue relentless, driving him wild. "Harder—shit, fuck me harder," he moans, his voice high, desperate, his body trembling, drowned in pleasure, the club a haze of leather and lust, our bodies slick with sweat, cocks throbbing, the tension unbearable, electric, pushing us closer to the edge but not there yet, not until I drive him further, make him lose it completely.

His hole clenches tight around my cock, hot and slick, pulling me deeper with every thrust, his moans loud and desperate, echoing over the club's pulsing bass. The air's thick with the scent of leather, sweat, and raw musk, neon lights casting sharp shadows across his tanned skin, his leather harness gleaming, straps digging into his pecs, nipples hard and flushed. My jacket's open, my bare chest slick with sweat, the leather cuff on my wrist creaking as I grip his hips, my leather pants unzipped, my cock buried in him, throbbing, leaking precum that mixes with his heat. His pants are low, bunched around his thighs, his cock bouncing, thick and veiny, leaking onto the floor, his boots scuffed, scraping the concrete as he braces against the wall, his ass pushing back, meeting every snap of my hips.

"Fuck, you're—shit, you're wrecking me," he groans, his voice hoarse, wrecked, his hands clawing at the wall, knuckles white, his body trembling, his hole clenching tighter, making my cock throb, aching to pound harder. I slap his ass, the leather stinging my palm, the sound sharp, making him cry out, his hips bucking, his cock twitching, leaking more, dripping onto the floor. "Harder—

fuck, give it to me," he pleads, his voice high, desperate, his eyes wild, glancing back at me, pupils blown, drowned in lust.

I grin, my lips crashing into his neck, sucking hard, leaving a mark, my tongue licking the sweat, tasting the sandalwood, the raw musk of him. "You want it hard, huh?" I growl, my hips snapping forward, pounding deep, the slick sound of skin on skin mixing with his moans, the creak of leather, the thump of the bass. My hand slides to his pit, fingers digging into the damp hair, inhaling deep, the musky scent hitting me like a drug, raw and masculine, driving my cock wild. I lick his pit, slow and deliberate, tasting the salt, the heat, and he moans louder, his body shuddering, his hole clenching, pulling me deeper.

"Goddamn, you're—fuck, you're filthy," he gasps, his voice breaking, his hands braced against the wall, his ass pushing back, taking every thrust, his cock pulsing, leaking, dripping onto the floor. I slap his face lightly, the sting making his eyes flash, his lips parting, his moan raw, needy. "You love this, don't you? Me licking your pits, fucking you like a slut," I murmur, my lips brushing his ear, nipping the lobe, my hand stroking his cock, keeping him on edge, the head flushed red, slick with precum, throbbing in my grip.

"Yes, fuck, yes," he moans, his voice high, desperate, his hips rocking back, meeting my thrusts, his hole clenching tighter, making my cock throb, aching to come but holding, just barely. I pull out, making him whimper, his hole clenching, empty and begging, and I spin him around, pushing him to his knees, his face level with my cock, slick with his heat, glistening with precum. "Suck it," I growl, my voice low, commanding, my hand grabbing his hair, tugging hard, making him moan, his lips parting, his eyes wild, locked on my cock.

“Fuck, you’re—shit, you’re huge,” he groans, his voice trembling, his hands grabbing my thighs, fingers digging into the leather, his tongue flicking out, licking the head, tasting the precum, sharp and musky. I moan, my hips bucking, my cock throbbing, aching for his mouth. He sucks the head, his lips stretching, his tongue swirling, clumsy but eager, and I groan, my hand tightening in his hair, guiding him, fucking his mouth, the wet heat driving me wild. “That’s it, big guy,” I growl, my voice thick, my hips rocking, my cock hitting the back of his throat, making him gag slightly, his eyes watering but hungry, his cock twitching, leaking onto the floor.

I slap his ass again, the leather stinging, and he moans around my cock, the vibration sending sparks through me, my cock throbbing, leaking more, dripping down his chin. “Fuck, you’re good at this,” I murmur, my hand sliding to his pit again, inhaling deep, licking the damp hair, tasting the salt, the musk, savoring the raw masculinity of him. I pull back, my cock slick with his spit, glistening, and push him back against the wall, his ass out, his hole exposed, pink and tight, begging for me. “You’re gonna take my cock again,” I growl, my hand stroking my cock, slick with his spit, pressing it against his hole, breaching it, slow and deliberate, making him gasp, a sharp, needy sound.

“Goddamn, fuck me,” he moans, his voice wrecked, his hands braced against the wall, his ass pushing back, taking every inch, his hole clenching, hot and slick, pulling me in. I pound harder, deeper, the slick sound of skin on skin filling the club, mixing with his moans, the creak of leather, the bass thumping. My hand strokes his cock, keeping him on edge, my other hand slapping his ass, the leather stinging, making him cry out, his hole clenching tighter, driving me closer to the edge. “Harder—shit, fuck me harder,” he pleads, his voice high, desperate, his body trembling, his cock pulsing, leaking, dripping onto the floor.

I lean in, kissing his neck, sucking hard, leaving another mark, my tongue licking the sweat, tasting the sandalwood, my hand sliding to his pit, inhaling deep, licking the damp hair, savoring the musky scent. "You're so fucking tight," I groan, my hips pounding relentless, my cock driving deep, hitting that spot inside him that makes his moans turn to cries, his body shuddering, his cock twitching in my hand, ready to burst. I slap his face lightly, the sting making his eyes flash, his lips parting, his moan loud, needy. "You love this, don't you? My cock in your hole, my tongue in your pits," I growl, my lips crashing into his, the kiss feral, tongues fucking, tasting sweat, musk, leather.

"Fuck, yes," he moans into my mouth, his voice breaking, his hands grabbing my jacket, yanking it open further, fingers roaming my chest, pinching my nipples, making me groan, my cock throbbing inside him. "I'm—shit, I'm gonna come," he gasps, his voice wrecked, his hips bucking back, meeting my thrusts, his hole clenching tighter, pulling me deeper. I pull out, making him whimper, his hole clenching, empty, and I push him to his knees again, my cock slick with his heat, glistening with precum, inches from his face.

“Suck it,” I growl, my hand grabbing his hair, tugging hard, guiding my cock to his lips, his tongue flicking out, licking the head, tasting the precum, his lips stretching, sucking hard. I moan, my hips rocking, fucking his mouth, the wet heat driving me wild, my cock throbbing, aching to come. “Fuck, you’re so good,” I groan, my hand slapping his ass again, the leather stinging, making him moan around my cock, the vibration pushing me closer to the edge. I pull back, my cock slick with his spit, and stroke fast, my hand a blur, my cock pulsing, ready to burst.

“Open your mouth,” I growl, my voice thick, commanding, and he obeys, his lips parting, his tongue out, his eyes wild, locked on mine. I groan, my cock throbbing, and I come, hot and thick, spurting into his mouth, filling it, dripping down his chin, the taste salty, musky, making him moan, his eyes fluttering shut as he swallows, savoring every drop. I keep stroking, the last spurts landing on his chest, splattering across his harness, the white cum stark against the black leather, dripping down his pecs, mixing with the sweat, glistening under the neon lights.

"Fuck, look at you," I murmur, my voice hoarse, my hand stroking his hair, gentle now, my cock softening, slick with spit and cum. I pull back, grabbing my leather jacket, wiping the cum from his chest with the sleeve, smearing it across the leather, the sight filthy, perfect. I stroke my cock again, squeezing out the last drops, letting them drip onto his harness, his abs, the leather pants bunched around his thighs, the cum pooling in the creases, glistening, marking him as mine. "Covered in my cum, wearing that leather like a fucking slut," I growl, my lips brushing his ear, nipping the lobe, tasting the sweat.

He moans, his voice wrecked, his hands grabbing my thighs, fingers digging into the leather, his cock still hard, leaking, dripping onto the floor. “Goddamn, you’re—fuck, you’re insane,” he gasps, his eyes wild, locked on mine, his chest heaving, cum dripping down his harness, his abs, the leather slick with sweat and my load. I grin, leaning in, kissing his lips, slow and deep, tasting my cum, his sweat, the musk of leather, the kiss sloppy, hungry, his tongue chasing mine, his moans soft, needy.

I pull back, zipping up my pants, the leather creaking, my cock still tingling from the intensity. “Keep that cum on you,” I murmur, my voice low, teasing, my hand brushing his harness, smearing the cum deeper into the leather, marking him. “Something to remember me by.” I wink, stepping back, my boots thudding on the concrete, leaving him on his knees, covered in my cum, his harness and pants slick with it, his cock hard, leaking, his body trembling, wrecked.

UNDERWEAR MISMATCH

I'm thirty-four, built like a rugby player who's kept the muscle but trimmed the bulk—broad shoulders, thick pecs, and a waist that's still tight, carved from years of deadlifts and early morning runs. My dark blond hair's cropped short, just long enough to run my fingers through, with a faint wave that's starting to show a few silver strands at the temples. My green eyes are sharp, always scanning, catching every detail, and my jaw's square, shadowed with a day's worth of stubble that's more grit than groomed. I'm gay, always have been, and I wear it like a second skin—confident, unapologetic, whether I'm in my fitted black tee and jeans or the charcoal suit I've got on today, tailored to hug every curve of muscle, the white dress shirt crisp, the silver tie knotted loose. My name doesn't matter; what does is the way my cock twitches when I catch sight of him across the gym, the new guy who's got me hard just from the way he moves.

He's a few years younger, maybe thirty, with a body that screams discipline—lean but powerful, like a boxer who's all sinew and speed. His black hair's buzzed close, accentuating the sharp angles of his face, and his dark brown eyes are intense, focused, with a flicker of something guarded, maybe even shy, when they meet mine. His skin's a warm olive, smooth except for the faint stubble along his jaw, and his lips are full, the kind you can't help but imagine wrapped around your cock. He's in a gray tank top, clinging to his defined chest, his biceps flexing as he racks a barbell, and his black gym shorts hug his thighs, thick and muscular, with a bulge that's impossible to ignore. He's straight, or so he says, with a fiancée he mentions too often, like he's trying to convince himself, but the way his eyes linger on me—

quick, heated glances when he thinks I'm not looking—tells a different story.

The gym's a haze of clanging weights and grunts, the air thick with the scent of sweat and rubber mats, the mirrors reflecting every flex, every bead of perspiration. It's late, past nine, and the place is thinning out, just a few diehards left, the fluorescent lights harsh against the black equipment. I'm finishing a set of pull-ups, my arms burning, my shirt damp, clinging to my pecs, when I catch him watching me in the mirror, his eyes flicking to my ass, then away, his face flushing slightly. My cock stirs, half-hard in my jockstrap, the black fabric tight under my gym shorts, and I drop from the bar, grabbing a towel to wipe the sweat from my neck, giving him a slow, deliberate grin.

"Nice form," I say, my voice low, carrying just enough edge to make it clear I'm not talking about his deadlifts. I saunter over, my sneakers silent on the mat, stopping a few feet from his bench, where he's adjusting the weights, his hands steady but his eyes betraying a flicker of nerves. "Those squats are doing you favors." My gaze drops to his thighs, thick and defined, the shorts riding up just enough to show a glimpse of tanned skin, and my cock twitches harder, pressing against the jock.

He laughs, a short, nervous sound, his hands pausing on the barbell, his fingers flexing around the knurled grip. "Thanks, man," he says, his voice deep, with a slight rasp that sends a jolt straight to my dick. "Just trying to keep up with guys like you." His eyes meet mine for a second, dark and intense, before darting away, and I catch the way his throat bobs, the faint flush creeping up his neck, staining his olive skin.

"Keep up?" I chuckle, stepping closer, close enough to smell his sweat, clean and sharp, mixed with a hint of cedar from whatever body wash he uses. “You’re outlifting half the guys here, including me.” I lean against the rack, my shirt pulling tight across my chest, my tie loosened, dangling against my abs. “Bet your fiancée loves the view when you strip out of those shorts.” It’s a bold jab, testing the waters, and I see his eyes widen, his flush deepening, his hands fumbling with the weight plates.

“She, uh, doesn’t complain,” he says, his voice quieter now, his eyes flicking to my chest, then lower, lingering on the bulge in my shorts before snapping back to the barbell. “But I’m not here for the compliments.” He tries to keep it light, but there’s a tremor in his tone, a crack in that straight-guy facade, and my cock’s fully hard now, straining against the jock, the outline obvious if he dares to look.

I grin, wiping the towel over my face, letting it hang low, brushing my crotch, drawing his eyes for a split second before he looks away, his jaw tightening. "Not here for compliments, huh? Could've fooled me, the way you keep checking me out in the mirror." I step closer, my voice dropping to a low drawl, my body inches from his, the heat radiating off his skin, his tank top damp, clinging to his pecs, showing the faint outline of his nipples, hard from the cool air or something else.

"Fuck off," he mutters, but it's weak, more reflex than rejection, and he doesn't move away, his hands still on the barbell, his knuckles white. "I'm not—shit, I'm not like that." His eyes flick to mine, then away, his face redder now, and I can see the bulge in his shorts growing, the fabric stretching tight, his cock clearly stirring, betraying his words.

"Sure you're not," I say, my grin widening, my hand brushing the towel against my thigh, close enough that it grazes his shorts, the contact subtle but electric. "But your dick's saying something else, man. Bet it's rock-hard under those shorts, just from me standing here." I lean in, my breath hot against his ear, not touching but close enough to make him tense, his shoulders stiffening, his breath hitching.

"You're full of shit," he says, his voice rough, but he's not pulling back, his body angled toward me, his eyes darting to my lips, then lower, to the bulge in my shorts, the jock doing nothing to hide my hard-on. His hands drop from the barbell, flexing at his sides, like he's fighting the urge to touch something—me, himself, anything to ease the tension coiling in his muscles.

I step even closer, our sneakers almost touching, the air between us thick with sweat and want. "Full of shit? Maybe," I murmur, my voice a low growl, my hand brushing his arm, just a graze, feeling the heat of his skin, the muscle flexing under my touch. "But you're not pushing me away, are you? Standing here, letting me get this close, your cock hard as fuck." My fingers linger, tracing the curve of his bicep, and he flinches but doesn't pull away, his breath uneven, his eyes dark with a mix of panic and lust.

"Fuck, man, you're—shit, you're trouble," he says, his voice low, almost a whisper, his hands twitching like he wants to grab me but can't quite cross that line. He adjusts his shorts, a futile attempt to hide the bulge, his cock clearly straining, the fabric damp with sweat or maybe something more. "I've got a fiancée, you know that. This isn't—" He cuts off, his eyes meeting mine, wide and conflicted, like he's drowning in the pull of this moment.

"Trouble's my specialty," I say, my voice a low purr, my hand sliding to his wrist, feeling his pulse race under my fingers, my thumb brushing the sensitive skin inside. "And that fiancée? She's not here, is she? Just you and me, in this gym, with that cock of yours begging for attention." I lean in, my lips inches from his, not kissing but close enough to feel his breath, hot and ragged, his eyes locked on mine, pupils blown wide.

He groans, a low, desperate sound, his hands flexing, one brushing my hip, hesitant, like he's testing the waters. "You're gonna get me in deep shit," he mutters, his voice rough, his fingers lingering on my hip, the contact sending a jolt through me, my cock throbbing in the jock. "I'm not—fuck, I'm not into guys." But his hand doesn't move, his fingers digging into my hip, pulling me just a fraction closer, his bulge brushing my thigh, the heat of it making my head spin.

"Not into guys?" I chuckle, my hand sliding to his chest, feeling the hard muscle under his tank, the rapid thud of his heart. "Then why's your cock so hard, huh? Why're you letting me touch you like this?" My fingers graze his nipple through the fabric, pinching lightly, and he gasps, his hips jerking, his bulge pressing harder against my thigh. “Bet you’re imagining what it’d be like, me peeling off that tank, getting my hands on that dick.”

“Fuck, stop,” he says, but it’s half-hearted, his voice trembling, his hand sliding to my waist, fingers slipping under the hem of my shirt, brushing the bare skin of my abs, the touch clumsy but hungry. “This is—shit, this is crazy.” His eyes flick to my lips, then down to my bulge, and I can see the conflict, the guilt about his fiancée, but it’s losing to the heat, the want, the way his cock’s straining, leaking through his shorts.

I grin, my hand sliding to his neck, feeling the sweat-slicked skin, the pulse hammering under my fingers. “Crazy’s good,” I murmur, my lips brushing his ear, not kissing but teasing, my breath hot against his skin. “Crazy’s what makes you grab me like that, makes you want to rip these shorts off.” I tug at his tank, pulling it up just enough to expose a sliver of his abs, tight and defined, glistening with sweat. His hand tightens on my waist, his fingers digging in, and I can feel his cock twitch against my thigh, the fabric of his shorts damp, sticky.

"You're—fuck, you're relentless," he says, his voice hoarse, his hand sliding higher, brushing my pecs, his thumb grazing my nipple through my shirt, sending a spark straight to my cock. "I shouldn't be—shit, I shouldn't be doing this." But he's leaning in now, his breath hot against my cheek, his lips so close I can taste the salt of his sweat, the cedar of his body wash, and my cock's throbbing, ready to burst through the jock.

"Then stop me," I challenge, my voice low, my hand sliding to his ass, squeezing the firm muscle through his shorts, feeling it clench under my touch. "Push me away, big guy. Tell me you don't want this." I press closer, our bulges grinding together, the friction making us both groan, his hand tightening on my pec, his thumb circling my nipple, bolder now, like he's giving in, piece by piece.

He doesn't push me away. Instead, his hand slides to my back, pulling me closer, his fingers digging into my spine, his bulge pressing harder against mine. "Fuck, I—I can't," he groans, his voice wrecked, his eyes wild, locked on mine. "You're making me—shit, I want it." His words are a confession, raw and desperate, and it's like a dam breaking, his hand sliding to my ass, squeezing hard, his fingers teasing the crease through my shorts, making my cock throb harder, leaking into the jock.

I laugh, low and dirty, my lips brushing his jaw, feeling the stubble scrape against me. "Want it, huh? Bet you're dying to feel my hands on your cock, stroking you till you're begging." I slide my hand to his bulge, cupping it through his shorts, feeling the thick, hard shape of him, the fabric damp with precum. He gasps, his hips bucking into my hand, his eyes fluttering shut for a second, his breath ragged.

“Goddamn, you’re—fuck, you’re too much,” he mutters, his voice trembling, his hand sliding under my shirt, fingers roaming my abs, tracing the lines of muscle, the sweat slicking my skin. His touch is bold now, no longer hesitant, like he’s crossed a line and can’t go back. “I’m not—shit, I’m not supposed to feel like this.” His eyes meet mine, dark and wild, and I can see the guilt, the thought of his fiancée, but it’s drowning in the need, the way his cock pulses in my hand.

I grin, my hand squeezing his bulge, stroking through the fabric, feeling it twitch, hard and heavy. “Feel like what? Like you wanna fuck me right here in this gym?” I lean in, my lips brushing his ear, my tongue flicking out to taste the sweat on his skin, sharp and salty. “Bet you’re imagining it, my hands on your cock, my mouth on your hole, making you moan louder than you ever have." My fingers tease the waistband of his shorts, slipping just inside, brushing the coarse hair at the base of his cock, and he groans, his hips rocking, his hand tightening on my ass.

"Fuck, you're—shit, you're gonna get us caught," he says, his voice high, desperate, but his hand doesn't stop, sliding to my thigh, fingers digging in, pulling me closer. "This is—fuck, this is wrong." But his eyes are locked on mine, pupils blown, and his cock's leaking through his shorts, the wet spot spreading, his body betraying every word.

"Wrong?" I chuckle, my hand sliding inside his shorts, brushing his cock through his briefs, feeling the thick, pulsing heat. "Feels pretty fucking right to me." I stroke him slow, deliberate, my thumb circling the head through the fabric, and he moans, loud and needy, his hips bucking into my hand. "Look at you, leaking already, ready to burst just from my touch." I lean in, my lips brushing his, not quite a kiss, just a tease, and he groans, his hand sliding to my cock, cupping it through my shorts, his fingers trembling but eager.

"Goddamn, man," he breathes, his voice shaky, his hand stroking me now, clumsy but bold, feeling the outline of my cock through the jock. "This is—fuck, I shouldn't, but you're making it so fucking hard to stop." His eyes meet mine, dark and desperate, and I can see the conflict, the guilt, but it's losing to the heat, the want, the way our bodies are pressed together, cocks hard, hands groping, the gym a haze of tension and desire.

I pull back, just enough to grab his tank, yanking it up, exposing his abs, tight and defined, glistening with sweat. "Hard's the point," I say, my voice a low growl, my hand sliding to his chest, pinching his nipple, making him gasp, his hips bucking. "Bet you're thinking about it—my hands on you, peeling off these shorts, seeing what's under all that straight-guy bullshit." My fingers tug at his waistband, pulling it down just enough to show the band of his briefs, black and tight, hugging his cock, the wet spot stark against the fabric.

He groans, his hands grabbing my shirt, yanking it up, exposing my chest, his fingers roaming my pecs, thumbs brushing my nipples, sending sparks through me. "You're—fuck, you're insane," he says, but it's half-moaned, his voice trembling, his hands bold now, squeezing my pecs, feeling the muscle, the sweat. "I'm—shit, I'm not supposed to want this." But he's pulling me closer, our bulges grinding together, the friction making us both moan, the air thick with the scent of our sweat, our arousal, the gym a pressure cooker of want and risk.

His hands are on my pecs, fingers digging into the muscle, thumbs circling my nipples with a boldness that's got my cock straining against the jockstrap, the black fabric soaked with sweat and precum. The gym's a furnace, the air heavy with the musk of our bodies, the clank of distant weights fading into a dull hum under the pounding of my pulse. His tank top's bunched up around his chest, exposing the tight ridges of his abs, glistening with sweat that catches the fluorescent light, his olive skin flushed with heat. My shirt's rucked up, my tie a loose knot dangling against my abs, the silver silk brushing his wrist as he gropes me, his touch hungry but still tinged with that straight-guy hesitation. His shorts are low, the waistband of his black briefs peeking out, the bulge massive, tenting the fabric, a wet spot spreading where his cock's leaking, desperate for more.

"Fuck, you're—shit, you're making me lose it," he mutters, his voice a low rasp, thick with need, his eyes dark and wild, flickering between my lips and the bulge in my shorts. His fingers trace the line of my pecs, slow and deliberate, like he's mapping me, learning the feel of another man's body, and my cock twitches, aching under his gaze. “This is—fuck, I shouldn’t be touching you like this.” But his hands don’t stop, sliding lower, brushing my abs, his thumbs grazing the trail of hair leading into my jock, sending a jolt straight to my dick.

I grin, my hand still on his bulge, stroking through his briefs, feeling the thick, pulsing heat of his cock, the fabric slick with precum. “Lose it? You’re already gone, man,” I murmur, my voice a low growl, my lips brushing his ear, close enough to feel his shudder, the heat of his skin against mine. “Look at you, groping my chest, your cock leaking like a faucet. Bet you’re dying to feel more.” My fingers squeeze his bulge, slow and firm, and he gasps, his hips bucking into my hand, his eyes fluttering shut for a second, his breath ragged.

“Goddamn it,” he groans, his hands sliding to my hips, fingers hooking into the waistband of my shorts, tugging them lower, exposing the straps of my jock, the black elastic stark against my skin. "You're—fuck, you're pushing me too far." His voice cracks, but his fingers are bold, slipping under the straps, brushing the sensitive skin at my hips, making my cock throb harder, leaking into the jock. His eyes flick down, catching the outline of my dick, and his flush deepens, his throat bobbing as he swallows hard.

I step closer, our sneakers brushing, the air between us electric, thick with sweat and want. "Too far? Nah, you're right where you want to be," I say, my voice a low purr, my hand sliding to his neck, feeling the pulse hammering under my fingers, my thumb brushing the stubble along his jaw. "Bet you're imagining what's under this jock, aren't you? My cock, hard as fuck, just for you." I lean in, my lips grazing his throat, tasting the salt of his sweat, the cedar of his body wash, and he moans, a low, desperate sound that hits me right in the gut.

“Fuck you,” he mutters, but it’s weak, his hands tightening on my hips, pulling me closer, his bulge grinding against my thigh, the friction making us both groan. “I’m not—shit, I’m not supposed to want this.” His fingers slide higher, brushing my abs again, then lower, teasing the edge of my jock, his touch tentative but hungry, like he’s fighting himself but losing fast. His cock twitches in my hand, leaking more, the wet spot on his briefs spreading, and I stroke harder, my thumb circling the head through the fabric, making him shudder.

I laugh, low and dirty, my lips brushing his ear, nipping the lobe, feeling him tense. “Not supposed to? Your dick’s begging for it,” I say, my hand sliding to his ass, squeezing the firm muscle through his shorts, feeling it clench under my touch. “Bet you’re thinking about me peeling these off, getting my hands on that cock, making you moan louder than you ever have.” My fingers tease the crease of his ass, brushing the fabric, not pushing further but close enough to make him gasp, his hips jerking, his bulge pressing harder against my thigh.

“Goddamn, you’re—fuck, you’re trouble,” he says, his voice hoarse, his hands sliding to my back, fingers digging into the muscle, pulling me closer, our chests brushing, his tank top rough against my bare skin. “I’ve got a fiancée, man. This is—shit, this is crazy.” His eyes meet mine, dark and wild, the guilt flickering but drowning in the heat, the want, the way his cock pulses in my hand, ready to burst but holding, just barely.

“Crazy’s my middle name,” I murmur, my hand sliding to his chest, pinching his nipple through his tank, rolling it between my fingers, making him cry out, a sharp, needy sound that echoes in the gym. “And that fiancée? She’s not here, is she? Just you and me, with your cock hard as fuck, letting me touch you like this.” I tug his tank higher, exposing more of his chest, the dark hair dusted across his pecs, glistening with sweat, and I lean in, kissing his collarbone, sucking lightly, tasting the salt of his skin.

He groans, his hands sliding to my ass, squeezing hard, his fingers bold now, teasing the straps of my jock, slipping under them, brushing the bare skin of my cheeks. “Fuck, you’re—shit, you’re making it impossible to stop,” he says, his voice trembling, his fingers digging into my ass, pulling me closer, our bulges grinding together, the friction electric, unbearable. His eyes flick to my lips, then lower, to the outline of my cock in the jock, and I can see the hunger, the curiosity, the straight-guy resolve cracking under the weight of this moment.

I grin, my hand sliding to his neck again, pulling him closer, my lips inches from his, not kissing but teasing, my breath hot against his mouth. “Then don’t stop,” I say, my voice a low growl, my fingers tugging at his shorts, pulling them lower, exposing more of his briefs, the black fabric stretched tight over his cock, the wet spot stark and growing. "Show me how much you want this, big guy. Let go." My hand strokes his bulge, slow and deliberate, feeling it pulse, thick and heavy, and he moans, his hips rocking into my hand, his eyes fluttering shut.

"Fuck, I—I can't," he gasps, but his hands don't stop, sliding to my chest, fingers roaming my pecs, thumbs brushing my nipples, sending sparks through me. "You're—shit, you're too much." His touch is bolder now, his fingers tracing the lines of my abs, slipping lower, brushing the straps of my jock again, teasing the edge of my cock, making me groan, my hips bucking into his hand. His cock twitches in my hand, leaking more, the fabric of his briefs soaked, and I stroke faster, my thumb circling the head, feeling it pulse.

I pull back, just enough to grab his tank, yanking it up and off, tossing it to the floor, exposing his chest fully, the dark hair matted with sweat, his nipples hard and flushed. “Look at you,” I murmur, my voice thick, my hands roaming his chest, pinching his nipples, making him gasp, his hips bucking. “All that muscle, that perfect fucking cock, and you’re letting me touch you like this. Not so straight now, are you?” I lean in, kissing his chest, my tongue flicking over his nipple, tasting the salt, the musk, and he moans, loud and shameless, his hands grabbing my shoulders, fingers digging in.

“Goddamn it, you’re—fuck, you’re killing me,” he says, his voice high, desperate, his hands sliding to my ass again, squeezing hard, pulling me closer, our bulges grinding together, the friction making us both groan. “I shouldn’t—shit, I shouldn’t be doing this.” But his fingers are bold, slipping under the straps of my jock, brushing my cheeks, teasing closer to my hole, the contact sending a jolt through me, my cock throbbing, leaking into the jock.

I laugh, my lips brushing his nipple, sucking hard, making him cry out, his hips rocking, his bulge pressing harder against my thigh. “Killing you? Nah, I’m just getting you started,” I say, my voice a low purr, my hand sliding to his ass, squeezing through his shorts, fingers teasing the crease, making him shudder. “Bet you’re imagining what it’d be like, my hands on your cock, my tongue on your hole, making you scream.” I kiss his chest again, slow and deliberate, my tongue tracing the line of his pecs, savoring the heat, the sweat, the raw masculinity of him.

“Fuck, stop,” he groans, but it’s weak, his hands tightening on my ass, pulling me closer, his fingers bolder now, teasing my hole through the jock, the pressure intense, making me moan, my cock aching. “This is—fuck, this is too much.” His eyes meet mine, wild and conflicted, but his touch is sure, his fingers circling my hole, driving me wild, his cock pulsing in my hand, ready to explode but holding, just barely.

“Then make me,” I challenge, my voice low, my hand stroking his bulge, keeping him on edge, my other hand sliding to his neck, pulling him closer, our lips inches apart. “Push me away, tell me you don’t want this.” I kiss his throat, sucking hard, leaving a mark, feeling his pulse race under my lips, his cock twitching in my hand, leaking more, staining his briefs. His hands slide to my hips, pulling my shorts lower, exposing more of my jock, his fingers brushing the bare skin of my thighs, the contact electric, making my head spin.

He doesn’t push me away. Instead, his hands slide to my chest, pinching my nipples, rolling them between his fingers, making me groan, my hips bucking into his touch. “Fuck, I—I want it,” he admits, his voice breaking, his eyes wild, locked on mine. "You're—shit, you're making me want it so bad." His words are a surrender, raw and desperate, and it's like a switch flips, his hands roaming my body, bold and hungry, his fingers teasing the straps of my jock, slipping under them, brushing my hole again, making me moan louder, my cock throbbing, ready to burst.

I grin, my lips brushing his ear, nipping the lobe, feeling him shudder. "That's it, big guy," I murmur, my hand stroking his cock faster, keeping him on edge, my other hand sliding to his ass, squeezing hard, fingers teasing his crack through the briefs, making him gasp. "Let go. Show me how bad you want it." I kiss his chest again, my tongue flicking over his nipple, sucking hard, and he cries out, his hips rocking, his bulge grinding against my thigh, the tension building, ready to snap but holding, just barely.

The gym's a haze of heat and want, our bodies slick with sweat, shorts low, briefs and jockstraps stretched tight, cocks hard and leaking, hands groping, pushing each other closer to the edge. His fingers are relentless now, teasing my hole, circling with a confidence that's got my knees weak, his touch rough but precise, like he's learning me inch by inch. My hand's on his cock, stroking through his briefs, feeling it pulse, thick and heavy, the wet spot spreading, his moans loud and needy, filling the gym, the air thick with the scent of our sweat, our arousal, the tension unbearable, electric, ready to explode but not there yet, not until I push him further, make him mine in this filthy moment.

His fingers are relentless, teasing my hole through the straps of my jock, circling with a hunger that's got my cock throbbing, leaking precum that soaks the black fabric, dripping down my thigh. The gym's a haze of sweat and heat, the air thick with the musk of our bodies, the fluorescent lights casting sharp shadows across his olive skin, his tank top long gone, his chest glistening, dark hair matted, nipples hard from my earlier teasing. My shirt's a crumpled mess on the floor, my silver tie dangling loose around my neck, my shorts barely clinging to my hips, the jock stretched tight over my cock. His black briefs are low, the wet spot stark, his cock straining, thick and veiny, leaking through the fabric, his shorts pooled around his sneakers, his thighs flexing, powerful and slick with sweat.

"Fuck, you're—shit, you're driving me insane," he groans, his voice a low rasp, cracking with need, his eyes wild, locked on mine, pupils blown wide. His hands slide to my ass, squeezing hard, fingers slipping under the jock, brushing my hole directly now, the contact electric, making me moan, my hips bucking back against his touch. "I shouldn't—fuck, I can't stop." His words are a confession, raw and desperate, his fingers bolder, circling my hole, pressing just enough to make my cock twitch, aching for more.

I grin, my lips brushing his jaw, tasting the stubble, the salt of his sweat, my tongue flicking out to trace the sharp line of his jaw. "Can't stop? Good," I growl, my voice thick, my hand stroking his cock through his briefs, feeling it pulse, hot and heavy, the fabric soaked. "Cause I'm just getting started, big guy." I kiss his throat, sucking hard, leaving a mark, feeling his pulse race under my lips, his moan loud and needy, echoing in the gym. My other hand slides to his ass, squeezing the firm muscle, fingers teasing his crack through the briefs, making him shudder, his hips rocking into my hand.

"Goddamn it," he gasps, his hands grabbing my face, pulling me into a kiss, his lips crashing into mine, hot and sloppy, his tongue plunging deep, tasting of sweat and desperation. His stubble burns my lips, the kiss all teeth and hunger, and I moan into his mouth, my cock throbbing in the jock, his fingers pressing harder against my hole, circling, teasing, driving me wild. "You're—fuck, you're too much," he mutters against my lips, his voice wrecked, his hands sliding to my chest, pinching my nipples, rolling them between his fingers, sending sparks through me.

I laugh, low and dirty, breaking the kiss to lick a slow stripe up his neck, savoring the salty tang, the cedar of his body wash, my tongue tracing the pulse hammering under his skin. "Too much? You're the one groping me like you're starving," I murmur, my hand sliding inside his briefs, wrapping around his cock, thick and veiny, slick with precum. I stroke slow, deliberate, my thumb circling the head, feeling it pulse, and he cries out, his hips bucking, his fingers digging into my ass, teasing my hole with more confidence now, making my head spin.

"Fuck, man, you're—shit, you're gonna make me lose it," he groans, his voice high and desperate, his hands sliding to my jock, tugging it down, exposing my cock fully, hard and leaking, brushing his thigh. His fingers wrap around me, stroking clumsy but eager, feeling the weight, the heat, and I groan, the contact electric, my hips rocking into his hand. "This is—fuck, this is crazy," he says, his eyes wild, locked on my cock, watching his own hand stroke me, like he can't believe he's doing this.

I grin, my lips brushing his ear, nipping the lobe, feeling him shudder. "Crazy's what makes your cock so hard, leaking all over my hand," I say, my voice a low growl, my hand stroking his cock faster, matching his rhythm on mine. "Bet you're imagining fucking me, aren't you? My cock in your mouth, my tongue in your hole." I kiss his chest, my tongue flicking over his nipple, sucking hard, tasting the sweat, the musk, and he moans, loud and shameless, his hands tightening on my cock, stroking faster, his fingers teasing my hole, pressing harder, making me moan louder.

“Goddamn, you’re—fuck, you’re filthy,” he says, his voice trembling, but his hands don’t stop, one stroking my cock, the other sliding to my ass, fingers circling my hole, bolder now, pressing just enough to make my knees weak. “I’m not—shit, I’m not supposed to want this.” His eyes meet mine, dark and wild, the guilt flickering but drowned out by the need, the way his cock pulses in my hand, leaking more, staining his briefs.

I pull back, grabbing his briefs, yanking them down, letting them drop to his ankles, his cock springing free, thick and veiny, glistening with precum, slapping against his thigh. “Not supposed to? Bullshit,” I growl, my hand wrapping around his bare cock, stroking slow, feeling it pulse, hot and heavy. “You’re so fucking hard, begging for it.” I lean in, kissing his chest again, my tongue tracing the line of his pecs, sucking his nipple, making him cry out, his hips bucking, his cock twitching in my hand.

“Fuck, stop—shit, don’t stop,” he gasps, his voice breaking, his hands grabbing my jock, pulling it off completely, letting it fall to the floor, my cock free, brushing his thigh, leaving a slick trail of precum. His fingers wrap around me, stroking faster, his other hand teasing my hole, circling, pressing, making me moan, my hips rocking back against his touch. “You’re—fuck, you’re gonna ruin me,” he says, his voice high, desperate, his eyes wild, locked on mine, his cock pulsing in my hand, ready to burst but holding, just barely.

I laugh, my lips brushing his nipple, sucking hard, then kissing up his chest, his throat, tasting the sweat, the heat. “Ruin you? I’m just giving you what you want,” I murmur, my hand stroking his cock, keeping him on edge, my other hand sliding to his ass, squeezing hard, fingers teasing his crack, brushing his hole, making him shudder. “Bet you’re dying for more, aren’t you? My tongue on your cock, my fingers in your hole.” I kiss his jaw, slow and deliberate, my tongue flicking out, tasting the stubble, and he moans, his hands tightening on my cock, stroking faster, his fingers pressing harder against my hole.

"Goddamn it, you're—fuck, you're right," he groans, his voice wrecked, his hands sliding to my face, pulling me into another kiss, hot and sloppy, his tongue plunging deep, swallowing my moans. His fingers are relentless, teasing my hole, circling, pressing, making my cock throb, leaking more, dripping onto his thigh. I pull back, grabbing his briefs from the floor, the black fabric damp with sweat and precum, and hold them up, my grin wicked, my eyes locked on his.

"Open your mouth," I say, my voice low, commanding, and his eyes widen, a mix of shock and lust, but he obeys, his lips parting, his breath ragged. I stuff the briefs into his mouth, the sweaty, musky fabric muffling his moan, his eyes fluttering shut, his cock twitching in my hand. "Fuck, that's it," I growl, my hand stroking his cock faster, my other hand sliding to his ass, spreading his cheeks, teasing his hole with my finger, brushing the rim, feeling it clench, hot and tight.

He moans through the briefs, the sound muffled but desperate, his hips bucking, his cock pulsing in my hand, leaking more, dripping onto the mat. I lean in, kissing his chest, my tongue flicking over his nipple, sucking hard, then licking a slow stripe up his throat, tasting the sweat, the musk, the raw masculinity of him. “You look so fucking hot like this,” I murmur, my lips against his skin, my finger pressing harder against his hole, not pushing in but teasing, making him shudder, his moans louder, muffled by the briefs. “Gagged with your own sweaty underwear, cock leaking, begging for me.”

I pull back, dropping to my knees, my lips brushing his thigh, kissing the tanned skin, tasting the sweat, my tongue tracing the line of muscle, moving closer to his cock but not touching, teasing, building the tension. His hands grab my hair, tugging hard, his moans muffled, desperate, his hips rocking, his cock brushing my cheek, leaving a slick trail of precum. I grin, kissing his thigh again, my tongue flicking out, tasting the salt, the heat, my finger still teasing his hole, circling, pressing, making him tremble.

"Fuck, you're—shit, you're killing me," he moans through the briefs, his voice high, muffled, his hands tightening in my hair, pulling me closer, his cock throbbing, leaking, begging for my mouth. I kiss higher, my lips brushing the base of his cock, not sucking, just teasing, my tongue flicking out, tasting the precum, sharp and musky, making my cock throb, aching against the mat. My finger presses harder against his hole, circling, teasing, feeling it clench, hot and tight, and he cries out, his hips bucking, his cock brushing my lips, desperate for more.

I stand, grabbing his face, kissing him over the briefs, my tongue pushing against the fabric, tasting the sweat, the musk, his moans loud and needy, muffled but raw. “You taste so fucking good,” I growl, my lips brushing his, my hand stroking his cock, keeping him on edge, my finger teasing his hole, pressing harder, making him shudder. “Bet you’re imagining my cock in you, fucking you right here, with your briefs in your mouth.” I kiss his neck, sucking hard, leaving another mark, my tongue tracing the pulse, feeling it race under my lips.

He moans, his hands sliding to my ass, squeezing hard, fingers digging into the muscle, pulling me closer, our cocks grinding together, the friction electric, unbearable. “Fuck, I—I want it,” he groans through the briefs, his voice muffled, desperate, his eyes wild, locked on mine. “You’re—shit, you’re making me want it so bad.” His words are a surrender, raw and filthy, and I grin, my hand stroking his cock faster, my finger pressing against his hole, teasing, circling, driving him wild.

I pull back, licking a slow stripe down his chest, tasting the sweat, the musk, my tongue flicking over his nipple, sucking hard, then kissing lower, tracing the ridges of his abs, savoring the heat, the salt. “That’s it, big guy,” I murmur, my lips against his skin, my hand stroking his cock, keeping him on edge, my finger teasing his hole, pressing harder, making him moan louder, muffled by the briefs. “Let go. Show me how bad you want it.” I kiss his abs, my tongue dipping into the lines of muscle, tasting the sweat, the raw masculinity of him, my cock throbbing, leaking, ready to burst but holding, just barely.

His moans are muffled, raw, vibrating through the sweaty black briefs stuffed in his mouth, his eyes wild, pupils blown, locked on mine as I stroke his cock, my finger teasing his hole, circling the tight rim, making his hips buck, his thick thighs trembling under the strain. The gym’s a furnace, the air thick with the musk of our sweat, the cedar of his body wash, and the raw, primal scent of arousal that’s got my cock throbbing, leaking precum onto the mat. His olive skin glistens, his chest heaving, dark hair matted across his pecs, nipples hard and flushed from my tongue. My silver tie dangles loose, brushing my abs, my jock long gone, my cock hard and slick, grinding against his thigh. His briefs are around his ankles, tangled with his shorts, his cock free, thick and veiny, leaking so much it's dripping down his shaft, pooling on the floor.

"Fuck, you're so hot like this," I growl, my voice low, thick with lust, my lips brushing his ear, nipping the lobe, feeling him shudder. "Gagged with your own sweaty briefs, cock leaking, begging for me." I pull the briefs from his mouth, the damp fabric trailing spit, and he gasps, his breath ragged, his lips swollen from the pressure. I toss the briefs aside, grabbing his hips, spinning him around, pushing him face-down over a bench, his ass up, cheeks spread, his hole exposed, pink and tight, glistening with sweat. "Time to change things up, big guy," I murmur, my hands squeezing his ass, spreading him wider, my cock throbbing at the sight.

"Goddamn, man—fuck," he groans, his voice hoarse, wrecked, his hands gripping the bench, knuckles white, his face pressed against the vinyl, sweat dripping from his brow. "You're—shit, you're gonna kill me." His tone's a mix of panic and need, his body trembling, but he's pushing his ass back, inviting me, his hole clenching, begging for more. His black gym socks cling to his feet, damp with sweat, the white soles stained from the mat, and I grin, my hands sliding down his thighs, feeling the muscle flex, the heat radiating off his skin.

I drop to my knees, my lips kissing the back of his thigh, tasting the salt, the musk, my tongue tracing the curve of muscle, moving higher, closer to his hole. "Fuck, you smell so good," I growl, my nose brushing his ass, inhaling the raw, masculine scent—sweat, musk, a hint of cedar, driving me wild. I kiss his cheek, my tongue flicking out, licking a slow stripe over his hole, tasting the clean, musky heat, and he cries out, a sharp, needy sound that echoes in the gym, his hips bucking back, chasing my tongue. "Yeah, that's it," I murmur, my tongue diving in, fucking his hole, wet and relentless, savoring the tightness, the way he clenches around me.

"Fuck, fuck," he moans, his voice high, desperate, his hands clawing at the bench, his socks sliding on the mat as he pushes back, grinding his ass against my face. "You're—shit, you're filthy." His words are slurred, drowned in pleasure, his cock twitching, leaking onto the bench, a slick puddle forming under him. I pull back, grabbing his ankle, lifting his foot, the black sock damp, clinging to his skin, the scent hitting me hard—sweaty, musky, so fucking masculine it makes my cock throb, aching to be inside him.

I press his socked foot to my face, inhaling deep, the smell raw and intoxicating, sweat mixed with the faint rubber of the mat, and I groan, my tongue flicking out, licking the sole, tasting the salt, the grit. "Fuck, your feet smell amazing," I say, my voice thick, my hand stroking my cock, keeping it hard, slick with precum. His eyes widen, watching me over his shoulder, a mix of shock and lust, his cock twitching harder, leaking more. "You like that, don't you? Me sniffing your sweaty socks, getting off on you," I murmur, sucking the fabric, the taste sharp and heady, driving me wild.

"Goddamn, you're—fuck, you're insane," he gasps, but his voice is needy, his hips rocking, his hole clenching, begging for more. I drop his foot, kissing up his calf, my tongue tracing the muscle, tasting the sweat, then licking higher, back to his ass, my tongue diving into his hole again, fucking deep, making him moan louder, his body trembling, his socks sliding on the mat. "Don't—shit, don't stop," he pleads, his voice breaking, his hands gripping the bench, his cock leaking, dripping, his thighs shaking.

I stand, grabbing my cock, stroking it slow, the head flushed and slick, and press it against his hole, not pushing in, just teasing, feeling the heat, the tightness. "You want this, don't you?" I growl, my voice low, my hand sliding to his cock, stroking in time with mine, keeping him on edge. "Want my cock in you, fucking you hard, right here on this bench." I lean in, kissing his back, my tongue licking a slow stripe up his spine, tasting the sweat, the musk, savoring the way his muscles flex under my lips.

"Yes, fuck, yes," he moans, his voice high, desperate, his hips pushing back, his hole clenching against the head of my cock, begging for it. "I'm—shit, I'm nervous, but I want it." His eyes meet mine over his shoulder, dark and wild, the guilt about his fiancée drowned out by the need, the raw hunger in his gaze. I grin, my hand squeezing his cock, my other hand spreading his cheeks, my cock pressing harder, breaching his hole, slow and deliberate, making him gasp, a sharp, needy sound that fills the gym.

“Fuck, you’re tight,” I groan, pushing in deeper, inch by inch, feeling his hole clench, hot and slick, pulling me in. He moans, loud and shameless, his hands clawing at the bench, his socks sliding on the mat, his body trembling as he takes me, his cock pulsing in my hand, leaking more. “Taking my cock so well, big guy,” I murmur, my lips kissing his back, licking the sweat, tasting the salt, my hips rocking slow, letting him adjust, savoring the tightness, the heat.

“Goddamn, it’s—fuck, it’s too much,” he gasps, his voice wrecked, his hips bucking back, meeting my thrusts, his hole clenching tighter, making my cock throb, aching to pound harder. I lean in, kissing his shoulder, sucking hard, leaving a mark, my tongue tracing the muscle, savoring the taste, the heat. My hand strokes his cock faster, keeping him on edge, my other hand grabbing his ankle again, lifting his socked foot, pressing it to my face, inhaling deep, the sweaty, musky scent hitting me like a drug, making my cock twitch inside him.

"Fuck, your socks are—shit, so fucking hot," I growl, sucking the fabric, tasting the sweat, my tongue licking the sole, the smell driving me wild, my hips snapping forward, pounding deeper, harder, making him cry out, his moans loud, echoing in the gym. "You love this, don't you? Me sniffing your feet, fucking you like this," I say, my voice thick, my cock driving into him, the bench creaking, his hole clenching, pulling me deeper.

"Yes, fuck, yes," he moans, his voice high, desperate, his hips rocking back, taking every thrust, his cock pulsing in my hand, leaking so much it's dripping onto the bench. I drop his foot, grabbing his briefs from the floor, the black fabric damp with sweat and precum, and stuff them back into his mouth, muffling his moans, his eyes widening, lust and shock mixing as he tastes his own musk, his cock twitching harder in my hand.

"Fuck, that's it," I growl, my hips pounding harder, my cock driving deep, the slick sound of skin on skin filling the gym, mixing with his muffled moans, the creak of the bench. I lean in, kissing his back, licking the sweat, my tongue tracing the curve of his spine, savoring the taste, the heat, my hand stroking his cock, keeping him on edge. "Gagged with your sweaty briefs, taking my cock like a fucking slut," I murmur, my lips against his skin, my cock pounding relentless, his hole clenching, tight and hot, driving me closer to the edge.

He moans through the briefs, his body trembling, his hips bucking back, meeting every thrust, his cock pulsing, leaking, ready to burst but holding, just barely. I pull back, grabbing his hips, flipping him onto his back on the bench, his legs up, socks in the air, his hole exposed, glistening with sweat and my precum. I press my cock against his hole again, pushing in deep, making him cry out, his moans muffled by the briefs, his eyes wild, locked on mine. “Fuck, you look so good like this,” I growl, my hips snapping forward, pounding hard, the bench rattling, his cock bouncing, leaking onto his abs.

I lean in, kissing his chest, my tongue flicking over his nipple, sucking hard, tasting the sweat, the musk, my hand stroking his cock, keeping him on edge. “You’re so fucking tight, taking me so well,” I murmur, my lips kissing up his throat, licking the sweat, tasting the cedar, my cock driving deeper, harder, making him moan louder, muffled by the briefs. I grab his socked foot again, pressing it to my face, inhaling deep, the sweaty, musky scent driving me wild, my tongue licking the sole, sucking the fabric, my cock throbbing inside him, pounding relentless.

"Goddamn, your feet, your hole—fuck, you're perfect," I growl, my voice thick, my hips snapping forward, pounding harder, deeper, his hole clenching, pulling me in, his cock pulsing in my hand, leaking more, dripping onto his abs. His moans are loud, desperate, muffled by the briefs, his body trembling, his socks sliding on the bench, his thighs shaking, his eyes wild, locked on mine, drowned in pleasure, the gym a haze of heat and want, our bodies slick with sweat, cocks throbbing, the tension unbearable,

His body's trembling, sprawled across the gym bench, legs up, black socks dangling in the air, his hole clenching around my cock as I pound into him, the slick sound of skin on skin mixing with his muffled moans, the sweaty briefs stuffed in his mouth. The gym's a haze of heat and musk, the air thick with the scent of our sweat, his cedar body wash, and the raw, filthy aroma of arousal that's got my cock throbbing, buried deep in his tight, hot hole. His olive skin glistens, his chest heaving, dark hair matted across his pecs, nipples flushed and hard from my tongue. My silver tie's a crumpled loop around my neck, my jock long gone, my cock slick with precum, driving into him with relentless thrusts, the bench creaking under the force. His briefs are tangled with his shorts around his ankles, his cock bouncing, thick and veiny, leaking precum that drips onto his abs, pooling in the ridges of muscle.

"Fuck, you're so tight," I growl, my voice thick, my hips snapping forward, pounding deeper, making him moan through the briefs, his eyes wild, pupils blown, locked on mine. I lean in, kissing his chest, my tongue licking a slow stripe over his nipple, sucking hard, tasting the salt, the musk, savoring the way his body arches, his hole clenching tighter around my cock. "Taking my cock like you were fucking made for it," I murmur, my lips brushing his skin, my hand stroking his cock, keeping him on edge, the head flushed red, leaking more, dripping onto his abs.

“Goddamn—fuck,” he moans, muffled by the briefs, his voice high, desperate, his hands clawing at the bench, knuckles white, his socks sliding on the vinyl as he pushes back, meeting every thrust, his hole pulling me deeper. His face is flushed, sweat dripping from his brow, catching in the dark stubble along his jaw, and I grin, my hand sliding to his ankle, grabbing his socked foot, the black fabric damp, clinging to his skin, the scent hitting me hard—sweaty, musky, so fucking masculine it makes my cock twitch inside him.

I rip the briefs from his mouth, tossing them to the mat, the wet fabric landing with a soft thud, and he gasps, his breath ragged, his lips swollen, glistening with spit. “Fuck, man, you’re—shit, you’re wrecking me,” he groans, his voice hoarse, wrecked, his eyes wild, locked on mine, a mix of lust and panic, his straight resolve shattered. I grab his sock, yanking it off his foot, the damp fabric warm in my hand, the scent raw and intoxicating, sweat mixed with the faint rubber of the mat. “Open your mouth,” I growl, my voice low, commanding, and his eyes widen, shock and lust mixing, but he obeys, his lips parting, his breath hitching.

I stuff the sock into his mouth, the sweaty, musky fabric muffling his moan, his eyes fluttering shut, his cock twitching hard in my hand, leaking more, dripping onto his abs. “Fuck, that’s it,” I murmur, my hips pounding harder, my cock driving deep, the bench rattling, his hole clenching, hot and tight, pulling me in. I lean in, kissing his neck, my tongue licking the sweat, tasting the cedar, sucking hard, leaving a mark, savoring the pulse hammering under his skin. “Gagged with your own sweaty sock, taking my cock like a fucking slut,” I growl, my hand stroking his cock faster, feeling it pulse, thick and heavy, ready to burst.

He moans through the sock, the sound muffled, desperate, his hips bucking, his hole clenching tighter, making my cock throb, aching to come but holding, just barely. I grab his other sock, yanking it off, pressing it to my face, inhaling deep, the smell raw and filthy, sweat and musk driving me wild, my tongue flicking out, tasting the salt, the grit. “Fuck, your feet smell so good,” I groan, sucking the fabric, my cock pounding harder, deeper, making him cry out, his moans muffled, his body trembling, his cock leaking, dripping onto the bench.

I pull back, flipping him onto his stomach again, his ass up, cheeks spread, his hole glistening with sweat and my precum, so fucking tight it’s driving me insane. I press my cock against his hole, pushing in deep, making him moan through the sock, his hands clawing at the bench, his body arching, taking every inch. “Fuck, you’re perfect,” I growl, my hips snapping forward, pounding relentless, the slick sound of skin on skin filling the gym, mixing with his muffled cries, the creak of the bench. I lean in, licking his back, my tongue tracing the sweat-slicked muscle, tasting the salt, the musk, savoring the way his body flexes under my lips.

“Goddamn, you’re—fuck, you’re too much,” he moans through the sock, his voice high, muffled, his hips rocking back, meeting every thrust, his hole clenching, pulling me deeper. I grab his cock, stroking fast, my thumb circling the head, smearing precum, and he cries out, his body trembling, his socks discarded on the mat, his bare feet sliding, toes curling. I kiss his shoulder, sucking hard, leaving another mark, my tongue licking the sweat, the heat, my cock pounding harder, deeper, making him moan louder, muffled by the sock.

I pull the sock from his mouth, tossing it aside, and he gasps, his breath ragged, his lips swollen, glistening with spit and sweat. “Fuck, I—I can’t hold it,” he groans, his voice wrecked, his eyes wild, locked on mine over his shoulder. “You’re—shit, you’re gonna make me come." His words are a plea, raw and desperate, and I grin, my hand stroking his cock faster, my cock driving deep, hitting that spot inside him that makes his moans turn to cries, his body trembling, ready to explode.

"Not yet," I growl, pulling out, making him whimper, his hole clenching, empty and begging. I grab his hips, flipping him onto his back, his legs up, bare feet in the air, his cock bouncing, leaking onto his abs. I lean in, kissing his mouth, my tongue plunging deep, tasting the sweat, the musk of the sock lingering on his lips, the kiss sloppy, all teeth and hunger. "I want you to come in my mouth," I murmur, my lips brushing his, my hand stroking his cock, keeping him on edge, my other hand grabbing his discarded sock, pressing it to my face, inhaling deep, the smell driving me wild.

“Fuck, man, do it,” he gasps, his voice breaking, his hands grabbing my hair, pulling me down, his cock throbbing, leaking, begging for my mouth. I kiss down his chest, my tongue licking the sweat, the musk, sucking his nipple, then lower, tracing the ridges of his abs, savoring the taste, the heat. I reach his cock, my lips brushing the head, tasting the precum, sharp and musky, and I groan, taking him into my mouth, sucking hard, my tongue swirling over the head, tracing the veins, feeling it pulse, thick and heavy.

“Goddamn, fuck,” he moans, his voice high, desperate, his hands tightening in my hair, his hips bucking, fucking my mouth, his cock throbbing, leaking more. I suck harder, my tongue working relentless, my hand stroking the base, keeping him on edge, my other hand grabbing his sock again, pressing it to my face, inhaling deep, the sweaty, musky scent making my cock throb, aching to come. “I’m—shit, I’m gonna come,” he cries, his voice breaking, his body trembling, his cock pulsing in my mouth, ready to burst.

I pull back, just enough to kiss his cock, licking the head, tasting the precum, then sucking hard, taking him deep, my throat relaxing, feeling him hit the back, gagging slightly but not stopping. He cries out, a raw, desperate sound, his hips bucking, his cock pulsing, and he comes, hot and thick, filling my mouth, spurting down my throat, the taste salty, musky, so fucking him. I swallow, savoring every drop, my tongue swirling over the head, milking him dry, his moans loud, echoing in the gym, his body trembling, spent.

I pull off, my lips slick, grinning, wiping my mouth with the back of my hand. He's sprawled on the bench, chest heaving, abs slick with sweat and precum, his cock softening, glistening with spit and cum. I grab his briefs and socks from the mat, the black fabric damp, reeking of sweat and musk, and drape them over his chest, the socks across his pecs, the briefs over his abs, a filthy trophy of this moment. “Keep ‘em,” I say, my voice low, teasing, my eyes locked on his, watching his flush deepen, his eyes wide, a mix of shock and lust. “Something to remember me by.”

I stand, grabbing my jock, pulling it on, the black fabric clinging to my sweat-slicked skin, my cock still half-hard, buzzing from the intensity. I slip my shirt back on, leaving it unbuttoned, my tie loose, and grab my shorts, stepping into them, smoothing the fabric over my thighs. He’s still lying there, covered in his dirty socks and briefs, his breath ragged, his body wrecked, his eyes following me, conflicted but hungry. I wink, sauntering toward the locker room, leaving him on the bench, the gym silent except for the faint hum of the lights, the air heavy with the scent of our sex, the moment locked tight in my chest, a forbidden thrill that’s burned into us both.

CHOKEHOLD

I'm thirty-eight, built like a boxer who's never missed a sparring session—broad shoulders, thick pecs, and a lean waist sculpted from years of training and street fights. My dark brown hair's cropped short, military-style, with a few silver flecks at the temples, giving me a grizzled edge. My blue eyes are sharp, always scanning, catching every twitch in a suspect's stance, and my jaw's square, shadowed with stubble that's rough from days on patrol. I'm a cop, all grit and discipline, my black uniform snug, the badge glinting on my chest, the utility belt heavy with cuffs and a holster, my boots polished but scuffed from the beat. I'm gay, always have been, but I keep it locked down on the job, my desires buried under the weight of duty—until tonight, when I spot him in the alley, and my cock stirs, straining against my uniform pants, the black fabric tight, no room for secrets.

The alley's a narrow strip of shadow behind a dive bar, the air thick with the stench of spilled beer, cigarette butts, and urban grit, the neon sign flickering above, casting red and blue hues across the damp concrete. It's past midnight, the city humming with distant sirens and muffled music, and I'm off-duty but still in uniform, my patrol car parked a block away. He's leaning against the wall, a street fighter type, maybe thirty-two, with a body that's all lean muscle, like a pitbull—wiry, powerful, built for a brawl. His black hair's tousled, falling into his eyes, which are green, sharp, and defiant, glinting with a challenge that makes my blood pound. His skin's pale, a few scars crisscrossing his knuckles, his jaw sharp, dusted with stubble. He's in a tight black tank top, showing off his defined arms, veins popping, and ripped jeans that hug his thighs, the bulge obvious, thick and tempting. His sneakers are worn, caked with dirt, and a leather bracelet on his wrist screams trouble. He's no stranger to a fight, and the way he's eyeing me, like I'm prey, has my cock half-hard, pressing against my zipper, the uniform doing nothing to hide it.

"Got a problem, officer?" he calls out, his voice low, taunting, a smirk curling his lips as he pushes off the wall, stepping closer, his posture all swagger, his eyes locked on mine. My hand rests on my belt, fingers brushing the cuffs, a reflex, but my gaze rakes over him, catching the way his tank clings to his pecs, the faint sheen of sweat on his skin, the bulge in his jeans shifting as he moves. My cock twitches, and I shift my stance, trying to hide it, but his eyes flick down, catching the outline, his smirk widening.

"Maybe I do," I say, my voice steady but rough, laced with an edge I can't quite control, my eyes narrowing as I step closer, boots thudding on the concrete. "You look like you're asking for trouble, standing out here like that." I let my gaze linger on his bulge, deliberate, making it clear I'm not just talking about a fight, and his smirk falters, a flush creeping up his neck, his eyes darkening with something that's not just defiance.

He laughs, a short, sharp sound, his hands flexing at his sides, knuckles scarred and ready. "Trouble? You're the one staring, cop," he says, his voice dripping with challenge, stepping closer, close enough that I can smell his sweat, clean and sharp, mixed with a hint of smoke from the bar. "What's the matter? Uniform too tight?" His eyes drop to my crotch again, blatant now, and my cock throbs, straining against the fabric, the zipper biting into my skin.

I step closer, our chests almost touching, the air between us electric, thick with tension and the scent of sweat and leather. “Keep talking, and you’ll find out how tight,” I growl, my hand brushing my cuffs, the metal cool against my fingers, my eyes locked on his, catching the flicker of heat, the curiosity in his green gaze. “You think you can take me?” I let my fingers graze his arm, just a touch, feeling the hard muscle, the heat of his skin, and he tenses, his breath hitching, but he doesn’t pull away, his bulge growing, the jeans stretching tight.

“Take you?” He grins, his voice low, teasing, his hand brushing my chest, fingers grazing my badge, the contact sending a jolt through me, my cock twitching harder. “I’d have you on the ground in seconds, officer.” His fingers linger, tracing the edge of my uniform shirt, brushing my pec, and I catch the way his cock stirs, the bulge in his jeans obvious, a faint wet spot forming where he’s leaking, his defiance melting into something hotter, hungrier.

I grab his wrist, pinning it against the wall, my grip firm, the power play making his eyes widen, his breath catching, his cock twitching in his jeans. “Big talk for a guy who’s already hard,” I say, my voice low, rough, my lips inches from his, my free hand brushing his hip, grazing the bulge in his jeans, feeling the thick, pulsing heat. “Bet your cock’s begging for more, isn’t it?” I lean in, my breath hot against his ear, nipping the lobe, tasting the salt of his sweat, and he moans, a low, needy sound that hits me right in the dick.

“Fuck you,” he mutters, but it’s weak, his voice trembling, his wrist flexing against my grip, his body leaning into mine, his bulge pressing against my thigh, the jeans rough, the heat intense. “I’m not—shit, I’m not into guys.” His words are a reflex, but his eyes betray him, locked on my lips, then dropping to my bulge, the uniform pants stretched tight, my cock throbbing, leaking precum that soaks the inside. His free hand brushes my chest again, fingers digging into my pec, feeling the muscle, the sweat, and I grin, my hand squeezing his bulge, stroking through the denim, making him gasp, his hips bucking.

"Not into guys?" I chuckle, my voice a low growl, my hand releasing his wrist, sliding to his neck, feeling the pulse hammering under my fingers, my thumb brushing the stubble along his jaw. "Your cock's saying something else, tough guy. Leaking like a fucking slut just from my touch." I stroke harder, my thumb circling the head of his cock through the jeans, feeling it pulse, thick and heavy, and he moans, his head tilting back, exposing his throat, sweat glistening in the neon light.

"Goddamn it," he groans, his hand sliding to my waist, fingers brushing the utility belt, grazing the cuffs, the contact sending a jolt through me, my cock throbbing, aching for more. "You're—fuck, you're trouble." His voice is hoarse, his fingers bolder, slipping under my uniform shirt, brushing my abs, feeling the sweat-slicked muscle, his touch hungry, no longer hesitant. His eyes meet mine, green and wild, the defiance fading, drowned in the heat, the want, the way his cock pulses in my hand, leaking more, soaking the denim.

I grin, my hand sliding to his ass, squeezing the firm muscle through the jeans, feeling it clench under my touch, the denim rough against my palm. “Trouble’s my job,” I murmur, my lips brushing his ear, my tongue flicking out, tasting the sweat, the smoke, making him shudder. “And you’re begging for it, aren’t you? Standing here, letting me grope you like this, your cock hard as fuck.” I tug at his tank top, pulling it up, exposing his abs, tight and defined, glistening with sweat, and he moans, his hand tightening on my abs, fingers digging in, his bulge grinding against my thigh, the friction electric.

“Fuck, man,” he breathes, his voice trembling, his hand sliding to my chest, pinching my nipple through the uniform shirt, making me groan, my cock throbbing, leaking more, soaking the inside of my pants. “This is—shit, this is crazy.” His eyes flick to my lips, then lower, to the bulge in my pants, the uniform stretched tight, the outline of my cock clear, throbbing, and I catch the hunger, the curiosity, the tough-guy facade cracking under the weight of this moment.

"Crazy's what makes you grab me like that," I say, my voice low, my hand stroking his bulge, keeping him on edge, my fingers teasing the zipper, pulling it lower, exposing the base of his cock, the dark hair damp with sweat. "Bet you're imagining my hands on your cock, my mouth on your hole, making you scream." I lean in, kissing his neck, sucking lightly, tasting the salt, the smoke, feeling his pulse race under my lips, his moan loud, needy, echoing in the alley.

"You're—fuck, you're gonna get us in deep shit," he says, his voice hoarse, his hand sliding to my ass, squeezing through the uniform pants, fingers teasing the seam, brushing my crack, making my cock throb, aching for more. "I'm not—shit, I'm not supposed to want this." His words are weak, the thought of consequences fading under the heat, the want, the way his cock pulses in my hand, leaking more, soaking the jeans.

"Then stop me," I challenge, my voice low, my hand sliding inside his tank top, brushing his bare chest, pinching his nipple, rolling it between my fingers, making him gasp, his hips bucking. "Push me away, tell me you don't want this." I stroke his bulge harder, feeling it pulse, thick and heavy, my other hand grabbing his wrist again, pinning it against the wall, the power play making his eyes flash, his breath catching, his cock twitching against my thigh.

He doesn't push me away. Instead, his free hand slides to my bulge, cupping it through the uniform, feeling the thick, pulsing heat, his fingers trembling but eager, stroking the outline of my cock, making my head spin. "Fuck, I—I want it," he admits, his voice breaking, his eyes wild, locked on mine. "You're—shit, you're making me want it so bad." His words are a surrender, raw and desperate, and it's like a dam breaking, his hand stroking my bulge harder, his fingers teasing the zipper, brushing the bare skin above, sending a jolt through me.

I laugh, low and dirty, my lips brushing his jaw, kissing the stubble, tasting the sweat, the smoke. "That's it, tough guy," I murmur, my hand sliding inside his jeans, brushing the base of his cock, the dark hair damp, his cock straining, leaking more, soaking the denim. "Show me how bad you want it." I tug at his tank top, pulling it higher, exposing his pecs, the faint hair dusted across them, glistening with sweat, and he moans, his hand tightening on my bulge, stroking faster, the alley a haze of heat and want, our bodies pressed together, uniforms and jeans creaking, cocks hard and leaking, hands groping, pushing each other closer to the edge.

His hand grips my bulge, fingers digging into the black uniform pants, tracing the thick outline of my cock, the fabric stretched tight, soaked with precum that's making the zipper bite into my skin. The alley's a grimy cocoon, the neon bar sign flickering above, casting jagged red and blue shadows across his pale skin, his black tank top rucked up, exposing the lean ridges of his abs, glistening with sweat. My badge glints on my chest, the utility belt heavy, cuffs clinking as I shift, my boots scraping the damp concrete. His jeans are unzipped, the bulge massive, throbbing, a wet spot spreading where his cock's leaking, his scarred knuckles flexing, his green eyes wild, locked on mine, defiance and lust warring in his gaze. The air's thick with the stench of beer, smoke, and our sweat, the distant hum of the city barely cutting through the tension crackling between us.

“Fuck, you’re—shit, you’re pushing me too far,” he rasps, his voice rough, trembling with need, his fingers stroking my cock through the uniform, slow and deliberate, making my hips buck, my breath hitching. “This is—fuck, I shouldn’t be doing this.” His words are shaky, but his hand doesn’t stop, sliding to my hip, fingers brushing the bare skin above my belt, sending a jolt straight to my dick, making it throb harder, leaking more, the precum pooling inside my pants.

I grin, my hand still pinning his wrist against the wall, the power play making his eyes flash, his breath catching, his cock twitching in his jeans. “Shouldn’t? Your dick’s begging for it,” I growl, my voice low, edged with authority, my free hand sliding to his chest, fingers digging into the muscle through his tank top, brushing his nipple, hard and sensitive. “Bet it’s rock-hard, leaking like a fucking slut just from my touch.” I lean in, my lips grazing his ear, nipping the lobe, tasting the salt of his sweat, the faint smoke clinging to his skin, and he moans, a low, needy sound that hits me right in the gut.

“Goddamn it,” he groans, his free hand sliding to my ass, squeezing through the uniform, fingers bold now, teasing the seam, brushing my crack, making my cock throb, aching for more. “You’re—fuck, you’re trouble, officer.” His voice cracks, his fingers digging into my ass, pulling me closer, our bulges grinding together, the denim and uniform fabric rough, the friction electric, making us both groan, low and desperate. His eyes flick to my lips, then lower, to the badge on my chest, the sweat beading on my pecs, and I catch the hunger, the curiosity, his tough-guy front crumbling.

I release his wrist, my hand sliding to his neck, fingers curling around the back, feeling the pulse hammering under his stubble, my thumb brushing his jaw, rough and warm. “Trouble’s my beat,” I murmur, my voice a low purr, my lips inches from his, not kissing but teasing, my breath hot against his mouth. “And you’re eating it up, aren’t you? Letting me pin you like this, your cock leaking in those jeans.” My fingers tug at his tank top, pulling it higher, exposing more of his chest, the faint hair dusted across his pecs, glistening with sweat, and he moans, his hand tightening on my ass, his fingers teasing closer to my crack, sending sparks through me.

"Fuck you," he mutters, but it's weak, his voice trembling, his hand sliding to my chest, fingers brushing my badge, then lower, grazing my nipple through the uniform, making me groan, my cock throbbing, leaking more, soaking the inside of my pants. "I'm not—shit, I'm not into this." His words are hollow, his eyes betraying him, locked on my bulge, the uniform stretched tight, the outline of my cock clear, throbbing, and his hand moves, cupping it again, stroking slow, feeling the heat, the hardness, making my head spin.

"Not into it?" I chuckle, my hand sliding inside his tank top, brushing his bare chest, pinching his nipple, rolling it between my fingers, making him gasp, his hips bucking, his bulge pressing harder against my thigh. "Bullshit. Your cock's screaming for it, leaking all over those jeans." I lean in, kissing his neck, sucking lightly, tasting the salt, the smoke, leaving a faint mark, feeling his pulse race under my lips. His moan is louder, needier, echoing in the alley, his hand stroking my bulge faster, his fingers bold, teasing the zipper, brushing the bare skin above my belt.

"You're—fuck, you're gonna get us caught," he says, his voice hoarse, his hand sliding to my back, fingers digging into the muscle, pulling me closer, our chests brushing, his bare skin hot against my uniform, the badge pressing into his pec. "This is—shit, this is crazy." His eyes meet mine, green and wild, the defiance fading, drowned in the lust, the want, the way his cock pulses in my hand, leaking more, soaking the denim, the wet spot stark against the fabric.

"Crazy's what makes you grab me like this," I murmur, my hand sliding to his ass, squeezing hard, feeling the muscle clench through the jeans, my fingers teasing the seam, brushing his crack, making him shudder. "Bet you're imagining my hands on your cock, my tongue on your hole, making you scream." I tug at his jeans, pulling the zipper lower, exposing more of his bulge, the dark hair damp with sweat, his cock straining, thick and veiny, begging to be touched. I stroke through the denim, slow and deliberate, my thumb circling the head, feeling it pulse, and he moans, his head tilting back, his throat exposed, sweat glistening in the neon light.

"Goddamn, you're—shit, you're relentless," he groans, his hand sliding under my uniform shirt, brushing my abs, fingers tracing the sweat-slicked muscle, his touch hungry, no longer hesitant. "I'm not—fuck, I'm not supposed to feel like this." His fingers dig into my abs, sliding lower, brushing the waistband of my pants, teasing the bare skin above, sending a jolt through me, my cock throbbing, leaking more, the precum pooling inside my uniform. His eyes flick to my lips, then lower, to the bulge in my pants, and I catch the hunger, the curiosity, his tough-guy resolve cracking under the weight of this moment.

I grin, my hand sliding to his face, cupping his jaw, my thumb brushing his lips, feeling the soft, full curve, the stubble scraping my skin. "Feel like what? Like you wanna rip this uniform off me, get your hands on my cock?" I murmur, my voice low, my lips inches from his, not kissing but teasing, my breath hot against his mouth. "Bet you're imagining it, my hands on your dick, my tongue in your hole, making you lose it." I tug at his tank top, pulling it off completely, tossing it to the concrete, exposing his chest fully, the faint hair matted with sweat, his nipples hard, begging for my touch.

“Fuck, stop,” he says, but it’s half-hearted, his voice trembling, his hand sliding to my bulge again, stroking harder, his fingers teasing the zipper, brushing the bare skin above, making my cock throb, aching for more. “This is—fuck, this is too much.” His eyes meet mine, wild, conflicted, but his touch is bold, his fingers slipping under my shirt, brushing my pecs, pinching my nipple, making me groan, my hips bucking into his hand. His cock twitches against my thigh, leaking more, the wet spot spreading, his jeans soaked with precum.

“Then make me,” I challenge, my voice low, my hand stroking his bulge, keeping him on edge, my fingers teasing the base of his cock, feeling it pulse, thick and heavy, through the denim. “Push me away, tell me you don’t want this.” I lean in, kissing his chest, my tongue flicking over his nipple, sucking hard, tasting the sweat, the musk, and he moans, loud and needy, his hand tightening on my bulge, stroking faster, his fingers bold, tracing the length of my cock through the uniform, making my head spin.

He doesn't push me away. Instead, his hand slides to my neck, pulling me closer, our lips inches apart, not kissing but teasing, his breath hot against my mouth, his eyes wild, locked on mine. "Fuck, I—I want it," he admits, his voice breaking, his hand stroking my bulge harder, his fingers teasing the zipper, slipping inside, brushing the bare skin at the base of my cock, sending a jolt through me. "You're—shit, you're making me want it so bad." His words are a surrender, raw and desperate, and it's like a dam breaking, his hand sliding to my ass again, squeezing hard, fingers teasing my crack through the uniform, making my cock throb, leaking more, soaking the inside.

I laugh, low and dirty, my lips brushing his jaw, kissing the stubble, tasting the sweat, the smoke. "That's it, tough guy," I murmur, my hand sliding inside his jeans, brushing the base of his cock, the dark hair damp, his cock straining, leaking more, soaking the denim. "Show me how bad you want it." I pinch his nipple, rolling it between my fingers, making him gasp, his hips bucking, his bulge pressing harder against my thigh. His hand tightens on my bulge, stroking faster, his fingers bold, teasing the zipper, brushing my cock directly now, the contact electric, making my head spin.

"Goddamn, you're—fuck, you're gonna ruin me," he groans, his voice hoarse, his hand sliding to my back, fingers digging into the muscle, pulling me closer, our chests pressed together, his bare skin hot against my uniform, the badge pressing into his pec. "I shouldn't—shit, I shouldn't be doing this." His eyes meet mine, wild, conflicted, but his touch is sure, his fingers slipping inside my pants, brushing the base of my cock, feeling the heat, the hardness, making me moan, my hips rocking into his hand.

I grin, my hand sliding to his ass, squeezing hard, fingers teasing his crack through the jeans, brushing his hole, making him shudder. "Ruin you? I'm just giving you what you want," I murmur, my lips kissing his chest, my tongue flicking over his nipple, sucking hard, tasting the sweat, the musk, savoring the way his body arches, his cock twitching against my thigh. “Bet you’re dying for more, aren’t you? My hands on your cock, my tongue on your hole, making you lose it.” I kiss his collarbone, sucking lightly, leaving another mark, feeling his pulse race under my lips.

“Fuck, yes,” he moans, his voice high, desperate, his hands grabbing my face, pulling me closer, our lips inches apart, not kissing but teasing, his breath hot against my mouth. “You’re—shit, you’re making me want it so bad.” His words are a confession, raw and filthy, and I grin, my hand stroking his bulge, keeping him on edge, my fingers teasing the base of his cock, feeling it pulse, thick and heavy, the denim slick with precum.

His lips are so close I can taste the smoke on his breath, his green eyes wild, burning with a mix of defiance and raw hunger, his hand stroking my cock through the uniform, fingers bold, digging into the black fabric, tracing the throbbing outline, precum soaking the inside, making the zipper bite harder. The alley’s a gritty haze, neon flickering overhead, casting jagged red and blue across his pale skin, his tank top gone, his lean chest glistening, faint scars crisscrossing his pecs, nipples hard and flushed. My badge presses into my chest, the utility belt heavy, cuffs clinking as I shift, boots grinding on the damp concrete. His jeans are low, unzipped, his cock straining, thick and veiny, leaking through the denim, a wet spot spreading, his scarred knuckles flexing, his body trembling with need, pressed against the wall, my hand on his ass, squeezing the firm muscle, teasing his crack through the jeans.

"Fuck, you're—shit, you're driving me insane," he rasps, his voice rough, cracking with lust, his fingers sliding inside my pants, brushing the base of my cock, the contact searing, making my hips buck, my cock throbbing harder, leaking more. "This is—fuck, I can't stop." His words are desperate, his hand bold, stroking my cock directly now, skin on skin, feeling the heat, the hardness, his thumb grazing the head, smearing precum, sending a jolt through me, my breath hitching.

I grin, my hand gripping his neck, fingers curling tight, not choking but firm, the power play making his eyes flash, his lips parting, his moan low and needy. "Can't stop? You're fucking begging for it," I growl, my voice thick, my lips brushing his jaw, tasting the stubble, the salt of his sweat, my tongue flicking out, licking a slow stripe up his throat. “Your cock’s leaking like a slut, screaming for my hands.” I slap his ass, hard, the sound sharp over the alley’s hum, making him gasp, his hips jerking, his bulge grinding against my thigh, the denim rough, the friction electric.

“Goddamn it,” he moans, his hand sliding to my chest, fingers ripping at my uniform shirt, buttons popping, exposing my pecs, slick with sweat, his fingers digging into the muscle, pinching my nipple, making me groan, my cock throbbing, aching for more. “You’re—fuck, you’re too much, officer.” His voice trembles, but his fingers are bold, slipping lower, brushing my abs, tracing the sweat-slicked muscle, his touch hungry, no longer hesitant. I grab his wrist, pinning it above his head again, my other hand stroking his bulge, feeling the thick, pulsing heat through the denim, my thumb circling the head, making him cry out, his body arching against the wall.

“Too much?” I chuckle, my voice low, my hand sliding to his pit, fingers brushing the coarse hair, damp with sweat, the musky scent hitting me hard, raw and masculine, driving my cock wild. “You’re the one grinding on me, your dick hard as fuck." I lean in, my nose burying in his pit, inhaling deep, the smell intoxicating, sweat and smoke and pure him, making my head spin. I lick the hair, tasting the salt, the heat, and he moans, loud and desperate, his body shuddering, his pinned wrist flexing against my grip, his cock twitching in my hand, leaking more, soaking the jeans.

"Fuck, man," he gasps, his voice high, wrecked, his free hand grabbing my hair, tugging hard, pulling me closer, his pit pressed against my face. "You're—shit, you're filthy." His words are slurred, drowned in lust, his cock pulsing against my thigh, the denim soaked, his precum dripping, staining the concrete. I pull back, slapping his face lightly, just enough to sting, his eyes flashing with shock and heat, his lips parting, begging for more.

"Filthy? You love it," I growl, my lips crashing into his, the kiss hard and sloppy, all teeth and tongue, tasting the sweat, the smoke, swallowing his moans. My hand strokes his bulge, keeping him on edge, my fingers slipping inside his jeans, brushing the base of his cock, the dark hair damp, his cock straining, thick and veiny, leaking more. "Bet you're imagining my mouth on your cock, sucking you dry," I murmur against his lips, my hand releasing his wrist, sliding to his other pit, inhaling deep, licking the damp hair, savoring the musky scent, driving me wild.

"Goddamn, yes," he moans, his voice breaking, his hands grabbing my uniform, yanking it open further, fingers roaming my chest, pinching my nipples, making me groan, my cock throbbing, leaking more, soaking the inside of my pants. "You're—fuck, you're making me lose it." His touch is desperate, his fingers bold, slipping inside my pants, brushing my cock directly, stroking slow, feeling the heat, the hardness, making my hips buck, my head spin.

I pull back, grabbing his jeans, yanking them lower, exposing his cock fully, thick and veiny, slick with precum, slapping against his thigh. "Lose it? You're already fucking gone," I growl, dropping to my knees, my lips kissing his thigh, tasting the sweat, the musk, my tongue licking a slow stripe up to his cock, not touching it, just teasing, brushing the dark hair at the base, inhaling the raw scent of him. "Look at this cock, leaking like a faucet, begging for my mouth." I lick the base, slow and deliberate, tasting the precum, sharp and musky, and he cries out, his hands grabbing my hair, tugging hard, his hips bucking, his cock brushing my cheek, leaving a slick trail.

"Fuck, do it," he groans, his voice high, desperate, his hands tightening in my hair, pulling me closer, his cock throbbing, leaking, begging for my mouth. I grin, kissing his thigh again, my tongue flicking out, tasting the sweat, the heat, my hand stroking his cock, slow and firm, keeping him on edge, my other hand sliding to his ass, squeezing through the jeans, teasing his crack, brushing his hole, making him shudder. "Goddamn, officer, you're—shit, you're killing me," he moans, his voice wrecked, his body trembling, his cock pulsing in my hand, leaking more, dripping onto the concrete.

I stand, grabbing his neck again, fingers curling tight, not choking but firm, the power play making his eyes flash, his lips parting, his moan loud and needy. "Killing you? I'm just getting started," I growl, my lips brushing his ear, nipping the lobe, tasting the sweat, my hand stroking his cock faster, feeling it pulse, thick and heavy, the precum slicking my fingers. I slap his ass again, hard, the sound echoing, making him cry out, his hips bucking, his cock twitching in my hand. "Bet you're imagining my cock in your hole, fucking you right here," I murmur, my lips kissing his neck, sucking hard, leaving a mark, tasting the salt, the smoke.

"Yes, fuck, yes," he moans, his voice breaking, his hands grabbing my uniform, ripping at the shirt, exposing more of my chest, fingers digging into my pecs, pinching my nipples, making me groan, my cock throbbing, aching to be free. "I'm—shit, I want it so bad." His words are a surrender, raw and filthy, his body trembling, his pit exposed as he raises his arm, the musky scent hitting me again, driving me wild. I lean in, burying my face in his pit, inhaling deep, licking the damp hair, tasting the salt, the musk, my tongue relentless, savoring the raw masculinity of him.

"Fuck, you're perfect," I growl, my lips against his skin, my hand stroking his cock, keeping him on edge, my other hand sliding inside his jeans, teasing his hole, brushing the rim, feeling it clench, hot and tight. I slap his face again, lightly, the sting making his eyes flash, his moan loud, needy. “You want my cock, don’t you? Want me to fuck you senseless,” I murmur, my lips crashing into his, the kiss feral, tongues fucking, tasting sweat, musk, smoke, swallowing his moans.

“Goddamn, yes,” he moans into my mouth, his voice wrecked, his hands grabbing my belt, fingers brushing the cuffs, yanking at the zipper, brushing my cock directly, the contact electric, making my hips buck, my cock throbbing, leaking more. “Fuck me, officer—shit, I need it.” His words are desperate, his body surrendering, his cock pulsing in my hand, leaking, dripping onto the concrete. I grin, my hand sliding to his ass, squeezing hard, fingers pressing against his hole, not pushing in but teasing, circling, making him shudder, his moans louder, needier.

I push him back against the wall, his ass out, jeans low, his hole exposed, pink and tight, begging for me. “You’re gonna take it, aren’t you?” I growl, my hand stroking my cock, slick with precum, pressing it against his hole, not pushing in, just teasing, feeling the heat, the tightness. “Begging for my cock, right here in this fucking alley.” I slap his ass again, hard, the sound sharp, making him cry out, his body trembling, his cock leaking, dripping onto the concrete. I lean in, kissing his neck, sucking hard, leaving another mark, my tongue licking the sweat, tasting the smoke, my hand stroking his cock, keeping him on edge, the alley a haze of heat and lust, our bodies slick with sweat, uniforms and jeans creaking, cocks throbbing, leaking.

His hole clenches, hot and tight, begging for my cock as I press against it, teasing, not pushing in yet, the alley a gritty haze of neon and sweat, the air thick with the stench of beer, smoke, and our raw musk. His pale skin glistens, his lean muscles taut, scars crisscrossing his pecs, nipples hard under the flickering red and blue lights. My uniform’s torn open, badge glinting, utility belt heavy with cuffs clinking, my boots grinding on the concrete. His jeans are low, his cock free, thick and veiny, leaking precum that drips onto the ground, his scarred knuckles flexing, green eyes wild with defiance and lust. My cock throbs in my hand, slick with precum, straining against the open zipper of my uniform pants, the black fabric soaked inside.

“Fuck, you’re—shit, you’re making me crazy,” he groans, his voice hoarse, wrecked, his hands braced against the wall, his ass pushing back, desperate for more. His body trembles, muscles flexing, his cock pulsing in my grip, leaking more, staining the concrete. “Do it, officer—fuck, I need it.” His words are a raw plea, his tough-guy front shattered, his hips rocking, urging my cock closer to his hole.

I grin, my hand gripping his neck, fingers curling tight, not choking but compressing, the muscle under my grip hard, his pulse hammering. “Need it? You’re gonna beg for it,” I growl, my voice thick, my other hand slapping his ass, the sound sharp, making him moan, his body shuddering, his hole clenching, begging. I step closer, my chest pressing against his back, my badge digging into his spine, my cock teasing his hole, the heat intense, driving me wild. “Bet you’re imagining me pinning you down, fucking you senseless,” I murmur, my lips brushing his ear, nipping the lobe, tasting the sweat and smoke.

“Goddamn it,” he moans, his voice high, desperate, his hands clawing at the wall, his muscles flexing, trying to push back, but I hold him firm, my grip on his neck tightening, a wrestler’s chokehold, not cutting air but asserting control, his body yielding under my strength. “You’re—fuck, you’re too strong,” he gasps, his tone laced with awe and need, his cock twitching in my hand, leaking more, dripping onto the ground. I slap his ass again, harder, the sting making him cry out, his hole clenching, pulling at the head of my cock.

“Too strong?” I chuckle, my voice low, my hand sliding to his shoulder, shoving him down, forcing him to his knees, then onto his back on the concrete, the rough ground scraping his skin. “Let’s see you fight back, tough guy.” I straddle his chest, my thighs clamping his ribs, muscles flexing, compressing his torso, the power play making his eyes widen, his breath hitching. My cock hovers over his face, slick with precum, throbbing, and his lips part, his tongue flicking out, tasting the air, hungry but hesitant, his green eyes flickering with conflict.

“Fuck, man,” he groans, his hands grabbing my thighs, fingers digging into the uniform, feeling the muscle, his touch bold but trembling, his cock hard, leaking onto his abs, glistening under the neon. “I’m not—shit, I’m not supposed to want this.” His voice cracks, but his hands don’t stop, sliding to my ass, squeezing through the fabric, teasing the seam, making my cock throb, aching for his mouth. I lean down, my hand grabbing his jaw, forcing his head back, exposing his throat, my lips crashing into his, the kiss hard and sloppy, all teeth and tongue, tasting sweat, smoke, and his raw need.

“You want it,” I growl against his lips, my hand tightening on his jaw, my thighs squeezing his ribs harder, muscles bulging, pinning him to the ground, the concrete cold against his back. “Your cock’s leaking, begging for me to own you.” I pull back, slapping his face lightly, the sting making his eyes flash, his moan loud, needy. My hand slides to his pit, inhaling deep, the musky scent of sweat and smoke hitting me hard, driving me wild. I lick his pit, slow and deliberate, tasting the salt, the heat, and he moans, his body arching, his cock twitching, leaking more, pooling on his abs.

“Goddamn, you’re—fuck, you’re filthy,” he gasps, his voice wrecked, his hands grabbing my hair, tugging hard, pulling me closer, his pit pressed against my face. I suck the hair, savoring the musk, my tongue relentless, my thighs clamping tighter, compressing his chest, making his breaths shallow, his moans desperate. “Do it—shit, do something,” he pleads, his voice high, his hips bucking, his cock brushing my thigh, leaving a slick trail of precum.

I grin, shifting back, my hands grabbing his wrists, pinning them above his head, my strength overwhelming his, a wrestler’s hold, his muscles straining but yielding, his eyes wild, locked on mine. “Something? Like sucking your cock till you scream?” I growl, my lips kissing his chest, my tongue flicking over his nipple, sucking hard, tasting the sweat, the musk, making him cry out, his body writhing under my weight. My hand slides to his cock, stroking slow, feeling it pulse, thick and veiny, slick with precum, and he moans, his hips bucking, his wrists flexing against my grip.

“Fuck, yes,” he moans, his voice breaking, his body trembling, his cock pulsing in my hand, leaking more, dripping onto his abs. I release his wrists, my hands sliding to his jeans, yanking them off completely, tossing them aside, his cock springing free, slapping his abs, leaving a wet streak. I lean down, my lips brushing the head, tasting the precum, sharp and musky, and he cries out, his hands grabbing my hair, tugging hard, his hips bucking, chasing my mouth. “Goddamn, officer, suck it,” he groans, his voice wrecked, his eyes wild, pleading, his cock throbbing, begging for more.

I suck the head, my lips stretching, my tongue swirling, slow and deliberate, savoring the taste, the heat, the way it pulses in my mouth. He moans, loud and shameless, his hands tightening in my hair, his hips rocking, fucking my mouth, the wet heat driving him wild. “Fuck, you’re—shit, you’re too good,” he gasps, his voice high, desperate, his cock twitching, leaking more, dripping down my throat. I pull back, my lips slick, grinning, my hand stroking his cock, keeping him on edge, my other hand sliding to his ass, squeezing the firm muscle, teasing his crack, brushing his hole, feeling it clench, hot and tight.

“Too good?” I growl, my voice thick, my hand slapping his thigh, the sting making him moan, his body shuddering, his cock pulsing in my hand. “You’re gonna take more than that.” I flip him onto his stomach, the concrete rough against his chest, his ass up, hole exposed, pink and tight, glistening with sweat. I press my cock against it, not pushing in, just teasing, feeling the heat, the tightness, my cock throbbing, slick with precum. “Beg for it, tough guy,” I murmur, my lips kissing his back, licking the sweat, tasting the musk, my hand stroking his cock, keeping him on edge, my other hand gripping his neck, compressing lightly, the chokehold making his moans sharper, needier.

“Fuck, please,” he groans, his voice wrecked, his ass pushing back, chasing my cock, his hole clenching, begging. “Fuck me, officer—shit, I need it.” His words are raw, desperate, his body trembling, his muscles flexing under my grip, his cock leaking, dripping onto the concrete. I slap his ass, hard, the sound echoing, making him cry out, his hole clenching tighter, pulling at the head of my cock. I press harder, breaching his hole, slow and deliberate, the tightness searing, making me groan, my cock throbbing, aching to pound deeper.

"Goddamn, you're tight," I growl, pushing in deeper, inch by inch, feeling his hole clench, hot and slick, pulling me in. He moans, loud and shameless, his hands clawing at the concrete, his body trembling, his cock pulsing in my hand, leaking more, dripping onto the ground. "Taking my cock like a fucking slut," I murmur, my lips kissing his shoulder, sucking hard, leaving a mark, my tongue licking the sweat, tasting the smoke, my hips rocking slow, letting him adjust, savoring the tightness, the heat.

"Fuck, it's—shit, it's too much," he gasps, his voice wrecked, his hips bucking back, meeting my thrusts, his hole clenching tighter, making my cock throb, aching to pound harder. I slap his ass again, the sting making him cry out, his body shuddering, his cock leaking, dripping onto the concrete. I lean in, my hand gripping his neck tighter, the chokehold firm, compressing his muscles, his breaths shallow, his moans desperate, echoing in the alley. "Harder—fuck, fuck me harder," he pleads, his voice high, his body surrendering, his cock pulsing in my hand, ready to burst but holding, just barely.

I pound harder, deeper, the slick sound of skin on skin mixing with his moans, the creak of my utility belt, the thump of distant music. My hand strokes his cock, keeping him on edge, my other hand tightening on his neck, the chokehold relentless, his muscles flexing under my grip, his body yielding to my strength. “You love this, don’t you? My cock in your hole, my hand choking you,” I growl, my lips crashing into his neck, sucking hard, tasting the sweat, the musk, my tongue licking a slow stripe up his spine, savoring the raw masculinity of him.

“Yes, fuck, yes,” he moans, his voice breaking, his hands clawing at the concrete, his ass pushing back, taking every thrust, his cock pulsing, leaking, dripping onto the ground. I slap his thigh, the sting making him cry out, his hole clenching tighter, pulling me deeper, driving me wild. “Goddamn, officer, don’t stop,” he pleads, his voice wrecked, his body trembling, drowned in pleasure.

His hole clenches tight around my cock, hot and slick, pulling me deeper with each thrust, his moans raw and desperate, echoing in the grimy alley, neon flickering overhead, casting red and blue across his pale skin, his lean muscles trembling, scars glinting on his pecs. My uniform's ripped open, badge digging into my chest, utility belt clinking, boots grinding on the concrete. His jeans are gone, his cock hard, thick, and veiny, leaking precum that drips onto his abs, pooling in the ridges, his scarred knuckles clawing at the ground, green eyes wild with lust and pain. My cock's buried in him, throbbing, slick with precum, the black uniform pants soaked inside, zipper biting my skin.

"Fuck, it's—shit, it's too much," he gasps, his voice wrecked, high and strained, his body shuddering, his hole clenching tighter, the resistance fierce, my cock stretching him wide, too big, making him wince with every thrust. "Goddamn, officer, you're—fuck, you're huge." His words are a mix of awe and agony, his ass pushing back, taking me, but his moans sharpen, pain lacing the pleasure, his muscles flexing under my chokehold, my fingers compressing his neck, not choking but controlling, his breaths shallow, ragged.

I slow my thrusts, easing up, my hand loosening on his neck, feeling his pulse hammer under my fingers, his body trembling, slick with sweat. "Hurts, huh?" I growl, my voice low, thick with lust, my lips brushing his ear, tasting the sweat, the smoke clinging to his skin. "Your tight little hole can't handle my cock." I slap his ass, lighter this time, the sting making him moan, his hole clenching, still begging despite the pain. I pull out slow, my cock slick, glistening with precum, his hole winking, pink and stretched, glistening with sweat and my precum, making my cock throb, aching to dive back in.

"Fuck, yeah, it—shit, it hurts," he groans, his voice hoarse, his body slumping against the concrete, his ass up, red from my slaps, his cock pulsing, leaking onto his abs. "You're—fuck, you're too big, officer." His green eyes meet mine over his shoulder, wild, conflicted, lust battling the ache, his lips parted, swollen from our kisses, glistening with spit. I grin, my hand stroking my cock, keeping it hard, slick with his heat, my other hand grabbing his hair, tugging him up to his knees, his face level with my cock.

"Then you're gonna suck it," I growl, my voice commanding, my hand tightening in his hair, guiding his lips to my cock, the head flushed, leaking, brushing his mouth. "Show me how much you want it, tough guy." His eyes widen, hesitation flickering, but his tongue flicks out, tasting the precum, sharp and musky, and he moans, low and needy, his hands grabbing my thighs, fingers digging into the uniform, feeling the muscle, his touch bold but trembling.

"Goddamn," he mutters, his voice wrecked, his lips parting, taking the head, sucking slow, his tongue swirling, clumsy but eager, the wet heat driving me wild, my cock throbbing in his mouth. "You're—fuck, you taste so good," he groans, his voice muffled, his lips stretching, taking me deeper, his throat relaxing, gagging slightly but not stopping, his eyes locked on mine, green and hungry, the hesitation fading. I moan, my hips rocking, fucking his mouth, the slick sound of spit and precum mixing with his moans, the alley pulsing with our heat.

"Fuck, that's it," I growl, my hand tightening in his hair, guiding him, my cock hitting the back of his throat, making him gag, his eyes watering but burning with lust. "Suck that cock like you mean it." I slap his face lightly, the sting making him moan around my cock, the vibration sending sparks through me, my cock throbbing, leaking more, dripping down his chin. His hands slide to my ass, squeezing through the uniform, fingers teasing the seam, brushing my crack, making my cock twitch, aching for more.

I pull back, my cock slick with his spit, glistening, and shove him onto his back, the concrete rough against his skin, his cock bouncing, leaking onto his abs, his thighs spread, hole still red, stretched, begging. "You're not done," I growl, swinging my leg over him, straddling his face, my cock hovering over his lips, my hands pinning his wrists above his head, the wrestler's hold making his muscles strain, his body yielding under my strength. "We're gonna sixty-nine, tough guy. Suck my cock while I work yours."

"Fuck, officer," he moans, his voice high, desperate, his lips parting, taking my cock again, sucking hard, his tongue swirling, tasting the precum, the musk, his hands flexing against my grip, his cock throbbing, leaking onto his abs. I lean down, my lips brushing his cock, inhaling the raw scent, sweat and musk and him, my tongue flicking out, licking the head, tasting the precum, sharp and heady. He cries out, his moan muffled around my cock, his hips bucking, chasing my mouth, his cock pulsing, begging for more.

"Goddamn, you're—shit, you're killing me," he groans, his voice wrecked, his lips stretching around my cock, sucking deeper, his tongue relentless, the wet heat driving me wild. I suck his cock, taking it deep, my throat relaxing, feeling it pulse, thick and veiny, slick with precum, the taste sharp, musky, making my cock throb in his mouth. My hands release his wrists, sliding to his thighs, spreading them, my fingers teasing his hole, brushing the rim, still stretched, red, and sensitive, making him moan louder, his cock twitching in my mouth, leaking more, dripping down my throat.

“Fuck, you taste so good,” I growl, my lips against his cock, sucking hard, my tongue swirling over the head, tasting the precum, my fingers pressing against his hole, not pushing in, just teasing, circling, feeling it clench, hot and tight. He moans around my cock, the vibration sending sparks through me, my cock throbbing, leaking, dripping into his mouth. His hands grab my ass, fingers digging into the uniform, pulling me deeper, his throat gagging but taking me, his tongue relentless, driving me closer to the edge.

“Goddamn, officer, don’t—fuck, don’t stop,” he moans, his voice muffled, high and desperate, his hips bucking, fucking my mouth, his cock pulsing, leaking more, dripping down my throat. I slap his thigh, the sting making him cry out, his hole clenching under my fingers, his cock twitching in my mouth, ready to burst but holding, just barely. My tongue swirls over the head, sucking hard, savoring the taste, the heat, my fingers teasing his hole, pressing harder, circling, making him shudder, his moans louder, needier.

I pull back, my lips slick, grinning, my cock still in his mouth, his lips stretching, sucking hard, his tongue relentless. “You love this, don’t you? My cock in your mouth, my tongue on your dick,” I growl, my hand stroking his cock, keeping him on edge, my fingers pressing against his hole, teasing, circling, feeling it clench, still sore but begging. I lean down, licking his cock again, slow and deliberate, tasting the precum, my tongue tracing the veins, feeling it pulse, thick and heavy, driving him wild.

“Fuck, yes,” he moans around my cock, his voice wrecked, his hands tightening on my ass, fingers teasing my crack through the uniform, making my cock throb, leaking more, dripping into his mouth. “You’re—shit, you’re too much.” His words are slurred, drowned in pleasure, his cock pulsing in my mouth, leaking, dripping down my throat. I slap his thigh again, the sting making him moan louder, his hole clenching under my fingers, his body trembling, drowned in lust, the alley a haze of heat and musk, our bodies slick with sweat, uniforms and bare skin grinding, cocks throbbing, leaking, the tension unbearable, electric, pushing us closer to the edge but not there yet, not until I drive him further.

His lips stretch around my cock, sucking hard, his tongue swirling, relentless, the wet heat driving me wild, my cock throbbing, leaking precum down his throat. His pale skin glistens, lean muscles trembling, scars glinting on his pecs under the flickering neon, his cock pulsing in my mouth, thick and veiny, slick with precum, dripping onto his abs. My uniform's torn open, badge digging into my chest, utility belt clinking, boots grinding on the concrete. His jeans are gone, his cock hard, leaking, his scarred knuckles clawing at my thighs, green eyes wild, burning with lust and surrender. The alley's a gritty haze, thick with the stench of sweat, smoke, and raw musk, the neon sign casting jagged red and blue across his body, his hole red, stretched, still sore from my cock.

"Fuck, you're—shit, you're too good," he moans around my cock, his voice muffled, wrecked, his hands digging into my ass, fingers teasing my crack through the uniform, making my cock throb harder, leaking more. I pull back, my cock slick with his spit, glistening, and shove him onto his stomach, the concrete rough against his chest, his ass up, hole exposed, pink and tight, glistening with sweat and my precum.

“Goddamn, officer,” he gasps, his voice high, desperate, his body trembling, his cock leaking onto the ground, “it’s—fuck, it’s too much.”

“Too much?” I growl, my voice thick, commanding, my hand gripping his neck, fingers curling tight, the chokehold firm, compressing his muscles, his breaths shallow, ragged. “You’re gonna take it, tough guy.” I slap his ass, hard, the sound sharp, echoing in the alley, making him cry out, his hole clenching, still sore but begging. I press my cock against it, the head flushed, slick, teasing the rim, feeling the heat, the tightness, my cock throbbing, aching to drive in deep.

“Fuck, it hurts,” he groans, his voice wrecked, his hands clawing at the concrete, his ass pushing back, conflicted, wanting it but wincing, my cock too big, stretching him wide. “You’re—shit, you’re gonna wreck me.” His words are a plea, laced with pain and need, his body trembling, his muscles flexing under my grip, his cock pulsing, leaking, dripping onto the ground. I grin, my hand slapping his ass again, the sting making him moan, his hole clenching, pulling at the head of my cock.

“Wreck you? That’s the fucking plan,” I growl, my lips brushing his ear, nipping the lobe, tasting the sweat, the smoke, my hand tightening on his neck, the chokehold relentless, his moans sharper, needier. I push in, slow at first, breaching his hole, the tightness searing, making me groan, my cock throbbing as his ass resists, still sore, but I don’t stop, driving deeper, inch by inch, stretching him wide. He cries out, a raw, desperate sound, his body shuddering, his hole clenching, fighting the intrusion but taking it, his cock twitching, leaking more, dripping onto the concrete.

“Goddamn, it’s—fuck, it’s too big,” he moans, his voice high, pained, his hands clawing at the ground, his muscles flexing, trying to push back, but I hold him down, my thighs straddling his hips, mounting him, my strength overwhelming his, a wrestler’s dominance, his body yielding under my weight. “Please—shit, slow down,” he gasps, but his hips rock back, betraying his need, his hole clenching, pulling me deeper, the pain mixing with pleasure, his moans louder, rawer.

"Slow down?" I chuckle, my voice low, my hips snapping forward, pounding harder, deeper, the slick sound of skin on skin filling the alley, mixing with his cries, the creak of my utility belt, the thump of distant music. "You're taking it, slut. Every fucking inch." I slap his ass again, the sting making him cry out, his hole clenching tighter, making my cock throb, aching to drill harder. I lean in, kissing his back, my tongue licking the sweat, tasting the musk, sucking hard, leaving a mark, my hand stroking his cock, keeping him on edge, feeling it pulse, thick and heavy, leaking more.

"Fuck, officer," he moans, his voice wrecked, his body trembling, his ass pushing back, taking every thrust, the pain fading under the pleasure, his hole stretching, yielding to my cock. "You're—shit, you're destroying me." His words are slurred, drowned in lust, his cock pulsing in my hand, leaking, dripping onto the ground, his muscles flexing under my chokehold, his breaths shallow, his moans desperate, echoing in the alley. I pound harder, relentless, my cock drilling deep, hitting that spot inside him that makes his cries turn sharp, his body shuddering, his hole clenching, pulling me in.

“That’s it, take it,” I growl, my hand tightening on his neck, the chokehold firm, compressing his muscles, his body pinned under my weight, my thighs clamping his hips, mounting him like a beast. “Your ass is mine, tough guy.” I slap his thigh, the sting making him moan louder, his hole clenching tighter, his cock twitching in my hand, leaking, dripping onto the concrete. My lips kiss his shoulder, sucking hard, tasting the sweat, the smoke, my tongue licking a slow stripe up his spine, savoring the raw masculinity of him, my cock pounding, drilling, wrecking his ass, the tightness driving me wild.

“Fuck, it hurts—shit, don’t stop,” he pleads, his voice high, desperate, his hips bucking back, meeting my thrusts, his hole clenching, taking every inch, the pain fueling his need, his cock pulsing, leaking more, soaking my hand. I grin, my hand sliding to his pit, inhaling deep, the musky scent of sweat and smoke hitting me hard, driving my cock wild. I lick his pit, slow and deliberate, tasting the salt, the heat, and he moans, his body shuddering, his hole clenching tighter, making my cock throb, aching to come but holding, just barely.

"You love this, don't you? My cock wrecking your hole," I growl, my lips against his skin, my hand stroking his cock faster, feeling it pulse, thick and heavy, ready to burst. I slap his ass again, hard, the sound sharp, making him cry out, his hole clenching, pulling me deeper, the alley pulsing with our heat, the neon casting shadows across his trembling body. "Beg for it, slut. Tell me you want my cum," I murmur, my hips pounding relentless, my cock drilling deep, the slick sound of skin on skin mixing with his moans, the creak of my belt, the thump of the bass.

"Fuck, yes—cum in me, officer," he moans, his voice wrecked, his hands clawing at the concrete, his ass pushing back, taking every thrust, his hole clenching, begging for my load. "I want it—shit, I need it." His words are raw, filthy, his body trembling, his cock pulsing in my hand, leaking, dripping onto the ground. I pound harder, deeper, my cock drilling his ass, the tightness searing, driving me closer to the edge, my hand tightening on his neck, the chokehold relentless, his moans sharp, desperate.

“Goddamn, you’re tight,” I groan, my hips snapping forward, pounding ruthless, my cock throbbing, aching to come, the heat of his hole overwhelming, his muscles flexing under my grip. I slap his thigh again, the sting making him cry out, his hole clenching tighter, pulling me in, his cock twitching, leaking more, soaking my hand. “Take it, slut—take my fucking cum,” I growl, my lips kissing his back, sucking hard, leaving another mark, my tongue licking the sweat, tasting the musk, my cock drilling deep, hitting that spot that makes his cries turn raw, his body shuddering.

I groan, my cock throbbing, and I come, hot and thick, spurting deep inside his hole, filling him, the heat searing, my cock pulsing with every jet, marking him as mine. He moans, loud and shameless, his body trembling, his hole clenching, milking my cock, his cock pulsing in my hand, leaking but not coming, his body wrecked, spent. I keep thrusting, slow now, savoring the tightness, the heat, my cum slicking his hole, dripping out, staining the concrete, glistening under the neon.

“Fuck, you—shit, you wrecked me,” he gasps, his voice hoarse, his body slumping against the concrete, his ass red, stretched, leaking my cum, his cock still hard, dripping precum onto his abs. I pull out, my cock slick, glistening with cum and his heat, and stand, zipping up my uniform, the black fabric soaked, my badge glinting, my boots scraping the ground. I grin, my hand brushing his ass, smearing the cum, marking him, his body trembling, his green eyes wild, locked on mine, drowned in lust and exhaustion.

“Keep that cum in you,” I murmur, my voice low, teasing, my hand slapping his ass lightly, making him wince, his hole clenching, leaking more of my load. “Something to remember this by.” I step back, my uniform torn, chest slick with sweat, the alley heavy with the scent of sweat, cum, and smoke, the neon flickering above. I turn, boots thudding on the concrete, leaving him sprawled on the ground, his ass wrecked, leaking my cum, his cock hard, his body marked by my hands, my chokehold, my cock, a filthy, pervy memory burned into us both, the night sealing our forbidden clash in this gritty, neon-lit haze.

Printed in Dunstable, United Kingdom

70167739R00313